ACKNOWLEDGMENTS

No one is an island.

As a podcaster, I've met a number of authors who took their knowledge, experiences, passions, and values, and funneled these into beautiful books that I had the honor to read. They inspired me to take the plunge.

Many thanks to the Southwest Ohio Writers Club for the discussions, tangents, and workshopping that has helped me sharpen my craft, and for the opportunity to meet awesome local wordsmiths I now consider friends.

Thank you to the critique partners and beta readers who have given hours of their time to read my unfinished works, and have generously provided me with both encouragement and hard truths.

I appreciate the patience and support of friends and family members who have listened to me talk endlessly about writing for the past few years...and surely got tired of my special interest but didn't say it.

My brother, Ervin Johnson II, has persevered in his manga enterprise, Shining Otaku, for the past several years, and continues to do so. His devotion to his passion inspires me to do the same.

BOOK ONE
A LOSANTIVERSE NOVEL

MAKE ME FREE

JAYE POOL

TARTANIUM
PRESS

MAKE ME FREE

Cover design by GetCovers

Published by Tartanium Press
PO Box 33113 | Cincinnati, OH 45233

ISBN: 979-8-9923291-0-0 (eBook)
ISBN: 979-8-9923291-1-7 (Paperback)
ISBN: 979-8-9923291-2-4 (Hardcover)

Library of Congress Control Number: 2025900791

First Edition: March 2025

10 9 87 6 5 4 32 1

My sister, Vanessa Johnson, has been incredibly encouraging, and has always been there with practical questions, thoughts, and advice. I appreciate her so much.

My mother, Venita K. Johnson, has believed in me for as long as I can remember. She never let me say, "I can't." I can, Mom, and I have.

Last but certainly not least, my dear husband, Jon Pool, has worn many hats – idea guy, soundboard, editor, cheerleader. But the best hat is loving, amazing partner. Hub, I love you.

In memory of

Ervin B. Johnson
Jackie Daniel

This novel is dedicated to those who struggle to fit in, fail to be understood, and could never understand why.

You are seen. This novel is for you.

PROLOGUE

Losanti, Ohio is a boomerang town. It exists as a place to begin, and to end, but not to live.

Located on the southwestern edge of the state of Ohio facing the neighboring commonwealth of Kentucky is the city of Losanti. Midwestern but with a touch of the South, its flair can be heard in the distinctive accent of its natives. The signature blend of brewing hops and turned eggs wafts through the air, welcoming all who enter.

The locale is known for two things – its incredible, painful *mundanity*, and ranch dressing.

Losanti is often the stand-in for many a TV show or movie, the sleepy town where you blink and then you miss it. Its downtown area along the riverfront can double as a city center in any other mid-sized metro.

No monuments have ever been erected to great Losantians of the past and no real landmarks exist, except perhaps the billion-dollar football stadium residents are still angrily paying for with increased sales tax after several decades.

The one thing Losantians are proud of is their ranch dressing. Yes, but not just *any* ranch dressing. Losanti is the home of Ohio Valley Ranch, the most beloved ranch dressing in the United States.

Like most other things in Losanti, this dressing is quite ordinary, but this is the beauty of the brand. Ohio Valley Ranch is so ordinary, it offends the least number of consumers, making it the safest choice from coast to coast.

We all know a town like Losanti — a burg lacking true distinction, but whose natives believe it to be the best place one could ever dream of living.

In 1997, seventeen-year-old Luke Phillips called Losanti *home*. He was born and raised there, along with his parents Gerald "Cam" Junior and Elizabeth, known as "Libby," as well as his older brother Gerald III, nicknamed "Trey."

Trey was attractive, a cunning opportunist with a knack for finding himself in the right place at the right time. While Luke was the smarter of the two, he was not so lucky. His appearance was *average*, and his accomplishments were found wanting. His parents never passed up an opportunity to remind him of that fact.

Luke attended Denbytown High School, a public secondary school on the northern edge of the city. In twelfth grade, he met Morgan Haas. He was captivated at first sight by the attractive new transplant from, well, everywhere and nowhere at the same time.

Morgan was a "military brat." Her father Jim was an Army careerist of over twenty years, reaching the level of Lieutenant Colonel. Her mother Nancy meticulously kept a tidy home and cared for Morgan and her seven siblings. Of the eight total children, five were biological and three were adopted. Morgan was the youngest, born in South Korea and adopted as a baby. As a military family, the Haases were always on the move, on or near Army bases all over the United States.

Soon after they met in fifth-period civics class, Luke and Morgan forged a romantic relationship. He thought her pretty enough, an athletic beauty of African American and East Asian extraction with jet-black curly hair and vibrant deep brown eyes. More importantly to him, his friends thought she was incredibly attractive, which elevated his status among his peers. Morgan, for her part, felt that Luke, of German and English background, with his brown mop-top haircut and brilliant blue eyes, was *okay* in appearance. What she truly loved, however, was his hypnotic, tenor singing voice, and that he could tell a captivating story.

While the couple believed they were in love, their pairing was without the blessing of their parents.

Luke's mother and father, pillars in their Southern Baptist congregation, would never approve of him dating "the world's way." Morgan was not the image they had in mind of a future daughter-in-law. Their desire was for their youngest son to meet a godly, Baptist woman from *good stock* to court – not date, but court – and marry. Until then, temptation was to be avoided at all costs.

The thing was, Morgan *did* in fact come from a Christian family. Her parents were devout Calvinist Christians in the Reformed tradition, with deep roots in Western Michigan's Dutch community. These strong regional links endured despite moves necessitated by her father's military service.

Like Luke's parents, Morgan's father and mother wanted their daughter to marry an upstanding Christian mate. However, their idea of an "upstanding Christian mate" did not include a Baptist like Luke, especially an underachiever from a middling place like *Losanti*.

In the world of the Phillipses and the Haases, Baptists and Calvinists did not mix. Yet Luke and Morgan had no concern for petty doctrinal disputes.

Their parents believed that the end of high school was the end of the couple. Unbeknownst to them, they secretly applied to the same colleges. Both were accepted to the University of the Great Lakes, a respected public institution in Upper West Osceola, Michigan, and started shortly after high school graduation in 1998. At Great Lakes, they joined a student organization, Christian Kingdom. Christian Kingdom, or "CK," was an evangelical campus ministry with chapters at colleges and universities all over the globe. They planned to earn their degrees and perhaps marry and spend the rest of their lives together, God willing.

Unfortunately for Luke and Morgan, God was not so willing.

Having discovered the ongoing romance, Luke's parents demanded he end his relationship with Morgan. Over the Christmas holiday in December 1998, he called her on the telephone and did as he was told. His parents were present to ensure the job was done.

The two were heartbroken, but remained friends. Yet, over time, their faith faltered, Morgan's especially. Neither could understand a God who would keep them apart for *reasons*.

Then, during their third year at Great Lakes, Morgan's parents felt she was not as devoted to God as she was to enjoying her freedom as a young adult at a secular university. One weekday in October 2000, they showed up at Morgan's residence hall unannounced. As Luke watched from a distance, they forced her to pack up, pulling her out of school, and away from him permanently.

GONE
NOVEMBER 2001

"Hi, friend."

The caramel-shaded doll spoke. Just out of the box, the brand-new toy donning a pale pink jumpsuit sat atop the blue metal bucket. Its deep brown eyes shifted mechanically from side to side.

"Hi, Baby Talk," the young girl sheepishly responded to the doll. Turning away from it, she fixated on a set of Hot Wheels on the sidewalk. *Red one here. Orange one there. Yellow one there. My favorite,* she thought to herself. She carefully lined up each toy car end to end around the mound of sand covering the crack of the sidewalk.

As she moved the final car, the shimmer of a lone dragonfly came into view. Upon the sight, the girl hopped back startled, the skirt of her red, white, and blue dress lifting slightly, exposing the edge of her silk ivory slip.

"Ann!"

Upon hearing her name, the child looked back to see who called to her, her braided brunette pigtails swinging. In view was a large box truck parked in the driveway of a pink stucco ranch-style home with a lone palm tree in front. The voice belonging to a mahogany-toned, Rubenesque woman with a moist Jheri curl. "Annie, grab your toys. We're about to take off."

"Okay, Mommy." Ann picked up the talking doll by the arm, and then the bucket, flipping it right side up. She then lined the cars on its bottom and placed the doll inside. *Stupid fly. Whoops, can't say stupid. Mommy says we don't say that. It's not in our 'vo-cab-yu-lair-ee.'*

"Baby, let's go." A towering, freckle-faced man with tightly coiled sandy red hair lumbered towards the girl. As the man picked up the child, he smiled and told her, "We'll stop by Mickey D's on the way out of Fort Lauderdale, and we're gonna get you some chicken nuggets."

"Dad…"

"Annie!" Ann was jolted awake.

She turned her head to the direction of her bedroom door, where there stood the same woman in the dream but with a few lines in her face, now with pin-straight, wrapped sable hair and wearing a bleached sheath dress and matching pumps. The older woman gently informed her, "The limo is here."

With haste, Ann rose from bed and finished getting ready. She glanced in the mirror and caught a glimpse of an adult woman.

She sprayed her brunette curls with leave-in conditioner and placed her arms in each sleeve of her pink bolero jacket. She then adjusted the skirt of her white fit and flare dress to fit over her expansive hips. For the finishing touch, she slid into her ivory kitten heels and swiped her purse on her way out the door following her mother.

"Okay, Mom. Is Michelle ready?" she asked.

Her mother sighed. "Yes, Shelley's downstairs."

"Are *you* ready?"

"I don't know if I'll ever be ready, but time stops for nobody."

"I know Mom, I know."

"Every time I would return to Detroit, it was always for a funeral. Somebody's always dying."

Ann recalled these words from her father as the sleek black limousine carrying herself, her mother, and her sister, all dressed in ivory, turned right on East Grand Boulevard, and stopped in front of the stately funeral home. The driver parked directly behind the hearse with a casket inside, prepared for the procession to the cemetery following the service.

With her mother and sister leading, she stepped into the doors of the funeral home and turned right into the decorated parlor. As they entered the cream-walled hall, they each received a glossy obituary. Her aunts, uncles, cousins, and her father's many friends, were in the parlor to greet the bereaved immediate family.

Once seated at the front of the room, Ann opened the obituary, which was adorned by her father's smiling face in front, and read it:

Marshall Harris Corbin of Detroit, Michigan, passed away on Tuesday, November 6th, 2001, at the age of 49. Marshall was born July 30, 1952 in Detroit to Estelle and Palmer Corbin, who predeceased him, and grew up in the Boston-Edison district of the city. He graduated from Detroit Cathedral High School, class of 1970, then went on to earn a bachelor's degree in government from the University of the Great Lakes in Upper West Osceola, Michigan, in 1974, and a juris doctor from Gulf State College in Florida in 1978.

Marshall built a fulfilling career as an attorney specializing in family law at Fishbein and Bishop and was admitted to the bar in three states. He was also well-traveled, having visited five continents during his lifetime. He loved sports such as baseball and football, and played defensive back for the Great Lakes Buzzards, his university football team.

He married Sherrye Wilkins on January 29th, 1984, and became the father of two girls, raising them to walk upright in the Lord.

Marshall leaves behind his loving wife Sherrye, his daughters, Ann and Michelle, his siblings, Marie (Eddie) Hall, Louie (Eliza) Corbin, and Jeanie Williams, and a host of nieces, nephews, cousins, and friends.

As they sat down, Sherrye whispered, "We reserved the biggest room here, looks like it still wasn't enough." There was not an empty seat in the house, and mourners who arrived a touch too late stood in the back.

The funeral director, dressed in black, shuffled to the podium next to the grey and silver-lined casket and removed a piece of paper from his inside suit jacket pocket. He opened it and read aloud.

"Good morning, it is my honor to welcome every single one of you to this homegoing celebration for Marshall Harris Corbin, who entered into rest on Tuesday, November 6, 2001." He cast his eyes down on the casket, which was closed per Marshall's wishes.

Next to it was a large display of white and red flowers, and next to that a giant board with a collection of photos from various points in Marshall's tragically short life. The pictures included a black-and-white shot of Marshall as a child playing football, a year-book portrait from high school, a sepia photo of him flexing, presumably in his late teens or early twenties, and a color professional snapshot of himself as a young adult with his mother and siblings. The board also featured a wedding picture of himself, Sherrye, and Ann, a family image where he posed with his wife and two children, and numerous candid Polaroids and snapshots from the nearly fifty years Marshall lived.

In irritated distraction, Ann thought, *This is beautiful, but we should've had the funeral at our home church.*

Charity Community Church had been the church home for the Corbin family since the mid-nineties. A nondenominational evangelical Christian congregation located on Detroit's far east side, it was mere blocks from the family home in the East English Village neighborhood. Charity was a formerly Baptist institution that held fast to a suburban, mostly homogeneous demographic in a gradually diversifying urban enclave.

The family attended church infrequently prior to joining the congregation. Marshall dabbled in various religions during his lifetime, including several varieties of Christianity, two sects of Islam, Buddhism, and a benign spirituality divorced from organized religion. Sherrye, on the other hand, lived as an enthusiastic, Bible-believing Christian who prayed without ceasing and strongly believed she would be raptured – beamed up to heaven while avoiding death – once the world inevitably ended right soon. Yet despite her personal devotion, she loathed all-day Sunday church services much like the ones she had experienced in her younger days tarrying at Pentecostal revivals.

A neighbor recommended Charity Community Church to Sherrye, which led her to attend. Their quick services that released congregants in plenty of time for afternoon Detroit Lions games fit the bill. In support of his wife, Marshall attended as well.

In addition to the abbreviated time commitment on Sunday mornings, the Corbins were attracted to Charity because the members were pleasant and opportunities were available to give service, which excited Marshall in particular. A vibrant children's ministry was available for young Michelle to attend, as well as Vacation Bible School in the summers.

Ann rarely attended church as a teen, as she enjoyed sleep and was skeptical of the existence of God. But after deciding to become a Christian during her first year at the University of the Great Lakes, she attended Charity during summers and school breaks.

As long as you didn't need anything, Charity was good enough.

The day after Marshall passed away, Sherrye called the church to inform them of his death and to arrange for Pastor Ron to preside over a funeral to be held at Charity. After all, they had been active members for six years, dutifully tithed, and gave above and beyond in financial offerings and volunteer service. Marshall even volunteered and provided legal help to members who needed it.

"Charity Community Church, Marilyn speaking. How may I help you?" a lady answered the call.

"Hi, Marilyn, this is Sherrye Corbin. My husband Marshall, he's a member and on the church legal team. He died yesterday."

Marilyn sighed. "Welp, I'm sorry to hear that."

"Thank you. I'm calling because we want to hold the funeral at the church sometime within the next week or so. Marshall worked closely with Pastor Ron and held him in high regard, so, if possible, we would like to have him officiate. If not, one of the other ministers is fine. How would we go about arranging that?"

"No," the office manager stated matter-of-factly.

Sherrye was flabbergasted. "What?"

"No," Marilyn reiterated. "Pastor Ron is on vacation and the pastoral staff and assistant ministers are busy. The sanctuary and chapel are both unavailable. Goodbye."

Sherrye was then met with the harsh *buzz* of a dial tone. "I didn't even give her a date..." she voiced softly.

Over the next week, no call came from the pastoral staff or any of the ministers. No sympathy card appeared in the mail. Nothing from a church the Corbins called home for the past several years.

Sherrye was readily willing to forgive. Ann, not so much. It was awful enough that God did not answer when she prayed fervently for her dear father to live that fateful day, to keep her teenage sister Michelle from being forced to survive the rest of her childhood without a father, not to leave her pious and devoted mother a widow way too soon. Instead, God decided that November morning was Marshall's time to meet him face-to-face. On top of that, the dismissive way the church, the same church her parents devoted their time and tithe to, treated him in death was a real kick in the teeth.

Dad deserved better than this. Charity Community Church is dead to me.

While Charity Community Church had forgotten Marshall, it was crystal clear that the overflow of people in the parlor of Detroit's Hillman Funeral Home had not. The funeral home assistant had run to the office copier to make additional prints of the obituary to accommodate the overflow. The director dictated the details of Marshall's life, which Ann wrote with the input of Sherrye.

"Uh Mom, am I supposed to include just when you and Dad got married, or am I supposed to include when he was married to my birth mother, too?" Ann asked a few days previously, as she was typing up the obituary on the home computer.

Sherrye softly clarified, "Just ours, sweetie. You don't get into all of that in obituaries. Just the highlights, the good things."

"Okay," Ann obliged.

At the funeral, following the reading, an instrumental selection played "Goin' Up Yonder." As the hired keyboardist tapped the keys on the walnut spinet piano, many who already knew the words sang along. "We're goin' up a-yonder! We're goin' up a-yonder! We're goin' up a-yonder, to be with my Lord!"

After the spiritual ended, the time had come for any mourner who desired to give remarks about the deceased to approach the podium. Several attendees stepped up to the wood-paneled podium and shared fond memories of Marshall. Attendees giving remarks included the partners from Marshall's law firm, friends from the mayor's office and the Wayne County Court, childhood friends, old teammates from his time playing football at Great Lakes, and friends from his bodybuilding days in the seventies.

Then, Michelle rose to take the podium. Through tears, she shared with the crowd, "My dad was awesome. He was always there for me, he would teach me things, we would go places together, and he would tell me stories about going to a bunch of different countries, and other stories about his life too. He talked about how much he cared about the kids he represented, and how hard it was. He cared a lot about people, and he cared a lot about us. He worried a lot about my sister when she went away to college."

Her eyes landed on her father's siblings, Marie, Louie, and Jeanie, and their families. The siblings were significantly older than their late brother; sixteen, fifteen, and ten years older, respectively. Marshall was the baby out of the four, which made his sudden departure from this mortal coil particularly harrowing for them.

The articulate twelve-year-old paused and directed her next words to Louie. "Uncle Louie, Dad said that you were more like a father to him than an older brother. He looked up to you and you meant so much to him." She then declared through heavier tears, "I miss you, Dad!" She returned to her seat and cried on her mother's shoulder.

As Ann somberly patted her sister's back, she could never forget the morning her father left the land of the living.

November 6, 2001

Ann was away at college at the University of the Great Lakes, her father's alma mater, in mid-Michigan. She was fast asleep in her dorm room on a school night, but the loud ringing of the landline telephone roused her.

She peered at the digital clock. *Quarter to four. Weird.* Half asleep, she rolled over and picked up the receiver.

"Hello?" Ann answered groggily.

"Annie, this is Mom."

"Uh, hi, Mom," Ann muttered.

"This is urgent," Sherrye reported, voice wavering. "Your father fell at home and we're at the hospital. Your father is dead."

"Are you serious?" Ann responded, the news not registering in her mind.

"Yes. You need to get home as soon as you can."

"Okay, I love you."

"I love you too."

After hanging up, Ann sat upright on the bed. While slowly taking in the news from her mother, she felt numb. As she bought a ticket and rode a charter bus to her hometown later that morning, she felt numb. On the worst day of her life, she felt numb.

The week was emotionally fraught for the entire family, but Ann knew she needed to remain strong for her shocked mother and crushed sister. She helped Sherrye choose a funeral home and accompanied her family to the facility. She chimed in to help guide the process while her mother made the arrangements, all covered by Marshall's generous life insurance policy.

Ann wrote the obituary, cooked dinner for her family to make sure they ate to keep up their strength, and assisted in picking out their customary white outfits for Marshall's homegoing. After all, since he was presumably going to heaven, death was supposed to be a celebration rather than a sad occasion.

She felt the weight of the week and took temporary comfort in the memories she had of her father. *Just a little while longer.*

August 1993

It was a sunny Saturday morning, and Marshall drove around town conducting his daily errands, including to the bank, to the park, and to spend time with his multitude of friends around town. As was the case much of the time, thirteen-year-old Ann, "Mini Marshall," tagged along with him.

While driving through the city, Marshall reflected on life, as he often did, and told stories of times past in the city he so loved. "Back when I was a kid, Annie, this area was a lot different. Lots of people, lots of businesses, everybody watched out for each other," he recalled. The teen stared out the passenger side window at the boarded-up homes, barren lots, and gutted storefronts that dotted the east side avenues.

Continuing along East Warren Avenue, he pointed out an area to his daughter. "Annie, not far from here was a neighborhood called Black Bottom, and it was where most of us Black folks lived. But it wasn't called Black Bottom because we lived there. It was called that because of the soil. It was dark because it was fertile, it was full of nutrients, and it was the lifeblood of the Indians who were here first. The soil was vital for them to grow crops."

During the drive, he pointed out the Black-owned businesses and local institutions that he had been fond of that had long since closed. "Things were good," he remembered. "We had our own, we were self-sufficient, until they tore down the neighborhood for the freeway. That changed everything for us. Our community was never the same. It wasn't just the unrest in '67, it was the freeway."

"What about the freeway?" Ann asked.

"When I was a kid, I used to live on a street that was close to downtown in Black Bottom. Your grandparents migrated up here from Mississippi in the 1940s and they owned a bar in Paradise Valley. It was called the Snippity Snap Saloon, close to where we lived, and your Auntie Marie bartended there too. Things were okay for our family. Then, the government decided they were going to build a bypass into downtown from the Chrysler Freeway," Marshall explained, referring to the section of Interstate 75 that runs through the City of Detroit.

"You're talking about 375?"

"Yes Annie, they built I-375 right on top of our neighborhoods just to have a shortcut into downtown from the Chrysler Freeway. And it wasn't much of a shortcut either. We were forced out of our homes, and our businesses were gone. It shattered the community. We all scattered around the city. Our family eventually rebuilt by getting into real estate. Your Big Mama did well for herself, even once your grandfather died, but it's impossible for an entire community to do that."

"Oh, wow," she voiced, astonished.

"People always talk about the rebellion...what *they* call the 'riots,' being what killed Detroit. No...Detroit was dying long before that. The freeway was the beginning of the end."

As the service wrapped up, Ann continued thinking of her father in life. The times they had as a close father and daughter duo had come to an end, and everything reminded her of the loss.

After the funeral, everyone proceeded to their vehicles to join in the procession to the cemetery where Marshall would be laid to rest. The pallbearers lifted the hefty casket and took it out of the funeral home. Once outside, the men slid it into the shiny hearse. Sherrye, Ann, and Michelle followed, taking their seats in the limousine behind it. The other mourners lined up along East Grand Boulevard. The procession line grew so long that it wrapped around the corner and continued for two additional city blocks.

Once the hearse began moving, so did the limousine and the participating cars. Several minutes later, the lengthy funeral procession continued up Woodward Avenue, passing Detroit's mile roads until crossing Seven Mile Road, then turning left, arriving at Woodlawn Cemetery.

Woodlawn Cemetery was the place of eternal rest for the Corbin family, including her paternal grandparents and other relatives. Ann stared out the window quietly as the limousine passed through the black wrought iron gates. For a brief moment, her thoughts drifted to an earlier time with her father, when the passing of another loved one was the topic of discussion.

July 1989

One weekend when Ann was nine years old, she and her father spent the day at Belle Isle, an island park on Detroit's riverfront. They were sitting on the grass near the edge of the Detroit River.

Marshall pointed to Windsor, Ontario, Canada, which could easily be seen on the other side of the river. "You see how close that looks?"

"Yeah," Ann answered. "It's like you can touch the other side."

"Annie, that distance is a lot further than it looks. I had a cousin named Jerry. We grew up together, and he was an excellent swimmer. He went to Cass Tech and he was on the high school swim team. He was so good, he was going to try out for the Olympics."

"Oh, wow," she marveled.

"Well, one time Jerry was with his friends out here on Belle Isle. And he bet them that he could swim from here to Windsor. I'm sure he thought he could easily win the bet because he was confident in his talents. You don't become successful if you're not confident."

"So, Dad, did he make it?"

He took a deep breath. "Well, he went out there, and he did his best, but the distance is longer than it looks. A lot longer. Jerry got tired out swimming across the current. He lost steam...and he drowned."

Ann peered out at the expanse.

Marshall added, "They never found the body. There is nothing underneath his gravestone."

Once arriving at the cemetery for Marshall's burial, the queue wound through the manicured grounds at a leisurely pace, stopping at a location where two rows of folding chairs were set up next to a platform, covered by a small tent.

The pallbearers left their cars first to move the ornate casket up the gentle incline to the green platform. After it was placed atop the platform, the limousine was opened so that Marshall's immediate family could sit in the first row.

For Ann, Michelle, and Sherrye, the brief walk felt like an eternity. Once seated, the other mourners left their vehicles to converge on the hill to pay final respects to Marshall Harris Corbin.

The place where he would be laid to rest was near the gravestones of other members of the Corbin family. Ann glanced at the plot where his mother was buried. This observation brought to mind the first time she experienced death.

April 1985

"When your Big Mama died, she left her body, so she's in heaven now," explained Sherrye gently as she pressed Ann's untamed curls.

"Heaven?" inquired the five-year-old.

"Yes sweetie, heaven. That's where God is. Sit still. Move your head down. Just need to get the kitchen."

The child complied silently.

Sherrye continued working on her daughter's hair, carefully straightening the short hairs on the back of her neck using an extremely hot pressing comb. "Big Mama's in heaven. That's where Jesus is, and she's gone to be with Jesus."

"Okay, Mommy."

"When we go to the funeral, you'll see Big Mama's body laying down in a casket."

"What's a casket?"

"A long box with a lid, where dead people's bodies go to rest. Her body will be in the casket, but it won't be her. She's not in there. Her soul, the real her, she'll be with Jesus."

The sanctuary of Zion Hope Missionary Baptist Church was very *blue*. The crushed velvet upholstery adorning the tall windows, the pews, the choir seats, and the thrones for the deacons and the pastor, were a sky shade of blue. The floor was covered in shag carpeting dyed a similar color to match. Lacquered redwood trimmed the seating, which was filled with wailing mourners. A white casket with gold finish was elevated on a dark wooden pedestal, the lid open to show the visage of an elderly woman clad in pink.

A kindergarten-aged Ann, wearing a silk black and white dress with bows, walked up to the casket with her parents. She placed her right hand on her grandmother's, which lay stiffly over the left. Big Mama's hands were oddly cold, not a bit like the warm hands that would hold a young Ann on her lap in life. She remembered her mother saying that her grandmother was no longer in her body. Now, touching her chilly fingers, she *felt* that.

"Annie, tell Big Mama goodbye," Marshall uttered through tears and sniffles of his own.

"Goodbye, Big Mama."

Quietly, Ann sat with her mother and sister at the burial site, where her father's casket was lowered into a deep, dark hole. The funeral director recited, "We therefore commit the body of Marshall Harris Corbin to the ground. Earth to earth, ashes to ashes, dust to dust. From dust you were made, and to dust you shall return."

A lone tear rolled down her face. "Goodbye, Dad."

After the events of the day, the Corbin family, minus their patriarch, retired to the family home on Grayton Street. Sherrye and Michelle entered their respective bedrooms to rest.

Ann proceeded to her childhood bedroom, still decorated with posters representing the interests she loved as a teenage girl. Images of Tupac Shakur, TLC, R. Kelly, and the 1997 Detroit Red Wings still adorned the painted beige walls. A chest-high pine bookshelf filled with her favorite books sat opposite her white-framed daybed.

She softly shut the door, removed her dress clothes, and changed into her green plaid pajama bottoms and matching long-sleeved sleep shirt. She then left her room and headed down the creaky stairs into the living room.

There, she sat alone on the felt brown couch watching television — or really, the television was watching her. Jay Leno performed his Tonight Show monologue on the bubble screen. She enjoyed watching him with her father as a teen, but only the monologue because she needed to go to bed early on school nights.

Now by herself, she could finally sit with her feelings. The house was too quiet. *Dad is really dead.* She had held the weight of her immense grief as much as she could, but it was now all too real. She was a daddy's girl whose daddy was gone. She wept.

The footsteps were barely heard creeping down the staircase. Sherrye took a seat next to Ann and grabbed her hurting daughter, holding her close as she finally expressed the pain of loss. In that moment, she realized that they would be okay. They would go on together as a family, and Marshall would be there in spirit.

Ann's mind and heart went to how her father was so close to his dear mother, that even long after her death, he would speak to her in his prayers to the Almighty. Much like the Catholic saints, whose role is to intercede on behalf of devoted believers, Marshall looked towards the ancestors, especially his mother, to give him guidance, comfort, and peace. And it was now that she understood.

Our ancestors become saints because it is how we keep the departed alive forever.

ONWARD CHRISTIAN KINGDOM
NOVEMBER 2001

A week after the funeral, Ann rode a Greyhound bus back to Upper West Osceola to continue her studies at the University of the Great Lakes. Once she arrived on campus about two hours after departure, the bus dropped her off at the roadside stop, marked only by a small sign.

She only waited at the stop for a few minutes when a brown Toyota Tercel pulled up to the curb. Ann knew that car anywhere. It belonged to her closest friend, Terah Sanders. Terah was also from Detroit, and they had been best friends since high school. She also attended the university and they shared a dorm room that year.

Ann slid her luggage into the back seat and sat up front with her friend.

"Thanks, girl!"

"No problemo! Anytime!" spoke Terah in a sweet, almost singing voice, as she shifted into first gear and headed toward their residence hall.

"How was your test?" Ann asked.

"Mmm, it was a'ight. Prayerfully I passed, it counts for half my grade." The exam kept Terah from attending the funeral of Ann's father. Invoking her deep evangelical Christian faith, a faith they shared, she continued, "All I can do is give it to God."

"Amen."

"How was the bus ride back?"

"Not bad, it was about what you'd expect."

"Mmm-hmm." Terah nodded while moving her long box braids away from her face.

"You know, I'm sure looking forward to getting back to my normal routine."

"I hear you. It'll probably keep your mind off things."

"Oh yeah, for sure. Really wanting to get back to my Stata project," Ann was anxious to finish a major course assignment using her favorite statistical software.

"Girl, not gonna lie, it amazes me how you enjoy math, of all things," Terah marveled. "See, that's why I'm an urban planning major. No math...well, at least, not a lot of it."

"Yeah, it's not for everybody, but it's fun, especially stats. It's math with a story, it's math with meaning behind it, you know what I mean?"

"I hear you."

Once they arrived at Packard Hall, their dormitory, on campus, Terah began the hunt for an open student parking space. These parking spots were usually in short supply, but this time, one happened to be available, so they were in luck. Terah swiftly pulled into the open space. "Ooh, thank you, Jesus," she whispered, thrilled at her good fortune.

"Do you think you'll make it to Christian Kingdom large group meeting?" inquired Terah.

"Eh, I dunno. Part of me wants to sleep so bad, but I've done enough of that. Gotta get back into the swing of things. I suppose I'll show my face."

The friends were active participants in Christian Kingdom, a global, interdenominational Christian campus ministry. Christian Kingdom, or CK, held large group meetings on Thursday evenings and small group Bible studies on other nights during the week. The Great Lakes chapter was particularly noteworthy because of its cultural diversity. The evangelical trend of "racial reconciliation" had greatly impacted it, leading to campus leadership efforts to diversify the fellowship. Their initiatives resulted in an influx of international students, as well as students of Asian and Latino descent, to a chapter that was once nearly all-white.

While the ministry was ethnically diverse, Ann and Terah were *the* Black representation in the chapter. This occasionally led to uncomfortable moments among group members.

October 1999

One Friday afternoon, Terah strolled into the dorm room she shared with Ann during their second year in college.

"You're not gonna believe this, Annie."

"Oh, what's up?" Ann responded while perusing online bulletin boards on her computer.

"So, I ran into Megan Tsong from CK. Saw her on my way back from class."

"Oh, okay..."

"So, apparently, she's having a party tonight. And we're actually invited."

"Huh...that's a first. Folks from CK don't really invite us to anything unless it's our peeps."

"Yeah, I know, girl."

"But Terah, do we really wanna go?"

"Yes, yes we do. We got invited; Megan's being nice, so we should honor that. It's just off campus. I got the address. It's at seven."

Ann looked up from the monitor. "'Kay...what are we supposed to wear?"

"She said it's a costume party, but costume's optional."

"I mean, we could try to come up with something."

"Sure, we *could*."

"Shouldn't we bring something?"

"Megan said to just bring ourselves. They already got food and drink covered."

"Are you sure? I don't want us to show up empty-handed and come off rude or something."

Terah grew slightly annoyed. "If she wanted us to bring something, she should say something."

Later that day, Ann found a witch's hat in their shared closet and matched it with a dusky sweater, jeans, and boots. Terah opted for a white lab coat she used for her chemistry prerequisite to pull off dressing as a doctor. The two then walked to the party, five minutes away.

The destination was a subdivided house in the middle of the block just off campus. It was three stories and appeared to be a little worse for wear, with weathered tan siding and a wooden balcony jutting out from the top floor. The friends stopped in front of the building.

Terah looked down at the note. "Okay, it says to climb the stairs to the third floor. The one with the balcony."

Ann grimaced slightly, concerned about the makeshift wooden stairs. "Alright, that's it then. Not loving those stairs, though."

"It'll be fine."

They made their way up the stairs carefully. As they continued their ascent, the music grew increasingly loud, intensifying the shaking motion on the outdoor staircase the closer they got.

"Geeze," Ann moaned, "why's that music so loud?"

Terah rolled her eyes and said something Ann couldn't hear.

"What?"

Terah got louder. "It's a party, Annie!"

Once at the top, Terah knocked on the door. After a few moments, the door opened.

"Hi!" A young man looked down slightly at the women. "Who are *you?*"

"Hi, I'm Terah, and this is Ann. Megan invited us."

"Megan?"

"Megan Tsong."

Just then, Megan, who was wearing a black cat costume with whiskers, came to the door. She looked up at the man who opened the door. "Linh, it's fine. These are my friends."

"Oh, okay." He stepped away.

"Don't mind Linh," Megan spoke loudly. "He's fine, just a little weird sometimes. Anyway, glad you guys could make it. Come on in. Snacks and drinks are at the table over there, and feel free to mingle, dance, have fun!"

"Thanks, Megan!" Terah responded with gratitude and loudness.

Fighting nerves, Ann made a beeline to the refreshment table, grabbed a red plastic cup, and filled it from the punch bowl. As she stood there drinking and munching on plain potato chips from a bowl next to her, she scanned the room while Terah mingled with the other guests.

This is weird, she thought. It caught her eye that many of the guests, who were mostly Asian and white, had their faces painted black and were wearing bright red lipstick. Some wore black afro wigs of various sizes. Their "costumes" were rounded out by baggy clothes and gaudy gold chains. *I hate this. I really hate this.*

A young man sauntered up to her. He wore a white hoodie plastered with pink bunnies. His clear green eyes looked her up and down. "Enjoying the chips?"

"Sure, I guess."

"Chips ain't gonna love you, but I sure will. Wanna head in there?" He pointed to a hallway to which Ann could see no end.

She tried to speak, but no words departed from her mouth.

"Missed your chance, fatty." He strolled away, snickering.

A half hour later, Terah came back to retrieve her friend. "You see these people? This is bull," she said in Ann's ear.

"I hate this," she whispered back loudly.

"Don't I know it?"

Ann led her furious friend out the door and down the stairs. Upset and feeling insulted, they returned to their residence hall.

The next day, they vented to each other about their experience at the event.

"That party was foul," Ann snarked.

"It really was," Terah agreed. "Megan called me after we got back, guess she noticed we didn't stay long. I told her we took ourselves on home."

"Huh. So, lemme guess, she said, 'The party was fine?'"

"Yeah, pretty much. I told her how we both felt about the blackface, and she was like, 'It was fine. You're making a big deal out of nothing.'"

"Ugh. Of course she did."

"Wish I was surprised."

A few days after Megan's party, Ann departed from her morning Math 315 session once it was over and walked across The Mall, a large grassy area in the middle of campus surrounded by the Main Library and several classroom buildings.

"AC!"

Ann heard a loud, somewhat deep voice in the distance. *Only one person calls me that.* She turned around and caught a glimpse of Luke Phillips.

"Wait up!"

"Of course, Luke!" she called back, smiling at the average, athletic man.

"Hey, AC, what's up?"

"Not much, how's it going?"

"Good, good. Wanna grab lunch at Buzzard Lake?"

She looked up at him and paused for a moment, captivated by his bright eyes, which shifted shades with the light, the sun, the moon, and the mood. "Uh...yeah, sure."

The friends visited the Buzzard Lake Cafe, a campus cafeteria offering takeout meal plan options. Once their food was ready, they headed outside to Buzzard Lake, a manufactured campus water installation best known for hordes of students swimming in it on football game days for good luck. They sat on a bench by the lake and enjoyed their lunch.

"How was your class this morning?" he asked.

"Not bad...it's math, can't complain. You had your photography class this morning, right?"

"Yeah, I did."

"How did that go?"

"Excellent – got an 'A' on my black and white portfolio project. Wanna see?"

After she nodded, opened his backpack, pulled out a portfolio, and handed it to her. When she opened it, she perused several photos, including a photo of Buzzard Lake on a bright fall day, and a few landscape photos of The Mall while leaves were falling from the trees.

"Luke, these are great. I told you that you have a talent for this."

"I do alright. Anyway, check out the one on the last page."

Ann flipped to the final snapshot, which was of her sitting cross-legged on a thick, concrete wall which supported the Main Library stairs. She was staring straight ahead, the photo capturing her in profile. The strong winds blew against her face, and her big brunette curls flagged behind her.

"Y'know, my professor told me that was his favorite."

She blushed, then quietly closed the folder and handed it back to him.

Luke then changed the subject. "So...did you go to Megan's party the other day?"

"Yeah. Terah came with, but we didn't stay long," Ann mentioned.

"Oh, okay. I got an invite for it, but I didn't bother. Costume party – not my scene."

"I hear you. I didn't even know about it until Terah told me. I guess she ran into Megan and she invited us last minute. You didn't really miss anything."

"Oh, okay, cool. How bad was it?"

"Uh, it was stupid bad. I mean, dudes in, like, blackface."

"Blackface?"

"Yeah, blackface. Like, these were white and Asian people with faces painted coal black with bright red lipstick pretending to be Black people. They thought they were being funny."

Luke made a disgusted face. "Oh, that's bad. Really bad. Seriously?"

"Yeah. For real. Truth be told, thinking back, I wonder if we were just invited as a joke. Sometimes I wonder why I even bother with CK at all, other than you, Terah, and our other friends."

"I can see why you'd be offended by that, but is it really a CK thing, though? Sounds like it's just Megan and her roommates, and they're not in CK...they aren't even Christians."

"Yeah, but, like, there was the time last spring when Steve Lopez asked me and Terah to come with him and some other CK people to see that new movie *The Skulls* after Tuesday small group. But then when we got there, the theater was close to full, and nobody saved any seats for us, just for themselves."

"Really?"

"Yeah. So, we had to sit far away from the group. They didn't even acknowledge us when we showed up. We only went because they invited us and we thought it would be cool to bond with them. I wasn't exactly dying to see that movie."

"That sucks...that really does. Hopefully, that was just a mistake. Steve's pretty cool."

"You'd think, but there was the time when we had finished up large group meeting and I stuck around to help clean up. This was, like, a month or so ago. Megan, Steve, Mei, and some of the other CK student leaders were standing around, and I think it was Mei who made a comment about a Black guy in her class asking her out. She was like, '*ewww.*' She said that even if she liked him, there was no way she would date him since she couldn't bring him home to meet her parents."

"Yikes."

"Yeah, I know. And every single person standing around said pretty much the same thing, that they wouldn't date Black people for that reason."

Luke was stupefied.

"Um, you know, I get it...we like who we like. But I feel like no matter what kind of person I am, if I'm a strong Christian or if I'm serious about my purity, it doesn't matter because being Black trumps everything."

He sighed. "I'm sorry, AC."

Ann shrugged. "It is what it is. I go to CK to worship God, but also because of you, Terah, and our group of friends. You guys *are* awesome. The rest of them...I don't know. I try, but I just don't fit in. It's always like that."

"Y'know, those reasons make sense, but why keep putting yourself through this? Sounds awful, honestly."

"I dunno. Good question. I mean, we're supposed to forgive, right?"

"Yeah, I guess that's true."

"You know, I do my best…and maybe I'm stubborn, I dunno. Not fitting in is nothing new to me, but my parents always said, 'Don't quit.' That stuck with me, I guess."

He nodded while chewing his bratwurst.

"But the other thing is, I wanna support Terah. She feels called to be a bridge-builder within CK so she can make a real difference. You know, diversity 'on earth as it is in heaven.'"

"Yeah, I know what you mean. But you gotta take care of yourself, too."

A few hours after returning to campus from her hometown following her father's funeral, Ann threw on her "campus uniform," consisting of dark blue jeans from The Avenue, a plain pink tee, a light blue pullover hoodie with a "UGL" logo and buzzard mascot, and Doc Martens. After getting dressed, she took off on her five-minute walk to Milliken Hall, a classroom building in the center of campus where the Christian Kingdom large group meeting would be held.

Once she arrived, she entered the cavernous auditorium, stopping to compose herself. The room was furnished with bolted-in seating with small movable desktops for notes attached to the seats. At the front was an overhead projector, turned on and ready to go, its light shining on a screen pulled down from the wall. A microphone, acoustic guitar, keyboard, and basic drum set were also plugged in at the front, along with sound equipment.

"Hi, Ann!" called out Cristina Molina. "Good to see you back! Missed you last week!"

Ann waved back.

Alyssa Van Hooten turned her head to see her, then jumped up and ran to hug her. Her curly blonde locks were bouncing behind her. "I heard about your dad. I'm so sorry." Luke walked up, along with another friend, Paul Chu.

"My condolences, Ann," Paul said, giving Ann a firm side hug.

"Thanks, Paul."

Luke approached her. "I'm sorry you lost your dad, AC. I don't really know what to say, but lemme know if you ever wanna talk."

Ann nodded. "Thanks, Luke. I appreciate you saying that."

Others also greeted the grieving young woman with their condolences, and she softly thanked everyone. *All this attention feels weird...I hate being the focus like this. But I get it, and I appreciate that they're trying to comfort me.*

Once seven o'clock rolled around, it was about time for the Christian Kingdom large group meeting to start. The worship band, consisting of Paul on guitar, Megan on keyboard, a woman named Sri Dharma on vocals, and a young man named Kyle Tracey on drums, started their Christian contemporary music set. Craig Dombrowski, a staff leader known as "Brother Craig," controlled the projector, sliding transparent slides with lyrics onto the glass at the appropriate times. The team performed three selections for the attendees to sing together, including "How Great is Our God," "I Want to Know You More," and Ann's favorite, "Better is One Day."

After the opening songs, the worship team sat down, and Brother Craig approached the podium. Towering over the podium he gave what was essentially a religious sermon. He read from the book of Job in the Bible. This ancient story was about how God and Satan bet on the likelihood that Job, a man devoted to God, would renounce his deity if he lost every blessing he had been provided, including his family and his health.

This felt a bit on the nose for Ann, given her recent loss. *Great.*

"The devil seeks to steal, kill, and destroy. He desires to separate us from the Lord. We are not promised a comfortable life. Goodness, we're not even promised tomorrow!" Running his fingers through his spiky bleach-blond hair, he continued preaching. "But when we're facing hard times, whether they're small or big, we wanna turn to the Lord in prayer and ask him to use our pain for his glory. Amen?"

"Amen!" the group shouted.

"He may not answer your prayers the way you expect. But Jesus Christ and his sacrifice on the cross, that is *the* answer. He has not abandoned you; he has not forsaken you, he is here, he is here with you, and he is who you need to rely on, even when you have nothing else, just like Job. Amen?"

"Amen!"

Then, Brother Craig shared, "One of our own, Ann Corbin, has returned to campus today and is here with us. Her father died about two weeks ago. As we know, death is not the end for those of us who believe, but the beginning of a glorious eternity with the Lord."

I hope Dad is with the Lord. Ann knew that her father believed in a higher power, but he was a bit of a spiritual wanderer, dabbling in several faiths and philosophies throughout his life. The prayer in the auditorium brought to mind conversations she had with him about his beliefs.

January 1997

One day when Ann was sixteen, she was bored and looked for something to occupy her time. So, she rifled through the incredible multitude of books that her father owned. Found on bookshelves in the family home were tomes about several topics. Some were spiritual in nature, including *Siddhartha*, *The Qur'an*, and *The Urantia Book*. She even noticed a few controversial books, including *The Turner Diaries*, *The Communist Manifesto*, and *Message to the Blackman in America*. After thumbing through each of them, she brought the bunch to Marshall, who was busy writing at his office desk.

"Dad, why d'you have these books?"

"Which books?"

"These ones. Some of them are about other religions, and you know Mom won't like that...and there's a lot of bad stuff in some of them. Do you believe all this?"

Marshall sat back in his reclining chair and chuckled. "Good question, Annie. Lemme see these."

She handed him the stack of books, and he quickly skimmed through each.

"So, you know how I listen to talk radio, right?" he asked. "Even the hosts that say really prejudiced shit about us Black folks?"

Ann nodded. "Yeah."

"We listen to it, but not because we're toms and believe that shit about ourselves and our people. We know better, or at least we *should*. We listen to it because we want to understand all sides of things, including the side of the folks we disagree with. We even want to know what our enemies, and those who hate us, think. We don't want to be blindsided. It makes us prepared; it makes us more effective. You know what I mean?"

"Yeah Dad, I think I get it."

"It's the same thing with books. You don't want to just read things you agree with a hundred percent. Knowledge is power, we don't want to limit our knowledge because it comes in a package that we don't fully agree with."

She nodded as he handed her back the books.

"Don't limit what you read. It doesn't matter how you feel about it as a whole, or whether the authors were good or bad people," he explained. "Folks are complex, folks are complicated. Most folks live their lives in shades of grey."

"Hmm...okay."

"Annie, take what is useful to you. Take what you can and throw the rest away."

While Brother Craig had given his words of assurance from the podium, Ann felt less than assured. He then called her down to the front of the room.

When she got there, he, as well as Rhonda Bevins, the other staff leader known as "Sister Rhonda," and several students proceeded to the front, laid hands on her, and prayed fervently for her father, her, and her family.

For Ann, the prayers and touch were comforting, as this made her feel the presence of God. But a tiny yet significant piece of her feared deep down that her father's spirituality placed him out of reach of the grace of a loving God. Guilt steadily crept in, guilt that perhaps she did not fight hard enough to save him from himself.

STEPHANIE
DECEMBER 2001

The Saturday before autumn semester final exams, Ann and Terah enjoyed a late Saturday lunch at Romney Commons, a cafeteria near their residence hall.

"Terah, you thinking about going to the CK Christmas party tonight down at the Great Lakes Union?" Ann asked while eating a slice of pizza.

"Eh, I dunno. It sounds cool, but who's all going?"

"I know Luke said he's going, and then Paul, Alyssa, and Cristina are going, too. I dunno about anybody else, but not gonna lie, I'm over the rest of them," Ann responded while drinking a small glass of Faygo RedPop.

"I get it. The crew's good enough for me."

"Oh, Sister Rhonda said we're supposed to dress nice. We're celebrating the Lord's birthday."

"Okay, cool."

After returning to their dorm room, Ann raided her closet and found a long-sleeved, dark purple wrap dress that formed a deep "V" shape in the cleavage area and with a hem that met her knees. The outfit was rounded out with short sable heels. Standing in front of a full-length mirror, she used a wet Denman brush to style her shoulder-length hair.

Terah put on a winter white long-sleeved, high-necked silk blouse with a long, black suede pencil skirt and heeled boots. She pulled her hair up into a slick bun and smoothed the edges with Lets Jam gel.

Once dressed, she looked at her friend's chiffon dress and shook her head. "Annie, you're not going out like that, are you?"

"Uh...what? What d'you mean?"

"That's a bit low-cut, girl."

"It's not that bad, is it?"

"Kinda. Lemme help you out." Terah swiped a safety pin from her desk and adjusted the neck, using the pin to make sure the cleavage was covered and did not slip. "There. Nice and modest."

After getting ready, the friends walked to the Great Lakes Union, a three-story student meeting and conference building on the eastern edge of campus. The Christian Kingdom event was held in a small conference room on the ground floor. Ann and Terah walked in and noticed the silver garland, ornaments, and Christmas decorations hung around the room. Five circular tables were scattered about, covered with red and green tablecloths, and dotted with tinsel and sequins. A rectangular table sat off to the side, complete with crockpots, containers, bags of snacks, and two-liter soft drinks.

"Wow, they did it big," Terah remarked.

"For sure. I'm guessing there was a lot left in the student org budget for the semester."

The friends spotted Paul, Alyssa, and Cristina sitting at one of the circular tables. Paul waved at them. "Hey guys! We're over here!" he called out.

They walked over and sat at the table. "How long have you been here?" Terah asked.

"Oh, not that long," Cristina responded. "Maybe ten minutes?"

"Is Luke still coming?" Ann inquired.

"Always thinking about Luke," Alyssa quipped.

"It's nothing..just asking."

"He's coming," Paul reassured her. "You know how he is sometimes. He gets caught up in things and it takes him time to pull away."

About five minutes later, Luke strolled in, wearing a purple dress shirt, lavender tie, black pants, and shoes. He held a small silver camera in his hand. Once the friends flagged him over, he sat in the free seat next to Ann.

"Sorry I'm late. Had to pick up batteries for my camera. The line at Rite Aid was ridiculously long, probably 'cause of the Great Lakes-Michigan State game."

"It's fine," Ann replied. "You didn't miss anything."

"It *is* the final game of the season, isn't it?" Paul asked.

"Yeah."

"You're twinning," Paul quipped.

Ann and Luke glanced at each other.

What the hell? We're both wearing purple, we're matching like a cutesy couple.

The two then trained their eyes on Paul, slightly annoyed.

"Hey! It's true."

"It's a coincidence, I swear," Luke responded.

Ann joined in. "Yeah, there's no way I would've known what Luke was gonna wear."

"But great minds do think alike."

The friends ate and chatted about their final exams and daily lives. They even stepped out onto the dance floor, along with other students from Christian Kingdom. Luke and Ann stood against the wall while watching the crowd move to the music.

He leaned towards her and confessed, "I can't dance."

"I doubt I'm any better than you, but give me the right song, and I'll get out there. Can't say I'm any good, but it's fun. It's a nice feeling having the beat move through you. It's worth trying."

After a few minutes, "My Eyes Don't Cry" by Stevie Wonder began blaring through the speakers.

"C'mon Luke, let's go!"

"Oh no, I can't," he resisted.

"Hear me out. This is a line dance, and it's super easy. Just line up over there with me, and follow everybody else," she explained, pointing out a spot on the floor where they could easily join in.

"I dunno..."

Ann pulled Luke to the dance floor to join in the line dance. She was easily able to find her rhythm. After a few small missteps, he got the hang of it as well.

After the song was over, the friends sat back down at their table.

"Y'know AC, gotta admit, that was fun."

"Told ya."

"And it wasn't that hard, either."

"I knew you'd pick up on it fast. What made you think you couldn't dance? C'mon...I know better."

He smirked. "Welp, I don't have much dancing experience. My family's Baptist, they're weird about dancing. They believe it leads to temptation. So, even though my high school had dances, I couldn't go."

"Not even prom?"

"Nope."

"Don't feel too bad. I would've gone to prom, but my high school sweetheart backed out at the last minute."

"That's crappy of him. You didn't deserve that."

"Thanks." She shrugged. "It happens. So, looking forward to winter break?"

"Yeah, kinda. My parents are flying out to California to see my brother."

"You're not going?"

"Nah. All they're gonna do is brag on him more and puff out his chest. I'm gonna be at home by myself. I'll go see my hometown friends and probably spend Christmas with Paul and his family."

"Sounds fun."

"Yeah, for sure. What about you?"

"Um...I'm going back home to be with my family. It's the first Christmas without my dad," she lamented.

"Oh yeah. That'll be tough."

"Yeah, I'm sure it'll be hard, but you know, death is a part of life. It is what it is."

"Welp, if you need anybody to talk to, you got my number. That's what friends are for."

"Sure, I'll keep that in mind."

Just then, Ann felt a hand on her shoulder.

"Saw y'all out there on the dance floor. Lukie baby, I didn't know you had it in you!" Paul joked.

Luke laughed. "Paulie, I don't!"

"That's a lie. You were busting moves I've never seen out of you. Channeling your inner Backstreet Boy."

"Ha ha," Luke snarked. "But yeah, AC got me out there, and she brought it out of me."

"I see, I see! Guys, can you believe this is gonna be our last CK Christmas party together?"

"Why do you have to be so sentimental, bro?" Luke remarked.

"I hear you, man, but honestly, these moments matter. It's time we're never gonna get back. And you brought the camera, so I'm sure that deep inside, you know I'm right."

"Okay, bro, whatever."

"I'm really gonna miss y'all."

"We still have another semester until graduation," Luke pointed out.

"Sure, but that's gonna go by so fast."

"You're not wrong, Paul," Ann agreed. "The past few years here at Great Lakes have really flown by, you know what I mean?"

"For sure."

Luke then spoke up. "Welp, let's break out the camera, then." He called out to Cristina, who was returning to the table. "Tina! Could you take a picture of the three of us?"

"Yeah, sure!"

Paul leaned in between Ann and Luke, and all smiled for the camera.

After the photo was taken, they took turns snapping photos of the room, the dancing, and each other. Once the party ended, Ann left with Terah, Luke, Paul, Alyssa, and Cristina.

"It's weirdly quiet out here for a Saturday night," Cristina noted.

"Especially since they had the football game earlier...I'm surprised I'm not seeing anyone else around," Alyssa observed.

Once in the middle of the Quad, the group stopped.

"Cristina and I need to study," Terah noted. "We have a Monday exam to get ready for...it's for our sociology class, so we're headed to the library."

Cristina added, "It's gonna be a super hard final, so we'll have to use all the time we have to prepare. Take care, guys!"

After Terah and Cristina split off from the group, the four friends looked at each other. "I don't like how quiet it is," Luke observed.

"I hear you, man," Paul concurred. "I don't think Alyssa and Ann should be walking back to their dorms by themselves."

"I'm good," Ann tried to reassure them.

"Nah, AC," Luke pushed back. "I'll walk you to your dorm. Paulie, will you be okay walking Alyssa to hers?"

"Yeah. We might hang out for a bit in her dorm room, and then I'll meet you back at our apartment."

"Alright. See you later tonight."

The friends split off to head to their respective destinations.

Watching Paul and Alyssa walk away, Ann turned to Luke. "Do you think it's a good idea for them to be alone in her room like that?"

Luke was incredulous. "Eh, what would be the problem?"

"I mean, they're in a relationship. Wouldn't that be a tempting situation for them? Won't they fall into sin?"

"Nah, I don't think so. Paulie's a solid Christian, very honest, you know that. I mean, he confessed to masturbation in front of large group." He chuckled.

She tried to stifle laughter to no avail. "That's true. I guess you're right."

"Yeah, he'll be fine. Alyssa too. Besides, her roommate Vicky's usually there. She's a bit of an introvert, so she hardly ever leaves the room unless she has class. She'll either be studying or watching TV.

The most that'll happen is that the three of them will be together watching taped episodes of General Hospital."

"Ugh, that sounds boring."

"Yeah, for sure. But at least it's not tempting to anybody but old housewives."

Once arriving at Ann's residence hall, they stopped in front.

I really hope Luke asks to come up and hang out.

"Alright, I'm gonna head on back to my apartment."

Damn.

"Okay, sounds good. Be safe."

"I will. And like I told you earlier, if you need to talk or anything, don't hesitate to give me a call."

"Thanks, Luke."

"Anytime." He gave her a warm embrace. "Oh, by the way, AC, you look lovely tonight."

"Thanks, Luke. You're not so bad yourself...twin."

He smiled and then left in the direction of his apartment off-campus.

Before entering the dormitory, Ann looked down and noticed that the safety pin had fallen out and that her cleavage was quite visible.

Oh no!

The next morning, Ann woke up to a ringing telephone.

It's seven in the morning. It's not even time to get up for church.

She picked up the phone. Upon hearing her mother Sherrye on the other end, she felt a twinge of anxiety.

I've already lost Dad. I can't take losing anybody else so soon.

"Hi, Mom...is everything okay?"

"Yes, sweetie. I wanted to call and make sure you're okay."

"Of course. Why wouldn't I be?"

"You don't know?"

"No..."

"There was a riot at Great Lakes."

"What?" Ann sat up in bed.

"Yeah, it was on the news this morning. You know how I'm still having trouble sleeping since your dad died?"

"Yeah."

"Well, I was up this morning, and I was watching TV, and it was all over the national news. They were burning couches and cars, and a lot of students got arrested. All that because they lost to the Spartans."

"Wow, that's insane. I had no idea. We had a Christmas party last night and headed straight back to my dorm room afterwards, so I saw none of it."

"That's good. Anyway, Annie, I'm looking forward to you coming home next week."

"I am, too."

Over winter break, while school was out due to the season's holidays, Ann returned to Detroit to spend time with family. It would be her first Christmas without her father. She anticipated the season would be incredibly difficult, and knew she needed to be with her family.

Two hours after leaving campus with Terah, they arrived in their East English Village neighborhood. The enclave was well-maintained and middle-class. It was the home of many of the city's civil servants, including police officers and firefighters, as well as engineers and other professionals working for the "Big Three" American auto companies.

By the early 2000s, the loosening of residency requirements in the previous decade led to some civil servants moving out of the neighborhood and into the suburbs, but for the most part, the clean and proud character of the locale remained. The streets were filled with meticulously-kept Tudors, Cape Cods, colonials, and bungalows. These nice homes, mostly built in the early to mid-twentieth century, sat on fairly small lots, with paved driveways and serviceable one-car garages.

Ann's family home on Grayton Street was a humble colonial with baby blue cladding and stark white window trim, soffits, and fascia, located a block north of East Warren Avenue, a main thoroughfare. Terah lived on Bishop Street, the next street over, in a small red brick bungalow with yellow chrysanthemums in front, on the other side of East Warren.

One morning, Ann woke up to the smell of bacon and biscuits. She loved it when her mother made breakfast. In her pajamas and bonnet, she headed down the stairs and strolled into the kitchen. At the gas stove stood Sherrye, in a green overcoat and a light green scarf over her hair, cooking the first meal of the day.

"Good morning," Ann greeted her mother.

"Morning darling," Sherrye responded sweetly. "How did you sleep?"

"I slept okay. I kept the TV on and eventually fell asleep."

Ever since Marshall's death, Ann needed noise to sleep. Her physician prescribed Prozac to ease her anxiety and help her rest at night. She took the medication as prescribed, but the vivid nightmares she experienced as a side effect led her to taper off the pills with doctor's approval. In the absence of pharmaceutical help, the noise of the television helped her get some semblance of rest.

"How did you sleep, Mom?"

"Well, I always get up very early now. Ever since your father died, I just can't sleep through the night. No matter how early or late I sleep, I always wake up around two in the morning and can't fall back asleep."

"That's rough." As Ann looked around the kitchen, she asked, "What can I do to help?"

"You can go ahead and wash dishes for right now. You know I like to keep up with the dishes while I'm cooking."

She cleaned the dishes. "What are you making right now?"

"Ah, I'm making bacon, eggs, and grits. Biscuits are in the oven."

"Ooh, that sounds delicious!"

"I'm setting aside some hard-boiled eggs and well-done grits just for you."

Ann was thrilled to hear of the eggs and grits. She had a visceral dislike of scrambled eggs and loose grits. The issue was not the taste, but the texture. Only hard-boiled eggs and well-done grits felt quite right in her mouth. "Aww, thanks Mom, I appreciate it."

"Of course, dear."

A few minutes later, Michelle trudged down the stairs in blue plaid pajama pants and a solid shirt.

"Hi, hun!" called out Sherrye.

"Hi, Mom," mumbled Michelle. She sat at the perfectly set polished dining room table, her raven and auburn ombré micro braids in a plump bun.

Breakfast was ready a short time later. After setting the table and sitting with her children, Sherrye said, "Let's bow our heads and pray."

The family lowered their heads for prayer.

Sherrye prayed. "Heavenly Father, I thank you for waking us up this morning, and for our meal that we take in for the nourishment of our bodies. Thank you, Jesus, for both my girls being here at home. We praise you and thank you, in Jesus' name, Amen."

Everyone then ate the tasty spread.

"Do you wanna go to Uncle Louie's today?" Michelle asked. "I told him you would be in town and he wants you to stop by."

"Okay, sure."

She smiled. "All right, we'll do that this afternoon." She turned to Sherrye. "Do you wanna come with us?"

"No, that's alright, Shelly, I'll stay here. But you and your sister should go and see your uncle and aunt. Go ahead and take your father's car. Tell them I said 'hi.'"

That afternoon, Ann and Michelle hopped into Marshall's powder blue Buick LeSabre and headed west. The roads were cleared by several weeks' worth of traffic after a period of heavy lake effect snow earlier in the month.

The sisters took Eight Mile Road, the thoroughfare on Detroit's northern border separating the largely beleaguered city from suburbs that were, overall, quite posh. However, there existed pockets of nicer enclaves within city borders, and one of these great Detroit neighborhoods was their destination.

While driving down Eight Mile, Ann and Michelle viewed the snow layers on the homes, lawns, businesses, and parking lots lining the thoroughfare. After a half-hour drive avoiding freeways due to their desire to take the scenic route, the siblings arrived in Palmer Woods, an affluent section of the city just west of Woodward Avenue, the street that bisects Detroit. The neighborhood was also near two cemeteries, including the one where Marshall was laid to rest less than two months previously. The small bedroom community consisted of mansions and large homes built primarily in the early 1900s that sat on manicured lawns along curved, quiet streets.

Ann turned left into the spacious driveway of a substantial Tudor home with perfectly landscaped, snow-topped rose bushes in front, the car coming to rest on the left side of the shoveled pavement. The sisters got out and strolled to the front door. Ann pressed the doorbell, and Louie opened the door to greet them.

Once inside, they all proceeded to the sitting room, where Louie's wife Eliza was waiting. She gave them a broad smile.

"Hey Shelley, hey Annie! So good to see you!"

"Hi, Auntie Liza! I'm happy to see you too!" Ann responded.

"Auntie Liza, I said I'd get her over here!" Michelle told her, feeling accomplished.

The siblings sent spent much of the afternoon catching up with their uncle and aunt. During the course of their conversation, Ann shared her plans for post-university life.

"So, I think I'm going to stay in Upper West Osceola for a bit. There are some data analytics jobs in and around the university that I'll be qualified to do," Ann shared.

"Doesn't that involve computers?" Eliza asked.

"Uh, yes. It involves researching data, analyzing it to answer questions, and pointing out patterns and trends, that kind of thing. There's a lot of statistics involved, so it's pretty much a computer-based field."

"I thought you were going to law school?" Louie interjected.

"I don't know, Uncle Louie. It's something Dad wanted me to do, but I'm not sure. I need some time to figure that out."

In part, Ann's apprehension regarding a potential future as a lawyer was due to her budding Christian faith. While she dreamed of becoming an attorney for much of her life, doubts were planted in her mind. *What about public speaking? Will the law profession conflict with my belief in Jesus Christ?* She was having second thoughts.

February 2001

Months before Marshall's death, Ann found herself contemplating life after college. She was studying for the LSAT consistently as she made plans to go to law school, either at Great Lakes' Fieger School of Law or potentially at a school in New York, since her aunt Marie and uncle Eddie lived there. She also kicked around the idea of attending Gulf State College in Florida, since that was where her father received his *juris doctor*.

She discussed her future with her closest college friends. Terah and Luke supported Ann's initial plan for law school, but Paul was not so sure.

"Eh, you should probably think twice about getting into law," Paul mused. "It's full of crooks and shady people."

"Um..." Ann took time to gather her thoughts. "My dad's an attorney. He's in family law and he sometimes represents kids. He's not a crook and he's not 'shady' either."

He issued his mea culpa. "Sorry, wasn't trying to offend you. Didn't mean to put it like that. It's just that sometimes, you hear about lawyers doing things like covering up for criminals."

"Uh...everybody has the right to an attorney, even if we don't like what they're being accused of doing. If we convict in the public and not give people a fair trial with representation, it becomes easy for innocent people to go to prison, or worse depending on the state."

"I know what you mean. Look, Ann...whatever we're thinking about doing for a career should be brought to God, I think. If you wanna be a lawyer, it wouldn't hurt to run it by Brother Craig or Sister Rhonda, or maybe even your home church pastor."

"Yeah, maybe you're right. I'll talk to one of them."

A few days later, she attended Bible study at Sister Rhonda's house close to campus. Ann spoke with her after the meeting. They sat on a purple sofa in her living room, where a variety of toys were strewn around the floor. Her rambunctious kindergarten-aged daughter Hannah and her excitable son Adam, who was two years Hannah's junior, were playing.

"So, you wanted to talk to me about something," said Rhonda.

"Yes, I did. So uh...I'm trying to figure out what to do after I graduate next year. I've planned on going to law school for as long as I can remember. But I was talking to Paul, and he was saying I probably shouldn't do it because he says lawyers tend to be shady criminals. I mean, I don't think I have to be shady or a criminal if I became a lawyer, but would there be a concern spiritually?"

"Mommy, look! Mommy, look!" Adam interrupted, holding up a blue and yellow toy train.

Rhonda picked up her young son to give him attention, then responded to Ann. "That's a great question. I think God appreciates that we want to include him in our decision-making. Your dad's a lawyer, right?"

"Yeah."

The staff leader thought aloud, tying her her dark, wavy hair into a long, thick braid. "A lot of times, we see what our parents do, and we want to follow in their footsteps. The question is, is this what you're being called to do?"

"Hmm, good question. My dad helps a lot of people, he's an advocate for kids. But I *hate* public speaking. Not all attorneys are in courtrooms, but still...I don't know. I've been thinking about data analytics. I love numbers and finding out new things, and not gonna lie, I think I would like the challenge of working in a mostly male field."

"Welp, it looks like we have a lot to pray about. You see, it's not just about what *you* want to do, but what *God* wants you to do. And you may have to figure out how your career affects other callings like marriage and motherhood. God willing, you'll meet a young man who loves Jesus, who you're called to marry. And then, of course, God will call you to be fruitful and multip—"

"Mommy, I want the train!" interrupted Hannah, who got up from the floor and tried to reach for her brother's toy vehicle.

"No kiddo, your brother's playing with that right now. You have some other toys right there on the floor that are just for you," Sister Rhonda pointed out to her daughter.

"I don't want that; I want the train!"

"Trains are for boys. See, your toy kitchen and Barbie dolls are there in the corner. Go play with those."

Hannah sat and sulked.

Sister Rhonda turned back to Ann. "Sorry about that."

"Oh, that's okay."

"So, I was saying, you'll want to make room in your life to have a family of your own, but God's timing is everything. As of right now, since you're not in a relationship and set to be married soon, it's healthy to consider a career. You'll hear some pastors and others who advise everybody that they should either be in ministry or running their own business. And if you feel led to do either of those things, those are wonderful callings. But God is the God of all arenas, and he needs his people everywhere."

Ann nodded. "That makes sense."

"If he wants you to be a lawyer, that's great, be the best Christian lawyer you can be. If he wants you to be in data analytics, be a data analyst for the Lord. Let's pray about it."

After the women finished praying, they hugged, and Sister Rhonda reassured her softly, "You'll be okay. God's got you."

While visiting her uncle and aunt, Ann explained her altered plans in detail.

"I've been leaning towards data analytics. I've been researching and it's a growing field, with the internet and all. The data industry is expected to be a big deal in the near future, and I'll be on the cutting edge of that."

"That sounds great," affirmed Eliza. "Just be careful, it's a risk. Remember how just a few years ago there was the dot-com bubble, and that burst. At least with law, you'll always have a job. Everybody needs lawyers at one point or another."

"Yeah. Everybody was talking about how much money they could make from the internet, and then the dot-com bubble burst and it all fell apart," Louie elaborated. "Just be careful."

"I will."

They continued their conversation during the visit, including sharing cherished memories of Marshall, as Perry Mason, Louie's favorite show, played on the large-screen box television. Then, he brought up another subject.

"Annie, have you thought about meeting your mother?"

"Huh?" Ann looked up at her uncle, perplexed.

"Your mother, Stephanie."

"Louie, stop. You're going to confuse Michelle," Eliza admonished her husband in a hushed tone.

"Auntie Liza," Michelle interjected. "I already know Ann has a different birth mother."

"Oh, okay. I didn't know what your father told you."

"Mom and Dad talked about that with the both of us."

"Um, to answer your question, Uncle Louie," Ann replied, "to be honest, I haven't thought about it."

"Oh, why not?" Louie asked, confused.

"Because...why would I?"

Louie rocked back a bit on the cocoa suede couch contemplatively. "What did your dad tell you about your mother?"

"Well, he said that he and my birth mother were married for a short time, she lost her mind, they got divorced, she felt he would be the better parent, so she stopped contesting custody and then she was 'poof' — in the wind."

"Oh boy. Damn it, Marshall," he grumbled to himself while rubbing his forehead. "It wasn't like that at all."

"Uncle Louie, I don't think Dad would lie about that," Michelle opined.

"I'm sure your father didn't *lie*, Shelley. When you get older, you'll find out that adults can be complicated."

Louie retrieved a green photo album from the dark-stained mahogany bookshelf. Then, sitting next to Ann, he cracked it open. The album included several pictures she had never seen before. He then pointed out a specific one. It was of a petite, toned woman with a clear fawn complexion, deep brown eyes, and dark brunette, tightly curled hair to her shoulders. She wore a sleeveless, fitted polyester dress with a sketched dragonfly pattern. The hem brushed an inch above the knee. The woman stood in front of a bungalow, smiling weakly.

"Have you seen a picture of your mother before?"

Ann nodded. "Yes, but it's been a long time."

"If you ever want to know what *really* happened, you can always come see me."

"Okay, Uncle Louie."

"You know, Annie...your Big Mama would always say, 'The truth shall make you free.'"

Ann felt a bit rattled after the visit to see her uncle and aunt. Her thoughts stayed with her throughout the day and into the evening.

I feel like an orphan. Dad isn't here because he died. My birth mother is gone without being dead. Sure, I had a mom because Mom stepped in and raised me. I will forever appreciate that. But what if I hadn't lucked out? What if Mom hadn't treated me like she had given birth to me? What if I had gotten a mean stepmother instead? Or if it was just Dad and me, and I didn't have a mom at all? Stephanie would never know. Does she even care?

She was so pretty. I'm sure she was embarrassed of me...look at how fat I am, and how weird I look! How do you carry a child for nine months, give birth, then you decide to disappear from your child's life? I don't understand, I can never understand that.

Unable to sleep, Ann crept downstairs and shuffled into the kitchen of the home she grew up in. She searched the freezer for something to eat. *Oh, those mozzarella sticks...perfect!*

She proceeded to the beige gas-powered stove, moved the standing pot of cool cooking grease to the front left burner, and turned the burner to medium flame. After several minutes, she dumped several breaded cheese sticks into the oil and watched them sizzle. Once fully cooked, she fished the sticks out of the pot and plated them.

While her snack was cooling, she opened the refrigerator, retrieved a two-liter Faygo carbonated fruit punch bottle, and poured the tall glass halfway. She then picked up a bottle of Faygo orange pop and filled up the glass the rest of the way. *No ice. I hate diluted pop.* Now finished, she sat down to enjoy her mozzarella sticks and pop in peace.

"Ann — what are *you* cooking this time of night?"

Ann nearly jumped out of her skin. She then turned around in her chair to see her mother in the kitchen doorway. "Hi, Mom, uh...what are you doing up?"

"I smelled the food from all the way upstairs."

"Oh."

"Annie, I don't want to sound like your father, but you know you should watch what you eat a bit more. You don't want to end up like him."

"I know, Mom."

Weight was always a sore subject for the young woman, as she was criticized for it both at home and at school. It was one of many traits she possessed that made her the subject of derision, and therefore, often sat at the forefront of her mind.

Generally, acceptance was elusive as she was growing up. She was not a popular child in her fairly diverse elementary school. She could not relate to most of her classmates, no matter how hard she tried, and was bullied often.

Many of her white classmates took verbal jabs at her overweight body, which at the time was only ten to twenty pounds larger than most of her classmates, as well as her nervous speech patterns, which they mocked relentlessly by stuttering at her, "uh uh uh uh uh." She was commonly called "Stay Puft" and "Goodyear Blimp" by these classmates.

Some of her Black classmates made fun of her too, but for different reasons. While light skin was largely favored among this set of classmates, especially for girls, any advantage Ann's beige skin tone would have given her was offset by her Afrocentric facial features and her curvier body type, coupled with her unusual grey eye color. The combination was off-putting in their view. In addition, many of her Black classmates believed she spoke too "proper," and that her grades in class — mostly 'A's — reflected a desire to "act white."

Ann spoke the way she did because Marshall and Sherrye, due to their own upbringing, class, and education level, did not allow her nor her sister Michelle to use "slang" in their presence, especially in their formative years. The youngest Corbin's saving grace was that, as an extroverted social butterfly, she could easily 'code-switch' — that is, she could converse in standard English with her parents and authority figures, yet easily slide into speaking the dialect of her peers in the neighborhood and at school. Ann, however, was more introverted and socially awkward, making an audience-dependent shift in speech incredibly tough.

In addition, her intense anxiety made it tough to keep from using crutch words such as "uh," "um," and "like." For a brief period, her parents placed her in speech therapy, and her speech improved somewhat over time. Unfortunately for her, the speech therapy was stopped after a few sessions, as her parents were in denial that their daughter had a problem besides simply *shyness*.

Once in high school, Ann still faced the wrath of bullies on occasion, but now had a solid core of friends. Terah, in particular, was her first high school friend and was one of the few friends who were constant in her life.

Ann's size was a constant concern for her parents, especially her father. Marshall's own weight had increased over the years. He stopped going to the gym after the birth of his children, but still ate the same as he did while bodybuilding. This led to many health problems by the time he reached his forties, such as type 2 diabetes, hypertension, and vertigo. He did not want his children to face the same health challenges he encountered.

She knew that her father's push for weight loss came from a good place, but he had trouble practicing what he preached. That meant watching her parents and sister eat delicious, fattening foods while she was stuck eating plain rice cakes and "pizza" made from English muffins, tomato paste, and fat-free cheese, among other concoctions from a cookbook of diet foods for children.

To supplement efforts to slim down Ann's pudgy figure, Marshall pushed her to participate in sports, signing her up for volleyball, basketball, and track and field. However, she hated every minute of it, as she had absolutely no athletic ability, and her coaches and teammates constantly reminded her of it. Yet, it was not for lack of trying. She worked incredibly hard to improve, attending every practice and pushing herself beyond her limits each time, but was rewarded by riding the pine pony on gamedays.

This intense monitoring of the girl's diet and exercise, as well as her inability to find acceptance, led to a disordered relationship with food. This started with sneaking snacks from the kitchen once home from grade school. Then, in high school, Ann would buy junk food on her way home, or secretly take forbidden foods from the kitchen.

A night owl, Ann had the habit of creeping into the kitchen after everyone else was asleep and making fried foods she would be scolded for eating during the day. Most of the time, she got away with it. But occasionally, not so much.

April 1996

One Saturday night when Ann was sixteen, she sat downstairs alone and watched the police procedural "Homicide: Life On the Street," and then the eleven o'clock news, waiting out her family until they retired to bed. After the news was over, she headed to the kitchen, quietly pulled out a box of breaded chicken tenders, and fried them on the stove, a few at a time in two batches, six in total.

Everybody's asleep. I'm hungry...I'm gonna have my tenders in peace.

She then sat at the small kitchen table with her plate of chicken and was about to bite into one.

"Annie – you know you shouldn't be eating that."

Ann jumped, startled. "Dad, how did you know?"

"The smell is all over the house."

"What did Ann make?" asked nine-year-old Michelle, who had now made her way downstairs.

"Looks like chicken tenders," Marshall responded. He then grabbed the plate of food from the table and ate it himself. He then turned to Michelle. "Want some?"

"Yeah," she responded, taking a piece and eating it while smirking at her shamed sister.

"You can still eat these."

Ann shook her head, dejected. "No Dad, you can have them."

"Don't let me stop you."

"No, I'm sure. Goodnight." She left the kitchen and trudged upstairs to her bedroom, frustrated, alone, and sad.

Experiences such as the one she had in adolescence led Ann to redouble her efforts to hide her compulsive eating.

In college, free from the watchful eye of her father, her binging increased. Without the guardrails set in place by her family, she availed herself of the many restaurant takeout and delivery options around the University of the Great Lakes. She continued hiding the magnitude of her eating from peers to avoid their critiques or judgmental stares. As a result, she gained the freshman fifty – yes, the freshman *fifty* – and her weight continued to climb. Food was how she coped with her feelings.

Upon Sherrye's callout of Ann that December evening, she fidgeted and averted her eyes. "I already know, Mom."

Noticing the reaction, her mother changed the subject. "So, how was your trip to see your Uncle Louie and Auntie Liza? How are they?"

"They're doing pretty good. It was nice visiting them. Uncle Louie brought up my birth mother."

Sherrye raised an eyebrow. "Really?"

"Yeah, he did."

"What did he say about her?"

"He asked me if I wanted to meet her."

"Do you?"

"Honestly, I don't know why I would wanna do that."

"Eh, I'm sure he brought it up now since your father's not here to say something to him. But I do think that one day you should meet her, I've told you that. I think it's important."

"Yeah, you've said that."

"To be honest, I wish your uncle had let you come to him when you were ready. It's been less than two months since your father died."

"True, Mom. I guess so," Ann responded, staring regretfully at her cooling mozzarella sticks.

"I see you look upset. I hope it wasn't the comment I made about your weight. You know it's all about your health and I wouldn't be a good mother if I didn't worry about you."

"I get it. It's just that...um...I got a lot on my mind. I really miss Dad, and I'm about to be finished with college and I don't know what I'm gonna do next. And then this whole thing...I don't know how I feel about my birth mother. I've got too many questions, but at the same time, none at all." Ann sighed and shook her head. "I just don't know."

Sherrye sat at the table and placed her hand gently on Ann's arm. "I know, Annie. Have you thought about talking to someone, like counseling? You saw somebody in high school and it seemed to help you."

Ann sighed. "Eh, maybe I should, Mom...maybe I should."

PORKIE
JANUARY 2002

Therapist Mara Strong sat in her chair facing her client. "Good afternoon, Ann. Come in and have a seat."

She quietly sat and took off her green pea coat.

"Ann, I understand you lost your father recently. My condolences," the therapist expressed.

"Thank you."

"How are you feeling right now?"

I could lie, or I could just not open up. I mean, I don't know if this woman is safe. But then, what's the point of not being fully honest in therapy?

Ann answered, "Eh, I don't really know right now. My dad and I were so close. Sometimes, it felt like he knew me better than I know myself. The thing is, a part of me knew this was coming."

"When you say that you knew this was coming, what do you mean by that?"

"Um...when I was a kid, I always thought my dad was invincible. He was heavyset – I guess I get that from him – but he was strong. He worked out a lot. He went to the gym. And he was always pushing me to get involved in sports at school, even though I don't have an athletic bone in my body. But then, maybe a year or two ago, he started looking *weak* to me."

"When you say he looked 'weak,' what do you mean by that?"

"You know, he was diabetic, and his health was catching up to him. He walked slower. He was having trouble with his balance. Sometimes, he would get kind of foggy. I could see it, but I didn't wanna admit to myself that something was wrong."

Mara gently moved a strand of her straight brown bob from her face. "So, you're saying you could see the health challenges your father was facing, but you did not want to face that he might be dying?"

Ann nodded. "Yeah, pretty much. The other thing is that the reality of my dad being dead is setting in."

"In what ways?"

"I mean, I can't pick up the phone and call him anymore. When I go home, he's not there. There's an empty seat at the dinner table where he always sat. My sister asks me questions she can't ask him anymore. Then, there's also the future stuff."

"The future? Please tell me more about that, Ann, if you're comfortable."

"Uh...if I ever get married, my dad won't be able to walk me down the aisle. If I have kids, my dad won't be here to meet them. But then, I think to myself, 'Why am I even worried about things like getting married and having kids? It's not like I'm good enough for anybody to notice me."

"When you say you don't feel that you're 'good enough,' what do you mean by that?"

Ann looked down and fiddled with the strap on her pink Jansport backpack. "You know, I always feel like no matter how hard I try, even though I know there are good things about me, none of that matters."

"What are those good things?"

"Uh...I'm a solid Christian who has kept my purity."

"Purity?"

She nodded. "Yeah...like, I'm still a virgin."

"Oh...okay. Is there anything else you see as a good thing about yourself?"

"Um...I listen to people...I try to understand them, see things from different points of view. I'm flexible – I mean, I try to do things other people like because I want to see them happy. I'm a loyal person. I work hard in school and I have a lot of drive. But none of it matters."

"What makes you think the things you like about yourself don't matter?"

"Because no matter what I do, I can't get any guy to notice me. They just see that I'm fat and that I'm strange-looking, and that I'm just weird, and nothing else matters. Who I am as a person doesn't matter. I might as well be invisible."

Mara shifted her slight frame. "Ann, could you tell me more about that?"

Ann sighed. "I guess so. See, it's been like this for a very long time."

Summer 1992

"Hi, Mom!" Ann greeted her mother as she got into the front passenger seat of her red and grey Ford Aerostar.

"Hi, Annie!" Sherrye started up the minivan. Michelle, who was a toddler, was in the back seat, strapped securely into her booster car seat. "How was school?"

"It was okay. This girl in my class, Maya, passed gas in my face."

"She didn't mean to, did she?"

"Mom...she meant to. She did that and laughed at me."

"That's rude. Kids can be mean."

"Could you and Dad go up to the school? I'm always getting made fun of. I don't care if they don't wanna be friends. I just wish they would leave me alone."

"No, dear. We did that at Saint Mark's, and it just made things harder for you, especially since the principal was friends with your bully's father. You're at Saint Martha's now. You're in middle school, you need to learn how to fight your own battles."

Sullenly, Ann stared out the window as they traveled home.

"Annie, I meant to tell you. Grab that envelope on the dashboard. It's for you. It's from Great Lakes. I think it's about that SoM program."

As a lover of math with excellent grades, Ann's school counselor advised her to apply to the Summer of Mathematics program, or SoM, hosted at the University of the Great Lakes. SoM was a six-week residential program for high-achieving middle school students of color, where they would participate in math-centered workshops, engage in activities such as walking tours and field trips, and stay in one of the campus dormitories.

The teen picked up the white envelope, opened it, and read the letter inside:

THE UNIVERSITY OF THE GREAT LAKES

OFFICE OF MINORITY AFFAIRS
SUMMER OF MATHEMATICS PROGRAM
May 11, 1992
Dear Miss Corbin:
On behalf of the Office of Minority Affairs at the University of the Great Lakes, we are excited to offer you placement in the Summer of Mathematics Program (SoM) for Summer 1992. The program duration is from Monday, June 22 to Sunday, August 2, 1992, and is free of charge to participants. More details regarding the program will be provided in a separate packet arriving within a few days. Please have your parent or guardian respond confirming your participation by calling (517) 555-7801 during business hours or using the enclosed postcard postmarked no later than Friday, May 29, or you will lose your placement and it will be offered to a waitlisted applicant.

Parent or guardian: Please call us at (517) 555-7801 during business hours if you have any questions about your child's participation in the program.

Sincerely,
William Freeman, PhD
Director, Office of Minority Affairs
The University of the Great Lakes

"Mom, I got in!"

"Oh, I had no doubt, sweetie. I knew you would. Let your dad know when he gets home."

This marked the first time Ann would be away from home without her parents for a significant period. She was excited because this was a new adventure and the first time she would be staying on a college campus. There would be boys, too, which was an exciting prospect for a preteen girl attending a same-sex private school. At the same time, she was extremely nervous. She knew no one else attending, and as an awkward, shy teen who already found it difficult to fit in with her peers, it was not always easy for her to strike up friendships.

Since Marshall had to work that June day, Sherrye, with Michelle in tow, drove Ann to Great Lakes to drop her off at SoM. When they arrived at McDonald Hall, the campus dormitory where she would be staying, they were guided by a residence counselor to a two-person dorm room. One side of the floor housed the girls, while the other side of the floor housed the boys, and each side had its own designated community bathroom.

Shortly after her family left and she began to settle in, a teen with a brown suitcase in hand stood in the doorway and said sweetly, "Hey, girl!" She then took another look at the solid hardwood door, where colorful tags included the names of the two occupants. "Ann, huh?"

"Uh...hi. That's me."

"Hey, I'm Jennifer!" She walked in, sat her suitcase down, and hugged her. "Where you from?"

"Um...Detroit."

"What side of town?"

"East side."

"Okay, I got people over there. Seven Mile and Dequindre."

"Oh, I know where that is," Ann recalled. "I'm on the far east side, Warren and Cadieux."

"Oh, you're in *that* part of Detroit," Jennifer responded, side-eying Ann. "You bougie."

"Nah, not really. So, uh...where you from?"

"Saginaw."

"Okay cool, how's it there?"

"They say it's more ghetto than the D, but it's a'ight."

As were most of the group's meals during the program, dinner the first night was held in the cafeteria located on the first floor of the residence hall. As the roommates took their seats at a table, Jennifer introduced Ann to a friend, LaTeisha, from her high school in Saginaw.

A chocolate-hued, thick-bodied girl with box braids, smirked slightly. "'Sup?"

"Hey, nice to meet you," Ann responded

"Yeah. You too."

As the girls continued to chat, they heard a voice.

"Wassup, ladies!"

The girls turned around to see a chunky, bronze-toned boy with a high-top fade and the beginnings of a rat tail. He had a smirk on his face as if he were trying to be cool. A gangly boy with slicked-back hair stood next to him, expressionless.

"I'm Tavion, and this is my boy, Hector."

Hector bobbed his head in acknowledgment. "'Sup?"

The girls introduced themselves and the boys sat down with them. While eating their meal of hamburgers and fries, they learned more about each other. Tavion was from Detroit's west side – West Warren Avenue and Wyoming Avenue. Hector was from Jackson, a city west of Detroit and south of Michigan's capital, Lansing, which was home to a notorious state prison. The boys had been involved in similar state academic programs while in elementary school, and because of that, they already knew each other.

Over the week, the workshops proved exciting for the students, including Ann. Her favorite workshop was physics, where the students worked on creating aerodynamic toy cars powered by CO_2 cartridges. While she enjoyed the science and hands-on activities of the workshop, she looked forward to it for a different reason.

"That's real nice, Ann. Love the design," Tavion noticed.

"Thanks, Tavion. Your car looks nice too. Very aerodynamic."

"Yeah, thanks. I love this kind of stuff. My dad's an engineer at GM, and we create all kinds of fun toys in our garage at home. So, I got some practice."

"So, um, what can I do to make mine better?"

Tavion picked up Ann's car. "Mmm, shave a little off here, and make sure you place the hole for the cartridge just right."

The two continued their chats each day in physics while crafting their cars to successfully race the track assembled by the organizers. She was smitten by his brains and smooth demeanor and could not wait to gab about him to her new roommate.

"So, Ann," Jennifer began while lying in her bed one night later that week, "There's a lot of fine dudes here. I got my eye on Donte, that tall light-skinned dude with them silk shirts. He's so fly!"

Ann, in her own bed, turned to face Jennifer. "I mean, he's not bad. But you know, I think I like Tavion."

"Oh, really? What you feelin' about him?"

"I mean, he's really smart, he knows things, he's fun to talk to. I like his voice, it's smooth."

"What about how he looks?"

"Uh, he's cute, I guess. I dunno. But that's not why I like him."

Jennifer furrowed her brow. "Okay…"

The following Wednesday, Ann strolled into the classroom excited to paint her toy car. She planned to color it a slick shade of red. But Tavion's workstation, which was typically next to hers, was moved three tables over.

Ann thought to herself, *Did I miss something?*

She looked around to see him returning to the room. He walked over to the table where his materials had been moved, sat down, and began preparing his workstation.

Ann approached her crush. "Hi, Tavion!"

No response.

"Uh...what's going on?"

Tavion averted his eyes and quietly mumbled, "Nothing."

"Oo-kay."

"I heard you wanna be with me," he said quietly. "I don't wanna be in a relationship right now. But we can be friends."

How does he know? Ann was puzzled as she returned to her table in silence. *Boys don't like me, and it sucks. It's nothing new. But how did I get rejected yet again when I literally told him nothing?*

She was disappointed and confused, but what was she going to do? *At least he said we could be friends.* But as time went on, the confusion only deepened.

Over the next week, Ann attempted to talk to Tavion as if they were friends, but he was not as receptive and gregarious as he was before the rejection. One evening before bed, she shared her feelings with her roommate.

"I don't get it. He said we could be friends, but he's being all weird around me."

"Girl, he wrong for that," Jennifer affirmed. "If he didn't wanna be cool with you, he shouldn't have gave you hope like that."

"Hope?"

"Yeah, hope. Like, if y'all are friends, something more'll happen later."

"That makes no sense. I dunno. I get it, he doesn't wanna be with me. But I never told him I liked him. I ain't say shit to him."

"I dunno, girl. I sure ain't say nothing to him 'bout that. But maybe you came off like you did, and he just knew."

"Ugh. But yeah, if he doesn't wanna be friends, it's whatever. But I wish I knew why he lied to me."

Two weeks later, on a Friday morning, Ann woke up to her alarm. The routine would be a little different than the typical daily itinerary. Instead of the workshops, the SoM group would be going on a field trip to Detroit to visit the Museum of African American History.

Weird, Jennifer's not up here. She must've gone down early to meet up with LaTeisha.

After washing up, showering, and pulling her tightly curled brown hair into a ponytail, she jumped into her clothes, including an orange summer jumper, which felt a lot looser on her than it did before arriving at Great Lakes four weeks prior. *Must be all that walking.* Ann felt accomplished. After jumping into her white K-Swiss high tops, she headed downstairs. This morning, they were going to have pancakes and bacon out on the buffet. *Tasty.*

Ann descended down the stairs and walked inside the open double doors to the cafeteria. As she proceeded to grab her tray, silverware, and plate, she looked around and noticed something that made her stop dead in her tracks.

LaTeisha had not arrived at breakfast yet, but Jennifer was not alone, or even with the other girls. She was sitting next to Tavion. They giggled and fed each other pieces of bacon.

I thought he didn't want to be in a relationship right now. And not only he lied, but he's getting with my roommate? How could she do this to me? I thought we were friends.

LaTeisha then entered the cafeteria. She looked over at Jennifer and Tavion, then glanced at the betrayed teen, snickered, and walked away.

On the van during the two-hour trip to Detroit, Ann was forced to endure seeing her crush and her roommate stare at each other dreamily. At the museum, while the other students were studying the artwork and exhibits, she sat on a bench, alone with her intrusive thoughts. *Why? How could he lie to me? She must have told him I liked him and then swooped in.*

Occasionally, the two waltzed into her line of sight — he with his baggy jean shorts and yellow and blue striped Polo shirt, wearing knockoff Cool Water cologne, she in a teal, spaghetti-strapped minidress with a form-fitting white tee underneath. The sight made her feel sick to her stomach.

After the museum trip, the group stopped at Sanders Hot Fudge, an ice cream parlor in the Village, a shopping district in the affluent Detroit suburb of Grosse Pointe. Ann barely noticed the residents staring suspiciously at their group, who appeared out of place in the wealthy, homogeneous district. She was laser-focused on Tavion and Jennifer sharing a large, delicious hot fudge sundae.

When the young students returned to campus and the confines of McDonald Hall, Ann used a public telephone in a tucked-away carrel and called her parents. She spoke with her mother for a few minutes, getting caught up with the happenings back home, which were not much. Then, Sherrye handed the phone over to her dad.

After a couple of minutes, Marshall said, "Baby, I can tell something's wrong. What's going on? Do you want to go home?"

"No Dad, I don't wanna go home. But I don't wanna talk about it."

"Must be a boy."

Ann hesitated. "Yeah. I liked a boy, he said he didn't want a relationship, but then he got with my roommate."

"Did you tell your roommate that you had a crush on the boy?" he asked.

"Yeah, why?"

Marshall sighed. "One of the things I had to learn when I was younger is to keep my love interests to myself, even when people act friendly towards you. See, people do things like that. They pretend to be your friend, and then use what you say against you."

Ann took a deep breath, regretting her decision to divulge the details of her situation. "Okay, Dad."

"And you know what else? About that boy. That knucklehead is immature, most boys are at that age. When you get older, things will change for you. You'll meet more mature boys. You'll meet someone who sees how special you are. But right now, don't worry about boys."

Sherrye overheard Marshall. "Is Ann upset about a boy?"

He responded, "Yeah, a boy up there at camp rejected her."

"She needs to stop worrying about these boys and keep her nose in the books. See, that's why she's at Saint Martha. Boy crazy."

After Ann got off the phone with her parents, not feeling the least bit better, she went upstairs and closed the door. As she took her ponytail down, there was a knock on the door. She got up and answered it.

"Hi, LaTeisha. Jennifer isn't here."

"I'm not lookin' for Jennifer. I'm lookin' for you."

"Uh, okay. What's up?"

"*So*, we went and asked all the boys in the group, all eight of 'em. About *you*."

"What? Why?"

"Just cuz. Anyway, none of 'em think you're cute. They said you jiggle and your grey eyes make you look weird, like you a funny-looking white girl. You sound white too, what's up wit' that?"

Ann was speechless.

LaTeisha continued, smugly. "They said you ugly, and you know what they rated you? A negative two hundred and fifty-six. Fatass." She then strolled away, giggling.

Furious, Ann slammed the door. She was so over it. She was over her roommate, her roommate's new boyfriend, her roommate's friend, and every other student at SoM. She was beyond over it. She hated every single one of them. Most of all, she hated herself.

She turned off the room light, lay in her stiff university-issue bed, and sobbed uncontrollably. She desperately wanted to go home. Her parents would undoubtedly make her feel worse about the sin of attempting to connect with her peers, but at least she would be free of the relentless taunting, at least for a moment. However, her unwillingness to show weakness to her bullies won out over self-preservation, so she chose to tough out the remainder of the program.

∽

Mara looked at her client sympathetically as she shared her story. "I'm sorry that happened to you. Children can be incredibly cruel."

Ann shrugged and looked down. "Eh, it is what it is."

"You said your mother called you 'boy crazy.' Do you know what she meant by that?"

"Uh...my parents said that all the time once I started liking boys. It wasn't like I was sleeping with them or anything, and I still got good grades. I guess they just didn't understand why I would be sad when I got rejected by the boys I liked. They just saw me as 'boy crazy' and they decided to send me to an all-girls school for both middle and high school."

"How did that make you feel?"

"Uh...it was yet another area of my social life where I felt like I wasn't good enough, but they didn't get it. I dunno...looking back, I don't think I was *that* different than other kids. I just had a harder time getting into relationships. Still do."

Mara nodded. "At least from what you shared, it doesn't sound like you were 'boy crazy.' Puberty is often a challenging time in life. Kids develop romantic crushes. Regardless of how old you are, it's natural to want your feelings reciprocated, and it's disappointing when that doesn't happen. You weren't 'boy crazy,' Ann. Your feelings were valid. I'm sorry the younger you didn't get to hear that from your parents."

"Thanks. You know, when my dad said things would get better, I know he meant well, but I feel like he lied."

"Why do you feel that way?"

"I'm twenty-two now, and it's not like things have gotten much better since I was twelve."

"Tell me more about that."

Ann stared intently out the window, where she trained her eyes on the stately campus buildings and the patterns in the architecture.

"I started making a few friends when I got to high school. I still got made fun of, but at least I finally had a clique. Then, when I was a senior, I finally got a boyfriend."

Mara nodded. "Could you tell me more about him, Ann?"

"Welp, I had an after-school job at a peanut and candy shop near Eastern Market, you know, the big farmer's market in Detroit. Um...this guy Jake worked there too. He was, um, like, my age. He went to the brother school to Saint Martha's, Bishop McNamara. I liked him a lot. I loved his sense of humor, and he made me laugh. But then, he started getting his laughs at my expense."

July 1998

As Ann ran down the staircase into the living room, she called out, "Dad?"

"Yes, Annie?" Marshall turned to face his daughter while watching sitcoms on television with his wife.

"May I borrow the car?"

"Sure. Where are you going?"

"Um, I'm going with Daryn to see the new Austin Powers movie. It's gonna be a good one, at least it looks like it from the ads."

"When's the showtime?" Sherrye asked.

"Uh, eight o'clock, but we're going to Sun Cinema, you know, the cool theater on the west side with the stadium-style seats. And we're getting a bite to eat near the theater."

"Okay, sounds good," Marshall said approvingly. "Your curfew is still midnight."

"What? Why, Dad? I'm eighteen and I've already graduated from high school!"

"Annie, you haven't started college yet," her mother noted. "Besides, you still live under our roof. Listen to your father."

"Okay, Mom. I'll be back by midnight."

About an hour later, Ann swiped her purse and the keys to Marshall's LeSabre, and left the house.

Her first stop was to pick up her good friend, who lived a couple of streets over from Ann on Yorkshire Street. When Ann pulled up, a girl her age with long, dark relaxed hair was sitting on the porch steps waiting.

"Hey, Daryn!" Ann called out to her.

Daryn smiled as she approached the car. "Hey, Annie!"

"Door's unlocked. You ready to go to the party?"

"Yeah, it sounds cool."

"K. We're gonna go get Jake and Brandon, and then we're gonna head over to Lenox Park."

"Jake's coming?"

"Yeah, of course. His friends are throwing the party."

Daryn rolled her eyes. "You know how I feel about him. He's bad news."

"Look, I know you don't like him, but give him a chance. And his boy Brandon is cool. I got you."

"Alright, I'll deal. But next time, count me out. I want no parts of Jake."

Ann then made the five-minute trip to the nearby suburb of Grosse Pointe City, one of the five Grosse Pointes, and pulled up at a small Tudor on Rivard Boulevard. Once she parked in front of the house, two young men strolled to the car. Daryn moved to the back seat. A fairly short young man with shoulder-length blond hair and green eyes entered the front seat. A taller man with dark brown hair and brown eyes, sat in the back with Daryn.

"So, Jake – staying over Brandon's for the weekend?" Ann asked.

"Yeah, Porkie. I went over there after work yesterday. My parents didn't bother to come get me, they're prolly drunk again. So, I'm staying there 'til at least tomorrow. I'll figure something out."

"Wow, that's some shit. Kinda figured something was up. I tried to call you, and your mom sounded really annoyed."

"Yeah, that's her. She's kind of a bitch." Then, Jake gave his girlfriend instructions. "Alright, before we go to the park, we gotta stop by the party store over here on Mack. Then we need to go to the spot to score some pot."

Ann sighed. "Okay."

She stopped at a corner store on the Detroit side of Mack Avenue, facing Grosse Pointe Park. Jake walked in and bought a pack of Newport cigarettes. On his way back to the car, he spoke to an older man loitering outside the store. He gave the man some cash and returned to the car.

"Okay, let's wait for a second," Jake advised.

The man entered the store, then a few minutes later, walked out and approached the car. Jake rolled down the car window, and the man passed him a brown bag.

"Thanks, dude. Keep the change."

"No problem, man."

Jake opened up the bag. Inside was a bottle of eighty-proof Stolichnaya vodka. "Stoli! This is gonna be the shit!" he marveled. Then, he stashed the bottle underneath the seat. He opened up the pack of cigarettes, took one out, and lit it, flicking the embers out the open window.

A few minutes later, the LeSabre crept down a nondescript side street in an eastside Detroit neighborhood much rougher than what the girls were used to. When they were halfway down the second block, Jake said, "Stop the car."

"What?" Ann responded, confused. Many of the homes on the block were boarded up or torn down. Food wrappers, empty cups and beer cans filled the shaggy, crabgrass-covered lawns.

"Porkie, stop the car now," he reiterated.

She pressed the brakes, stopping the car in the middle of the street. A few seconds later, several young men and boys as young as ten years old ran out from the shadows and swarmed the car. Jake and Brandon spoke to a boy and exchanged cash for several tiny clear plastic bags.

"Alright, let's get outta here."

Ann sped out of the neighborhood, relieved that the police did not pull her over. Then, at her boyfriend's directive, drove over to Lenox Park, which was located on the riverfront, one mile from the border the city shared with the Grosse Pointes.

It was shortly after dark and the small park was empty, save a group of about a dozen older teenagers and twenty-somethings sitting at a picnic shelter playing alternative music, smoking, and drinking beer.

Ann and Daryn were unfamiliar with this crowd, as these were Jake and Brandon's friends from the nearby suburbs. Jake brought them over to the group.

"Jake! Brandon! You got pot?" asked one teen boy in the crowd, who was thin and fairly short like Jake.

"Yeah, Trent, I got some," Jake told him, pulling out the small bags. "Who's got the 'shrooms?"

"Greg...yeah, Greg," Trent said, pointing to a large young man with red hair and a scraggly beard sitting on top of a picnic table."

"Yeah, Jake, I got it. Told you I'd bring it. It's a nice night to trip balls." Greg then looked over at Ann and Daryn. "Who are the girls?"

"Oh, yeah...guys, this is my friend, Ann..."

"Friend?" Daryn interjected. "She's your *girlfriend*."

Brandon added, "Hey, c'mon dude. No shame if you're dating her."

Jake rolled his eyes. "Alright, my *girlfriend* Ann, I call her Porkie, it's a cute name, isn't it?"

The group stared at Jake.

Slightly embarrassed, Jake took a deep breath. "Okay whatever, and uh...this is her friend Daryn." The crowd, consisting of both young men and women, waved and spoke to the girls.

The two continued mingling with some of the partygoers while Jake and Brandon disappeared into the nearby woods with a few others. One girl in the crowd who remained behind was very chatty and took a particular interest in Ann.

"Hi, Ann – I'm Katrina!" said a very thin adolescent with straight hair with chunked blonde and black color. She appeared unsteady as she was sitting on top of a picnic table with a can of budget beer in her hand.

"Hi, Katrina."

"Have a beer! They're...right over there." Katrina lifted her arm and pointed shakily to a large blue cooler with a white lid next to the table.

Ann grabbed a can of Natural Light from the cooler, popped it open, and tasted it. It was her first time trying beer, and it reminded her of seltzer water.

"So," the inebriated girl asked, septum piercing bobbing, "how d'you know Jake?"

"Uh...he and I work together at the Peanut Factory over at Eastern Market. That's how we met."

"Oh, that's cute! Jake and I, we went to school together, until...until he got kicked out."

"What? I thought he changed schools 'cause he moved to Roseville."

"No, he got kicked out...uh...it was his junior year...his *first* junior year. I was...uh...a freshman. That's why he's still got one more year, even though he's eighteen. Didn't they j-just move to Roseville last summer?"

"Yeah, I think so."

Katrina reached for the vodka, which was sitting in the cooler with the beer cans, and poured some into her open can. "Jake's...uh...kind of...a liar."

Ann sighed. *Yeah, I know.*

"You...you know what?" Katrina continued. "You're r-really pretty."

"Thanks," Ann replied with suspicion.

"You...know...what else? Stop letting him call you...Porkie. He's being...mean. You're too nice, you're...b-better than that."

"It's not a big deal. He doesn't mean anything bad by it."

"Uh...I dunno about that." Katrina shrugged, then got off the table. "Well, anyway...n-nice to meet you. I'll see you around!" She stumbled off into the wooded darkness.

Ann and Daryn sat on one of the benches, drinking cheap lager and listening to loud alternative rock music played from a boombox.

"This party's lame," Daryn remarked.

"Yeah, I know. I'm sorry. I thought it would be different, like more fun. Figured Jake and I would spend time together, we'd get you hooked up with Brandon or one of the dudes here, and it would just be cool."

"Eh, none of these dudes are my type. And you know how I feel about Jake, so it's not like his boys are any better."

Ann shrugged. "I guess."

After a while, Daryn checked her watch.

"Annie, it's 11:30."

"What? Shit. Brandon's right over there, but I gotta go find Jake."

Ann wandered around the darkened park to find her boyfriend. After a few minutes, she looked behind a small bush and noticed Jake with his pants pulled down to his knees, vigorously pumping a visibly passed-out Katrina.

What the fuck?!

Ann quietly stepped away from what she saw. Shocked and heartbroken, she was too timid to confront her significant other. She found Brandon, who was leaning against a tree smoking a glass bowl, and spoke with him.

"It looks like Jake is, uh...busy. You wanna ride home? I need to get home by midnight."

"Nah, I'm good. I'll stay with him. I'm sure we'll find another way home. Thanks, though."

She then returned to Daryn, saying somberly, "Let's go."

In the car, through tears, she told her friend what she witnessed.

"Annie...that girl was knocked out?"

"Yeah, she sure was."

"Whoa...he's skeezy," Daryn pointed out.

"I...I didn't know what to do when I saw them. I didn't expect to see that, you know?"

"I know, but shit...I don't know why you even give him the time of day. He's a terrible person. He calls you out your name and he disrespects you right in your face. Fucking 'Porkie'...'"

"He says 'Porkie' is supposed to be cute. You know what really sucks? I told him that I wanted to lose my virginity to him, but he said I was 'too good' for that, that it would be 'like fucking the Virgin Mary.'"

"You know he's full of shit, right? It's clear he's not into you like that, and he's just using you for your car since he's a bum who can't drive. Find somebody else."

"What if there *is* nobody else? What if he's the best I can do? You know how hard it's been for me to find a dude who actually wants to date me."

"What dates have you and Jake been on? When have you two actually gone out in public, as boyfriend-girlfriend? You know, where you go to the movies, or out to dinner, or something he actually pays for?"

Ann was quiet.

"That's what I thought. Look, you think he's the best you can do, but that's bullshit. He's not. Not by a long shot. But even if he was, alone is better than this dude."

"I guess. Um...let's roll down the windows so we can air out the car."

Once Ann made it back to her neighborhood, she dropped off her friend and then headed home. It was ten minutes before midnight when she crept through the door. Sherrye was on the living room couch waiting up.

"Hey, Annie!"

"Hi, Mom."

"How was the movie?" Sherrye asked.

"It was fine," Ann said, quietly. She was attempting to make a beeline up the stairs to her bedroom.

"Why do I smell smoke?" Sherrye asked.

"Smoke?" Ann said. *Shit.* "Uh, no."

"I know I smell smoke. Marshall!" Upon hearing his name, he came downstairs.

"Do you smell smoke on Annie?" Sherrye asked her husband. He sniffed. "Uh, no."

Sherrye was confused. "Hmm, maybe it's just me."

"I know you've said you smell smoke on occasion ever since you quit a few years ago," Marshall reminded his wife.

"May I go upstairs?" Ann asked in a tired voice.

"Sure, Annie," Sherrye responded.

Ann began her ascent, but as she heard her parents continuing to talk amongst themselves, she stopped and quietly sat on the landing near the top of the stairs, out of view.

"You know what, hun? I think Ann went to see that boy Jake again," Marshall posited to Sherrye.

"I know."

"I shouldn't have let her borrow the car. He's a degenerate. He has nothing going for him, and I know he's on drugs. I can tell. He looks like some of the parents involved in my court cases. I don't know why she still talks to him after he backed out of her senior prom. It should've been over then. I don't get it."

"Marsh, I'm sure you're right, and she did go see him tonight," Sherrye agreed. "But if you keep trying to keep her from him, all you're going to do is drive her right into his arms."

"I...I know. I just don't want her to ruin her future."

"Look, we've taught her sex ed, we've told her we'll get her on birth control if she needs it, and she knows how condoms work. She'll be okay."

"I don't even wanna think about that, hun."

"I know, but it's the reality. Just wait this out. Once she goes away to college, she won't even be thinking about him. They'll be done and over with. Just be patient. It'll be okay."

After this, Ann went to her bedroom. She stripped into her pajamas, turned off the lights, and cried herself to sleep.

Mara took a deep breath. "That must have been a painful time for you."

"It was." Ann recounted, "Looking back at everything years later, I wish I had said something when I saw Jake with Katrina while she was passed out. I was too much in my own feelings to see the reality of the situation. Sometimes I wonder if everything that has happened since...my bad luck with guys, and especially my dad dying, is my karma for not doing the right thing."

"Ann, it's not your fault. Jake was the one who chose to take advantage of someone who was vulnerable. We often like to think that we would respond in a particular way if we witness a crime, are victimized, or experience some type of trauma, but it rarely turns out that way. We have fight or flight responses, and yours was flight."

"I see."

"It's important to forgive yourself. You did the best you could at the time. And life happens...there isn't always a reason. When bad things happen, it's not 'karma' or payback for your past." Mara then switched gears. "I would like to ask you something else. You said that Jake gave you a nickname. How do you feel about the nickname Jake gave you?"

"I didn't like it, and I told him that, but he said he didn't mean anything by it, and I was being too sensitive. I let it go because I didn't want to make him upset and break up with me."

"Ann, that is emotional abuse. Name-calling and degradation are forms of abuse. Not all abuse is physical. And if you're in an abusive relationship, it's not always easy to see when others are being victimized by your abuser."

"Hmm, I never thought about that."

"Also, it seems that in your adolescence, quite a few people in your life were dismissive of your feelings."

"Yeah, I guess."

"Ann, it's okay to stand up for yourself."

"I guess, but I feel like I don't know how to do that without making people upset."

"Setting boundaries can lead to conflict at times, but it's healthy to set them."

Ann nodded.

Mara continued. "Did you end your relationship with Jake at that point?"

"No, I didn't. I didn't break up with him until a few months later, when I was in my first semester here at UGL. I was at a revival my friend invited me to—"

"A revival?"

"Yes, a revival. It's this event where Christians get together, pray, and wait on the Holy Spirit – God – to do supernatural things. I felt like I heard an audible voice from God telling me that I needed to end my relationship with Jake."

"An audible voice?"

"Yes...but not like a 'voice' voice, like you're talking to me right now. It was more like a spiritual voice, it's hard to explain. I'm not actually hearing voices. But anyway, my parents didn't like Jake, my friends didn't like Jake. Everybody wanted me to break up with him. Then I heard that voice, and I realized that if I wasn't even listening to God, something's wrong. So, I called Jake and I told him it was over."

"Good for you, Ann."

Ann looked out the window. "Thanks."

"Did you maintain communication with Jake after that?"

"Yes...kind of, but not by choice. The first summer after freshman year, I came back home and worked at the store. Jake had gotten fired in the meantime; I heard he was stealing stuff. But he just showed up at my job wanting to talk to me. I told him I was at work and there was nothing to talk about, and then he got trespassed. After that, he finally got the message. Haven't heard from him since. Thank God."

THE ONE

Each year, members of the Christian Kingdom campus ministry would use their spring break week, which fell on the second week of April, to attend Christian retreats at fellowship-owned centers across the country. At these annual retreats, dubbed Infinity, students would praise and worship God through song, read the Bible, attend workshops and sermons conducted by ministry staff, pray, and meditate.

Nestled in East Tennessee's Smoky Mountains was Honeycutt Estate, the property used by Christian Kingdom's Great Lakes chapter, as well as others in the Midwest and Southeast regions. The grounds consisted of several acres of trails, lakes, and streams, a working horse stable, rustic sleeping cottages, and a large, white-sided plantation house built in the mid-1800s, where students would converge to enjoy group workshops, Bible studies, praise and worship time, and meditation sessions focused on hearing from God.

At nineteen years old, Ann was no stranger to listening to the voice of the divine. After all, she ended her relationship with her high school school sweetheart, Jake, upon an apparent command from the Great I Am. But Infinity held a special place in her heart. At her first spring retreat, God spoke to her one more time — or at least she believed so.

April 1999

This year marked the first time Ann, Terah, Luke, and Paul attended the Infinity religious retreat. Prompted by the conservative Texas Pentecostal Bible College chapter of Christian Kingdom, each of the Infinity retreats that year featured their favorite minister as guest speaker. The speaker was Bethany Shank, a charismatic speaker, given the title "Prophetess," whc was known in Pentecostal Christian circles for her riveting teachings on sexual purity.

Prophetess Bethany's talk during the week the Great Lakes chapter attended was called "Jesus Orders Your Steps." She shared that she had run away from home and traveled across the country, smoked marijuana habitually, and was involved in several sexual encounters in her youth, not all of which were consensual. She recalled to the crowd that she had endured a great deal of trauma as a young person due to her upbringing. She told tales of growing up living a "hard life": impoverished in rural Texas and raised without her parents, who had developed an addiction to illicit drugs and left her and her nine siblings in the care of her elderly, ailing grandparents.

She spoke to the group of approximately thirty college students about her "formerly promiscuous" lifestyle. which changed miraculously when she found and accepted *the Lord*. She then went on to describe how her life had been transformed once becoming a *saved* evangelical Christian.

Prophetess Bethany paced around the wooden stage erected behind the big house, her closed-toed heels clacking around with intention, donning a silk fuchsia blouse tucked into a sharp flowing black skirt that hit just below the knee, and her long, bleached blonde hair flowing in the wind. Her words carried strongly in a raspy voice that emerged from her thin lips glazed with two lines of magenta lipstick. The stage lights flooded the platform, drowning the dark of the evening.

"I was no longer running out here whoring around with men! I was no longer opening up my legs to every Tom, Dick, and Harry!" projected the prophetess. "I was now saved! I *am* now saved! And sanctified! Amen?"

"Amen!" roared a captivated crowd.

"But the book of Genesis makes it clear that God does not want for man and woman to be alone. I was now delivered from my old ways, *but* I was not designed to be alone."

Groans of agreement could be heard from the audience.

"So, I was faithful, and I prayed, I prayed to our Lord Jesus Christ, I prayed that I would be a Proverbs 31 woman," she uttered, referencing the Bible chapter outlining the behavior of a godly woman. She continued, "I prayed that I would be a woman of purity and virtue, a 'help meet' for a man after God's own heart."

The prophetess stopped and stared intensely at the crowd. "Then, one night, I was in my prayer closet, and I was praying hard for a godly husband with everything I had, and everything I didn't have. And the Lord spoke to me, and he told me, 'My dear daughter Bethany, I have a man for you. A man of God. Your assistant pastor right there, at your church, Pastor Troy — he is The One.' And it wasn't just a thought in my head, I heard that voice...like you hear me talkin' to you right now. It was real, I could *hear it*."

Some of the students gave each other strange looks, while others nodded along.

"So, right now you might be like, 'Bethany, you done lost your everlovin' mind. You heard God actually *talk* to you? Time for those men in white with them butterfly nets!'"

The crowd chuckled.

"But I'll tell you what happened. The very next day was a Sunday. And after Sunday morning service, Pastor Troy sure did walk up to me and told me I was beautiful, and he would love to get to know me, and from there we set our sights on marriage. And now, amen, now, I married Pastor Troy Shank, and we have been married for ten years, and we have three wonderful children together. Praise Jesus!"

The group then erupted in cheers, clapping, and shouts of "Amen!" and "Hallelujah!"

Maybe there's hope for me yet.

During a workshop two days later, a group of ten students were instructed to find places within the spacious living room that doubled as the main meeting space, while additional students were placed in other rooms of the big house. Each student would be left alone to stand, kneel, sit, or lay prostrate, and be in silent prayer and meditation.

Ann chose a corner space with a busy yet soft oriental rug. She sat, legs crossed, closed her eyes, and raised her hands, palms up towards the ceiling, with elbows resting on her denim-clad thighs. She waited on the voice of God, as she was encouraged to do from listening to the guest sermon. She knew in her heart that God was capable of speaking directly to her. After all, it had happened once before. She waited, and waited, and waited – and then, there it was.

"Be patient," whispered the still, small voice, "Luke is The One."

Luke?

Not that Ann minded. From the first time she met him, she was absolutely smitten.

January 1999

Terah enrolled in an English course to fulfill a general education requirement during her second semester at Great Lakes. In class, the professor assigned a project where students were asked to pair up in order to create and act out a sketch. The completed sketches would be performed at the end of the semester.

She knew Luke, another first-year student taking the course, from Christian Kingdom, which she started attending on her own at the beginning of the school year. She approached him to pair up for the sketch project, and he readily agreed.

While writing the sketch together during the first week of class, they realized they needed a third person to help act it out. Terah wrangled her roommate and best friend to assist.

"So, Annie, I got this project I'm working on for English class with this guy I know from Christian Kingdom."

"That's cool, Terah," Ann replied while typing an assignment on her desktop computer in their dorm room. "What kind of project?"

"It's a sketch. We're writing it and then we're gonna act it out the last week of class."

"That sounds like fun. I'd love to sit in on the performance if they allow visitors. I definitely wanna support you. Just let me know when you're doing it."

"How about this...we need a third person to act out the play. A girl. You wanna join us?"

Ann turned around to face Terah. "Um...I dunno. I mean, I'll be in front of people. You know how I feel about that. This is for your class, so I know it's important. What if I mess things up for you guys?"

"It'll be fine. And it's healthy to stretch yourself, face your fears, stuff like that."

Ann rolled her eyes. "Alright, but only because you're my best friend."

That evening, Terah brought her friend to the basement of their residence hall, where there was a large open space and a brown table with wooden chairs in one corner. At the table sat a young man waiting for them.

"Hey, Luke!" Terah called out.

"Hi, Terah! You brought somebody." Luke smiled. "Cool."

"Yes, Luke, this is my best friend Ann. Annie, this is Luke, we know each other from CK, and we're doing this project together for our class."

Ann smiled and waved, "Hi, Luke."

Luke's eyes turned hazel, reflecting the retro brown of the basement area. "Hi, Ann, great to meet you."

While the three sat around the table, Terah handed Ann a copy of the script. "Okay, Annie, you're gonna read this part. You're reading the parts that say 'AC.'"

"Easy enough."

"Yeah. It stands for Anna Claire. Luke's gonna be Prince Albert. I'm gonna be the genie Khadijah."

"Prince Albert?" Ann side-eyed Terah.

"Yeah. It sounds like a princely name."

"Terah...do you know what a Prince Albert is?"

"No. What are you talking about?"

Ann then swiveled her head to face her friend's classmate, who was snickering. "Um...Luke, right?"

"Yeah."

"Sorry, Luke...I'm not always the best with remembering names, so I wanted to make sure. I'm sure it'll stick soon."

"I get it, Ann. I'm kinda like that too."

"So, um...do you know what a Prince Albert is?"

"Yeah...I was trying to figure out how to explain it to Terah, but it's...well...y'know..." Luke replied, outwardly cringing. "Maybe you can explain it since you're both girls. I'm a guy, that'll be a little weird."

She looked at Terah. "You want me to tell you now or wait until later?"

"Eh, tell me now."

"It's a penis piercing."

Terah's mouth was agape.

Ann snickered. "Look, it's your sketch, you can keep the name."

Luke added, "Honestly, I don't mind it. Let's keep it. The class might get a kick out of it when we perform it."

Terah shrugged. "Alright, I suppose we'll keep it. Luke, you could've told me!"

"How was I gonna come right out and tell you a Prince Albert is a penis piercing?"

"I guess like *that!*" Terah giggled as Ann and Luke howled.

Once they calmed down and skimmed the script, Ann asked, "So what's this sketch about?"

"Basically, it's about a girl who encounters a genie and wishes for her true love. The genie grants her this 'true love' who's a prince. But he's also a killer."

"What?"

"So yeah, you get stabbed by Prince Albert in the end."

Ann started laughing all over again.

"What?"

"So lemme get this straight — I ask a genie for my true love, and I get stabbed by penis jewelry? Then, that makes me a—"

"Dick!" As the word slipped out of Luke's mouth, he lost it and laughed heartily, his face turning beet red.

Ann had a smirk on her rosy face, while Terah doubled over in guffaws.

When Luke regained his composure, he said, "Okay, let's get started with the line for 'AC.'"

After joining the class project, Ann began attending Christian Kingdom meetings. At these meetings, she heard the message that Jesus died for her sins — the wrongdoings she had committed in her life — and that accepting him as "Lord and Savior" would provide her with a community of believers where she would belong, and an eternal afterlife in heaven. She had already been attending Sunday church services with Terah, and believed she had heard the voice of God instructing her to end her relationship with Jake during a revival held by the church. Yet hearing "the gospel" in campus ministry sealed the deal for her.

Shortly thereafter, Ann dedicated her life to Jesus Christ and became an evangelical Christian. Having endured a great deal of bullying and social rejection in adolescence, she viewed her new-found faith as a fresh beginning and embraced faith in an entity greater than herself.

As she spent more time with Luke, she found herself falling for him. Other than his reflective eyes, he was not the kind of man who would stand out in a crowd for his gorgeous looks. He was not particularly charming, either. However, it was not his looks or charisma that attracted her to him.

She found, as their friendship blossomed, that he was more than ordinary, at least in her view. He knew a lot of random facts and was quick to share them. He had traveled to various states around the country and to two continents outside North America. She was enthralled by his storytelling and captivated by his intellect. They could have deep philosophical conversations with ease, yet laugh together at cringe and corny jokes. When he wanted to, he could sing — but only when he wanted to. And he was *fun*.

Ann fell for him hard.

At Ann's first Infinity, she became convinced that Luke was The One — in other words, her God-given soulmate. Yet, despite this, she was also convinced that he did not feel the same way about her, based on her history of experiencing romantic rejection. That said, she did not know for sure. At her second Infinity in the spring of the year 2000, she would gain the courage to find out.

April 2000

While in their second year at Great Lakes, Luke drove Ann, Terah, Paul, and Alyssa to Infinity 2000.

"Luke, have you read *Dating Is Wack?*" Paul asked,

"*Dating is Wack?* What's that?" Luke inquired while focusing on the road.

Alyssa explained, "It's a book by Justin Chatsworth."

"Yeah," Terah jumped in. "He's a young minister, I think out of Ohio. That title is so corny like he's trying to be cool, but it's a weird book."

"Yeah, he's young, but he's anointed — God's flowing through him and he's using him for great things. Justin Chatsworth really knows what he's talking about."

"Right, so anyway," Paul continued, pulling the book out from the backpack in front of him, "the book is called *Dating is Wack: Courtship's Where It's At*, and it's about Christian romantic relationships. Chatsworth says we shouldn't date, we should 'court' instead."

"What's 'courting?'" Luke asked.

Paul explained confidently. "Courtship is a model of pure Christian relationships that invites accountability and visibility by parents and pastors. So, in courtship, unlike dating, you're not in a relationship *just because*, you're in a relationship because the goal is marriage. So, the family and the church are involved in matches and guidance prior to marriage. You're not going out *alone* with the girl, you're on group outings with her."

Alyssa shook her head. "I'm surprised you've missed the whole craze, Luke. I was hearing about it in high school, the book's been out a few years now."

"To be fair, Alyssa," Luke noted, "I went to a public high school, and I wasn't homeschooled."

"But you go to a Baptist church back home, right?" Paul pushed back. "I believe Chatsworth is Southern Baptist."

"Yeah, but I dunno. Halfway through high school, I stopped going to youth group. I was in Japan Club at my school, and that conflicted, especially when we started planning for our overseas class trip."

"It's a huge thing all across the country now, even at Great Lakes," Terah explained. "Now I don't think CK as an organization has made a statement on courtship versus dating, but a lot of other campus ministries have. The Seafarers have made courtship mandatory for their members, I think a couple of other ministries have too. But Mosaica has come out and said they disagree with the book because it's too legalistic."

"Mosaica's always been loosey-goosey though," Paul remarked snidely. "Too liberal and relativist."

Ann, sitting in the front seat, then spoke up. "Um...anyway, I got the book and I've been reading through some of it. What I don't get is why, uh...dating is supposed to be bad for Christians. I get that sometimes you can have new and better ideas, but you can have a good alternative without the regular way being bad."

"Good question, Ann. Chatsworth talks about this – so basically, dating's bad for Christians because there's no accountability from authorities like your parents or your pastor, since you're doing everything on your own. And that can lead to situations where a relationship can turn impure."

"Impure?"

Paul expounded, "Yeah, impure, so, like, touching, kissing, sex of all kinds. Chatsworth talks about how when you date, you can date whoever, even non-Christians, atheists, same sex, whoever, and even if it *is* another Christian, it's easy to slide into temptation and cause each other to sin. He claims that dating is spiritually *dangerous* for us as Christians. Courtship gives us the guardrails we need to tame our fleshly urges and enter into a healthy, pure marriage with a godly person."

Terah rolled her eyes. "Seems like a lot of work. I wonder if this boy has even tried it."

"He's married," Alyssa informed her regarding the book's author.

"Oh. Let's see how long that lasts."

Paul then said, "Luke, I'm finished with my copy, so feel free to borrow it when we get down to Tennessee."

"Yeah, sure, Paulie," Luke replied.

The discussion over *Dating is Wack* continued during the weeklong Infinity retreat.

"Of course we should court, Luke!" said Greg Travis, another Infinity member who was a year ahead of Luke, while he shifted on the ornate flowery couch in the sitting room of the big house. "Why wouldn't we want our parents involved? It's a bit wrong to sneak around behind everybody's back, don't you think?"

"Why does it have to be 'sneaking around,' though?" Luke retorted, resting on a recliner. "Why can't we just date whoever we want? Of course they should be Christians too and all that, but why can't we be trusted to make decisions for ourselves?"

"Because, brother," Kyle said, sitting comfortably on the floor with a Bible between his pretzeled legs, "the flesh is weak. If we date, we might decide on who we want to spend the rest of our lives with based on lust."

Ann, Terah, and Paul were passing through the sitting room. Paul's ears perked up and he stopped. "Guys, you're talking about *Dating is Wack*, aren't you?" he asked the group members in the space.

The other young men muttered, "Yeah."

"Welp," Paul joined Greg on the couch. "I agree with Kyle and Greg. Yes, it's hard to resist temptation and we need authority for that purpose. I think that's what Justin Chatsworth is really getting at here."

Luke responded, "I get that point, Paulie. But at the same time, if we can't be trusted to decide who we're gonna go out with, how can we be trusted to marry, have children and raise them, lead the church, and make any other big decisions for ourselves? There's got to be a happy medium, y'know what I mean?"

Ann sat on the floor and leaned her head on the side of Luke's recliner. Terah grabbed a chair, creating a circle in the well-decorated, antique space.

"Let's be serious," Terah started. "The boy who wrote it is barely even an adult. How is he talking about the 'right way' to da—"

"Not date," Kyle interjected. "Court."

"Whatever. It's the same thing, different name. Christians are out here buying just anything now, huh?"

Ann gave her thoughts. "Uh...I don't know if I would dismiss Justin Chatsworth like that. I mean, God can use anybody, right? Yeah, he's young, but it doesn't mean he doesn't have anything to contribute."

"Annie, I'm not saying he doesn't," Terah explained. "But there's something to be said for wisdom and life experience. This boy has none. Dude can't even drink. A twenty-year old is out here advising millions of people about their futures. It's wild."

"I dunno, Terah. I mean, on one hand, there's a reason why everybody's reading the book. There's probably something to it. I'm not saying I agree with all the courtship stuff, I mean, it has this whole part about your parents being active in your courtship, especially your father. But what if you don't have a father? Or parents at all? Or what if your parents aren't Christian? Then what? Are you S.O.L. or something?"

Greg responded, "Sis, parents would be ideal to oversee the courtship, but church authorities would probably step in for that part of the process if your parents weren't able to."

"That makes sense, I guess...I dunno, it's so involved."

Over the next couple of hours, the young students of Christian Kingdom's Great Lakes chapter continued to debate the merits of *Dating is Wack*.

"You know," Ann continued. "Um...I feel like this book is contradictory."

"Why?" said Greg.

Ann spun strands of her tightly coiled hair around her index and middle fingers. "Because, the whole point of courtship is that as young Christians, um…we're prone to making bad decisions on who we're looking to be with, so we need to have our parents and the church community involved in keeping us accountable and pure until marriage, right?"

Everyone nodded.

She continued. "But at the same time, the book is written in a way that assumes that Christian men will focus on women's physical appearance, and it doesn't take them to task for that. That's a worldly thing, though, and looks change. Isn't focusing on looks part of those 'bad decisions,' since according to the Bible, God says that he looks on the heart?"

Greg moved a strand of dark brown hair from his freckled face. "Not really. We're not God."

"But aren't we supposed to be striving to become more like God? We're all made in his image, so wouldn't focusing on looks take away from that?"

Paul uttered thoughtfully, "That's a really good question."

Greg then jumped back in. "I know what you mean, but that's because you don't understand men. It's in our nature to focus on physical appearance, kind of like how it's in women's nature to focus on whether or not a man can provide. It's a lot like the animals, it's innate."

"But aren't we supposed to be fighting against that nature though? The Bible has a lot to say about fighting against the flesh," Ann shot back. "We're not like the animals. We have free will, we're capable of rational thought, we should have the ability to think beyond our animalistic desires. The world focuses on the same exact things. How can we claim that we're set apart from the world, except when it's inconvenient?"

Kyle had a thought. "Okay, so Ann, let's say we don't use physical appearance to decide on the right woman, or women don't use finances to decide on the right man, what are we supposed to use?"

"Easy. We should focus on things like shared values, character traits like honesty and loyalty, things like that. Do you have similar interests, can you enjoy each other's company? Do we want the same things out of life? Do we bring each other closer to Christ? Those are ways we can be compatible. Too often, people look at surface things instead, and they miss their real soulmate who could be right in front of them."

"I guess that thought process makes sense," Luke uttered slowly.

"Yeah, I mean, why do you think the divorce rate is so high? The Christian divorce rate isn't any better than the one for non-Christians. People focus on the wrong things. If becoming a Christian transforms us, where is that transformation if, um...when we look to get into relationships, we hold onto the same standards the world does? It's as if we're saying we're changed people, except for *this*. Greg, that doesn't make any sense."

Soon enough, Ann would wish she had read *Dating Is Wack* in its entirety, and it was not because of an adolescent preacher's pronouncements on purity or the 'right' way to pursue a relationship in the church.

On the ride back from that year's retreat, Ann sat in the back seat with Terah and Alyssa, while Paul was in the front seat with Luke.

"I'm so not looking forward to finishing this semester," Luke complained. "These classes are kicking my butt, especially Econ 147."

Paul looked at him while chewing on a beef jerky stick. "Econ? Really? I thought you'd kill that one."

"Nah, man. Y'know, I thought so when I signed up for it. But it's brutal. So hard to pay attention. My mind just keeps drifting off to other things."

While listening to Luke and Paul's conversation, Ann had a thought cross her mind.

I know God is supposed to bring us together, but maybe I should help this along by being courageous and telling him.

"Bro, I'm hungry," Paul said to Luke as he finished his snack.

"Where you wanna stop?"

"I don't care. Where do the girls wanna go?"

"I'm good with McDonald's," Alyssa opined.

Terah spoke up. "We're getting close to the Ohio border. How about Riverview Coneys? We went to McD's on the way to Tennessee, why do we try something different since we're on our way back to Michigan?"

"What about you, AC?" Luke asked.

Ann was looking out the window at the rolling hills and lush green forests of Kentucky, paying no attention to the conversation.

"AC!" Luke called to her a little louder.

Ann jumped. "Oh, yeah...Luke, what's up?"

"We're stopping for food. Where do you wanna go? McDonalds or Riverview Coneys?"

"Uh...Riverview Coneys for sure. I've heard they're a lot different than Detroit coneys."

"They totally are. The coney sauce is made with sweet chili oil instead of chili powder."

"That's definitely different. It'll be nice to try something new."

"What do you think, Paulie?"

"C'mon Luke, you and I are from around here. I mean, how often do we get a chance to eat Riverview Coneys?"

"True," Luke agreed. "Are you good with that, Alyssa?"

"Yeah, sure."

"'Kay, Riverview Coneys it is!"

A few minutes later, Luke exited Interstate 75 in Northern Kentucky only a few miles from the Ohio border and pulled into a Riverview Coneys restaurant. Riverview Coneys was a popular restaurant chain in this region of the country. The car's occupants got out and flooded into the quiet, pre-evening rush diner, ordering their food to eat on the outdoor patio. After receiving their food, they went outside and sat at a circular blue metal table with an umbrella.

Paul tore into his chili and cheese-covered hot dog with glee. "Man, I missed this!"

"How?" Alyssa questioned Paul. "It's weird. Not like any coneys I've had."

"You don't understand," Paul responded with a full face of hot dog and chili. "These are Ohio coneys. They're amazing."

"Detroit coneys are better," Terah weighed in.

Ann turned to Luke and asked quietly, "Hey Luke, can I talk to you about something right quick?"

"Uh, yeah, sure."

Ann and Luke left the table and walked over to another part of the desolate patio.

"So, um, Luke," she stuttered while fidgeting. "I should probably tell you something."

"Of course, AC, whatever you want to tell me is totally fine," he responded.

Here we go...now of course, I can't tell him God wants us to be together though. He's gonna think I'm crazy.

"Uh, I like you, and I think it would be great if we started going out."

"Like...a relationship?"

"Uh, yeah."

"Hmm." Luke was quiet for a moment, then spoke again. "I'm not surprised."

"What?"

"Yeah, I'm not surprised you like me like that. I can tell, you wear your heart on your sleeve."

Ann looked over at Luke, a bit surprised yet frustrated at herself.

"You know Ann, you're a great girl, and you're so fun to be around. And I really like hanging out with you. But I don't see you in that way."

Ann cast her eyes downward.

Damn. Knew it.

"We can stay friends for sure, though, if you're fine with that."

"Yeah, of course. I just hope you mean it. If you don't and you're just trying to let me down easy, don't do that."

"No AC, I actually mean it. I do enjoy our friendship. And you know, things could change tomorrow, or six months from now, or years from now. You never know. Just not right now."

Well, at least the door is open for the future.

"Okay, sure. Thanks for hearing me out."

"No prob."

That night, back on campus, Ann saw Paul in the lobby of their dormitory. She sat by him and started talking.

"Paul, can I talk to you?" Ann asked.

"Sure, Ann — what's up?"

Ann took a deep breath. "I...I told Luke that I like him and I wanted to be with him."

"Ooh, why did you do that?"

"Because why not? If he wasn't going to say anything, I figured I might as well."

"Yeah...no." Paul shook his head. "That's not good. You don't wanna be the one to make the first move because men are driven to pursue women. It's their natural God-given role. Women are meant to be pursued. Didn't you get to that part in *Dating is Wack*?"

"No, I got through most of it while we were down in Tennessee, but I didn't see that part."

"You really wanna read that part. It's in the chapter Chatsworth writes specifically to women," Paul advised.

That night, while in bed in her dorm room, Ann pulled her personal copy of the bestseller out from her purple duffel bag and flipped the fairly thin pages to the eleventh chapter. She intently read the chapter the author devoted to women:

To my sisters in Christ: Women are the gatekeepers of sexual purity. God created men to pursue the beauty of a woman, as humanity is pursued by the God of the Bible. You are to use discernment and guidance from your earthly father to evaluate the brothers in Christ who may attempt to approach you for courtship. Choose based on the wisdom endowed to you by the Lord.

Ann continued to read the chapter, dismayed.

Sisters, you may ask, "Justin, what if a man never approaches me? What do I do then?" The difficult truth is that there is no guarantee the Lord will provide you with a husband. Men are designed by God to focus on physical appearance. They cannot control this. You may seek to enhance your appearance by improving your diet, engaging in physical activity, working towards or maintaining an ideal body size, using a modest amount of makeup, and growing out your crown. Your body is a temple, and a godly man will appreciate an adorned, preserved temple.

If you are asking this question, you may want to begin with these suggestions. But even for sisters in Christ who look like Heidi Klum or Kate Moss, being chosen for courtship and ultimately marriage is not a certainty. Allow yourself to be chosen. Do not attempt to usurp God's natural order.

Welp, I'm screwed.

FINAL INFINITY
APRIL 2002

The soothing tenor voice with a slight tinge of Kentucky twang caught Ann's attention.

"Ready, AC?"

She turned around in her dorm room to see Luke, who was wearing an orange linen shirt with short sleeves, the buttons partially opened to show a peek of a white tee-shirt, as well as a pair of relaxed-fit Levis with a brown belt and Air Force Ones. This time, his eyes were a piercing cobalt.

"Hey, Luke! Sure. Is your car in the lot?"

"Yeah. I already have my stuff packed up. Terah and Paulie are in the lobby waiting. They had me come up and get you."

"Okay cool. Let's go."

Ann came downstairs with Luke, and all four piled into Luke's midnight blue Saab station wagon.

"Can't believe this will be our last trip to Infinity Week," Paul mused wistfully. "It's such a restful way to spend our spring break. I'm gonna miss it."

"I know. It's incredible, isn't it?" Luke added while keeping his eyes on the road. "The quiet woods and streams. The horseback riding. And the Smoky Mountains are amazing!"

"Paul, I'm surprised you're not riding down with Alyssa," Ann noted.

"Nah, not this time. We're together, but we figured since this is the last Infinity, we'd ride with our best friends. So, she's with Megan and Cristina, and I'm riding with y'all."

"Cool!"

During Infinity 2002, members of the Great Lakes chapter of Christian Kingdom joined up with the chapter from Grace College, a small Christian Reformed college in Western Michigan, since their Spring Break fell the same week. These chapters converged in the scenic Smoky Mountains as they did each year.

The words she felt she heard from her first Infinity still looped in Ann's mind years later. *"Be patient. Luke is The One."* She was certain she heard them so clearly from God, much like the time God told her to break up with Jake. And yet, three years later, she and Luke were still friends. *Just friends.*

The rolling green hills of rural Kentucky slid past as she stared out the passenger side window. As Luke sped down Interstate 75, she could see the trees regrowing their shade.

Sister Rhonda says that we're supposed to have unwavering faith, and then God will give us our deepest desires. I really want to be with Luke, I'm supposed to be with Luke. God himself said so.

At dusk, the station wagon turned into the grassy lot by the big house at Honeycutt Estate and came to a rolling stop. The big house was clad in ivory siding and adorned with four matching columns. The outdoor stairs ascended to a wooden porch with whitewashed benches on each side, along with rocking chairs, each with well-loved pillows covered in deep red and gold. The front door was painted forest green with a gold doorknob. A brown, carved cross completed the look of the door. Several people, most of them in their teens and early twenties, were milling about in the grassy parking area as well as on and around the porch.

The four exited Luke's car. "We're here!" he exclaimed. As he walked toward the back of the station wagon to open the hatch, he stopped in his tracks.

"Luke! Luke! Oh my gosh, Luke! You made it!" An athletic, curvy young woman was waving her hands high in the air, capturing his attention. Ann could not help but notice how stunning she was, with long, straight ebony hair, almond-shaped eyes a sultry brown, smooth skin, pillowy lips, and a ninety-kilowatt smile.

Ann's face fell.

"Morgan? Oh my God! I didn't know you were coming!" Luke's voice matched the beautiful young woman's energy perfectly.

She ran and jumped on him, hugging him as he swung her around. Not exactly a Christian side hug.

She wasn't supposed to be here.

November 2000

When Ann first met Luke in early 1999, he and Morgan had ended their romantic relationship less than a month previously. When she learned of their past romance, she felt a sense of hope.

Maybe, just maybe, I have a chance with him.

On one hand, the fact that Morgan was Luke's ex-girlfriend showed that he was open to dating Black women, unlike many men

Ann encountered in the Great Lakes Christian community. On the other hand, having dated a woman of partial African extraction in the past would not necessarily mean he would be open to dating *her*. In most other respects, Morgan and Ann were very different, and Ann knew it. She knew she could never compete with her rival's captivating appearance, her outgoing nature, or her natural wit.

Everybody loved Morgan, including the man who stole Ann's heart. As long as she continued to be in close proximity and was still a fixture in Luke's life, there would always be a chance the relationship would be rekindled, and there was nothing Ann could do to stop it.

One night, during their third year at Great Lakes, Ann was studying in her room when she heard a soft knock on the frame of her open door.

"Uh...who is it?" she called out from her bed, sitting with her back turned away from the door.

"AC, it's Luke..."

She spun around to face Luke in the doorway, downcast and near tears.

"Come in, dude. What's wrong?"

He closed the door and sat on the bed next to her. "It's Morgan."

"What's up with Morgan? Is she okay?" Ann asked.

"Her parents came to pick her up today and take her home. They're pulling her out of UGL."

"What? Oh no! I hate hearing that. Definitely gonna miss her. Did she wanna leave or something?"

"No, she didn't," Luke disclosed. "She loved it here, but her parents felt like she was getting too distracted with 'worldly' influences and she was falling away from Christ, so they took her out. I watched her parents take her away."

"That's awful, Luke."

Morgan is finally gone. For a brief moment, Ann sensed an opportunity. *Maybe this is how God was supposed to bring us together. This is how it seems to work out. At least it does in rom-coms. Isn't this the moment when the love interest is sad and you're supposed to swoop in and make a move?*

Immediately after that fleeting thought, Ann was struck by a wave of immense guilt. *What is wrong with me? She's a sweet person. She didn't want to leave. And Luke misses her already. I need to get my mind right.* She was thoroughly conflicted.

"Y'know, it sucks so bad," he expressed. "I mean, we've been broken up for almost two years now, but it feels more real than ever now. She's really gone."

"I'm so sorry."

Luke then cried in earnest, and it was the first time Ann had seen him so vulnerable. She gently touched his shoulder and held his hand, and in a quiet, tender moment, allowed him to release his pain.

Day two of Infinity 2002 had just begun. Ann awoke with the rising of the spring sun. *What a beautiful day.*

She changed into brisk spring clothes, picked up her blue hardcover Bible, and set out for the morning, seeking a place to meditate before breakfast near the big lake. As she started out for her walk, she eyed Luke and Morgan riding on horseback from the barn, galloping towards the trail together. Upon seeing this, she became emotional.

Luke and Morgan look happy together. It's like they're made for each other. I'm so lame and unathletic. There's no way I could even get onto a horse, let alone ride one.

As she noticed Terah leave the cabin, she motioned her over. She gestured her head towards Luke and Morgan, who were heading away from them. She mouthed, "I need to talk." Her friend nodded her head and followed her.

They hiked towards a couple of stones by a nearby creek. Once they sat down on a large rock next to the creek, tears began streaming down Ann's face.

"I've been there for him all this time. I've been a great friend to him. We spend so much time together, how could he not see how great we would be for each other? But then, Morgan just gallivants back into his life and then she's all that matters. It's not fair."

"How much do you trust God?" Terah asked.

"What?"

"How much do you trust God? If you truly believe that God told you Luke's 'The One,' why are you so worried about what he's doing right now?"

Ann huffed.

"You know how I feel about all this, Annie. God has his will for our lives, but we can make choices. Sometimes we want something so bad, we can hear our own voice in place of God's."

She angrily looked through Terah. "Are you saying this is all *me?* If it was up to me, I would've moved on. I've been asking God, 'If it's just my own will, take away my feelings for Luke.' But it hasn't happened."

Terah stared back at her friend empathetically. "Look, I'm not saying God didn't tell you that you're gonna be with him. I believe you. But you know, we have free will. You have free will, but so does he. I would just hate to see you waste your life on somebody who doesn't wanna be with you. You're too good for that. There are other dudes out here who do wanna be with you, good dudes. But you gotta be free from this whole thing about him being 'The One' in order to see that."

"It's hard, though. You know, it's the mixed signals. That's the hardest part."

"Mixed signals...what?"

"You know, it's like there's something there, and there are times when he makes it seem like something's going to happen. But then there are times when it doesn't. I just need him to be consistent. If he's going to only be a friend, be that. Just be consistent."

"If he really wants to be with you, he'll show you that and it won't be ambiguous."

"Yeah, I get it." Ann's eyes welled up. "Terah...what's wrong with me? Why am I not good enough? I'm too much and never enough."

"My heart hurts for you." She patted her friend's back. "But...I gotta ask, are you truly sure God told you Luke is 'The One?'"

"I'm a thousand percent sure. I have never been so sure of anything else in my life. It's not like I hear God talking to me all the time. If that was what was up, it means I lost my mind, y'know what I mean?"

"Yeah, I hear you. Welp, if God's gonna put you two together, you can't worry about what you're seeing right now. If it's meant to be, it'll happen. If it's not, it won't, no matter how much you want it."

"I know...but do you ever feel like God sees you as an after-thought?"

"Oh, no. Why do you say that?"

"A part of me wonders if God said, 'Luke is The One,' and then forgot what he promised. So many people need bigger things from him than I do. So he's focused on that and when it comes to me, 'eh,'" Ann explained, shrugging.

Terah shook her head in disbelief. "No, girl. God's not gonna abandon you, Annie. That's not how he works. He cares about the big and the small."

"I know, but here's the thing. It all feels like mixed signals to me. It's like there's something there, I can feel it, and there are times when he makes it seem like something's going to happen. But I need him to be consistent. If he's going to only be a friend, be that. Just be consistent."

"That all makes sense. But what I don't get is, why can't you just let it go? If nothing's happening, just let it go until it does."

"You don't get it—"

"Tell me, what don't I get?"

"See, it would be one thing if I just heard God say, 'Luke is The One,' and that's all I had to go on, but there's way more to it than that. Something's there between us. Not just a regular platonic friendship. There's been times he's even hinted at the idea of there being more, maybe in the future. But I feel like his problem is him."

Just then, two well-trained horses with deep brown coats strolled up on the other side of the creek.

"Hey guys!" Morgan called out.

Ann wiped her face with her shirt collar as if she were simply wiping off dirt. "Hey!" replied both of the women sitting on the rock.

Luke chimed in. "We haven't eaten breakfast yet. You wanna join us?"

Terah responded, "I still need to shower and get ready, so I'll have to pass on that. What about you, Ann?"

Ann sighed and looked up at the two on the magnificent equines. "You know what, that sounds good. I'll meet you both at the cafeteria."

As the two galloped away, Terah whispered, "The heck are you doing? Are you seriously gonna be their third wheel?"

"I hear you, but the last thing I want is for them to see me sweat."

"Girl, you can always say no. You're too proud for your own good."

After leaving the creek and parting ways with Terah, Ann headed to the cafeteria adjacent to the big house. Once entering, she stood in line with the other Infinity participants. Breakfast on this day was pancakes, scrambled eggs, a slice of breakfast ham, and two sausage links. She selected a plate with all of the available food items and poured herself a paper cup of orange juice.

After getting her meal, she sat at a table and saved space for Luke and Morgan. A short time later, the two strolled in, got breakfast, and came over to the same table. They sat next to each other, facing her.

"So, uh...how was your horseback ride?" Ann asked.

"It was great. We saw the sunrise, and it was nice to be out with nature, wind in our faces," Luke recalled fondly.

Morgan added, "We watched the deer too. They were frolicking around, so cute. The streams and the lake are quite pretty early in the morning."

Ann nodded. "That's really nice."

"You don't know what you're missing. You should come out with us sometime."

"Maybe so," Ann muttered, having absolutely no intention of getting up extra early or attempting to climb a horse. She then changed the subject. "Morgan, how has it been at Grace College?"

She sighed. "It's a Christian Reformed college, so it's about what you would expect. Conservative, theologically rigid. Kind of like the students I came down here with."

"I see."

"I mean, honestly..." Morgan leaned in so only her friends could hear. "If this was a retreat with just Grace kids, I would've gone straight home for break. But since I knew you guys would be here too, I decided to go, even if I had to suck it up and ride down here with these ignorant freaks."

"Fair," Luke commented.

The three continued to enjoy their breakfast.

Morgan smiled at Luke while holding her sausage-filled fork in her left hand. "So, Luke, how's the vet school process going?"

"Welp, good question Morgs. Still waiting to hear back. My parents keep asking me about it, but I figure that if I don't get in, I'll stick around near UGL, or even move over to the west side of the state, near Niles."

"Um...near Grace? Welp, I guess that's a plan."

"Eh, sure. Now, how about you? I know you said you were thinking about trying to find some work near the UWO region," he recalled, referring to Upper West Osceola, the home of Great Lakes.

She glanced down at her plate. "Um...we'll see. There are a lot of options."

"Yeah, well, uh...I'm thinking about staying in Mid-Michigan, lots of jobs are cropping up in my major," Ann interjected while moving around her scrambled eggs, which were too runny for her liking, with her fork.

Luke and Morgan looked at Ann without responding. *Ugh...they don't care. Should've kept my mouth shut.*

After breakfast, the three bussed their own table and left the cafeteria. Once outside, Morgan pulled on Luke. "Hey, let's talk." They waved Ann off and headed over to a wooden bench on the shore of the idyllic lake.

As she walked toward the cabin alone, she heard Terah, Alyssa, and Cristina chatting.

"Ann's still stuck on Luke, isn't she?" Alyssa assumed.

Terah shook her head. "Yeah. She's noticed him hanging out with Morgan a lot here at Infinity, and she's really not taking it well."

"I can tell. She's not great at hiding her feelings."

"True. Annie's a very 'what you see is what you get' kind of person, always has been, at least as long as I've known her. It's good because you always know where you stand with her, but it makes it easy for terrible people to take advantage of her."

"See," Cristina opined, "I don't get the appeal. Why is she so into *Luke*, of all people? He's average, nothing to write home about. And he's dry and...a little odd."

"Odd?" Alyssa questioned.

"Yeah, odd. He's the kind of guy who goes to a wild party and everybody thinks he's a narc."

"So...awkward?" Terah proffered.

"No, not awkward. Just strange...but anyway, the two of them? I just don't see it."

"Truth be told, Cristina, I don't see it either. But I think she likes him 'cause he's a smart dude and their humor's a lot alike. She always says she finds him interesting. He's not a bad guy at all. I just don't get the hype."

Alyssa had another thought. "You all know this, so this isn't news, but she had gotten out of a bad relationship not long before she met him, and she's not had the best luck with guys in general. She'd tell you that herself. What I'm thinking is that maybe he's the only guy she's liked that's actually been nice to her."

After overhearing the conversation, Ann approached the women. "Hey, what's up?"

"Nothing much. Just talking about your thing for Luke," Terah said.

"Yeah, I'm well aware," she responded flatly.

"Hey Ann, I know you're dead set on Luke being 'The One,' but do you think God would put you in a situation that makes you feel terrible?" Cristina asked.

"I don't think you understand, Cristina. It's not that I *want* Luke to be 'The One.' It's what *God* wants. Why would I *want* God to set me up with someone like Luke who isn't looking to be with me right now?"

The group was silent.

She continued. "See, God doesn't always put us in positions that make us feel comfortable. If we're comfortable, it might not be of him, right?"

"True," Cristina agreed. "But God does want good things for us. Actual good things. Ann, it's okay to want more, to expect more."

"Sure, but it's not like we deserve good things. It's not like any of that is guaranteed, you know what I mean? Aren't we called to humility?"

"Yeah. And I mean, I get we want to be humble, and I know we don't 'deserve' anything but eternal death. But at the same time, God wanted us saved for a reason, he sees great worth in us, and we're supposed to live and move in that reality. I know you like Luke, but you can and should expect better."

Alyssa added, "Yeah, not just someone who's nice to you, someone who truly sees you and values you and loves you for you."

"What makes you think I want the bare minimum? Sure, I haven't had the best relationship history, but it doesn't mean I'm settling for whatever," Ann pushed back. "There are actual things I like about him, and it's not simply because he's 'nice.'"

"I mean, I'm sure there's something you see in him that we don't. But trust that God desires better for you than a guy who breaks your heart. If Luke is truly the one, he won't be the Luke he is now."

After the unsettling conversation, Ann continued her trek to the cabin to retrieve her Bible, and a handful of gummy bears for good measure.

They really don't get it. I'm not some pathetic sow. I'm just trusting God.

Many of the graduating seniors felt wistful on the final full day of Infinity 2002. This would be the last year that most of them would be attending Infinity, and unless they planned to become staff leaders for Christian Kingdom, this would be the final major campus ministry event in which they would participate.

The entire group came together for a workshop just outside the big house. Brother Craig and Brother Steve, the new staff leader for the Grace College chapter, stood up onstage in front of the group near a corded microphone.

Brother Steve, a blond-haired, clean-shaven man in his mid-twenties, spoke. "This has been an amazing week here at Infinity 2002. It's inspirational seeing the Lord working in each and every one of you. And I'll tell you what...it's one thing to go through this as a student, but it's another seeing this as staff this year."

He continued, calling out his colleagues. "You — Brother Craig and Sister Rhonda — I appreciate God placing both of you here, for making me feel at home and for providing me with your wisdom and guidance."

Steve handed the microphone to Craig and stood aside.

"Thank you, Brother Steve, and we praise God for you stepping into a leadership role at Grace College." Brother Craig continued, speaking to the students. "As we close out Infinity 2002, we want to make sure we take the time to break out into small groups. In those small groups, you'll want to share what you need help with, and then your group will pray over you. Everyone in the group will get prayed over. Now each of you, starting here at the end, count off one through eight."

The students counted from one to eight and then looped the count until each was assigned a number. Ann was in group number five.

At the end of the count, Brother Craig explained, "Everyone with the same number will group together, so there should be eight groups of about five, there might be a couple with six. You can either congregate somewhere in this immediate area or your group can head inside the big house and find a place there if you want. The three of us staff leaders will walk around, intercede, and join in as

God leads. We're going to take as much time as we need because Jesus can't be put in our boxes. We move in *his* time, not our own."

Besides Ann, the other fives included Kyle from the Great Lakes chapter, along with three people from the Grace College chapter, including Brogan, Ellie, and a powder-shaded, ginger eighteen-year-old named Wesley. They walked over to a set of benches on the porch of the big house to commence the group prayer.

Each member shared the issues they sought prayer for, such as classwork-related struggles, feelings of persecution due to being "real" Christians in a "worldly" society, worries about the future, relationships with family and among family members, health, a vague category called "sexual temptation and sin" that no one dared elaborate on, as well as desires to meet the perfect Christian spouse.

When it was Ann's turn to disclose what she wanted prayer for, she told the group, "Well, uh...my dad passed away several months ago."

Words of comfort, such as "I'm sorry" and "My condolences" came from the group.

"It was sudden and it's been really hard for my family to deal with. He and I were close, and I'm still wrapping my head around him being gone." She also shared another challenge. "Um, I'm also struggling with companionship. I'm trying to do my best to wait for who God has for me, but uh...I feel like I'm not seen."

The others in the group laid hands on Ann, everyone closed their eyes and began to pray. "Father God," prayed Kyle, "we lift up your daughter Ann in prayer. We pray for her family, that they have peace that passes all understanding. That they are comforted by you, Jesus. We know that Ann's earthly father is in heaven, and for that we can rejoice. Let Ann take comfort that she will see her earthly father again in heaven with you, her Father in heaven."

Wesley now prayed. "God, oh Lord our God, we hope and pray that by your grace and providence, that Ann's earthly father was predestined to be with you in heaven." A few eyebrows were raised. Wesley peeked and saw the furrowed brows, then quickly finished his part with, "Uh, we believe he's in heaven, in the name of Jesus."

Ellie took over, "Dear Lord, we trust that as Ann continues to seek you, Father God, and desires you and you alone, you will give her the desires of her heart. You designed us to be in relationship, both with you oh Lord and with each other. Please build her up as a Proverbs 31 woman, a godly woman who will be the right help meet for a warrior after your heart, Jesus."

Then Brogan closed out the prayer. "Our Father in heaven, we know that nothing is guaranteed to us, we may pray for what we want to happen, but you are sovereign and your will may not be our own. Your will be done, Father God. Your will be done."

Brogan picked up his Bible and opened it up. He continued, "Not everyone is made beautiful. The book of Isaiah, Chapter 53 describes as such, 'He hath no form nor comeliness; and when we shall see him, there is no beauty that we should desire him. He is despised and rejected of men; a man of sorrows, and acquainted with grief, and we hid as it were our faces from him; he was despised, and we esteemed him not.'"

As he closed his Bible, he continued. "That was Jesus Christ. He was not beautiful, he was unremarkable, he was easy to reject. He never married and he died alone on the cross. Your daughter Ann was made in your image, to show us who you are and to be thankful.

Let her see herself in the person of Jesus, and lead her to give her desire for companionship to you."

After the group finished, Ann returned to her cabin. She changed into her pajamas, and before climbing into bed, pulled the gummy bear bag out of her bag.

Dad might be in hell — I sure hope and pray he's not. I hope I shared enough that he truly believed in Christ when he died. And I'm alive so that other Christians can be thankful that at least they don't look as unfortunate as me. That might be true. If so, that really sucks. It sure feels like it.

She proceeded to stuff handfuls of the confection down her throat. The gummy bears, while soothing for a moment, only made her feel worse once swallowed. Once the family-sized bag was empty, she placed her bedsheet over her head and wept quietly into her pillow.

On a rainy Friday morning, the time came to leave Honeycutt Estate, as Infinity 2002 was over. Terah and Paul felt energized, having recharged their batteries during the retreat, whereas Ann and Luke were more subdued.

For Ann, this year's trip only increased her anger at God for taking her father away from her and her family way too soon, and reinforced her latent self-loathing. Luke, for his part, was downcast, and had been for a few days.

The group packed Luke's Saab and said their goodbyes to everyone. Morgan came over and hugged their group. The hug she gave Luke, though, was a side hug, much the same as she gave her other friends from Great Lakes. At half past nine in the morning, the station wagon departed the mountains for its journey back to Michigan.

By the time the car passed through Lexington, Kentucky along Interstate 75, Paul and Terah were fast asleep in the back seat. Ann was up front in the passenger's seat, awake but quiet.

Unprompted, Luke spoke in a depressed tone. "Morgan found somebody else."

"Oh, really?" Ann replied quietly. "I'm sure that's gotta be hard for you."

"Y'know, AC, I...I didn't think it would be that hard. I mean, we've been broken up for three years now. But it's a whole 'nother thing when she's telling me she's found somebody else. It's...it's real now."

"I hear you." *I knew it. He's still not over her. Maybe everybody's right. But then. does that mean God is wrong?*

"Thanks. So, y'know how she took me aside to talk to me earlier this week?"

"Yeah."

"Before, she'd been talking about moving back to the university area. She talked about how she missed it there, and that once she was done with school, her parents couldn't keep her from going wherever she wanted to go."

Ann nodded silently.

Luke continued his thoughts as if in a vocalized stream of consciousness. "Well, she met a guy named Nadei, he's from Russia. He's a professor there but in a different department so I guess the school doesn't think them being together is unethical."

"Hmm, that's strange."

"Yeah, that's what I was thinking. But anyway, she told me this guy got offered some kind of job at the United Nations, so he might be moving to New York and he wants her to come with him."

"Ooh, I'm sorry, Luke. Is she gonna marry him?"

He sighed. "I dunno...she didn't say anything about that. I don't even know if he's gonna propose. But either way, she's pretty dead set on going with him to New York if he takes that job. And honestly, I don't know why he wouldn't. She said he's a visiting professor in government."

"That makes sense. I mean, the UN is a huge deal."

"Yeah. AC, I know I'm supposed to be over her, and maybe knowing she's moved on is the closure I need. I can finally be open to something new...maybe somebody that's truly good for me and that I'm supposed to be with. Y'know, God's trying to tell me something, and maybe I should start listening."

ABANDONED
MAY 2002

"So, Ann," her counselor Mara began, checking her notes, "you told me in our earlier sessions that you were raised by your father Marshall and your stepmother...is that 'Sherry?'"

"Uh...it's pronounced 'Shur-ree,'" she corrected her, gently rocking back and forth on the couch. "But yeah, they raised me."

"Okay." The therapist wrote a small note in her client's file. "You've said in previous sessions that you and your father were very close."

"Yes, we were. He was, like, my mentor, my role model, and like my best friend. He knew me very well, probably better than I know myself," Ann recalled, mournfully.

"And your relationship with your stepmother Sherrye is like a mother-daughter relationship?"

"Yes. I consider her my mother. Um...she's the only mother I've known and she's always been there for me. She's never treated me any differently than my sister Michelle. She's my mom."

"Is Michelle her biological daughter?"

"Yes, they had her together. But my mom doesn't make a difference between us."

"Okay. That's good that you have that type of relationship with Sherrye." Then, Mara moved the conversation in a different direction. "So, tell me a bit about your birth mother, you said her name was Stephanie?"

Ann's eyes anxiously bounced around the room. "Uh yes, Stephanie. Um...there's not a lot to tell, you know. My parents divorced when I was a baby and my dad got custody of me, and that was pretty much it."

"Did you always know about your birth mother?"

"Yes, my parents were always honest with me about my birth mother. We've never met, but I always knew she existed."

Mara crossed her stocking-clad legs. "How did you feel about your birth mother not being in your life growing up?"

"I don't think I felt anything, really. It's not like I missed out...I still had a mother and a father. I still grew up in a two-parent household. But sometimes, I used to wonder what happened to Stephanie. It's like she had me, she was here and then she was gone. I don't understand how a mother just drops out of her child's life like that."

"That's understandable to feel that way, Ann. Did your parents ever discuss your birth mother's absence?"

"Yes. My dad did."

October 1993

"One large hazelnut coffee, only fill the cup halfway," Marshall gave his order to the cashier at the Brotmann Bagel Company, a coffee and bagel shop nestled in the Village district in Grosse Pointe. He then looked down. "Annie, go ahead and order."

Ann then gave her order to the cashier. "I'll have a blueberry bagel and a hot chocolate."

After they received the food and drink, Ann located a table for two by the front window to the shop, while Marshall headed to the condiments counter, long-pouring sugar and filling the rest of his cup with half and half.

"Mom's not gonna like you getting coffee," Ann gently admonished her father. "All that sugar's not good for your health."

"Yeah yeah, I know," Marshall responded.

After taking their seats and enjoying their drinks, father and daughter spent about over a half hour chatting away, as they enjoyed doing on Sunday afternoons.

"You look so much like your biological mother," he commented.

The teen took a bite of her bagel. It was warm and tasty.

He went on. "I know that she would be proud of you. You're doing great in school, all 'A's, honor roll."

She looked up at him. "Would she, though?"

"Yeah, I'm sure she would. She was quite smart, just like you."

She sipped her hot chocolate, which was perfect for a crisp winter day, even without any snow on the ground quite yet. "What happened to her?"

Marshall took a deep breath, then tasted his cream and sugar with a splash of coffee. "Well, your biological mother was a good woman, but she was unwell, and she wasn't willing to get the help she truly needed. I couldn't fix it for her, and things just didn't work out. We ended up getting divorced, and she decided I would be the better parent, so that's how I got you. Stephanie truly loved you, Annie. She just didn't want to confuse you by staying in your life."

∽

Mara scribbled words down on her spiral notepad. "That must have been difficult to hear."

Ann slowed her rocking. "I guess. It was what it was. But I don't get it. Why not get help? Wasn't I worth getting better for?"

The counselor leaned in. "If you're uncomfortable sharing, that's fine, but when you say your mother was unwell – what do you mean by that?"

"Uh...sure. According to my dad, she had mental health issues. If she had a long day at her job, or if she had to entertain a lot of people, or if she needed to go to my brother's parent-teacher conferences, anything that involved crowds, or people she didn't know, she had a very hard time." Ann continued. "She would just lock herself in her room and cry, and uh...just not be able to do things."

"You have a brother?"

"Um...yes. He's a half-brother technically – we have the same birth mother. He's, like, ten years older than me, but I've never met him. His name is Lionel."

"How does having a half-brother you have never met make you feel?"

"I dunno. I wish I had a chance to get to know him. You know, I would like to meet him one day."

Mara continued. "That's understandable. So, from what I hear you saying, there was a lot of conflict between your father and your birth mother, and they divorced when you were still a baby."

"Yeah." Ann stopped rocking and looked straight at her therapist. "I was born to do one thing. I had one job, and I failed."

September 1996

One Sunday afternoon, sixteen-year-old Ann was upstairs in her bedroom writing in her journal, as she enjoyed doing. She wanted to listen to "One in a Million" by the singer Aaliyah, but the cassette tape she owned of the single was nowhere to be found. It was not in her Walkman, and she could not locate it in her storage tray of cassette tapes.

Retracing her steps from earlier in the day, she started her search in her parents' bedroom. She began looking in Marshall's walk-in closet first as she had retrieved a sweatshirt for her father from there at his behest. As she crawled on the floor, she noticed a small black footlocker underneath the hung clothes. She had always known it was there, but it was not until that moment that she was curious about its contents.

She pulled out the heavy footlocker, which was fastened but unlocked, and opened the latch. The footlocker included beige file folders full of legal-sized papers, as well as a small photo album with a forest green hardcover. She grabbed these folders, as well as the photo album, and spirited them away to her bedroom.

On the top of one stack of papers read:

STATE OF MICHIGAN
FAMILY COURT, WAYNE COUNTY
PETITIONER: MARSHALL HARRIS CORBIN
RESPONDENT: STEPHANIE FIELDS CORBIN

IN RE CUSTODY OF: ANN LEIGH CORBIN

For the next two hours, Ann pored over these papers, which detailed the custody dispute between her father and birth mother in excruciating detail. Extremely well-documented was each accusation of the other being terrible in one way or another. On page after page were call-outs that in the grand scheme of the situation appeared minor, such as Stephanie accusing her estranged husband of slacking on his strength training and eating too much, and Marshall being upset that his wife had not cooked his favorite meal in months. But then there were deeper accusations, such as accusations that she was overly anxious, reclusive, paranoid, and insane, and assertions that he was a narcissist who lacked patience and understanding, and that he was searching for any reason to have his spouse committed to the state asylum.

As Ann continued reading, she noted that there was a shared custody agreement, and it appeared to be going smoothly for several months. However, at a certain point during the divorce, Stephanie abruptly stopped showing up to take her daughter during her custody time. She also ceased appearing in court proceedings, and no attorney showed up in her stead. Marshall's lawyer requested a default judgment that sole custody be given to him, which the judge granted.

Ann found the papers strange. *It looks like the custody battle was pretty intense, but then after a few months, she simply quit showing up? That doesn't make any sense to me at all. Why just...give up?*

Ann then carefully opened the photo album. Plastered on glossy cardboard behind plastic were several photos dating back to the late seventies and early eighties that she had not seen before this. Quite a few were of Ann as a baby and toddler, in brown braided pigtails held together by rubber bands with colored plastic balls on the ends. A couple of these photos included her being held by both her father and a young, Jheri-curled Sherrye.

Then she noticed a few snapshots of her father as a young man, slightly pudgy but appearing strong, with a tight navy blue tee-shirt. Many of these pictures showed him together with a petite, light brown-skinned lady who appeared around the same age. The woman had dark brown eyes and a full ebony afro, and wore a white and blue plaid sundress. She had never seen this woman before, but she looked oddly familiar at the same time.

On another page was what appeared to be a professional school photo of a young boy. The boy was the complexion of copper, with black hair and brown eyes, but otherwise looked quite a bit like Ann as a child. *Who is this kid?* Ann carefully peeled back the plastic to expose the photo. She then carefully removed it and took a look at the back. She was happy to see something written there that might give her a clue, but when she began reading, she was left even more confused. In childlike writing, the inscription read:

Marshall,
Merry Christmas! I love you!
Lionel
Age 9

That's weird. Ann wanted answers, so she collected the stack of papers, along with the album, and headed downstairs to the only person she knew would have them.

"Dad, I found these papers. I guess they're custody papers...all this happened?"

Marshall, sitting at the dining room table with his work papers, perked up. "Dear, where did you find those?"

"They were in this old trunk in your closet. I was looking for my Aaliyah tape and saw them instead."

He sighed. "It's right here," he said, pointing to a cassette at the edge of the table.

She then handed him the papers and picked up the tape.

He continued. "About those papers..."

"What about them?"

He explained, "Okay, I know it's a lot of legal stuff about custody. I fought so hard to keep you, and so did your biological mother. We both love you so much."

"It looks like you two always had problems."

"Well, kind of. We got together because we were both single and we knew some of the same people. I also wanted to be a role model for her son — your brother. She had a little boy named Lionel from before we got together."

"Is that the kid in the photo album that sort of looks like me?"

"Yeah, that's him. He was a really good kid. We would go on bike rides, I'd take him to the gym with me sometimes, and we would read lots of books. He was like a son to me, a son I never had. You're a lot like him, Annie. I hate that I had to leave him behind when I left Stephanie. I regret that the most." Marshall then went back to Ann's question. "Anyway, things started falling apart once we got married. I really didn't know how she was before that. When we met it wasn't like that, she hid her issues well. But then our marriage fell apart fairly quickly."

"What do you mean?"

"Well, she would scream in the middle of the night, she would freak out sometimes. And sometimes she just wouldn't leave the house. She would get so scared. I couldn't understand it, it's not like there was anything to be afraid of. I tried to calm her down and bring her to reality, but it didn't help. You know, I tried to get her to see a psychiatrist and she said that they couldn't help her. She said that her mom had a lot of the same problems, and all they did was commit her."

"Wow."

Marshall continued. "Stephanie and I were about to split up not long after we got married, but then she ended up pregnant with you. We figured that having a baby would bring us closer and save our marriage. Don't know why we thought that. But anyway, that's how you were born. And it worked for a little while, but then things got worse, and then the marriage was over."

ISN'T IT MIDNIGHT
MAY 2002

An hour before the final weekly Christian Kingdom large group meeting of the school year, Ann, Terah, and Paul decided to pay a visit to the student cafeteria. Goulash was on the menu – Paul's favorite – and all three of them were quite hungry. After scooping out the dish of elbow macaroni, 70/30 ground beef, and bulk marinara sauce from the buffet, as well as an assortment of sides, the friends snagged a circular table in the sparsely filled dining area. As they enjoyed their meals, Luke approached them with only his blue backpack in hand.

"Hey, y'all!" After the group greeted him, he took a chair, spun it around, and straddled it. "You're not gonna believe this!" He unzipped his bookbag, removed and unfolded a letter, and then passed it around the table. "Take a look at this."

When the letter got to Ann, she read its contents:

OHIO VALLEY TECHNICAL UNIVERSITY
SCHOOL OF VETERINARY MEDICINE
May 15, 2002
Dear Mr. Phillips:
Congratulations! You have been selected from the wait-list for admission to the School of Veterinary Medicine at Ohio Valley Technical University for the class of 2006

beginning in August 2002. This offer of admission is contingent on satisfactory completion of your undergraduate program with a cumulative grade point average (G.P.A.) of 3.2.

Please fill out the enclosed acceptance form, sign and mail it to our office postmarked no later than Friday, June 3, 2002.

Sincerely,

Andrew P. Mills, PhD

Dean of Academic Affairs

Ohio Valley Technical University

Paul responded first. "Woohoo! You got into OVTU's vet school! Congratulations brother! God is awesome!"

Terah joined in congratulating him. "Such a blessing! I'm so happy for you! Didn't you say that it's really hard to get into veterinary school?"

"Yeah," Luke responded. "There's only thirty-two vet schools in the country and only ten percent of people who apply get in. It's truly a miracle. I was holding out for this one because I didn't get into Michigan State, Ohio State, or Arizona. They waitlisted me and I had to wait until after the April 15th regular admissions deadline to find out if I could get a spot there."

"Yeah, congrats Luke, uh...that's...that's great." Ann glanced at the letter again, then handed it back to him. "Ohio Valley Technical University, that's down in Losanti, Ohio, right?"

"Yeah."

"So...this means you're moving back to your hometown?"

"Yeah." He carefully placed the letter back into his backpack. "If I hadn't been accepted, I probably would've stayed here and maybe gone to med school or something. But God made it happen for me, didn't he?"

"Sure, seems like it," she voiced quietly. "How do you feel about moving back home?"

"Good question." His smile dimmed a bit. "Obviously, I'm not gonna move back in with my parents. I'll probably rent an apartment near campus, that would make the most sense. But I'm fine with it." Then he said with a bit of an edge, "I mean, I'm going to *veterinary school*. My brother can't get all the glory."

"Luke," Paul asked between bites of his ranch-coated fries, a bit oblivious to the shift in tone, "I'm trying to remember, what does your brother do?"

"Paulie, he's a professor of environmental sciences out in California. He's a big deal because he wrote his dissertation on this thing called the Global Positioning System, something he helped to advance while in grad school."

"What's this Global Positioning System?" Terah asked.

"Uh, it's this navigation system that works with these satellites the government sent to space back in the seventies and eighties," Luke explained. "I guess that when you use it, it's supposed to be better than maps, in terms of finding directions to where things are and where you're going. It, like, knows where you're located on earth, so people can find you and you can find where you're going. It can tell you how to get to your destination in real time, or at least close to it."

Ann noted, "I imagine that's gonna be a big hit."

He nodded. "Yeah...I admit, it is pretty cool. I guess it was something that was limited to the US military for years, but I guess they're rolling out versions of these things now for the civilian market. That's what Trey was working on."

"Not gonna lie, bro, that *is* impressive," Paul said, muffled by his last bit of fries.

Luke rolled his eyes. "Eh, we'll see how long it lasts. But I guess that was enough for him to impress my parents. They have one and showed it off, and they kept saying, 'Trey this,' 'Trey that.'"

While wiping her face with a napkin she pulled from the dispenser in the middle of the table, Ann asked, "Have you told your parents that you got accepted to vet school?"

"Yeah, that was the first thing I did. My mom seemed pretty happy and congratulated me. My dad..." he sighed. "All he could say was, 'Good luck son, hope you finish.' That was it."

"Oh, I'm really sorry to hear that your dad wasn't as happy as you thought he'd be. I hope you know we're all proud of you. You're awesome to *us*."

"Thanks, AC." Luke's smile returned.

"Ann, graduation is fast approaching. How do you feel about that?" asked her counselor Mara during an afternoon session.

"Um...I definitely wanna go into data analytics. I love the idea of working with formulas, equations, and models that have real-world implications. But, what I'm not sure of yet is *where*."

"Where...could you share more about that?"

"Yeah. So, uh...I originally planned to stay around town for a while. I even tossed around the idea of moving back to Detroit. My family's still there, and my best friend Terah is moving back too. But I dunno, there's a whole world out there." She looked down while twirling the string of her light blue hoodie around her right finger. "I feel like my life needs a reset."

Mara responded, "A reset? Could you elaborate on that?"

"Well," Ann continued, "I've lived in Michigan for most of my life. And I've always felt like my life is one-dimensional and predictable. I've always been great at things that are concrete, stuff I could work hard doing and achieve, such as school, work, stuff like that. But it's hard to fit in with actual *people*."

"When you say it's hard to fit in, what do you mean by that?"

"You know, I have a few friends, which is great. But I'm in a campus ministry where I feel like an outsider. Dating and relationships feel unattainable, I can't even get guys to look at me. I feel like the day I started going through puberty, finding guys attractive was a curse. I don't know what it's like to like someone and actually have them like me back. I want to love and be loved in return."

"Hmm. It sounds like you've experienced a great deal of rejection when it comes to being a part of a group, and also when pursuing romantic relationships. That sounds difficult."

"It is."

"Okay, that's understandable. Now, what is it about changing your surroundings that leads you to believe your situation will change?"

"Eh...I don't know. I wonder sometimes if 'The One' is somewhere else. I mean, there are billions of people on earth, almost half of them men. Maybe the guys will be different somewhere else. No one will have to know I'm weird and awkward. Maybe I can finally lose weight, and guys will find me attractive. I just feel like if I stay here in Michigan, everything will stay the same, and I'm going to end up dying alone."

Mara moved around in her chair. "As you know, one of the things we've discussed in previous sessions is the need to dig deeper and gain the insight needed to cope with your reality and improve upon it. And that is often very tough work."

"I understand that."

"Sometimes fresh starts can be helpful. There may be some relationships that are unhealthy and need to end, and distance helps with that. There may be opportunities in other places that may not exist here. But when we're making those decisions, what we want to avoid is believing that changing our outside environment will fix challenges that are internal. I hope that makes sense."

"It does."

"Unfortunately, rejection is an experience we all face in one way or another in the course of our lives. Of course, we can always work on our health, improve ourselves inside and out, we can do things that will make us feel confident, strong, energetic, and accomplished, we can always 'level up,' so to speak. But even then, rejection can and does still happen."

Ann continued to twirl her hoodie string but was now looking up at her mental health professional.

"Ann, the key is not avoiding rejection, because I'm sorry to say, you can't. No one can, but the goal is to keep rejection from defining who you are and your worth in this world. It's valid to feel hurt when someone does not accept you as part of their group, or if someone doesn't want to be in a romantic relationship with you, but after acknowledging that hurt, you want to be able to keep moving forward. A huge part of that is defining and accepting who you are as a person independently of what others have to say about you or even how they treat you."

"Okay."

"When you're considering moving somewhere else, you want to be honest with yourself about your intentions. If you're doing it so you can find where you'll be accepted, or to have a better chance of meeting a significant other, even if you do find those things elsewhere, it may not necessarily change anything on the inside. Some people feel rejection and loneliness even when they're surrounded by family, friends, and romantic partners."

She doesn't get it. "I hear you, but I mean, most people can easily connect with other people. They can find groups and gel with them. And it's like everybody is in and out of relationships. They get with somebody, they break up, and then they quickly find somebody new. But that's not how my life is. Honestly, how can I accept myself when nobody else does?"

Mara was quiet for a moment, then responded. "That is a very good question. It's very easy to look on the outside and see that there are people who appear to have an easier time than you with making the connections you're looking for. But everyone has their own struggles and triumphs. There's a saying, 'Comparison is the thief of joy.' Yes, it's cliche but it's so true."

Ann nodded, still twisting her hoodie string, like hair fitted on a curling iron.

"Instead of focusing on what others around you have that you don't, think about what you *do* have, and figure out what you might want from your life. Where do *you* want to go? What do *you* want to do? What can *you* do that gives you pride? What activities bring *you* joy? These are all questions you should ask yourself as you make decisions on the next step in your life."

A week later, Ann parked herself in the computer lab located in the school library, with only herself and the IT attendant, who was sitting at a desk near the lab door. It was the last Friday night before graduation week.

Like the other students at the University of the Great Lakes, Ann was already finished with her final examinations, but she was still trying to sort out her plans after graduation. She logged onto the computer, popped in a Zip disk where her resume was located, and perused online advertisements for jobs.

She then opened a second browser window and searched, "Cities with the most data analytics jobs." While scanning the top results, she noticed an online article entitled, "Five Best Cities for Data Jobs."

Intrigued, she read the piece:

Big Data is the wave of the future. Data-related professions such as computer scientist, data engineer, data analyst, statistician, and more are typically high-paying and in demand. Now is the time to take advantage of this fast-growing field. Below are the top five locations in the United States to obtain employment in data-related fields:

1. Silicon Valley/San Francisco, California

2. Seattle, Washington

3. Dallas, Texas

4. Losanti, Ohio
5. New York, New York

Losanti, huh?

Losanti, Ohio: Known for its trademark Ohio Valley Ranch dressing and classic Big Ohio Ballpark, this hidden gem along the Ohio River is a fast-growing destination for Fortune 500 firms utilizing data analytics and data engineering. Don't sleep on the wealth of opportunity here.

She searched job postings in the southwest Ohio city, scanned the descriptions and requirements, and then noted which ones she may be qualified to perform. While the data jobs article was still visible on the screen, she heard someone say her name.

"Ann, what's up?"

She looked over her right shoulder. "Oh, hey Paul — what are you doing here? I'm surprised you're not out enjoying the night with everybody else."

"Well, today was a big day. Uh...it was a bit spontaneous, but I asked Alyssa to marry me, and she said 'yes!'"

"Oh my gosh — congratulations!" She hugged him.

"Thanks, Ann. I'm quite jazzed."

"Do you guys have a wedding date?"

"We're looking at June 22nd, it's a Saturday," he disclosed.

"That's quick."

"Oh yeah, I know, but we wanna get married quickly. We love each other, and, as the Bible says, it's better to marry than to sin."

"True."

"So yeah, it'll be in Niles, Alyssa's hometown. I came down here to the lab to start doing my part to help plan the wedding."

"That's exciting."

"For sure. Make sure you give one of us your address as soon as you can, so we can send you an invite. We definitely want you to be there."

"Of course, will do. Looking forward to it...I'll definitely be there. So, what are your plans after the wedding? Where are you going on your honeymoon?"

"We're gonna skip the honeymoon for now, 'cause right after the wedding, we're moving down to Florida."

"Oh...why Florida?"

"I got a job waiting for me down there pending graduation."

Ann voiced her excitement. "Excellent! Where in Florida?"

"Uh, Jacksonville."

"Neat! I was just curious because I lived in Florida briefly when I was a kid. It was further south, um...Fort Lauderdale."

"Oh, that's cool," Paul then glanced at the monitor and noticed the article. "Reading about Losanti, huh?"

Slightly embarrassed, she clicked on another tab to hide that one.

"Hmm, a job in Losanti, too," he called out.

Ann blushed. "You know, Paul, it's not what it looks like. I'm just sorting out my options."

"Ugh, you're still into Luke."

She sighed. "No, I'm over him. We're just friends, I'm fine with that."

"Are you sure?"

"Am I sure *what?*"

"Are you sure you're fine with you and him being just friends? I hope you don't think moving down there will lead to a relationship."

"Oh...no." She shook her head. "No way. I'm not stupid, and I can take 'no' for an answer." *But if I move to Losanti, God will see that I'm stepping out on faith, and he'll honor that. He'll get more time to put things in motion.*

She truly believed that Luke, deep down, felt *something* for her, and she knew in her heart that this feeling was not simply all in her head.

September 2001

On a Tuesday morning during the fall semester of Ann's fourth and final year at the university, she was sound asleep in her dorm room. Only one of her classes was scheduled that day, Sociology 512 – Statistics in Sociology, held in the afternoon. Because of this, she took advantage of the opportunity to catch up on rest.

Knock knock.

She woke up. She rolled around in her lofted bed and tried to ignore what she heard. *I'm just gonna pretend I'm not here. I'm sure it's not important.*

Just as she was finally drifting back to sleep, she heard yet another noise.

Knock knock knock knock knock!

She jolted wide awake. *Are y'all serious?* She called out, "What? Who is it?"

"It's Alyssa! Ann, it's important! Open the door!"

"Alright, I'm coming."

She climbed down the ladder from her bed, missing the bottom rung in her haste and falling to the floor.

"Ow!"

After dusting herself off, she trudged to the door and opened it, clad in her pajamas.

"What's up?"

Alyssa ran inside the room and motioned frantically to the 24-inch Sony bubble-screen television on her dresser. "Ann – turn on your TV!"

Ann picked up the remote control and clicked on the television. "Uh...Alyssa, what's going on?"

"Turn to CNN!"

She groggily did was she was told.

"Guys, could we replay the tape right now?" the news anchor called out to the crew behind the camera. "Do we have the tape right now of the second plane impacting? We're going to roll that tape in just a second."

"The heck's going on?"

Alyssa broke the news softly. "Ann, two airplanes flew into the World Trade Center in New York. They're trying to figure out what happened. They're not sure if it was an accident or terrorism."

"Two planes?"

"Yeah, two planes."

"Ah well, it's probably terrorism then. I mean, it's two of 'em."

About a half hour later, Terah came running through the door. "Holy shit — oops — I mean shoot."

"It doesn't even matter right now, yo," Ann calmly stated, still with her eyes trained on the television alongside Alyssa.

"It's crazy out there," Terah continued. "People are trying to use their phones, but nobody's getting through."

"Yeah, I'm not surprised. A few of the girls in my dorm are freaked out, they know people in New York who might be in those buildings," Alyssa observed.

"Not gonna lie...right now, I'm worried about my family in New York. I have an aunt and uncle there, and cousins. My aunt and uncle are retired, and my cousins are contractors and not white collar guys, but you never know," Ann shared.

"I hear you," Terah said. "We can only pray. Pray for them, and pray for people in New York right now."

The young ladies sat in Ann and Terah's dorm room watching the coverage of the cataclysmic event and praying periodically. Throughout the day, more information would be revealed regarding what would become known as "September 11th," a series of four coordinated terrorist attacks involving the hijacking of airplanes that would fly into the Twin Towers of the World Trade Center and the Pentagon that occurred on September 11, 2001. The fourth plane did not make it to its intended destination due to the heroic actions of passengers onboard, and as a result, crashed into a field near Shanksville, Pennsylvania. All aboard the airplanes died, along with nearly three thousand other victims in the buildings and on the ground.

Classes at the University of the Great Lakes were cancelled for the rest of the day, as well as the remainder of the week. Many students rushed to call their families, Ann and her friends included, but the lines stayed busy, and it took hours to get through.

When Ann finally reached her family, they were all safe, including relatives in New York City and Virginia. Most of her friends and dorm mates were also lucky in that regard, though unfortunately, she knew of two students who lost loved ones in the attacks.

In the early afternoon, an email blast went out to all Christian Kingdom members that Brother Craig and his wife Rebecca would be opening their home to ministry students and anyone else who wanted to commune with them. Once Terah received the email, she, Ann, and Alyssa changed clothes and headed there around three o'clock.

Once the ladies arrived at the home, a two-story Craftsman just off campus, Ann noticed that several students were already there, including Greg, Kyle, Megan, Paul, and many others. Sister Rhonda, her husband Freddy, and their children also came over. Luke showed up a half hour later. The night was full of sharing their experiences, expressing their feelings, and engaging in fervent prayer.

At half past four in the afternoon, the young children of the staff leaders began to get restless. In response, Brother Craig spoke up. "I'll pay for pizza for everybody, but I'm blocked in the driveway right now. Can anybody run down to Vito's on the other side of campus and pick them up?"

Luke stood up. "I brought my car with me and it's on the street. I can do it."

"That sounds great. Thanks, Luke. I'll call them now."

Craig picked the off-white cordless phone from its charging holder and dialed the number to Vito's. However, instead of the anticipation of a ringing phone, he was hit by the annoyance of a busy signal.

"Ope, I forgot that the lines are all tied up. Here's a fifty spot." Brother Craig handed Luke a crisp fifty-dollar bill. "That should cover a couple of their giant 24-inch Bambino pizzas. One pepperoni, one cheese — I think that'll work. Head on down there and wait however long it'll be. I have a feeling there are a lot of folks with the same idea."

"Alright."

"Oh," Craig added, "Tell them to keep the change. It's been a hard day for everybody, and it'll be nice to make it a little bit brighter for someone."

Luke then looked to Ann, who was sitting on the floor between Terah and Alyssa, and said, "AC, you wanna come with?"

"Yeah, sure."

From the floor, Paul piped up. "Alyssa and I can come along too."

"Thanks, but we need to save room for the pizzas. They're gonna be pretty huge. AC and I got it."

Paul cocked his head. "You have a station wag—"

Luke put his hand up. "Paulie, *we're good.*"

To that, he shook his head but otherwise remained silent.

Luke and Ann went to Vito's, a local pizzeria two blocks away from the eastern edge of campus, to order the huge pizzas. After parking the car down the street, the two hiked up to the restaurant and walked inside.

The dimmed pizzeria was empty, other than the two friends and an older gentleman behind the counter. All the dark wooden chairs were stacked on top of the matching tables as if the establishment were closed.

"Hey!" the man at the counter greeted them. "It's gonna be three hours. We're slammed as hell. You good with that?"

Luke called back, "Yeah, that'll be fine." He placed the order and gave the man at the counter his first name and phone number.

"Not gonna lie," the man said, "we gotta lotta people tryin' to get through, but it's so busy."

"I hear you," Ann responded. "We uh...we tried to call ahead and got a busy signal."

"Yeah, I'm not surprised," the pizza man quipped. "We're having trouble callin' out too, I think it's those attacks in Manhattan. So, I'll tell you, come back in, uh...two and a half hours at the earliest, three's betta."

Luke nodded. "Alright, that's fine."

"You know, it truly is a crazy night."

"Yeah, it sure is. It sure is."

Once Luke and Ann were outside, he turned to face her. "AC, we've got, like, three hours to kill. You wanna go for a drive?"

Ann shrugged. "Hey, why not?"

Luke turned over the ignition and pulled down his windshield visor to expose a cache of compact discs. He slid one out and popped it into the CD player installed in the dashboard, then rolled down the windows, shifted the Saab in drive, and started up the northern road out of town. Soon, bars, restaurants, and apartment buildings transformed into open fields and lush forests.

Flowing out of the car stereo was the song "Seven Wonders" by Fleetwood Mac. He chuckled. "Fleetwood Mac is my guilty pleasure. Don't tell anybody."

"It'll stay between us."

"I had to get outta there for at least a little bit. It's a lot to take in, AC. It's a lot. And when things get to be too much, going for a drive makes me feel better, helps me clear my head a bit."

"I hear you. Are you missing anybody in the attacks?"

"No, I'm real lucky...blessed, I guess. I have a small family. Not a lot of aunts, uncles, or cousins. The few I have are mostly down in Losanti. And then, y'know, there's my parents and my brother. So, I lucked out."

"Same here. I mean, uh...my family's bigger, and I have relatives in New York City and Virginia not too far from DC, but none were at the World Trade Center or at the Pentagon or anything. But Luke, this *is* scary."

"Yeah," Luke continued driving. "I found out in class this morning. We got let out early. When I was walking back to my apartment, I was just waiting for a plane to fall out of the sky and hit campus. It's so unreal."

"Oh yeah, I know," Ann responded, gazing out the window at the darkness forming over the horizon.

After a little while, he turned right onto a two-lane highway. After about twenty minutes, they came upon a tiny gravel lot where he turned off and parked. He then left the keys in the electric-only position within the ignition and turned up the volume on the car stereo.

"Follow me," he said.

"Aren't you worried about somebody running off with the car?"

"Nah, we're not going that far. You see the lake right there?"

Ann focused in the direction Luke was pointing and noticed a sparkling body of water backed by a gorgeous green forest. "That's amazing!"

"It's gorgeous for sure! Let's go."

The friends exited the station wagon and strolled over to a dry patch close to the shore. With "Little Lies" playing in the background, the two sat on the grass and took in the surroundings. While experiencing the calm of the environment, they began contemplating their respective futures.

"Luke, a part of me is looking forward to graduation. I'm excited to be starting my career in data analytics. My dad and my uncle want me to go to law school. But the more I thought about it, and the more I've prayed about it, there's like, no way. I'm not gonna say I won't revisit law in the future, but I'm not rushing to go to law school right now. I didn't even bother taking the LSAT. So, they're just gonna have to deal. It is what it is."

Luke laughed. "Y'know, I can respect that. Shit, I wish I could tell my parents, 'Hey Mom and Dad, I wanna be a documentary filmmaker.' But they would just call me a loser or whatever, and they'd compare me to my brother Trey. Y'know, not all of us can move out west and invent things."

"Sure, but you don't have to be like your brother. You've got your own talents and things you're good at. You have great qualities that make you 'you.' And anyway, as far as me doing what I want, I'm not that special. I guess I'm used to being a bit weird and I suck at conforming. No matter what I do, I'm not gonna fit in anyway, so why try?"

"Yeah, I get it."

"But anyway, if you were to be a documentary filmmaker, what sorts of stories would you wanna tell?"

"Easy. Human interest stories. Slice of life stuff. Observing how other folks live in other places. The environment, the scenery, all of that fascinates me. Following somebody else's life, some subject, something where the film can tell a story, that's what I would love to do, but there's no way. What chance do I have to make a living doing something like that?"

"Well, you *are* looking to go to vet school. It's not like your chances are that much better since the acceptance rates are so low and there aren't that many vet schools."

"Sure, you're right. But I tell you what, vet school sounds more impressive at the supper table than filming the lives of auto workers in Detroit or Flint for public access TV. Besides, if I don't get into vet school, med school is my backup, I've already been accepted at UGL for med school."

"Really? Why hadn't you mentioned that before?"

"'Cause it's not my first choice; it's my safety net."

"Hmm, who else can look at med school as a freaking safety net?" she chuckled.

"Somebody that's just two points below genius," he bragged.

"Are you serious?"

"Yeah, for sure. I was tested when I was a kid. I was so close, but not quite to genius level."

She furrowed her brow in approval. "Wow, that's impressive. Anyway, Luke, it sounds like you have things all planned out. I truly admire that you have the ability to chart out your life. I suck at that sometimes. Eh, a lot of times if I'm honest. I just hope that one day, you'll feel free to do what truly makes you happy, rather than worry about other people's judgments."

"I wish it was that easy. I dunno, maybe one day it will be." Luke looked up at the sky, which was dotted with stars. "A day like today puts things into perspective, you know what I mean?"

"Yeah, it really does. It's easy to go through life as normal...you know, go to class, study, go out with friends, go to large group, go to small group, call home, see family every once in a while, and it's just like, it's easy to take it all for granted. And then something like this happens. I mean, it was just a normal day. It was just a normal day."

After a pause, he inched closer to her and placed his arm around her. Leaning in on each other, they relaxed on the edge of the calm, beautiful lake, and took in the surroundings, soaking in the serenity during a time of chaos.

The bright sun slid behind the tall trees, and the song "Isn't it Midnight" played from the windows of the station wagon. He rose to his feet and held his hand out to her. She gazed into his eyes, which were now silver, much like her own, took his hand, and stood up as well.

For what felt like a beautiful eternity, the two slow danced. Only illuminated by the waning crescent moon, Luke and Ann were in sync, their souls bonding into one. On such a day full of fear and uncertainty, they sought safety and comfort in each other.

Once the song ended, he gave her a close, deep hug. He whispered in her ear, "You're stunning, AC."

Oh my God...it's really happening.

Ann was frozen, as she could not believe what she heard. Luke leaned in, their lips but an inch from each other. Then, as if catching himself, he stepped back.

Awkwardly, she checked her watch, and upon noting the time, sighed deeply. "It's time to go back, huh?"

He looked at his own watch to confirm. "Yeah, afraid so."

They then returned to the Saab and went back into town. They were silent on the way back, but while steadying the car with his left hand, Luke took his right hand and held Ann's left hand. All too soon, they were within city limits, with the nighttime traffic and bright lights.

Stepping into the restaurant, the same man at the counter greeted them.

"Hey guys! Welcome back!"

"Hi, how have things been since we left?" Luke asked.

"Crazy busy, slammed. Hasn't really let up."

"Can I ask you something, sir?"

"Yeah, shoot."

"I gotta ask, are *you* okay? Have you been affected by what's going on?"

The man's expression shifted into a mixture of sadness and relief at the same time. "You know what? You're the first guy tonight to ask me that. Uh...I'm sure you can tell by my accent – I'm from New York – Brooklyn. My wife and kids, they're here with me in Michigan, but my brothers and sisters and their families, a lot of 'em are still out east. I've been havin' a tough time gettin' ahold of my people, so right now I got no idea. But I went ahead and opened up anyway for takeout, figured it would keep my mind off stuff, at least for tonight."

"That's completely understandable."

"Man, thanks for askin.' You know, couples like you make my night. It's like I tell my wife – in all the madness, at least we got each other."

Luke and Ann smiled.

The man continued, "Oh, I'm pretty sure your pizzas just came up. You're Luke, right?"

"Yeah."

The man turned around to the pizza rack and grabbed two giant boxes. "Here you go. Thirty bucks."

He gave the restauranteur Brother Craig's fifty-dollar bill. "Keep the change, sir."

"Wow — thank you! Appreciate it."

"Of course."

"Have a safe night, guys!"

"You too," the friends responded.

Ann helped Luke load the boxes in the hatch of Luke's Saab. They then returned to the group at Brother Craig's house.

The two walked inside the house with the pizzas. "Wow, y'all were gone awhile!" Brother Craig said, grabbing the box Ann was holding.

"Yeah, they quoted us three hours," Luke explained.

"Wow, that was a lot of time to kill. I didn't expect that. You could've come back here and waited if it was gonna be *that* long."

"I know, but it was fine." Luke gave a knowing glance to Ann. "The time flew by amazingly fast."

Ann held onto the memory of affection amidst mayhem as she decided on her future following graduation. She and Paul continued to converse while in the computer lab after it slipped that she was considering a move to Losanti.

"Losanti's an interesting place. I hope you know what you're getting into," Paul warned.

Ann was concerned by Paul's statement. "Why do you say that?"

He smiled wryly. "Don't get me wrong, Losanti's not a *bad* place. But it's got its quirks. I'll put it this way...if you're not from there, it may take a bit to get acclimated and find a crowd to hang out with. And all in all, it's not the most exciting of places to live."

"To be fair, I'm just looking to move there to work."

"Sure, but you still have to live there. Again, it's not *terrible*. It's one of those cities that'll *do*, if you know what I mean."

"No, Paul. No, I don't. What do you mean?"

"Well," he sighed, "it's okay. Not bad, not good. It's not as exciting as Detroit."

"Detroit's not exciting."

Paul begged to differ. "Eh, I think it's pretty fun – you've got a bunch of sports – the Red Wings and the Pistons are good. You've got techno, the auto show, the Henry Ford Museum and Greenfield Village, the Motown Museum, all kinds of stuff. I guess when you're from there, you don't notice. You're used to it."

"Sure, I guess," Ann conceded. "But maybe that's why you don't think Losanti's exciting. You're from there so you're used to it."

"Touché."

"But yeah, if I find a job there, that could be where I'm headed. From everything I've read, it sounds promising."

"Sure...and you'll be down there with Luke."

Ann faced the computer monitor and shrugged. "Yeah Paul, I guess so."

OHIO WELCOMES YOU

JULY 2002

After three rounds of interviews, Ann received a formal job offer letter from The Nichols Agency, a major marketing firm located in the heart of Losanti, Ohio. She would be making an excellent starting salary, and it sure helped that the city's cost of living was quite low compared to most other regions in the United States.

Through a series of visits, she was able to snap up a decent one-bedroom apartment in Norris Park, an eclectic, yuppie neighborhood up a steep incline just east of downtown Losanti. The unit was on the second floor of a walk-up apartment building with unit entrances open to the outside. The exterior had orange and aqua trim, resembling a sixties-era Howard Johnson's motel.

The interior was dated yet renovated. The walls were painted white, and new brown carpet had been laid throughout the living room, hallway, and bedroom. The galley kitchen included an apartment-sized refrigerator, gas stove, double sink and dishwasher, and garbage disposal, complete with Formica countertops, brown top and bottom cabinets, and hardwood flooring. The bathroom was tiled beige, tan, and white, with a tan serviceable sink, mirror, and medicine cabinet, as well as a white built-in tub and shower.

But more than any other feature, she was excited that the property management company allowed pets: Up to two pets were permitted, including dogs of any size, if they were well-behaved. So, once she got settled in her new digs and prepared her home for a pet, she headed to the Losanti Humane Society to select a new furry companion.

While at the facility, she noticed a lanky dog of less than a year old, an ebony-coated male with deep brown eyes that laid down subdued with his head raised, that the other prospective pet owners there that day continued to pass by, overlooking him. She had always found black dogs beautiful, and this was a particularly adorable one. She walked up to the dog's kennel, and he perked up, wagging his tail excitedly.

"Could you tell me about Charlie over here?" Ann asked the vet tech.

"Oh, this little guy?" he replied. "His name is Charlie, he's a Labrador retriever. He's pretty active but well-mannered, and he's housebroken."

"Uh...how did he come to be in the shelter?"

"Well, Charlie was found abandoned as a pup with his litter mates in Michigan. It was a hoarding situation. We had room for him and a few of his litter mates down here. So, they came down here a few months ago. His siblings have already been adopted out, but not him. Unfortunately, black dogs tend to be hard to place."

"Could I spend some time with him?"

"Of course!"

Ann was taken to a colorful room resembling a child's playroom but with toys for dogs, such as ropes, squeaky tennis balls, ramps, and the like. Several minutes later, Charlie was brought to her in the room. He walked up to her carefully and sniffed her, and his tail wagged. She petted him and then sat down. He went to her and laid down next to her for pets. She then got him to play with the squeaky toys.

"I'll take him."

After filling out the paperwork and paying the one hundred dollar adoption and neutering fee, Charlie was now Ann's dog. She was thrilled to have a canine buddy of her own.

Two weeks after Ann's move to Losanti, she continued to settle into her new home. She was busy unpacking one of her moving boxes, labeled "Living Room," when she found an old picture of her with her father in a frame. She was only three years old, and they were sitting on the Florida beach.

She sat on her futon, stared at the photo, and thought to herself, *I miss you Dad. I wonder if the pain will ever go away. I doubt it will.*

She placed the framed photo on her end table, and just then, her cell phone rang. Seeing that Luke was on the other end of the line, she answered.

"So, I saw on Myspace you're moving down here to Losanti," Luke mentioned.

"Yeah, I'm actually here now. Been here for about a week or two."

"That's cool. What part of town?"

"Uh, Norris Park, not far from downtown."

"Where in Norris Park?"

Ann elaborated. "I'm on Sharpe Street, just off Hilltop Station."

"Oh wow...then I'm right around the corner from you. I live on Hilltop Station near the record shop. Sweet!"

"Awesome!"

"What are you doing right now?"

"Not much, just unpacking, but it's not, like, time sensitive or anything."

"I can swing by now. Is that cool?"

"Uh, that's great. But just know I'm not completely unpacked, and I have a dog now."

"Oh, that's so nice! What kind of dog?"

"He's a Labrador. He's a rescue, his name's Charlie."

"That's awesome. Anyway, see you in a little bit."

After the phone conversation, Ann ran to take a quick shower and change her clothes. A few minutes later, she heard a knock on the door and Charlie barked. "Coming!" she called out.

She was brushing her hair as she sprinted towards the door and opened it.

"Hi, Luke!"

"Hey, AC! Welcome to the neighborhood!"

The dog looked up and wagged his tail.

"Luke – this is Charlie."

"Aw, he looks nice and strong. Silky coat."

"He's friendly, but you *are* a new person to him, so you'll want to pet his back."

"Yeah, of course." He approached the dog and gave him his hand to sniff. Then, as he continued to wag his tail, Luke gave him pets, which made the dog happy.

"Uh...have a seat. Sorry for the mess, I'm still unpacking. Just a few boxes left."

"Oh, that's fine. Don't worry about it." He sat down on Ann's futon. Ann sat on the other end, still unpacking.

"So yeah, I've been here since, like, last week Tuesday."

"That's cool. Paulie and I were talking and he mentioned you were coming down here. Why didn't you tell me?"

"Of course Paul would tell you." *That guy can't keep his mouth shut.* "Anyway, I mean, I guess it wasn't that big a deal. I'm doing my thing and you're doing yours, and the thing is, you're in vet school, I'm sure you're busy. I didn't want to be a bother."

"Of course not, it's fine. Besides, classes don't start for another couple of weeks."

"Oh, that's cool."

"Besides, we're friends. Why wouldn't I want to hang out with you?"

"Uh, I dunno."

Luke took a deep breath. "AC, I gotta ask, what would make you wanna move here to Losanti of all places?"

"You know my degree's in statistical math, right?"

"Yeah."

"So apparently, Losanti is one of the top places in the country for data-related jobs. And I got hired over at The Nichols Agency."

"Oh, I've heard of them. They're always being cited by news stations and papers. They do a lot of polling. That's pretty important. Congrats!"

"Thanks, Luke."

"So...has anybody given you a tour of the city since you moved here?" Luke asked.

"No, not yet."

"Alright, let me show you around."

Ann and Luke walked outside, where his station wagon was parked on the street.

"Losanti's a car city," he informed her. "Public transit here is shit. Did you bring a car down here when you moved?"

"Yeah. It's parked right in front of yours." She pointed to a Volkswagen New Beetle painted neon green.

"Oh, the green New Bug. I like that."

"Yeah, it's cool. Saw them at the auto show in Detroit a couple of years ago, and when I got the job down here, I figured I had to get one."

"Yeah, I get it. It's nice. Anyway, let's hop in my car, I'll show you around a bit."

Ann and Luke entered the Saab. He pulled the car out of the space and began cruising around the city.

"Losanti's nothing like UWO. It's hilly, nothing like Michigan, and in the winter it's a little treacherous so you wanna be careful. There's not a lot of snow 'cause we don't have the lake effect and it's a bit south of Michigan. But the hills make it scary. And the drivers. Y'know, Losantians can't drive for shit, not even in the rain."

She laughed nervously. "Good to know."

"So right now, we're in Norris Park, which you already know. We're on the east side of the city. The east side is a bit easier to navigate 'cause it's more developed. More stores, businesses, and so on."

"So, what's on the west side?"

Luke laughed. "Not a whole lot, honestly. I mean, it's a bit cheaper to live on that side of town, but it's less developed and more conservative. If you get lost out there, God help you."

"Yikes!"

"Not trying to scare you. I mean, it's not that bad, but it is...different. It's rural, it's...y'know, hillbilly. I'll show you after we're done with the east side and downtown."

"So, uh...what part of town are you and Paul from?"

"Well, we're both from a little further out from here," Luke explained. "Paulie's from Vanderbilt, which is kinda northeast of here. It's pretty upscale, like upper middle class. I'm from Denbytown, which is kinda north-northwest, it's solid middle class – very much a bedroom community, a mix of blue collar factory folks and white-collar pencil pushers."

"Dude, you sound like a real estate agent," she quipped, chuckling.

"Y'know, maybe I missed my calling," he noted sarcastically. "Losanti's a city of neighborhoods, and people don't branch out a whole lot. High school sports are big here, and people judge you by what high school you went to."

"Really? Even adults?"

"Oh yeah. Even sixty-year-olds do it. Don't be surprised if you see grandpas dressed head-to-toe in their high school colors. It's crazy."

"Wow. I mean, um, Detroit can kind of be like that, but not to the same degree. There's the big three high schools, Cass, King, and Renaissance — they're public but you have to test into them unless they're your neighborhood school."

"Yeah, we have a few schools like that here too."

"Okay, so there's those, then there's pretty much everywhere else. I went to Saint Martha's, which is an all-girls Catholic school, but since it's in the city of Detroit, it had seen better days by the time I got there, and it's closed down now."

"Wow, I can't imagine them closing down a Catholic school here. They're pretty popular in Losanti."

"Oh, okay, that's definitely different. A lot of the Catholic families in Detroit are moving to the suburbs, so it's killing off the private schools in the city. But in any case, for the most part, nobody cares where you went to high school. In Detroit, it's more about what side of town you're from, maybe the neighborhood depending on which one, like Palmer Woods or Indian Village, those are a bit more upscale than most Detroit neighborhoods."

"Yeah, Losanti's gonna be weird for you."

"So, what do they do if you tell them that you didn't go to high school here?" she asked.

He cringed. "Oof...they don't know what to do with you then."

"It's that bad?"

"Yeah. A lot of people here don't wanna bother with outsiders 'cause they can't pigeonhole them, but don't worry, you'll find some decent people. Now another thing is, AC, that if you wanna know what kind of neighborhood you're in, step into their Lovett's," Luke explained, referring to the local grocery store chain. "So, we're now in Vanderbilt. I'll show you."

Luke turned into the nearest Lovett's parking lot and stopped the car in an open space. He and Ann got out and went inside the supermarket.

"Whoa!" Ann marveled at the shiny, large grocery store. Luke grabbed a handbasket, and the friends headed over to the produce section. She perused the shelves and was amazed at the availability of various types of fresh fruits she had not seen at her local Lovett's, including dragon fruit, pomegranate, and plantains. She also noticed stands dedicated to gourmet cheeses, olives, and artisan breads. "What is this, God's Lovett's?"

He chortled. "We're in Vanderbilt. They have money here. Anything they could possibly want, they get. But y'know, if we go to one of the Lovett's on the west side, chances are they'll look outdated and sparse, even more so than the one in Norris Park."

"That's crazy."

"Yeah, it totally is," he agreed. "But that's Losanti. It's a strange place to live, but I'm used to it. It's home."

After purchasing a few items at the Vanderbilt Lovett's, the friends continued the drive around the city.

"AC, you wanna bite to eat?"

"Hmm, I dunno. Are you hungry?"

"Yeah, I'm starving. There's a place along the river on the west side that's pretty good, called Tiki Hut. They have drinks too. And we can sit out on their deck along the river."

"Eh, sounds good, why not?"

Luke and Ann then traveled to the west side of Losanti. As he continued driving along, the densely populated buildings of the east side and the high rises of downtown gave way to historic Victorian, Federal, and Italianate-style homes sitting on larger tracts of land, and vast, sparse fields of grass and woods.

"Oh wow, Luke. I see what you mean when you say the west side is less populated than the east side. Definitely different."

He nodded while continuing to concentrate on the winding road that skirted the banks of the Ohio River. "It is. It's more spread out, and some people out here raise chickens, and even cows and horses."

"And all of that's within city limits?"

"Yeah, for the most part. Some of it's suburban, but around here, you go from city to cornfields pretty quick. This part of town has a bit of a deer overpopulation problem, so you wanna be careful out here, especially at night."

"Thanks for the heads up."

"Sure."

The friends arrived at the Tiki Hut and got a table on the river deck.

"The river is so nice and serene. It's so cool we can see the Kentucky hills from here."

"Yeah, it's alright. It's kinda brown, though. I think the lakes and rivers up in Michigan are prettier."

"They're alright, I suppose, but the Ohio River truly does have its own beauty."

He shrugged. "I guess it's easier to appreciate something when you didn't grow up around it."

A server walked up to take their order. "Hi, welcome to Tiki Hut! Would you like to start off with something to drink?"

Ann looked down at the drink menu. "Sure! I'll have a Hefeweizen."

"Great! And for you?"

Luke responded to the server. "I'll go with a Dunkel. And can we have an order of pretzels for the table as well please?"

"Perf!" the server responded. A couple of minutes later, the server brought back their beers and pretzels and took their food order before disappearing again.

Luke took a sip of his Dunkel. "You know what, AC?"

"What, Luke?"

He looked intently into Ann's eyes. "I'm so glad you moved down here."

Ann truly enjoyed her new job at The Nichols Agency. Every day was different from the day before, as she performed regression analysis and multivariate modeling using survey datasets for the benefit of the firm's clients. These clients included several news stations, as well as commercial retailers and manufacturers. She loved being able to use her mathematics skills to produce data-rooted insights with meaning, and that made a difference in the real world. It was hard work, but to Ann, it was rewarding work, and for a new analyst, it paid well. She lived comfortably, and did not have to rely on her family to stay afloat.

The office, located in downtown Losanti, was on the 40th floor of the Werac Tower, a local landmark built in the Art Deco style just off Fountain Circle. As Losanti's downtown center, Fountain Circle, with a huge cast iron fountain with multi-colored lighting in its middle, was the place for city gatherings and events. During summers, rallies would be held there for various political and social causes. The annual Ranchfest hosted by Ohio Valley Ranch would also take place there. In winters, the Circle would be the home of a giant Christmas tree, and an outdoor skating rink would be set up for residents to enjoy the outdoor cold weather.

The Nichols Agency office had cubicles in the center of a large floor. On the perimeter were standalone walled rooms with space for team leads, managers, and executive leaders, as well as small "breakout rooms" often used for stand-up meetings, one-on-ones, and weekly team meetings.

It was half past three on a Friday afternoon in late July. Ann was wrapping up some work for the day when two men and a woman approached her cubicle.

"Hi, Ann!"

Ann turned around to see a tall, tanned woman with shoulder-length crimped brown hair. She recognized her as her coworker, Gwen Fagan. "Uh, hi, Gwen!" She then addressed the young gentlemen standing behind her, Rob McCown and Jason Davis. "Hi, Rob! Hi, Jason!"

Rob, a short, balding man with light peach skin, said, "We're going downstairs to The Losanti Shanty after work, looking to meet up there at, like, four o'clock. You wanna come with?"

"Sure!"

"Awesome sauce! See you there!"

After Ann wrapped up her work, she made her way to the first floor to the Losanti Shanty. The bar was dark and wood-paneled with a stage and karaoke machine, as well as an outdoor patio. After a moment, she found her coworkers Besides Gwen, Rob, and Jason, a few other colleagues, mostly men, were sitting at a table. Ann ordered a draft Framboise lambic beer and sat with her coworkers.

After greeting them, she listened to their conversations. Gwen and Rob were discussing the sci-fi TV show Firefly, while others were chatting about the Green Sox baseball game that would be played the next day, complaining about how the team just started the season the month before and going into Memorial Day weekend, they were already ten games under .500.

Jason, a shiny-domed man with dark, tanned skin and brown eyes, turned and chatted with her.

"I'm glad you came out. Since we're all on the same analytics team, we thought it would be great if you joined us, and we can get to know each other."

"Yeah, that totally makes sense. Thanks for inviting me out."

"Oh, no problem. So, what high school did you go to?"

"Uh, I didn't go to high school here," Ann explained. "I'm originally from Detroit."

Jason appeared to be in thought. "Oh, you're from the Motor City, huh?"

"Yeah. Born and pretty much raised."

"I see. I grew up here in Losanti, but I have an auntie up there in Detroit, in Delray. I spent some time up there during summers back when I was growing up."

"Oh okay, I know where that is, southwest side. Not too far from Mexican Village."

He smiled. "They've got the best Mexican food."

"Sure do, especially the nachos, haven't found anything like those anywhere else."

"So, where in Detroit did you grow up?"

"Uh, over on the far east side, near Grosse Pointe."

"Oh, you're from the bougie part of Detroit!"

Ann blushed. "I dunno if I would say that, but..."

Another coworker, Brian Kraut, jumped into the conversation. "Oh, so I heard you're from Detroit, Ann?"

"Yeah."

"Oof. Was it rough up there? I heard it's really dangerous."

Ann rolled her eyes. "Eh, I mean, it's like most other cities, it's got its good parts and bad parts. The neighborhood I grew up in was fine, still is."

"Oh, really?"

"Yes. Really." She then took a swig of her beer.

One of Ann's pet peeves was one she shared with many native Detroiters. Because of the city's reputation amplified by the national news media, it was all too popular to vilify it as being dangerous and infested with blight and crime. Yet, while many from outside Detroit saw it as a prime example of urban failure, she viewed her hometown as the land of proud, hardworking people exhibiting grit and determination. It was where she was from, and where her family thrived.

To Ann, Detroit was *home*.

Shortly after this exchange, Gwen and one of the other coworkers in the group decided to perform karaoke. They walked up to the machine, pressed a few buttons, and then sang "Come On Eileen" by Dexys Midnight Runners. The table turned towards them and cheered for their off-key rendition, screaming "Go Gwen! Yeah Chris!"

When Gwen and Chris finished, they walked back to the table and the other coworkers high-fived them. Then Gwen looked to Ann and said, "Go up girl, you should try it!"

"Uh...I don't know about that. I can't sing."

"It doesn't matter, go ahead!"

Ann sighed and said, "Okay, sure." She headed up to the karaoke machine onstage and scanned the selections on the monitor. She eyed a new song on the list that received a lot of radio airplay, "A

Thousand Miles" by Vanessa Carlton. She selected it and started to sing.

As she belted out the lyrics, the table of coworkers continued with their conversations at the table. No cheers or even heckling came from the table, or anyone else at the bar for that matter. Once the song was over, she sat down, and everyone continued their conversations, not acknowledging her performance or even noticing she returned to the table.

Wow, really. Nobody even noticed I got up there. It's like they were trying to get rid of me. It was not about the praise, as she knew she could not sing. But she only went up to perform because she thought that was what others in the group did to fit in. Yet *she* tried, and it was as if she did not exist. After a few more minutes, she paid her tab and headed home.

On the short drive to her apartment, a Taco Bell fast food restaurant caught her eye, and she craved it. She turned in and went through the drive-thru, ordering a twelve-taco combo with a large Pepsi.

Once Ann arrived home, she took Charlie out for a potty break and gave him his nightly kibble. After taking care of her canine companion, she got onto the computer to play video games and started in on the tacos. Each taco tasted better than the one before, each crunch was more satisfying than the last. The cheap meat hit the spot, and the cheese was perfect. Swallowing the feelings of apparent rejection felt even better.

SWARM OF GUPPIES
SEPTEMBER-OCTOBER 2002

"So, you wanted to tell me about this guy you're seeing," Ann brought up to Terah as they caught up on each other's lives one September evening.

"Oh yeah, Jimmy." Terah's smile could be felt through the telephone.

"How's all that going?"

"Annie, he's everything I could've wanted. He's twenty-seven, born and raised here in Detroit, he went to Cass Tech, and he's got a bachelor's from U of M."

"He went to Cass for high school and graduated from Michigan? That's impressive."

"Heck yeah. And he's a good time. He's funny and we have some great conversations. He's got a car and he lives on his own...girl, he owns a condo on the riverfront," Terah raved.

"Nice...very nice. That's on our side of town, huh?"

"Yeah. He's not too far from my house."

"Convenient."

"It sure is. And when we go out, he takes me to some upscale places. Like, last Saturday, we went to the Caucus Club for dinner."

"Wow...isn't that some fancy steakhouse in downtown Detroit?"

"Oh yeah. It's very nice. The food was exquisite. And not gonna lie, it's ruined steak for me. It's like I can't go to Longhorn ever again!" Terah laughed.

"Oh dang! Must've been some amazing steak!"

"Oh, it was. But yeah, Jimmy...he's all this greatness in one package. He looks so good. He's got smooth and clear brown skin and he's got nice eyelashes and a neatly trimmed beard, and he's toned...mmm!"

"Nice!"

"But it's not just about how he looks. He's so loving, he shows he appreciates me. Very generous, it's like I want for nothing. And I'm gonna be meeting his family soon."

"Oh, he sounds great, seems like things are working out great for you two."

"Oh yeah...things are wonderful."

"So, what does he do?"

"He's an automotive engineer, he works at Ford," Terah explained.

"Wow, that's a solid job right there. Any kids?"

"Nope. No kids."

"Sounds like a unicorn." Ann was impressed. "Now remind me, where'd you meet him?"

"So, you know I've been on 'Swarm of Guppies.'"

"Uh...what's that?"

"It's a free dating website. I know people can get kinda weird about online dating and all, but I mean, why not?"

"I hear you."

"So anyway, Jimmy messaged me, and I saw he fit a lot of what I'm looking for, and he lives pretty close, so I messaged back and we went from there."

"That's great." Then Ann's tone became more serious. "Terah, I gotta ask, is he a Christian?"

She hesitated. "I mean...he's not into religion all like that. But he respects mine, that's what's important."

"Aren't you concerned about being 'unequally yoked,' as it says in the Bible?"

"I mean, kinda. But let's be for real. The church is full of hypocrites, and lemme not get started on Christian Kingdom."

"Huh? What do you mean?"

"Girl...you don't know the half...talking 'purity culture' but dating non-Christians, dudes getting with kids..."

Ann was taken aback. "What? Kids?! The hell?!"

"Yeah...Annie, sounds like you were out of the loop."

"Apparently."

"Let me put you up on game. Brother Craig and Rebecca? You know how they would tell us how they met in a Pentecostal church back in their hometown?"

"Uh-huh..."

"Welp, he was the youth group leader at the church. And Rebecca? She was one of the high school kids in the youth group."

"Whoa..."

"Yeah. Literally as soon as she was out of high school, they got married, and just a couple months after that, Nathan was born. You do the math."

Ann paused for a moment, then she understood. "Ew, that's gross."

"It is. They're almost twenty years apart. She's like, twenty-four."

"Twenty-four? Only two years older than us? That's crazy. I...I had no idea. She seems so...mature."

Terah sighed. "When you get married to some older guy and pop out a baby right after you turn eighteen, that ages you, you know what I mean?"

"Yeah...I guess that makes sense."

"And then look at Greg. You saw how he's engaged on Facebook, right?"

"Yeah, I hope she's not a kid, too."

"Oh...no no no. He didn't do *that*. But she's not a Christian. He met her in grad school, she's an atheist. He blogs on Xanga and he writes about how hot she is. She's from Europe and she used to model for Guess Jeans."

"Girl...you remember back in college when he was all about courtship and doing everything by the book?"

"Oh yeah, he was on that *Dating is Wack* bull harder than everybody else. You want me to keep going? There's Megan..."

Ann was still in a state of cringe. "Nah, nah, Terah. I'm good."

"See, thing is, when the rubber meets the road, our true beliefs come to light. I believe in Jesus and that hasn't changed, but this stupid obsession with sex and purity in the church, at the end of the day, it's a lie to control the flock. The people preaching it the loudest don't believe it themselves."

"Makes you think, I suppose..."

"It does. That's why my conscience is clean." Terah then pivoted. "So, Annie, have you thought about doing the whole online dating thing?"

"Hmm, maybe. I dunno. I mean, I'm still hoping things will work out with Luke. But I am starting to wonder if I really did hear from God, or if it was just something I wanted."

"See, I'ma be real with you. You've been into him for a really long time now. He's kinda strung you along, so it's like you have reason to keep the faith, but he won't pull the trigger on a relationship. I know you care about him and you think you're supposed to be with him, but you gotta love yourself more."

"I dunno. It's just hard."

"I get it. Maybe it's best for you to move on and stop waiting on him. Date other people, don't even worry if they're Christian or not. Just meet somebody."

"I'm not trying to be desperate and meet *somebody* just to say I met somebody."

"No, I don't mean it like that. I mean that you should put yourself out there and meet people. And that makes it more likely that you'll meet not just anybody, but a nice dude who will love you and appreciate you for the great woman that you are."

"I suppose. It's just that if the Lord did say Luke is The One, I don't want him to think I lack faith."

"I know, but the thing is...if God really wants y'all together, he'll make that happen regardless of what you do right now."

"Yeah, Terah...maybe so."

"So, when you get a chance, scan a nice picture of yourself into the computer and email it to me. Then I'll help build you a profile. We got this."

"How's vet school?" Ann asked Luke while they sat on the back patio of the Hula Hut, a Hawaiian-themed bar located in their neighborhood.

"Uh, it's not too bad. It's ridiculously busy. I'm telling you AC, I can see why it's hard for people to get in. It kicks your ass."

"Oh, I'm sure. But it's definitely an accomplishment. Before you know it, you'll be a bonafide vet!"

He sighed while nursing a draft Guinness. "That's true. So, how's your job?"

"It's cool. I like the work and the people are cool enough."

"You said you're at The Nichols Agency, right?"

"Yeah."

"Hmm. When I'm reading the Washington Post and even the Losanti Sun, they're always posting stats. I always wonder to myself if you're the one who's behind them."

"Sometimes. A lot of what I do ends up in papers and even on the evening news."

"That's so amazing! You have so much to be proud of. I'm sure your dad is looking down and proud of what you're doing."

"That means a lot to me, Luke. Thank you. I sure hope so. Anyway, I'm glad you reached out to me."

"Yeah, I'm glad too. It's always a great time hanging with you."

When Ann got home from the outing, she took care of her dog, then hopped on her desktop to check her email. As she scrolled through her messages, she happened on one from Swarm of Guppies.

What kind of horseshit is somebody gonna say now?

While many women would say they receive a lot of attention on dating websites such as Swarm of Guppies, Ann did not have the same experience. Her online profile included a photo of her from the waist up wearing an off-white sweater, minimal makeup,

and a brilliant smile. Her profile, which Terah assisted with, read
as follows:

- **Sex: Female**

- **Age: 22**

- **Location: Greater Losanti/Southern Ohio**

- **Ethnicity: Black/African American**

- **Body Type: Plus**

- **Religion: Christianity**

- **Status: Single/Never Married**

- **Match Desired: Men, 21-32, any ethnicity, any
  body type, any religion, Single/Never Married or
  Single/Divorced or Single/Widowed**

- **Seeking: Long-Term Relationship**

- **Bio: Hi, I'm Ann and I'm new to Losanti. I like
  hanging out with friends, travel, video games,
  learning about history, and more. My Christian
  faith is important to me. You do not need to be
  Christian, just respect my beliefs. I'm open to
  new experiences, dating and potentially something
  more serious with a great guy. Is that you?**

While Ann was hoping for the same luck as her best friend, that response proved to be elusive. The few notifications she did get seemed like a waste of time. And then, there were the mean messages:

> lol fatty

> are you black bc I don't date black chicks

> Ur eyes r steel like the Terminator. Scary.

She received other strange ones, such as a guy she knew in elementary school reaching out to her to catch up because he recognized her, and another man who wanted to share a multi-level marketing sales pitch.

But the email she received that day was a bit different. The photo included featured an average-looking, heavyset young man with brown hair and green eyes. The message read:

> Hi Ann, I'm Trevor, I'm 21 and I'm a hometown boy born and raised here in Losanti. I live in Norris Park, just up the hill from downtown. You're pretty and you sound fantastic from what you wrote, so I want to get to know you better. Please send me your number so we can chat further and go out sometime.

He's a little bit younger than me, but that's not bad. He seems nice enough, so why not?

She responded:

> Hi Trevor! Thanks for reaching out, I'm in Norris Park too! I would like to chat and

get to know you too. Feel free to give me a call (879)555-8549.

Immediately after she sent the email, her phone rang. She picked up quickly, hoping it was her new match.

"Hello?"

"Hi, Ann, it's Alyssa! Just checking on you, girlie!"

"Hey, chica! How's married life treating you?"

"It's great! We were over the moon seeing you at the wedding."

"It was so lovely – thanks for inviting me. You made such a beautiful bride."

"Thank you! Oh, by the way, I called to tell you — I'm pregnant!" Alyssa announced happily.

"That's wonderful – congrats!"

"Thanks so much! Paul and I are so excited."

"I'm sure you guys are. When's the baby due?"

"February...February 10th."

Wait a minute... Ann then cut her thoughts off at the pass. "Oh wow, that's coming up pretty soon then. Just a few more months."

"Oh, for sure."

"Do you know if it's a boy or girl?"

"We told the obstetrician that we didn't want to know the sex. As long as it's healthy, it doesn't matter."

"Ah, that'll be a fun surprise. So, how's Paul?"

"He's good. He's been working hard at his job, lots of late nights. He wants to get a nice financial cushion since we're building a family. But it's good."

"He's a civil engineer, right?"

"Yeah. Anyway, what's going on with you? How are you enjoying Losanti?"

"It's all right. Work's good. I'm trying my hand at online dating," Ann disclosed.

"Oh, you are? Finally gave up on Luke, huh?"

"Uh...it's not that deep. Just seeing who else might be out there."

"That's fair. Are you talking to anyone?"

"Not yet, but this guy just emailed me and I gave him my number."

"Hmm. *When* did he email you?" Alyssa uttered in a concerned tone.

The jumble of nerves bubbled up inside of Ann — the feeling of dread that always came from failing at some social convention unbeknownst to her. "He emailed me earlier today, I think it was sometime this afternoon. Didn't think to check. *Why?*"

Alyssa paused for a moment. "Oh girl, no...that was a bit too quick. It makes you look too eager. You should've let him wait at least overnight before responding."

"Why would I do that? It's not like I get a lot of guys emailing me with actual interest."

"That's so weird, Ann. I don't get why that would be. I've heard that women get lots of messages on these sites. What did you say in your profile? How long was it?"

"It wasn't long, it was pretty much to the point. And I didn't write it. Terah wrote it, and she's been doing great with online dating."

Once Ann read the profile aloud, Alyssa sat perplexed. "She did great with it, so I...I don't get it. You're nice and you're pretty. I don't know what the problem is."

"I know exactly what the problem is. It's my weight. Guys don't like fat girls. And I look weird, too."

"No. Plenty of heavier ladies attract men. And you stand out in a crowd, especially with those grey eyes. I'd kill for those. Plenty of men want someone who's not cookie-cutter. I don't think that's it."

"I can't think of anything else it could be, and I get rude messages that harp on my looks."

"That's stupid. Stop listening to negativity. Those messages are from miserable people who want to make you feel miserable along with them."

"I guess..."

"Girl – listen to me. You're unique. You don't look like everybody else, so? That's a *good* thing. You stand out. These guys sending you awful messages don't know what they're missing. If they just want samey-same and cookie-cutter, they're not worth your time anyway."

"Thanks Alyssa. Forever the optimist."

"Of course." Alyssa then shifted the subject slightly. "You remember Megan from CK?"

"Yeah."

"Her older sister Samantha has been trying her hand at online dating too. She's on this Christian dating service called eSympatico. And she's been getting a ton of hits. It's like her email's always exploding."

Ann rolled her eyes. "Yeah, Terah says the same thing about Swarm of Guppies, which is what I'm trying right now. Before she met her new guy from there, she would take breaks from online dating because she got too many messages and it was a lot to keep up with."

"Well, maybe you can try eSympatico, you just have to fill out a 198-question survey and then you're matched with wonderful Christian men."

"Eh, I tried that. I got literally no hits. None whatsoever."

"Darn," Alyssa lamented. "I'm sorry. That's gotta be hard."

"It was. And then by the time my thirty-day free trial was over, I was over it, so I went to cancel — they make you call them to cancel. It's stupid that you can sign up online but you can't cancel online. Anyway, I call them, and I about had an argument over the phone with customer service."

"What happened?"

"Okay, so I call, and I get to a customer service person, I tell them I wanna cancel. So, you know, they ask why. I tell them it's because I haven't matched with anybody. You know, the ones eSympatico says I match with, nobody messages me and I don't get any responses when I message them."

"Okay, makes sense."

"Yeah, but the lady on the phone is like, 'Well, we can't guarantee you'll get matches. We can't force members to message you or respond to you. Why would that make you want to end your membership?'"

Alyssa was in shock. "Wow, that's pretty unprofessional."

"Exactly. I couldn't believe what I was hearing. So, uh...I told her, 'I never said I expect for eSympatico to force anybody to message or respond to me. But if I'm not getting anything from the membership except rejection, why would I continue *and* pay for the privilege? That's stupid. Cancel the membership.' So, they finally did."

"I'm sorry you have so much trouble with online dating. Look, if these men don't want to give you a chance, it's on them. They're truly missing out on a wonderful woman of God. All I'm saying is that even if you aren't getting a lot of responses, you don't want to let men know that, or give them the impression that you're *too* available."

"I know. I just wish dating was simple and it wasn't full of people playing games, or these silly rituals where you can't show how interested you are in somebody. Why can't people just be direct — say what they mean, mean what they say, and be themselves?"

"I understand. You'll find the right person. You just have to keep putting yourself out there and trust God."

That evening, Ann received a phone call from a local number she did not recognize. She then flipped open her cell phone to answer.

"Hello?"

"Hi, is this Ann?" responded a voice that called to mind Cookie Monster from *Sesame Street*.

"Yes, this is her."

"Oh hi, this is Trevor."

The two conversed for an hour that night. That turned into long talks over the phone over the course of a week. She learned that Trevor, a Losanti native, came from a family of four — a married mother and father, and a twin sister, Trisha. He shared that he graduated from Southwestern High School three years earlier. Like many Losantians, he still carried high school pride years later. Now, he was an undergraduate student at Ohio Valley Technical University studying business administration and shared a four-bedroom house with three roommates a half mile from Ann's apartment.

The two began discussing plans to meet up Friday night at a local bar for drinks and hanging out. She was excited that she was finally getting out there, and now about to go on a proper date. *Alyssa means well, but she might be wrong about this one.*

A few days later, Ann left work excited for her first date with Trevor from Swarm of Guppies. At five o'clock, shortly after she arrived home, he gave her a call.

"Hi, Ann. What's up?"

"Nothing much. Just looking forward to our date tonight."

He took a deep breath. "About that...look, I know I talked about us going to the Norris Bar and Grill tonight at eight, but I'm a little short on money right now...had an unexpected bill come up. But I still want for us to meet. How about we meet over at the park?"

She felt a dose of disappointment. "I don't know. We can just wait and then you can take me out when you're able."

"Sure, but I would hate to bail on you tonight. We've been talking for a while and I'm dying to meet you. And besides, it's not like I have other plans."

I wanted us to meet at a public place. The park is not that, especially at eight o'clock at night. It's public, sure, but it's hidden where nobody can see us. I hope he's not ashamed of being seen with me. But he's got a good point. What else am I doing? Besides, I'm not trying to assume the worst of this guy.

"Uh...I guess so."

"Alright, great. Next time, we'll go to the bar. I always like paying for the first date. Just not in the position to do that this week. Let's meet over by the sled dog statue at eight."

That evening, Ann washed, moisturized, and brushed out her shoulder-length hair, put on a navy blue maxi dress with brown sandals, and added colored gloss to her lips. She then strolled to the park, proceeded to the obsidian-glazed sled dog statue surrounded by professionally landscaped orchids, sat on a wooden bench nearby, and waited. It was five minutes before eight.

When eight o'clock hit, a short, bulky young man with a slight yet noticeable limp shuffled his way toward her.

"Hi, Ann."

"Hi! You must be Trevor."

"Yeah, great to meet you."

Trevor sat next to her, his hands in the pockets of his pressed khaki pants. *He looks preppy, like a frat boy.*

He started with small talk. "It's a nice night, isn't it?"

"Yeah, it sure is. I like walking my dog out here." *I hope this 'date' isn't some hazing ritual.*

"Oh, that's great. I think that once I get my own place, I'll probably get a dog or cat."

The cool fall evening wind started to pick up, and the litter overflowing the trash cans in the park blew around. Goosebumps rose from Ann's skin due to the noticeable drop in temperature. *Damn, I really should've brought a sweater.*

The wind tousled his short blond locks. "It's getting kind of cold. Why don't you come to my house? It's just off the back side of the park. We can get warm and chat more comfortably there."

She hesitated. "Uh, I don't know. Are you sure about that? You know, you said you have roommates."

He smiled. "They'll be okay with it."

Despite her misgivings about going to his home on the first date, she agreed to follow him to his house. After leaving through the far gate of the park, he led her to an older Victorian home with turquoise cladding and pink trim. The exterior was immaculate, with a swinging bench on the spacious front porch, and rose bushes framing the stairs leading to the front door.

Looking over her shoulder, she was convinced someone would jump out of the bushes, point, and laugh at her like fraternity brothers treat fat girls in the movies. He unlocked the door and led her into the house. She was relieved that the cinematic surprise she anticipated did not materialize.

She followed him past the polished grand staircase down the hall to a small, outdated kitchen, painted white with a vinyl-topped card table in the middle that seated four.

"Ann, would you like anything to drink?" Trevor asked. "We have Natty Light, Coors, and Boone's Farm in the fridge. I'm going to get myself a Natty."

"Uh, I'll have that too."

He removed two cold cans of Natural Light beer from the refrigerator and handed her one.

"Thanks!"

"No problem."

She noticed a distinctive ring on his left pinky finger. The band was silver in color with a crown and a blue heart. "Interesting ring."

"Please?"

She was confused at his response. "Huh?"

"Ope, I'm sorry. I forgot you're not from here. A lot of us here say 'please' in place of 'what' or 'could you repeat that.' It's a Losanti thing, from the city's German heritage." he explained.

"Oh, didn't know that. Today, I learned." She chuckled. "Anyway, I was just saying your ring looks interesting. I've never seen anything like it."

"Oh, it's a Claddagh ring. It's Irish. I got it for high school graduation from my mom, we're Irish on her side of the family and our family crest is mostly blue. Means a lot to me."

After retrieving the drinks, she followed him up a smaller, narrow staircase just off the kitchen. Once at the top, they turned down the hall. A young man with a short fade walked out of one of the rooms, wearing only a towel around his waist and displaying his well-muscled upper body.

"Hey, Trev!" the man projected.

"Hey, Derrick! What's up?" Trevor called back.

"Nothing much. I see you brought yourself a girl home." Derrick then grinned at Ann. "Hey, how you doin'?"

"Hi," she responded, smiling weakly.

"Oh, she's just a friend of mine, we're just gonna go chill and watch a movie or something."

Just a friend, not a date.

Derrick nodded slowly. "Alright, bruh. I'm about to take a shower and head to bed. Gotta get up early tomorrow. Have a good night." He turned to Ann. "Nice to meet ya."

"Nice meeting you too," she responded quietly.

After Derrick entered the shared bathroom, Trevor led Ann inside his small bedroom and quietly shut the door behind him.

In the room, she observed a twin bed with blue sheets, a matching comforter and pillow, a heather foam fold-out sofa, and a medium-sized CRT television with a VCR connected to it. The TV sat atop a stand with several videotapes shelved underneath. The room also included a dark wooden built-in dresser and a mirror, along with a door to what was presumably a closet.

Trevor folded out the sofa to resemble a full-sized bed on the floor. Gesturing towards it, he said, "Just lay right here, get comfortable. We'll watch something. What kinds of movies do you like?"

Ann took off her sandals and reclined on the sofa. "I dunno, um...comedies are good."

He stooped to thumb through his movie collection. "Let's see...I've got *Clerks*, *The Big Lebowski*, the first *Austin Powers* movie, and *Dazed and Confused*.

"How about *Austin Powers*? I've never seen it."

"Great choice!" He then pulled the tape from the sleeve and slid it into the VCR. He set up the TV to begin playing the movie, turned off the lights, and lay down next to her, propping his head on the back of the sofa.

The movie began, and they watched for a few minutes. He then turned, his hazel eyes staring into hers.

"You're cute, Ann."

Really? I don't know about that. "Uh...thanks."

"See, I haven't dated in some time. I know I'm a little young, but I guess I'm not typical. I'm not a casual sex kind of guy. I like being in a real relationship before doing all that."

"Yeah, for sure, Trevor. I'm the same way." *It's not like I've done 'all that' at all, but it's weird to tell a guy I haven't really done much of anything.*

He leaned in to kiss her, and she took down her defenses. They continued to lock lips, and he reached out to lightly touch her arm, and then her shoulder. His hand traveled underneath her sundress to her strapless bra. Finding the front close snaps, he undid them, freeing her breasts. He cupped them with his cool hands and proceeded to move down the front of her sundress, uncovering them completely. He then stared at them in admiration.

"Oh, you have nice nips," Trevor said.

Ann smiled but had no words. *This is...new.* This was the first time a man had sought out her bosom. Jake, her boyfriend in high school, had not shown such an interest, only kissing her and declining to do anything more. But the attention Trevor was giving her in that moment was something she had never before experienced.

He placed his lips on each nipple. He sucked firmly, and then lightly nibbled one, and then the other, each bouncing back upon leaving his lips.

This feels...good.

He then moved her maxi dress down and slipped it off her body, which was now nude except for her black panties, which matched her undone bra. He continued to kiss and fondle her breasts.

I really like this attention, but we're not in a real relationship...hell, we haven't even gone out on a real date. He hasn't even been out with me in public.

Soon, his hands slithered southward.

Nah, I don't want to do this. Not like this.

"Uh...Trevor?"

Trevor, still fully clothed, including his turquoise shirt with a popped collar, looked up and responded softly, "Yes?"

"I...I should get going. I need to get back home and take care of my dog, I'm sure he's hungry."

He sat up while she reattached her bra and put on her dress.

"Ann, I hope I didn't scare you or anything."

"Oh no, it was great, I liked it."

"That's good. I did too. Next time, we'll go out to a restaurant or something nearby, and as things progress, we can do more."

"Sure. That'll be fun."

He led her to the front porch and gave her a kiss on the lips. "I had a very nice time."

"I did too," she responded with a small smile. "It was great."

"I'll call you tomorrow."

Ann headed for home and got a good night's sleep. As promised, Trevor called the next day and made a date for the next week.

The following Thursday evening, Ann was taking Charlie on a routine walk through the neighborhood when her cell phone rang. She saw it was Trevor calling and opened the clamshell to answer.

"Looking forward to tomorrow night?" she commented.

He hesitated, then responded. "Um, about that...well, uh...I told you about my twin sister Trisha, right?"

"Uh, yeah."

"So, she lives out in Chicago. She's going through a hard time there. Her boyfriend just broke up with her."

"Oh, I'm sorry to hear that."

"Yeah, they were together for like two years, and then he just kind of took off. You know, my sister and I are very close, and she wants me to drive up there to spend a few days with her."

"Oh, I understand. Go and spend time with her, it sounds like she needs you."

"I hate dipping on a date again, I'm so sorry. That's not who I am. I know it sounds like I'm full of shit but it's true."

"I'm sure you're telling the truth, Trevor. I mean, I know you've mentioned your sister before."

"Yeah, I appreciate that. Look, Ann...I promise I'll make it up to you and we'll go on a real date. I'll call you back this time next week, I promise."

After their conversation, she hung up the phone. She was a little sad, but it would only be another week, right?

It was a rainy October weekend, and Ann noticed that it had been three weeks since the last time she heard from Trevor. He had not called back since he told her he was traveling to Chicago to check on his sister, who was apparently mourning the end of her relationship. Ann decided that she would reach out to him instead to find out what happened.

She picked up her phone and called his cell phone. Once the call connected to his phone, the phone rang twice, then the call was directed to voicemail. "You have reached the voicemail of Trevor Stevenson."

Oh, it's like that? The one guy who actually responds to my Swarm of Guppies ad and he just ghosts me after I went over his house. He used me. I hate this. I really hate this.

The voicemail continued. "I'm not able to answer right now, but please leave a message and I'll give you a call as soon as I can."

The frustration of being blown off as an undesirable, throwaway object after their encounter really got to her. So, she unleashed her fury on his voicemail.

After the beep, she said, "Hi, Trevor, this is Ann. I thought you were going to Chicago for a few days, but I guess that was a lie. I wonder what else you lied about. If you didn't want more than something casual, or even if you didn't want to see me again, that's fine. But the least you could've done was tell me the truth. I hope you don't do this to anybody else. Have a nice life." She hung up the phone, and then shed a few tears in bed. Charlie trotted up to her, licked her face, then lay on the floor.

After calming down, Ann washed her face and jumped onto her computer enjoying her brand of relaxation, with Charlie lying down and chewing on his red Kong toy. She was focused, concentrating hard on building a new suburban home on an empty lot in her favorite video game, *The Sims*. As she was placing colorful shrubbery around the sides of the house, her phone rang. It was Luke.

"You wanna grab lunch over at Papa Dino's?" he asked.

I need to get out of this apartment. Lunch with Luke is perfect. "Yeah, sure."

"Okay, let's meet up in an hour. Is that cool?"

"Yeah, see you then."

An hour later, the friends met up at Papa Dino's, a local pizzeria within walking distance from where they both lived. They decided to share a small pizza with their favorite toppings, pepperoni and green olives, and a pitcher of Miller Lite. When their order arrived, each took a slice and began eating.

"Did I tell you that I've started talking to this girl in one of my labs?"

What? Ann was taken aback, as Luke had not discussed dating anyone since breaking up with Morgan years earlier. Nevertheless, she tried to mask her dismay. "Oh, that's great. Tell me about her."

"Yeah, her name's Shannon, she's smart and cute. She's a great time." He opened his clamshell cell phone, selected a photo to display, and handed it to Ann. A photo of a thin, elegant woman with freckles and luscious red hair stared back at her. *Of course. She's arm candy.*

"That's nice. I'm happy for you." Ann cut into her pizza slice, but the metal knife scraped against the plate making a jarring screech.

After a pause, Luke responded. "Thanks, AC. Have you been dating since moving here?"

"Yeah, I have...online dating."

"Oh, that's neat. Where have you signed up?"

"Uh, it's this site called Swarm of Guppies."

"Ah, I heard about that site. It's free, but from what my friends have told me, it's not too bad. More guys than girls. Have you gone on any dates yet?"

"Yeah." She looked down into the glass while drinking her beer. The alcohol loosened up her lips, like a truth serum of sorts. "Um, I was talking to this guy Trevor. We were supposed to go out on a date a few weeks back when he said he was leaving town for a few days to help out his sister. Never heard back."

"Ugh, I'm sorry about that. That's gotta be annoying."

"It is. I dunno. The whole process of trying to find somebody to date is tiresome. Whether I'm at the bar or the club or online, it's the same old shit. I wish I could just find a guy that I like and that actually likes me back. It seems so easy for everybody else."

"Have you taken a good look at what you want in a guy?"

"Of course I have. What do you mean?"

"Uh, don't take this the wrong way, but you could be asking for too much."

"What?"

"Y'know, you're a *big* girl. Maybe your standards are too high. You should probably rethink them."

"The hell does that mean? I'm hoping for mutual attraction, just like everybody else, it's not like I'm asking for the world. Being big doesn't mean I have nothing going for me."

"Look, AC, I'm not trying to be a dick. You've got a lot of awesome qualities. If you didn't, we wouldn't be friends. But guys are visual creatures, and they want to impress their friends and family with who they're with. I mean, it's something to consider."

"Luke...is how I look the only thing that matters?" Ann asked softly.

"No, it's not, but appearances do draw people in. And I mean, maybe the guy thought you were cute, but he was embarrassed to be seen dating you. I dunno, maybe if you lost weight, you might have better luck..."

All this time, and my looks are still the only thing that matters. I still don't measure up.

Ann went quiet as tears welled up in her eyes.

Luke sighed. "Sorry AC, didn't mean to hurt your feelings. I shouldn't have said that."

"It's fine," she murmured quietly, trying valiantly to put on a brave face. Inside, however, she was dying.

On her way home, Ann stopped at a local establishment near her apartment called Gorgeous Gorls Bakery. This boutique bakery sold cupcakes and full-size cakes of various sizes over the counter. They also took special orders for weddings, birthdays, and other events.

As she walked into the pastel-painted interior of the establishment, the smell of sugary goodness filled the air. She headed over to the counter and took note of several varieties of cupcakes, Danishes, and other pastries in the glass-covered case.

A young clerk greeted her from behind the counter. "Hi, welcome to Gorgeous Gorls Bakery! How may I help you?"

"Hi, uh...may I have six cupcakes?"

"Yes, of course. Which ones would you like?"

"One double chocolate, one white chocolate, one strawberry, two coffee mocha, and one tiramisu."

"Amazing choices!" The clerk opened the back of the case and selected the six cupcakes. "I take it coffee mocha's your favorite?"

"Yeah, for sure."

"Honestly, it's mine too, though they're all great." She packed the sweets up in a brown cardboard box, tied it up with twine, then placed it on the counter. "That'll be $5.99."

Ann paid, picked up the box, then returned home. Once safe in her apartment, she sat on the couch with Charlie at her feet and the box of confections next to her.

Luke's comments looped in her mind. His words cut to the quick. *All this time we've known each other and Luke only sees me as a fat girl who's an embarrassment and should just accept whatever I get. If how I look is all that matters, then what's the point? He's probably right, and no matter what I do, it doesn't matter. I'm destined to end up alone and unloved.*

She took each confection in her hand, one after the other, and ate each of them until the box was completely empty. With each rich, decadent, and delicious bite, she consumed her feelings of self-loathing, sadness, and despair.

MENDE
NOVEMBER 2002

Realizing she needed professional help processing her feelings about her life in Losanti, Ann sought out a new mental health therapist. The professional she selected, Belinda Cross, MA LPC, was located in her neighborhood of Norris Park.

On a Saturday morning, Ann woke up for her scheduled appointment. The therapist's office was a half mile from her home, so she decided to walk there. She packed her purse, including her wallet, cell phone, and asthma inhaler just in case, and left her unit. It was a crisp, fall day, and she observed the orange and purple leaves gently dropping to the ground as she strolled. After several minutes, she arrived at the building, which was a nondescript three-story office building in a lovely shade of concrete grey. She walked inside and checked the directory affixed to the wall to confirm her destination.

Suite 302. Okay, cool.

Ann felt a bit exhausted once she made it to the building. Out of breath, she decided to take the elevator to the third floor. Once there, she found Suite 302, which was behind a locked door. She pressed the intercom button.

"ThinkPointe Mental Health Services, how may I help you?" the receptionist asked through the intercom speaker.

"Uh, I have a nine o'clock for Belinda Cross. When I called, they said to be here fifteen minutes early."

The door buzzed open and Ann stepped into the plain, basic beige waiting room. The receptionist was behind a glass sliding window, which she slid open to speak with her.

"What is your name and date of birth?" asked the receptionist.

"My name's Ann Corbin, date of birth three...thirty...eighty."

"Do you have your ID and health insurance card?"

She passed her driver's license and insurance card through the window to the receptionist. After checking the cards, the receptionist scanned her ledger. "Okay Ann, here are the forms for personal information, emergency contact, health insurance, mental and physical health history, and family health history. Please fill these out and bring them back to me."

"Okay."

Ann took the papers, which were on a brown clipboard, along with a ballpoint pen. She sat down on a chair with a black metal frame and a lightly cushioned, beige upholstered seat, and began filling them out. When she got to the family information section, she again struggled to figure out how to best explain her family structure.

How do I explain that I have two moms? My birth mom is MIA and my stepmom is who I call 'mom,' and I don't even see her as a stepmother but my actual mother. That all doesn't fit on this form. God, this feels complicated. Shit.

After a moment of nervous consternation, she decided to label Sherrye as "mother" and Stephanie as "birth mother, don't know her." She gave the forms to the receptionist, who placed them in a folder and slipped it inside a tinted-clear file holder affixed to the wall.

A few minutes later, the door on the other side of the check-in desk came ajar. There walked out a slightly plump woman with light brunette hair twisted in Bantu knots.

"Hi, you must be Ann. I'm Belinda," she introduced herself with a friendly smile and slightly country lilt. "Follow me, my office is just this way." Ann rose from her seat and followed the counselor.

They entered a white room with blue commercial carpet. The space featured three chairs, one on the side of a dark table, and the other two opposite against the wall, similar to the ones in the waiting room, upholstered navy. On the table was placed a photo of a happy little girl, and on the side with the two chairs was a framed oil painting of an African mask, with a squat, shaded face, and elaborate headdress.

"Have a seat right over there," the therapist open hand gestured toward the seats, then sat next to the table. Ann took notice of the artwork as she sat down.

"That's a really beautiful painting."

"Thank you. It's a Mende painting."

"Mende?"

"Yes. The Mende are a tribe in Sierra Leone, and that's where the painting's from. It was one of the places in Africa where Black people were kidnapped and forced into the transatlantic slave trade. The painting helps keep me grounded, to remember where I came from."

"Wow," Ann nodded. "That's awesome. Never thought about that before."

After preliminary introductions, Belinda asked, "So, Ann – where would you like to start?"

"I have no idea. Where should I start?"

"Well, I'm here to help you, so you can start with what's most pressing, and we'll go from there."

"Um...so, I moved here a few months ago from Michigan, but it's been really hard to fit in down here. I feel like something's wrong with me."

"Okay. What brought you here to Losanti?"

"A couple of things. I graduated from college up in Michigan, University of the Great Lakes, and got hired for a job down here. And then, a guy friend from college lives down here. It's a bit of a long story, but I was so sure we would work out romantically. But now that I'm here, you know, I feel like I made a huge mistake."

"So, there's a man that you moved down here for?"

"Yeah...but it didn't work out...he doesn't see me the same way. So, I'm trying to make friends and find somebody new."

"What have you tried so far?"

"Um...I've been going to this church. It's okay, I like the Sunday service, but something's not connecting. Then, I've been going out after work with people from the office, and sometimes with a smaller group of girls from work on the weekend. We're always going to bars and clubs. I hate those places, but it beats doing nothing."

"What is it you don't like about the bars and clubs?"

"You know, it's like if you go to one, you've gone to all of 'em. It's like we go into the bar, drink, then people mingle, guys might go up to some of the girls, they flirt or whatever. And it's the same thing. People are nice and everything, but I'm ignored. It's as if I don't exist."

"That must be frustrating."

"Yeah."

Belinda leafed through Ann's file. "What I hear from you is that since moving to Losanti, you've tried social activities, but you feel you don't belong. And when you're in bars and clubs interacting with coworkers and strangers, you don't feel seen."

"Yeah, that's exactly what it is."

"What kinds of activities and hobbies do you enjoy doing?"

"I dunno. When I was in college, I was in campus ministry. I can't say I belonged there either, but I did have a small group of friends there...the guy I moved down here for was in that group. But I've been going to church here, it's alright, but at this point, I'm just not sure if it's for me."

"Ann, could you share more about your experiences with your current church?"

"So, my church now, Norris Park Christian Fellowship, it's a local church not too far from my home here in Norris Park."

"Oh okay, I've seen it. Tell me more about it."

"Yeah. Uh...it's got maybe a hundred people, small but not too small, and the teachings there are a lot like what I'm used to back in Michigan. Bible-based and all of that. They also have a singles ministry. But if I miss church, nobody notices I'm gone. And something about it...I guess it's not connecting, and I'm starting to wonder if church is really for me at all."

"What about it isn't connecting?"

"Uh...I dunno. The Fellowship focuses a lot on faith, kind of like my campus ministry did, and trusting in God that he listens to the prayers of those who believe. But I prayed so hard for my dad's health, and he's dead. And I've prayed for other things, but it's like God doesn't hear me or he doesn't care."

"What other things?"

"Love. I feel like God doesn't see me as a woman, so there isn't a man out there for me."

"I see. Could you please elaborate?"

"I'm trying to figure out the best way I can put this." Ann then inhaled deeply and continued. "For the most part, I don't feel connected to my identity as a woman. I know I'm a woman, I see a woman in the mirror. But, you know, I feel *connected* to being Black. But when people talk about being a woman, being a female, and the things that come with that, It's like I can't relate."

"Could you share more about that?"

"So, um, when I've been in church and other Christian settings, it's been, like, assumed that women are supposed to be extra feminine, look like some kind of model, aspire to be mothers. They always say that women tempt men to be sexual, a single woman's virginity is the most important thing about her, and she should guard it fiercely. But at the same time, men are 'visual,' they have sexual urges they can't contain, and women don't have them, so they have to 'tame' men. I relate to none of it."

"I see. What I hear is that you feel that there is a double standard for men and women in your faith?"

"Yeah, pretty much, but moreso that there are standards for women I don't fit into. When it comes to my interactions with men, I feel invisible, or even a last resort. People say women are overwhelmed with matches in online dating...ha," Ann laughed sardonically. "As you can see, I'm fat, and men *hate* that. My old friends from college are getting married left and right. Even in real life, I see my friends and coworkers getting hit on all the time. But none of that applies to me...hardly anything about being a woman applies to me."

"Okay, when you say it doesn't apply, could you elaborate a bit?"

"Sure. I like computer games and dogs, I'm not a huge hair and makeup person, I don't really do fashion, and I'm not into a lot of girly things. And as far as virginity and temptation and all of that, I don't feel like I'm tempting men to do anything but run away from me. My career is male-dominated, and the idea of becoming a mom scares me. I feel like a woman in the technical sense only. I have the parts and that's it."

"What scares you about motherhood?"

"Uh...well, it's not that I don't like kids. I just feel uncomfortable around them. They stare at me...they look at me funny, they say what's on their mind, and I don't know how to talk to them."

"Okay. So, about being a woman – there's a lot more to being a woman than the male gaze, stereotypical femininity, and motherhood, and your identity as a woman is something we can continue to explore in future sessions. Also, your faith may be something worth discussing as we continue meeting. What else do you enjoy?"

Ann sat with legs crossed, twirling a lock of her coiled dark brown hair. "Um...Belinda, I don't really know. Besides games and dogs, I like traveling and trying different types of food, and I enjoy philosophy and politics, at least to some degree...I have my interests but I'm willing to try most things at least once. But I can't imagine that any of it translates into actually meeting people. It was hard enough to find where I belonged in college. It's even harder in the real world."

"In terms of finding a group where you truly belong, it's really about finding your tribe — the kinds of people you can connect with and who connect with you. Losanti can be a difficult place for outsiders to make friends, so you're not alone. But with some effort and patience, you can find your people, and you can begin by trying new things."

"Okay."

"To give you a tangible action item – *The Almost CountryBeat*, it's the free arts paper they have at the flyer stand at the entrances of grocery stores and local restaurants – pick up one of those and they'll often have ads for various groups and events. That's a good place to start."

Ann nodded.

Belinda continued. "There are also online discussion boards and meetup groups for various interests, and some of them have in-person events, so that might be something else you'll want to try."

"Alrighty, I'll definitely look into that. Thanks."

"You're welcome. As you meet new people, be sure that you're allowing positive people into your life. Obviously, how you feel about yourself comes from within, but positive reinforcement helps."

DONUT SHOP
MARCH 2003

It was a brisk, cloudy Saturday morning. Ann was in bed and felt a warm, wet sensation on her face. She opened her eyes to notice Charlie licking her cheeks.

"Okay, okay buddy. I get it, I'll take you outside," she cheerfully said to the affectionate Lab.

While outside with her dog for a walk and potty break, she heard her phone ring from her pocket. She looked at the small display on the outside of the clamshell and noticed it was Luke. After their lunch conversation a few months previously, she distanced herself from him, as she felt hurt by his words. However, after several missed phone calls from him, she relented.

"So, there's this pub crawl over by Ohio Valley Tech since it's the weekend before Saint Patrick's Day. Wanna check it out?"

"What about Shannon?"

"She can't go. She's busy studying. Besides, you and I haven't hung out in a while."

Ann sighed. "Eh, you know there's gonna be a whole lot of people, really crowded. Not my kind of thing. Have fun, though."

"Alright, AC...I'll tell you what – we can just go to one of the bars by the school, drink for a little while. Then, we can go to Sunny's to grab some coffee and donuts. I'm sure that won't be too crowded, and we can people watch. Does that sound good?"

"Uh, sure. That's cool."

"I'll be by your place around five and we'll call a cab to go up there. Parking's gonna be insane and besides, depending on how much we drink, it won't be great for either of us to drive home."

"Fair. See you later on."

That evening, Ann and Luke caught a cab and were dropped off along Fries Avenue, which bordered Ohio Valley Technical University to the north. They strolled up the street, walking past young revelers, some already inebriated.

Then, the friends stopped in front of one of the bars. It was nondescript, save for a chalk sign near the door stating "St. Pat's Green Lager 16 oz - $3.50."

He turned to speak to her. "AC, this looks good, why don't we go here?"

"Uh, yeah. Sounds good."

They entered the dimly lit establishment and weaved through the throng of partiers. The smells of Cool Water cologne, Clinique Happy perfume, and sweat hung in the air. They found themselves at the far end of the bar lining the left-hand wall.

"Hi, what can I get you?" asked the bartender.

"We'll have two green beers," said Luke.

"Sure. Wanna open a tab?"

"Yeah." He handed his credit card over to the bartender.

After the barman brought back the glasses of clover-tinted beer, Luke handed one to Ann, then took one for himself.

"I'll get the next round," she said.

"Nah, I'll take care of the bill here. It's fine."

"It's the least I can do…I mean, you paid for the cab too."

"Don't worry about it, AC. I invited you out."

"Thanks. At the very least, I'll get the coffee and donuts at Sunny's."

"Alright – good deal."

Ann and Luke stood around and listened to the loud alternative music playing over the murmuring of the crowd.

He leaned over and spoke into her ear. "This beer's not so bad."

"Yeah," she replied close to his face so he could hear her. "It tastes like Miller Lite with green food dye."

"Y'know, you're probably spot on."

After about an hour in, and Luke sipping on his third beer and Ann nursing her second, they were bopping to "Cute Without the 'E'" by Taking Back Sunday. By this time, they had migrated to the front corner of the room closest to the entrance across from the bar. It allowed them to hear each other a bit better.

As she was captivated by the music, he tapped on her shoulder to catch her attention.

"Check that out." He discreetly pointed to two men standing near the entrance.

"You stepped on my foot!" yelled a young man wearing a cerulean button-down shirt with a popped collar and blue jeans.

"Ugh…sorry bro…didn't see you," replied another man in an orange fleece jacket and khakis.

"Watch where you're going next time, asshole!"

"What? Who are you calling an asshole?"

The man with the popped collar, who was slightly taller and larger than the man in fleece, stepped right in the other man's face. "You. You're the asshole. What are you gonna do about it?"

A small blonde woman who walked in with the man in fleece grabbed his arm. "Chris, it's not worth it," she pleaded. "Don't worry about him. Let's go."

Chris turned towards the woman to respond when the man with the popped collar took a swing, which landed square on his left cheek. He fell to the hardwood floor. The woman holding Chris back screamed in terror. The room fell silent, and all eyes were fixed on the altercation.

"Oh my God! Josh!" yelled a long-haired brunette standing behind the man with the popped collar. "What did you just do?"

Josh ignored the woman and hovered over Chris, who was on the floor holding his face. "The fuck do you think you are?" He leaned in and continued hitting the fallen man. A group of other men ran over and pulled Josh off of Chris and sat him in a chair.

The brunette went over to Chris and the blonde to try to diffuse the situation. "I'm...I'm so sorry...my boyfriend's trashed, and sometimes he gets crazy when he has too many."

Chris collected himself and got up, his cheek a bright red. "I can't believe that guy hit me!" He ignored Josh's girlfriend and locked eyes with the aggressor.

"Chris...don't do it...it's not worth it...don't do it..." the blonde told him.

"Nobody hits me and thinks he's gonna get away with it," Chris barked. He then ran and jumped on Josh. Both were swinging, pushing tables, and knocking over wooden chairs and beer glasses.

"We should go," Ann whispered to Luke.

"Nah...AC, this is getting good."

"No, this is getting dangerous. I'm ducking out. I'll wait for you at Sunny's."

"Nah, I'll come with."

After ducking out of the bar, the friends walked to Sunny's, only two doors down. When they entered the bright donut shop, they quickly noticed how empty, silent, and sterile it appeared.

"Wow," she uttered nervously. "No one's here."

"Yeah," he agreed. "It's so quiet. We should've stayed at the bar."

Once inside, they strolled to the counter. A middle-aged, ochre-toned woman wearing an apron shuffled out from the back storage room and walked behind the counter. She smiled and spoke to them.

"Hi, welcome to Sunny's! What would you like?"

Ann perused the available donut selection. "I'll have a double chocolate donut and a small coffee with cream and sugar."

The woman nodded. "Okay...sounds good." She then turned to Luke. "And you?"

"I'll have a glazed donut, a pack of 12 donut holes, and a medium coffee, cream, and sugar."

"Is that all?"

They nodded.

The woman then instructed them, "Go head up to the register, and I'll have your order for you in a moment."

They walked down to the register. After a few moments, the clerk met them with their order. She commented to Ann, "Has anyone told you that you have pretty eyes?"

"Thank you," she smiled lightly.

"You don't see a lot of *us* with natural eye colors other than brown. You remind me a lot of my best girlfriend's little girl. Her eyes are grey too."

"Oh wow. That's cool."

After receiving the total, she pulled her credit card from her purse and handed it to the clerk. She glanced at the card and paused. She studied her face, then looked down at the card again.

"Is everything okay?" Luke asked.

The woman snapped out of it. "Yes...yes, everything's fine. Sorry about that. Long, slow night." She ran the card and returned it.

The friends sat at the counter facing the storefront windows, where they could watch the pub crawlers walk up and down Fries Avenue.

She commented, "That was so weird. I don't know what to make of that. Does it look like I have two heads?"

"Of course not, AC. You're fine. You don't know her, do you?" he asked quietly.

"No...I've never seen that woman in my life. It's not like all of us Black people know each other," she laughed softly.

He chuckled as well. "I know, I know. But y'know, seriously...she was looking at you like she knew you or something."

"If that's the case, it's mistaken identity, I'm pretty sure."

"I dunno about that, you look pretty distinct."

To that comment, she rolled her eyes. *He didn't have to remind me that I look weird.*

A few minutes later, five police cars with sirens blaring and lights flashing passed by the donut shop and stopped just past the shop.

"Damn AC, I wanted to see how that fight turned out."

Ann shook her head. "See, that's stupid. You never know how that could've turned out. It could've gotten dangerous. Not trying to get caught up in that."

"It wouldn't have been that bad...just a couple of college guys who had too much to drink."

"Sure, but you never know. Back home, I learned that when people fight, it's in your best interest to make yourself scarce. You don't wanna be a witness. There's no such thing as fighting fair on the streets."

"Don't be so paranoid, AC. It's not like we live in Detroit."

"Sure, it's not Detroit, but crazy shit can happen anywhere. Even Losanti."

"Oh shit! They're getting wild already!" the clerk exclaimed, striding towards the glass door to get a better look at the scene on the street.

"Yeah, I'm pretty sure they're going to the Bronze Bull a couple of doors down," Luke explained to the server. "We just came from over there. A couple of guys were fighting and we ducked out."

"That's smart," the clerk remarked. "You don't wanna run to the trouble. You wanna get away from the trouble. Don't wanna catch strays and don't wanna deal with no cops."

Ann nodded and gave a smug look at Luke. "I told you it was better to get outta there."

The three watched out the window as police officers dragged out the two men who initially fought at the bar in handcuffs to awaiting police vehicles. Soon after, three others, including a woman and two additional men, were cuffed and taken away by law enforcement. A crowd of young people and locals formed on the street to watch the commotion.

As the squad cars left the scene and the crowd dissipated, the clerk sat down next to Ann. "I'm sorry, but I couldn't help but to overhear you two bringing up Detroit. Is your father Marshall Corbin?"

Ann was a bit taken aback. "Uh...yes."

The clerk took a deep breath. "Oh wow...I knew your father back in the day. How is he?"

"Uh, he passed away over a year ago."

"Oh no, I'm very sorry to hear that."

Ann shrugged. "Thank you, it was unexpected."

"Oh wow, that's too bad, I really hate to hear that." After a quick pause, the clerk asked, "Can I ask you another question? You don't have to answer if you don't want to."

"Um, yes, of course."

"Does the name Stephanie Fields ring a bell?"

"Yes...do you know her?" *What the...*

The clerk teared up. "Do I? Lord, I can't believe this is real. Stephanie's my best girlfriend, we've been friends since high school back in the late sixties. My name's Glenda. I remember you when you were a baby."

Ann was stunned into silence.

Glenda fished out a pad of sticky notes and a pen from her pocket. She wrote on the top sheet and then handed it over to Ann. "If you want to learn more about your mother, please give me a call. I'm sure that she would love to meet you, but you don't have to commit to that. It's up to you, don't feel like you have to call if you don't want to."

Ann looked at the piece of paper. It read:

Glenda Townsend
(741) 555-1949 (home)

A group of young women entered the shop, and Glenda rose to head back behind the counter to serve them. She looked over at Ann and Luke one last time. "Have a great night, and stay safe."

As the clerk turned her attention to other customers, Luke whispered in Ann's ear, "AC, what was that about?"

She sighed and stared straight ahead, not facing her friend. "It's a long story. I'll explain some other time."

Ann arrived home from the grocery store on a Sunday afternoon. To avoid making multiple trips to and from her car, she held several plastic grocery bags in each hand. She hobbled her way up the steel outdoor stairs, and then down the second-floor balcony to her unit. When she made it to her front door, she found herself fumbling with the unit key.

Why didn't I just do this in two or three trips? I'm so stupid.

As she continued to struggle, she heard someone yelling, "Hey, lemme help you!"

She stopped and looked around, trying to figure out where the sound came from. Then, a young man with straight onyx hair swept across his face emerged from next door. "Howdy neighbor!"

"Hi!" she responded, a little out of breath.

"Looks like you're having a hell of a time. Lemme help you out."

"Are you sure?"

"Of course!" The man held her bags while she gripped her keys and let herself into the apartment. The man brought in the groceries and sat them on her kitchen counter. Charlie sat in the living room and looked at the man, calmly wagging his tail.

"Thanks!"

"No prob!" He stopped as he was about to leave, and turned to face her. "By the way, what's your name?"

"I'm Ann, and this is my dog, Charlie. What about you?"

"I'm Ian. I'm just next door. I've seen you but hadn't had the occasion to introduce myself."

"Well, I'm glad you did. Thanks again!"

"It's no trouble at all. I'll see you around!"

"Oh, for sure!"

Ian then left her apartment and walked back to his unit. Ann then closed the door and smiled.

IN THE PRESENT
MARCH-APRIL 2003

Two weeks after the Saint Patrick's Day outing, Luke called Ann to invite her out to a bar in Mount Eve, a nearby neighborhood known for its hills overlooking downtown Losanti and the Ohio River, as well as its trendy bar and club scene. He suggested The Speakeasy, an establishment at the end of Carlton Avenue, the main thoroughfare in the area. They met up at the parking garage up the street and walked together towards the bar.

"AC, since it's your birthday tomorrow, I figured it would be fun to go out to Mount Eve to celebrate."

"Thanks, Luke! I appreciate it."

"Of course." He looked at her with a smile. "Since it's your day, drinks are on me."

"Thanks! So, where are we headed?"

"I read about this place in *The Almost CountryBeat* and y'know, from the way they describe it, I think you'll like it. It's supposed to be one of the up-and-coming bars in the city."

"Sounds fun." She kept up with him while holding her arms inside her sweater for warmth. "Wonder what makes it special."

"They've got all kinds of bourbons and bourbon cocktails, and y'know, the cool thing is, they have this bricked outdoor patio with a fire pit."

"Oh, that'll be neat. I love sitting outside. Wonder if they'll have heaters, too."

"They probably will. I mean, apparently they keep the patio open year-round."

The friends arrived at the eclectic bar, which was dimly lit on the outside, except for a small neon sign with the establishment's name. The entrance was a narrow, bricked tunnel that led to an outdoor area with a patterned red brick floor, metal tables with chairs, and cushioned chairs around a glowing firepit. Tall metal heaters blazed to warm up the patio area on the cool spring night. The bar was inside a glass-paneled dark wooden door, along with additional seating.

They ordered from the oaken bar. Once they got their drinks, they headed outside and sat by the crackling firepit, where they enjoyed conversation.

"So, how's school treating you?"

"Eh, it's fine. It keeps me busy," Luke explained. "It's hard learning the anatomy of all these different types of animals. I don't know how veterinarians do it."

"Cocaine?" Ann joked.

He snickered. "Yeah, probably. So, how's work been?"

"Um, it's been fine. They're giving me more projects, and I'm getting great reviews from my manager and our clients. You know, it's fun work. I love getting the raw survey results in from these polling firms like Gallup and Ipsos, and then being able to turn them into actual insights that the public can understand and take in."

"Yeah, I imagine so. It's like telling a story."

"Exactly."

"It's awesome to actually enjoy what you do. You're so lucky."

"I mean…it's cool. You know, I hope that for you one day too. So, how's the girl Shannon you're seeing?"

"Yeah…that didn't work out. I dunno, we're too different. I mean, she's hot, but she's kind of boring."

"I guess hotness isn't everything."

"Ugh, you're not wrong. My God, I swear I wanted to stab myself in the head when I spent time with her. Figured that should tell me we're not compatible."

"Oh, for sure."

"So, have you been seeing anybody?"

"No, not right now. Got a lot going on." *Not gonna make that same mistake again.*

"Oh, okay." He then changed the subject. "So anyway, remember that lady we met a couple of weeks ago at the donut shop, the one that wanted you to call her?"

"Uh…yeah."

"What was that about?"

Ann sighed.

"AC, you don't have to tell me if you don't want to."

"It's okay. So…the best way I can explain it is this. My parents got divorced when I was a baby, and I was raised by my father. My mother — my birth mother — wasn't around growing up and I've never actually met her."

"You must've when you were a baby."

She chuckled. "Sure Luke, but you know what I mean. Anyway, my dad remarried when I was pretty young, so the woman he remarried helped raise me, she's who I consider my mom, and she's who I call 'mom.'"

"Alright, that makes sense."

"So apparently, the lady at the donut shop is friends with my birth mother."

"Really? But you're from Detroit."

"Yeah. That's what's so weird about it. How did my birth mother's friend end up down here in Losanti, of all places? And then I end up running into her...it's crazy."

"Small world."

"For sure."

"So, have you called her?"

She shook her head.

"Why not?"

"Eh, I don't know, Luke. It's a lot. See, what gets me is that for most of the time I was growing up, we were living in the same damn city. I wasn't *that* hard to find. But she was never around."

"I hear you, but to be fair, AC, you're from Detroit, not BFE."

"True."

"Y'know, of course it's up to you. But for what it's worth, maybe you should give the lady a call. I'm sure she's got her own side to things. You might find out something you didn't know before, but you never know unless you reach out."

Ann's therapist Belinda peered down at her original intake sheet. "I understand your father passed away about a year and a half ago. I'm very sorry for your loss."

Ann stiffly nodded.

"You have a mother but also a birth mother you don't know. Could you share a bit more about that?"

"Uh...alright," Ann said, looking out the window. "Um...I was born, then my parents divorced. My dad remarried when I was around three, the woman he remarried is the only mom I've known, and um...she's always treated me like I was her own. My birth mother...well, I've never met her. She wasn't around growing up, so I don't know her."

"Did your father ever discuss your mother — your birth mother?"

"Uh...I know her name, her name's Stephanie. I was told that she had mental health issues and she thought my dad would be the better parent, so she just let him have me, and then she just *poof*, gone."

"How does that make you feel?"

"Not great," Ann smiled darkly. "You hear about 'deadbeat dads' a lot, but it's like I have a 'deadbeat mom' of sorts. It's different, though. I mean, she carried me for nine months and gave birth to me, and then when my parents split up, she just up and left. I guess what I can never understand is how you can do that...carry a kid, then just say, 'Here you go, you can have her,' and then disappear?"

"That feeling is understandable." Belinda nodded, writing down notes.

"If she put me up for adoption...um...you give them up knowing you can't take care of them and they'd be better off with parents that have the means to take care of them. But, I've seen the custody papers. There was a court fight, and then it's like she just gave up and was like, 'Go ahead, take her.' I don't get it."

"So, from what I'm hearing, you feel that your birth mother abandoned you?"

"Yeah, pretty much. I mean, my parents took good care of me, it's not like she left me with wolves. But I dunno, it bothers me."

"Yes, I can imagine that's painful for you."

"It sucks, but it is what it is."

"Ann...your feelings about your birth mother's absence are valid. It's okay to feel them. Since you're now an adult, have you thought about seeking her out?"

"Uh...not really. Funny thing is, I was out a week ago for Saint Patrick's Day, and I ran into a friend of my birth mother's. How that happened here in Losanti, I have no clue. But um...anyway, she gave me her number and said I could call her if I wanted to know more and possibly meet her. I guess she's still alive."

Belinda leaned in. "Ann, have you considered calling this friend?"

Ann shook her head. "Nah, not really."

"Why not?"

"Because...I hate phone calls, they make me nervous. Besides, what if I talk to her friend and find out that my birth mother doesn't want to meet me after all? Or what if we do meet, and it goes badly?"

Belinda took a deep breath. "Good questions. It seems that you're focused a lot on the 'what-ifs' – in other words, an uncertain future. Would you say that's accurate?"

"Yeah. I hate not knowing. I want to know what I'm getting into."

"That's anxiety. It sounds like you're trying to control the situation and protect yourself from hurt, which happens if you've experienced a lot of social rejection or have undergone trauma. The absence of a parent can be a form of trauma, and then losing your other birth parent can make you extra sensitive to that."

Ann nodded.

"I have counseled clients in similar situations who have reunited with parents or other family members. What happens at the meeting, and how the relationship develops after – it depends. Could it go badly? Sure. But it could also go well. It is a huge unknown, but you don't know unless you step out of your comfort zone. Regardless, the benefit is that you'll know more than you do right now, and that can provide you with closure and peace. Now, as far as your birth mother's absence is concerned, is your father's perspective the only one you have?"

"Yes. I only know what he told me when I was a kid."

"Okay. For your own healing, hearing the story from others may help. Even the best marriages can be complex, and the reasons for a marriage dissolving can be even more so. There may be more to your mother's absence than you've been told...or, maybe not, but at least you'll know."

"I understand."

"Ultimately, you want to be at a point where you can live in the moment. The past is a tool to learn from our mistakes, and we can make good choices to increase the chances of having the future we want. But, we can't change the past and we can't always control the future, so your main focus should be living in the present."

After a pause, Belinda continued. "From our initial session, it appears you have a great deal of anxiety. Anxiety doesn't go away, but you can manage it, and as we continue to meet, we'll work on ways you can do that. Does that sound good?"

"Uh...yeah."

"Now, to wrap up today's session, before the next time we meet, you may want to reach out to your birth mother's friend. She has given you the number, so she's inviting you to call. Hopefully, that will help ease at least some of your anxiety around that. Does this sound like a good plan, Ann?"

Ann took a deep breath. "I think I can do that."

HARRY
MAY 2003

Ann strolled into the office early on a bright May morning, warmly greeting her colleague as she approached her desk.

"Jason – what's up with all these decorations?"

"It's Cinco de Mayo! We're a piñata-hitting contest later on today."

"Sounds like fun."

"I think I read in the email we're supposed to have a taco bar too, so we don't have to figure out lunch."

"That'll be nice. Tacos are so good." Ann turned on her desktop computer to start her workday.

Rob walked in and joined his colleagues. "Hey guys! I've gotta say, it's nice that they converted the office to four-person cubes. Days go by a lot quicker."

"I hear you, bro," Jason responded.

Ann thought similarly. "Yeah, this isn't so isolating. It's nice."

Chad Mortensen, their supervisor, walked over to the four-person cube where Ann sat with Jason and Rob. After greeting his reports, he announced, "Team meeting's happening at ten in the Times meeting room. We've got a new guy joining our team and you'll get to meet him. He's taking that spot over there." He then pointed to an unoccupied desk next to Ann.

Once their manager walked away, Rob whispered, "Ooh, new guy. Hope he doesn't suck like the last one."

Ann chimed in. "Yeah, he *was* kind of weird."

"Oh, Mike? That guy smelled like straight up weed," Jason grumbled.

"He did, but it wasn't just that. Um...so he was supposed to follow up with the city papers for classifieds data for my Midwest Agenda Setting project, and the guy just...pretended to do it. And then when I called him out on it, he got so pissed, like he expected me to look the other way."

"He was just mad he got caught."

"Yeah, probably. But from what I heard, Mike had a hard time taking direction and feedback from women. But whatever, that guy's gone anyway. Hope the new guy won't be so ridiculous."

A few minutes before ten o'clock, the team filed into the Times room, a small meeting room just off the main working floor. Each member sat in a grey office chair surrounding a white oval table.

Right at ten, the door opened, and Chad entered, bringing with him a young man of husky build, wearing a blue button-up shirt and khakis, with a slight limping gait. Once in the room, the men sat down. As the man locked eyes with Ann, he turned pale.

"So," the supervisor began, "I got us together for a brief meeting so y'all can meet the newest member of the Nichols Agency, Trevor Stevenson. He'll be joining us as a junior member of our team, taking over the work Mike was doing."

Are you fucking kidding me?

"Hi, guys," Trevor greeted the group nervously.

Chad continued, "Trevor comes to us from Ohio Valley Tech, he's getting ready to graduate in a couple of weeks, and then he'll be joining us full-time." He then turned to Trevor. "This is the Press Data Analytics team. In-house, we're often referred to as PDA. As was discussed in orientation, we gather survey research data from political and market research houses, analyze it for notable insights and trends, and package it up for news outlets across the US and Canada."

Trevor nodded.

The boss turned to the rest of the team. "Go ahead and introduce yourselves. We'll just go around."

When it was Ann's turn, she introduced herself as if she had never met the new employee. "Hi, I'm Ann Corbin, I'm a senior analyst, and I've been here at Nichols for close to a year."

Chad provided instructions to the young man. "Trevor, at least in the immediate future, you'll be working closely with Ann. She's doing some great work on the Midwest region. We've got every confidence you'll perform well."

Shit.

"That...that sounds good," the new hire's voice quivered.

"Alright, that's everything. Trevor, you can follow the rest of the team to your cube. Your desk is there, and IT will be by shortly to help you get set up. I appreciate y'all."

The entire team, including Ann, got up and left the room. As the team returned to their work area, Ann smirked at her junior colleague. "I take it your sister's feeling better."

Trevor averted his eyes.

∽

"You have reached the voicemail of Luke Phillips. I wish I could answer my phone, but I can't. If you want to hear back from me, you can leave your name and number, and when I can use my phone, I'll call you. Thanks!"

Ann clicked on the button to end the call before Luke's voicemail began recording.

Huh. He usually calls me on the weekend to go out. I guess he's busy this week. Maybe he found somebody new, she thought to herself. *What to do on a Saturday night...*

She turned on her laptop computer and searched "BBW dating." Scrolling down the bright page of results, she located a message board website focused on dating in and around Losanti. She clicked onto the website, and searched the boards, locating one for "big, beautiful women." She browsed through the flirty messages back and forth of the big, beautiful women and the men who admired them. The idea of participating in this community enticed her. *A world where someone like me is paid attention to?*

Joining this well-traveled message board gave her a bit of an ego boost after the iffyness of Luke. However, this was not simply an online discussion board; this board was utilized for people to meet in person, both one-on-one and for planned social engagements.

For months, Ann noticed the announcements for these "BBW parties" in her inbox, gatherings involving shapely women and their potential suitors. The parties were held in the bar lounge of the Sprucedale Inn, a one-star motel in Martwenty miles west of downtown Losanti.

The emails included photo after photo of dancing buxom ladies, mostly in their thirties, forties, and fifties, and a collection of men touching their bodies seductively. But every time she received a notification in her email inbox, she would nervously click "delete."

This time, though, she hovered over the delete button, but instead of pressing it, she let go of her mouse and took a second look at the email. *Hell, it's not like I have anything to do tonight. It starts at eight-thirty and it's near the Indiana border. I've got a couple of hours before it starts.*

Charlie cocked his ebony head to the side as Ann got up from her chair and opened the door to her tiny yet cluttered closet. Furiously, she pushed her way through the articles of clothing that had not seen the light of day in months, perhaps years. Then she found the outfit: A black and green striped halter top and a basic, knee-length black skirt to match. *Sure. I suppose this works.*

Then, she hopped into the bathtub to shower. *That special soap would be great — you know, that super flowery kind from Bath and Body Works.* Ann lathered, imagining all the male partygoers turning their heads at her.

After brushing her eyelids with cerulean eyeliner, coating her adequate lashes with mascara, and lacquering her lips with pink-tinted lip gloss, Ann was ready. So ready.

Finally. Finally, they will see me.

Rolling up to the Sprucedale Inn, Ann noticed the freshly paved, filled parking lot, and the motel that, despite its one-star rating, appeared clean and well-maintained. The railings and room doors were adorned with a fresh coat of maroon paint, and the windows to the lobby sparkled.

Huh, this looks cleaner and busier than I thought it would be. Well hell...

She then glanced at the clock on her dashboard.

9:30. Shit.

She took a very deep breath. *Can't put this off forever.*

Grabbing her black crochet purse and slinging it across her right shoulder, she shut the car door and walked inside the front doors of the motel. As soon as she crossed the threshold, the loud reggae-inspired beats took over her senses.

Sean Paul — alright!

Ann pranced through the archway of the darkened bar. The room was decorated a shady crimson, with tables dotting the space. Most of the chairs were filled with corpulent women, some bigger than others, some blonder than others, all various shades of alabaster. The men, and there were fewer of them to be sure, varied greatly in shade, size, and age, and most were at the tables mingling with the ladies.

She looked down at her fawn-shaded arms. *This is a mistake, but I'm already here.*

Finding an empty stool at the bar, she claimed it and ordered her favorite drink, Cuervo and Sprite. She sipped her cocktail while listening to the music. Men were entering, but that one flocked to the tables. So did that one. And another, and another. A few even approached the bar, but either sat alone or flirted with the others seated there. Her glass was empty before she knew it, and still, no one approached her.

She ordered another Cuervo and Sprite.

Liquid courage coursing through her veins, Ann got up, smartly took her drink in her hand, and moseyed to the empty dance floor.

She stiffly danced to the groove of the bass-filled house music the hired disc jockey played. She struggled mightily to keep the beat.

As the first song flowed to the next, she felt a tap on her shoulder. She turned around to see a man staring at her with striking brown eyes.

"Hi," he whispered to her. "You're gorgeous."

"Uh...thank you."

He motioned her to a small table with two empty seats. Once there, the man spoke. "I happened to notice you. You look great and I want to get to know you."

"Oh cool, thanks. I'd like to get to know you too."

"Great. My name's Harry."

"Hi, Harry. I'm Ann, great to meet you. What do you do?"

He smoothed a lock of his grey-speckled hair behind his ear. "I'm an account executive for a company that supplies materials and curriculum to homeschool families internationally. What about you?"

"I'm a data analyst for a market research firm. Are you from around here?"

"Not really. I live about an hour northeast of here, in Adelphia. What about you?"

"Uh...I live in Losanti...Norris Park, not too far from downtown. Adelphia's really nice."

"Yeah, I like it there. It's a good family-oriented suburb, it's quiet, nice homes, low taxes." Harry sipped on his glass filled with clear liquid. "Norris Park is nice too. Plenty of people, kind of hilly, I used to party there back when I was in college. Does it still have a lot of bars?"

"Oh yeah. But it's not bad. It's close to my job. I work downtown, and everything is really close. It's also a great place to keep my dog."

"Oh, what kind of dog?"

"Uh...a Labrador retriever, he's a rescue."

"That's nice."

The two continued to get to know each other. Each ordered another drink.

"What's the thing you like most about what you do?" Ann asked.

"It's the travel, a hundred percent. I'm always flying out to Miami and Tampa for work. And sometimes I go out to the West Coast, like Northern California and Washington state. I even do a little overseas travel, nothing interesting though, just London on occasion. But all the places my job sends me to have fantastic aspects. Very beautiful."

"Oh, that's cool. Where's your favorite place to travel?"

"Florida for sure. I love the beaches, and it's a party all the time. What about you?"

"I haven't done a lot of travel, just some domestically, and I've been to Canada a lot since it was near Detroit, where I grew up."

"Detroit, huh?"

"Yeah."

"I've gone up there a few times for work. Gone to a few Pistons games in, what is it, Auburn Hills?"

"Yep – it's north of Detroit. Not much else out there but the arena."

"So, where else have you traveled?"

"Uh, I went to California with my family once when I was a kid. We went to the happiest place on Earth, and we also went down the coast as well. We made it all the way to San Diego. I'd love to go back as an adult."

"It's gorgeous out there. The Pacific is so deep and vast, and the beach is made of golden sand. Maybe, if things progress, we can go together."

She smiled and took a sip of her drink.

After a swig from his own glass, Harry commented, "So you look like you're seventeen, but I assume since you're in here, you're probably twenty-one."

"No," Ann corrected him. "I'm twenty-three. A lot of people say I look a little younger than I am."

"Yeah, I totally believe that. What would you think if I were to tell you I'm forty-one?"

"Hmmm. I'd be a bit surprised by that. You don't look forty-one."

"Yeah, I hear that a lot. Have you ever dated someone as old as me?"

"No, I haven't." *To be fair, it's not like I've dated a lot of someones.*

"Okay, there's something else I should tell you. Have you ever dated a married man before?"

Ann was taken aback. "No, and I don't know how I feel about that."

"Well, I'm married, but it's not a happy marriage. My wife cheated on me not too long ago."

"I'm sorry to hear that."

"It's all right. I was pissed, and honestly, I'm still pissed, but I can't leave her right now, I'm staying with her for the sake of the kids."

"Oh wow, that makes sense. So, why are you *here*?"

"Well," Harry took a draw of his rum and coke. "I find ample women to be quite beautiful. I like what I like. You see, what I had to come to terms with is that everyone cheats. Nobody's loyal. It's in our nature – humans are not made for monogamy." He took another gulp. "Anyway, I want to get to know you better. May I have your number? I would like to go out with you. How does Tuesday lunch sound?"

"Uh...sounds great," a slightly inebriated Ann agreed.

"I want to talk to you a bit more, but it's a bit loud in here. I'm parked outside, it's a BMW M5."

I really don't care about what kind of car this guy has. But whatever. "Sure."

The two partygoers strolled out to the parking lot, walking until coming across a waxed, white sedan. Harry opened the passenger's side door and Ann got in. After he closed the door, he made his way over to the driver's side and got in.

"It's nice in here, isn't it?"

"Sure."

"It's got leather seats, and they're heated, too." He leaned over to turn on the heating element. "Feel free to lean back. The control's on the side. It's push-button."

She found the seat adjustment control and leaned the seat back slightly.

"You're very cute, and I'm quite attracted to smart, career-minded women. Intellect really gets me going."

She beamed. "Uh...thanks, Harry. You're pretty nice-looking yourself."

Harry placed his right hand on Ann's nylon-clad thigh and leaned in for a kiss. Her lips met his. His hand began creeping up her thigh, and he slowly pulled down her stockings. He then rubbed the outside of her panties and his fingers slipped underneath.

That feels good. She instinctively spread her legs for his full access.

He continued to rub her gently yet firmly with his right hand, while he used his left hand to unzip the fly of his khakis.

She peeked at the large member and did not know what to make of the moment. The only other time she had seen anything like this, at least in person, was at the park when she was a teenager, and it was deeply plunged into someone else without their consent. But unlike the one belonging to her high school sweetheart, this one was excited for *her*.

He whispered in her ear, "Ann, you can touch it."

She leaned to the side slightly and touched it. It was fleshy yet solid.

"Go ahead, hold it, rub it up and down."

She then did as she was told, and did so gently.

"That's great. You're a natural."

Harry continued to rub Ann underneath her panties. A warm, tingling sensation flowed through her body. *This feels amazing.* He then slipped a finger inside.

"How does that feel?"

She exhaled. "That feels nice."

He moved the finger gently about. "Oh, that's tight. I'm gonna loosen you up."

He then went back to massaging her while she stroked him. Soon, she felt a strong surge of energy between her legs, and she moaned in ecstasy, gripping the passenger doorframe. At the same time, he achieved release.

After they were finished, he took out a few napkins in his center console and cleaned up after himself. "That was incredible, Ann. How was it for you?"

"It felt...wonderful."

"That's good. There's more where that came from. I want to take you out sometime, show you a nice time. And then we can do even more. Sound good?"

"It sure does." *This feels bad, but so, so good.*

Ann took Tuesday off from work. As she finished getting dressed, spritzing her neck with Be Delicious perfume, she heard a knock at the door. She peeked through the peephole and confirmed it was Harry.

Charlie sat up and emitted a deep growl.

"Stop, Charlie," she commanded the black lab, who then quieted down. She invited her date inside. He was clad in a blue button-up shirt, khakis, and brown lace-up shoes, as if he were ready for a typical day at the office.

"Hi, Ann! You look beautiful."

She felt her face getting warm. "Uh...thank you."

"Of course. Are you ready?"

"Yeah, just about. Come in and have a seat."

As the middle-aged man crossed the threshold, the dog quickly left his sitting position, growled and barked, and started towards him angrily. Ann caught him by the collar before he could attack.

"No, Charlie!" She then turned to Harry. "I'm so sorry. This is my dog, Charlie. I don't know why he's so upset, I've never seen him like this. Maybe it'll take time for him to get used to you. I'll move him to my bedroom."

"Don't worry, it happens sometimes. I used to have a couple of dogs myself, but I had to give them up after I got married. My wife's not a fan of pets."

She relocated the canine to her room, gave him a couple of toys, and closed the door. He was still barking but remained contained. "Okay, lemme grab my purse. Where are we going?"

"Oh yes – I know of a nice Asian fusion restaurant a couple of blocks from here. It's close enough to walk. If I park in your complex, will my car get towed?"

"No, it'll be fine, the property management doesn't care, and they're fine with visitors. Let's go."

The restaurant Harry had in mind was a small establishment called Papaya and Mango, in the heart of Norris Park close to many of the popular bars and clubs. Outside was a purple awning covering modern black-outlined windows. Light orange letters displaying the establishment name covered the awning.

The two were seated at a table for two, covered with a white tablecloth and maroon napkins holding polished silverware. For an appetizer, the two shared a sushi roll sampler, and for entrees, Ann ordered chicken fried rice, while Harry chose the beef yellow curry from the specials section of the menu.

"So, Ann, have you ever wanted to travel overseas?"

"Of course – I'd love to."

"Where would you like to go?"

"Uh...I'd love to backpack through Europe, that's a dream of mine. But I just haven't had the occasion to do it."

"You should go for it. Going overseas is fun, it'll open your eyes to a lot. There's a whole world out there and it's hard to experience it if you don't get a first-hand view."

"That makes total sense."

"The dish I selected is from Thailand, it's...good. But I've flown to Bangkok a few times. The food there is amazing. If you go off the beaten path, their dishes are not Americanized like it is here. Of course, the portions are smaller, but the quality is top-notch."

"That sounds nice. I'll have to go there one day. So, where would you like to go that you haven't gone to yet?"

"I'd say Italy."

"Why?" she asked.

He explained, "Ah, lots of old European architecture, old like centuries old, not America 'old.' Italy's also known for their delicious wine and great food. Different than Italian food here, and regionally dependent. I'd love to experience it firsthand."

"Sounds like you've really thought about this."

"Oh, I have."

After chatting and enjoying their meals, Ann and Harry headed back to her apartment. She turned the key and let him in.

Grrr!

Charlie stood stiff, his snout scrunched and teeth bared.

"Whoa!" Harry yelled.

"It's okay." She tried to reassure her dog, but he was still staring at the interloper, groaning with anger. The groans turned into ferocious barks. "C'mon Charlie, let's go outside." She turned to Harry and said, "I'm so sorry. Have a seat, I'm gonna run him out, then I'll just put him back in my room. I'll make sure the door's totally closed this time."

After taking care of Charlie, Ann returned to the futon next to her date. "So yeah, where were we?"

"Yeah, I was just about to touch you and make you feel nice and sexy."

"Hmm, I think I like that."

Ann and Harry kissed passionately while on the futon, then the moment progressed. He was quite ready. He stood in front of her. She touched it.

"Would you like to give it a nice mouth hug?" he asked.

"Sure, but I...I don't know what I'm doing."

"You've never given a blowjob before?"

"Uh...no."

"Okay. It's easy. You just put it in your mouth, you can lick it, suck it, let it run back and forth in your mouth. Just make sure you cover your teeth when you do it. Teeth on a dick hurt."

"Okay." She leaned in and fellated him, doing as instructed. *It tastes like soap.* He moaned as she performed.

After several minutes, Harry told her, "Okay, that was great for your first time doing this. Are you sure you've never done this before?"

"Um...yeah, I'm quite sure."

He then sat back on the futon and used his hand to motion her to a reclining position with her legs facing him. "Let me return the favor. Have you let anyone lick you?"

"No."

"You're gonna like this."

He placed his fingers between her legs, and then leaned in. She felt his warm tongue lick her vigorously. A few minutes later, that warm sensation she enjoyed in his car that night returned, stronger than ever.

"Oh my God, this is so good..." she vocalized.

He continued to pleasure her until she climaxed. *Incredible.* Afterward, he got on his knees and faced her.

"Are you ready?"

Oh, I'm ready. I can't believe this is happening.

Just as she opened her mouth to answer, Charlie scratched at the door, barked loudly, and would not stop. The mood shattered, she got up and hastily dressed.

"I'm so sorry about Charlie, I'm sure he's upset because he doesn't know you."

Harry sighed, standing up and retrieving his business casual outfit. "It's okay, don't worry about it. We'll set something up for the next party they're holding in Maryton; it's a week from Saturday. My wife will be out of town with the kids, so I should be able to get away for it. This time I'll get a room there."

"That'll be great."

"Then, we can go all the way."

At that moment, the gears began turning in Ann's mind. *I want this so bad. Harry makes me feel so good, and this might be my last chance at anything like this since Luke isn't going along with God's plan. Is he really The One? I don't even know anymore. At this point, I doubt God cares...not about me, anyway.*

He continued. "After my wife and I had our kids, I had a vasectomy. I've also been tested and I'm clean, so it's cool."

Second thoughts snaked in. *Harry's into me. He gets excited for me. But do I want to lose my virginity like this? In a shitty motel room? To a married man?*

"Eh, I hear you. I'm clean too, but I still think we should use condoms."

"Okay, that's fine. Whatever makes you feel comfortable. I'll call you."

After Harry left, Ann opened her bedroom door to let Charlie out. He ran out and sniffed around the apartment. Finding no signs of the interloper's presence, he wagged his tail happily as if everything were completely normal.

Ann slept in on a bright and early Saturday morning with Charlie curled up at the foot of the bed. She heard her phone vibrate, so she rolled over to view the notification. The phone displayed a text:

> Harry: **Got a room 4 the party next week. Can't wait to see u sexy**

She smiled to herself and texted back:

> Ann: **Cool, see you then ;)**

As she tried to go back to sleep, she was interrupted once again. *Ring!*

Ann rolled over groggily and checked her phone. *What the? Why is Paul calling me?*

"How's everything down there in Florida? How's married life treating you?" she asked.

"Oh, it's great, love it!"

"That's awesome. Congratulations on the baby girl! Isabella, right?"

"Yeah, Isabella Min-Seo."

"Aw, lovely name!"

"Thanks! We call her Bella."

"Oh, okay. How have you and Alyssa been holding up?"

"We've been alright. She's a real trooper. She's up all the time to feed the baby, even when I have to sleep for work, and we try to take turns changing her and everything. The baby's a real joy. We're both dog-tired, but it's so worth it. Parenthood is wonderful."

"That's great...happy to hear it!"

"Oh, and the rocker set you got us from the registry? Bella loves it. Sometimes we put her in there and set it to push, and it calms her right down."

"Oh, I'm so glad."

"Uh, anyway Ann, the reason why I'm calling is because I was talking to Luke last night," Paul explained.

Ann was confused. "Oh...okay."

"Hmm, not sure how to put this. So, he was telling me how...ever since you moved to Losanti, you two have been hanging out a lot."

"Um, sure. We hang out sometimes."

"Yeah. So, Luke was saying he was worried that you were clinging to him too much, like maybe you weren't over the fact that you and him aren't in a relationship. He just wants to be friends."

"What?"

"So, I don't know. Maybe you shouldn't call him so much? Start building a friend group there? I dunno."

"Huh?"

"Now, I know Losanti's not the easiest place to meet people, but I'm sure people find ways to do it—"

Ann felt the back of her neck heating up. "Look, Paul – I don't know what Luke's telling you, but he calls me a lot more than I call him. Most of the time when we go out, it's 'cause he's the one reaching out and coming by here. Believe it or not, I *do* have my own life here in Losanti. I don't get why he put you up to this."

"I dunno. That's what Luke told me."

"That's great and all, but you know – instead of presuming stuff about me, maybe you could've asked me about my side of things instead of calling me out of the blue to accuse me of something I'm not even doing."

"Ann, I'm not accusing you."

"You basically said I call him too much and I need to find my own friends. Lemme tell *you* something Paul – Luke is full of shit."

"Whoa! I'm sorry if it came off that way. It's just that Luke told me he was feeling smothered, but you know how he is. He's not good at telling people how he feels and what he wants. So, I agreed to help him out."

She calmed down slightly. "You know, I get it. You guys are best friends and you're doing him a solid. But Luke's a grown man. If he doesn't wanna hang out with me, he can tell me himself. Or better yet, he can stop calling me. While you're playing messenger, maybe you can go back and tell him *that*."

Paul sighed. "You know what Ann – you're right. That's fair."

After ending the call, Ann sat up in bed shaking. *What just happened? Luke really thinks I'm a burden...but he usually calls me.* Her mind then turned to food. *I'm hungry. It's almost ten, I think McDonald's is still serving breakfast.*

She donned a blue puffer jacket and gloves, grabbed her wallet, and hopped into her car. She drove to the fast food restaurant down the street from her. As she was sitting in the drive-thru line, she heard a knock at her passenger-side window.

"Shit!"

A middle-aged lady clad in a beige beanie and stained red coat stood at her window. She clicked the window control button to roll down the window. "Hi! Didn't mean to scare you."

"No, it's fine."

"Got any change to spare? Not gonna lie, I'ma go to the Dairy Union right over there and get me a St. Ides. I drinks." The woman pointed to the local convenience store on the corner.

Ann shrugged. "Eh, can't hate." *At least she's honest.* She dug inside her pajama pants pocket, pulled out a five-dollar bill, and leaned over to give it to the woman.

"God bless you!"

"No problem." Ann rolled her window back up as the woman skipped away.

A moment later, she pulled up to the drive-thru speaker and ordered.

"Good morning, welcome to McDonalds! May I take your order?"

"Uh...I'll have a sausage, egg, and cheese McGriddle meal."

"What drink?"

"Uh, small Hi-C orange."

"Anything else?" asked the cashier.

"Um...may I have another sausage, egg, and cheese McGriddle by itself, and two more hashbrowns?"

"Sure!"

"That'll be it."

"Your total is $6.58. Please pull around to the first window."

After Ann paid and received her meal, she drove back home, eating one of the hash browns in her car.

Once she returned, she ate the remainder of her breakfast while throwing small bits of cooled potato Charlie's way. Looking for a way to occupy her mind, she began searching on her laptop for assorted topics guided by her stream of consciousness.

While diving down the rabbit hole, she typed "Harry Richman Adelphia Ohio" in the online search bar. When the results popped up, a few hits on background check sites rose to the top, with Harry's legal name, Henry Francis Richman, along with his age and other individuals associated with him. One of the associated people listed was "Thanh Le Richman, 36."

Underneath the background check results was a result from a photo sharing website. Ann clicked on this result and flipped through the pictures. One in particular caught her eye. It was an outside candid snapshot of Harry in jeans and an orange fleece jacket smiling, sitting on shining silver bleachers next to a petite, dark-haired woman, apparently his wife, wearing jeans and a light aqua fleece jacket.

The adults were pictured with two happy young children: a boy also in jeans and an Old Navy fleece hoodie, and a girl likely no older than ten wearing a white and blue sports jersey with blue shorts, long white socks, and black soccer cleats.

As she took in the family photo, a powerful wave of shame came over her. The gravity of her involvement with Harry became powerfully real to her. *This is not who I am. But apparently, it is.*

As Ann wrestled with her conscience, the phone rang. Luke was the caller, so she sent it to voicemail.

A TALK LONG OVERDUE
MAY 2003

"Ann, I understand that you ran into a friend of your birth mother's about two months ago, and you were considering calling her. I just want to circle back on that in our session today. How is that going?" Belinda asked her client.

Ann's eyes became downcast. "I...I haven't done it yet."

"Okay. Could you tell me more about that?"

"Uh...well, I can't bring myself to pick up the phone to call her."

The therapist adjusted her seating position. "Okay. You've discussed previously that you have anxiety around phone calls. Is that just in relation to your birth mother's friend, or is that a more general fear?"

"Um...in general."

"Please share more if you're okay with that."

"I've always hated calling people. I mean, it's not the actual conversation, you know, unlessI'm calling a business or something. It's literally just the act of picking up the phone, dialing the numbers, and waiting for it to connect."

"What is it about the act of calling that makes you anxious?"

"I dunno...what if I'm calling at a bad time? What if I wake somebody up by mistake or I interrupt them? What if somebody else picks up? What if I say the wrong thing to them when I'm just trying to reach the person I meant to call?"

"Okay. As far as calling people at a bad time or saying the wrong thing, everybody does that sometimes. Besides, if someone is busy, they can always simply not answer the phone. I'm sure that there's been times you don't answer your phone if you're busy."

"That's true."

"How long have you felt this way?"

"Uh…" Ann twirled her brunette locks nervously. "Pretty much as long as I can remember. My parents were always trying to get me to call kids from school, or call my aunts and uncles. It's the same thing as how they would try to get me to talk to people in public. They always say I'm 'shy' and they say, 'Show yourself friendly.' I…I don't think it's that I'm mean or shy. It's just that I literally don't always know what to say to people, and half the time the things I say don't come out right anyway."

"I see."

"When I was, like, fourteen, my parents got me my own phone line for my birthday. Other kids would love it, but me? I didn't even *ask* for my own line. I guess they thought it would encourage me to call people more often and make friends."

"Did it work?" Belinda asked.

"Yeah, kinda. It took a while, but eventually, in high school, I ended up in a clique. Basically, we were all nerds and outcasts who didn't really belong anywhere else. It was me, Terah, Mykeisha, Zaire, and Daryn, and we would call each other. Then, when Terah and Zaire got their own lines, that was awesome. We'd get on three-way, four-way, and even five-way. And I didn't have to worry as much about doing something stupid if I got their parents when calling them, like calling my friend's mom by the wrong last name or forgetting to ask them how they were doing before asking for my friends and being told I was rude."

"I see. So, it sounds like you had anxiety around potentially saying or doing something socially unacceptable or forgetting a social convention, and upsetting or offending someone?"

"Yeah, pretty much."

"So, are there certain scenarios where phone calls are more difficult for you?"

"What do you mean?"

"Well, are there some calls you find harder to make than others? Is this just at home or also at work?"

"Well, I don't really have to make calls at work that much, I'm an analyst. But I've had jobs where I did make calls all the time. I mean, I had a customer service job for a while in college where I had to call and tell customers that their orders were running late. I got great evaluations when I was working there. I hate that kind of work, but I can do what I need to do if I absolutely have to. But I have a much harder time making personal calls to ask about something or make appointments for myself. Those get put off as long as possible."

"What happens when you make those types of calls?" Belinda asked.

Ann stared out the window, watching two bright cardinals perch on a tree branch. "Um...sometimes I freeze up as soon as they pick up. I forget who to ask for, or what I need or want. I forget to ask who I'm speaking with, all of that. It's pretty bad sometimes. But I tend to do better when I call people without an audience. The worst is when I have to make a call in front of family."

"Why is that?"

"When they're around when I call, as soon as I get off the phone, it's like, 'Oh, you should've said this,' 'You shouldn't have said that,' or, 'Why didn't you ask this, that and the other?' I'm sure they mean well, but it only makes me feel worse, like I'm incapable of taking care of myself or something. It feels embarrassing. That's why I try to make it a point not to be on the phone in front of them."

"So, what I'm hearing you say is that when your family members listen to your phone calls, they offer unsolicited criticism, which leads you to feel more anxious and insecure about making calls in the future. Is that a fair assessment?"

"Yes, exactly," Ann confirmed. "I don't think they realize that I can figure it out on my own. I'm doing okay down here without them trying to hold my hand, I don't need them to nitpick me."

"Okay. This will be something we'll begin to work through in our sessions if that's okay with you."

"Yes, that's fine."

"Perhaps this week, you can call your birth mother's friend," Belinda suggested. "If you're feeling nervous or anxious about calling her, it may help to remember that she probably welcomes your call, because she gave you her number and specifically asked you to call her."

The telephone number Ann received from Glenda two months earlier was still sitting on her desk at home, unused. She feared opening Pandora's box regarding her birth mother's absence, preferring the thorny comfort of her father's truth. Yet, in that moment, she realized that the one thing she sought to avoid throughout her life she needed to finally confront.

She opened up her cell phone, dialed the number, then hit "send" to make the call. After a couple of rings, a woman's voice answered, "Hello?"

Ann took a deep breath.

After they greeted each other, Glenda remarked, "I'm so glad you called. I see you're just like your mother. She hates phones too."

"Uh, I'm sorry it took so long. I hope I didn't call at a bad time."

"Oh, no," the older woman reassured her. "You're fine."

"I...I think I'm finally ready to know more."

"I'm glad. I'll be real with you. This probably needs a face-to-face rather than a phone call. It's a lot."

"Okay, Miss Glenda."

"You're welcome to come by my house. I'm off work during the day this Saturday. I'm in Avon Meadows. Are you free that day?"

"Yes, uh...Saturday's perfect. I'm in Norris Park. I've heard of Avon Meadows but I'm not super familiar. Isn't that somewhere in the middle of the city between the freeways?"

"Yes — it's between I-75 and I-71, north of downtown and OVTU. I'll give you my address and tell you how to get up here. How does 12:30 sound?"

"That'll be great. Thank you very much, I really appreciate this."

"Thank you, Ann. You have no idea how long I hoped for this day. We all have."

∾

Losanti was experiencing a mild and beautiful May day. Ann printed off directions to an address in Avon Meadows just off Interstate 71.

She pulled up to an unassuming bungalow with dark blue siding and stark white trim on a modest block. The garage was situated underneath the main floors, and the driveway led upwards towards the street.

With her car parked in front of the home, she walked up the long path of concrete stairs to the white front door and rang the doorbell.

Glenda answered, though instead of wearing an apron like she did the night of their encounter, she sported a pair of black slacks, an orange and red chevron blouse, and grey house slippers.

"Good afternoon, Ann! C'mon in!"

"Thank you, Miss Glenda."

As she closed the door, the homeowner took note of the Volkswagen in front of her house. "Ooh I tell ya...in Detroit, we wouldn't have been caught dead in a foreign car like that."

"Yeah, I know. Dad would always say that he got a Buick 'cause if he had to see a client at one of the factories, they wouldn't let him in with a foreign car."

"Sounds about right. And ooh, don't let it be Japanese – your car would be on blocks!"

"I know, right?" Ann chuckled.

Glenda exhaled. "Ah, a different time, a different place."

She guided her guest to a burnt orange sofa in the white-painted living room. The space was also adorned with a matching loveseat and floral sitting chair. The decor appeared to date back to the

1970s but was well-maintained. A plethora of indoor house plants rounded out the space.

After bringing back tall cups of iced sweet tea from the kitchen, she reclined in her favorite upholstered chair. "It amazes me how I would've run into you down here in Losanti, of all places."

"Uh, it was definitely a chance encounter, wasn't it?"

"Oh yes. How did you end up here? Did you grow up here in Losanti?"

Ann shook her head. "No, I've lived down here for less than a year. I grew up in Detroit."

"Really?"

"Oh, yeah. We moved back to the city when I was six, and I spent the rest of my childhood there."

"Oh wow, I'm shocked Marshall brought you back to town. I would've never thought that. Where'd you grow up in Detroit?"

"Uh, the far east side of the city, Warren and Cadieux near Grosse Pointe."

"Alright...that makes sense. You were on the other side of town. Ooh, he had you a long ways away from the old neighborhood."

"Yeah, we lived far away from the rest of my dad's family too. My uncle called our neighborhood 'Alaska.'"

Glenda chuckled at the comment. Then they began talking about Ann's father and birth mother.

"What do you already know about your mother?"

"Not a whole lot. My dad told me that pretty much, he and my birth mother were single, he thought she was attractive, and they got married. But she had mental health issues that she didn't want to take care of. They divorced not long after I was born. She said he would be the better parent, and it would be less confusing if she wasn't in my life, so she cut off all contact."

"Oh, I see. Well, there was more to it than that."

"Really?" Ann took a sip of sweet tea from a blue plastic cup.

"Yes, *really*. A lot more to it. See, Stephanie and Marshall grew up together in the same neighborhood."

Ann's eyes widened. "What? I didn't know that."

Glenda nodded slowly. "Yes, they sure did. They lived on the same block, they lived on Gladstone near Woodrow Wilson. And they went to the same elementary school too."

"He never mentioned that to me."

"Hmm, I wonder why. As a kid, Stephanie was very sweet, but quiet...and the thing is, kids can be mean when you're different and you keep to yourself."

"I know how that feels."

"She was left to fend for herself a lot by her family, that's what she would say. See, Marshall lived across the street from her, and he showed himself friendly...he was nice to her when most kids back then weren't. That meant a lot to her."

"That makes sense. He never talked about that...I had no idea. But he was comforting to me when I was a kid and I got made fun of by the other kids."

"That was the Marshall that Stephanie connected with. But anyway, when they hit middle school, he moved away. It was sometime in the sixties. He moved to the Boston-Edison neighborhood, I think he lived on Chicago Boulevard, and his mother put him in Catholic school."

"Correct me if I'm wrong, Miss Glenda, but that's not that far away though, is it?"

"No, it's not. Thinking back now, I mean, it was just a few streets over. But it was like a world away back then. I moved over on Gladstone later – I met Stephanie in seventh grade, so I didn't meet Marshall until we were grown. But yeah, where we lived was rough, but Boston-Edison was real nice. This was all before the '67 rebellion."

"Oh wow. So, how did they reconnect?"

"Well, in the seventies, Stephanie was into fitness, like body sculpting. Aerobics and things like that started becoming popular, but the thing with her is, when she gets into something, she *really* gets into it. So, she started getting a lot of muscles, now that wasn't as big for ladies back then, but she's never really cared about what's popular or what everybody else likes."

"Yeah, I totally get that," Ann said, chuckling.

"See, that's one thing about her, she sure dances to her own beat. Now anyway, back then, she got into bodybuilding. And there was an event at Cobo Hall in, uh...I think it was seventy-eight, seventy-nine? So she went, and I went with her. They didn't have a ladies' show, but they did have one for men, and your father was in it."

August 1978

"So, Glenda, I saw this flyer hung up at work, it's for the Mr. Chiseled Detroit exhibition contest," Stephanie excitedly told her friend. "It's happening this afternoon at two down at Cobo, it's $3.50 to get in. I'm sure I can have Lionel's grandmother watch him. Are you free today?"

"Yeah, sure."

"I'll be by at one."

When it was time to leave, Stephanie left her home on Gladstone and drove to Glenda's west side neighborhood near Joy Road and Schaefer Avenue. She pulled up to her friend's brick bungalow in her tangerine Mercury Bobcat to pick her up, and then they headed to downtown Detroit.

After parking, the ladies bought tickets at the box office and walked into a large room inside Cobo where the Mr. Chiseled Detroit show was held. They found seats together in the third row and sat in the folding chairs.

While many of the women in the audience were there to support their significant others or to ogle the sculpted bodies of the male competitors, Stephanie was there for a slightly different reason.

As the first group of men walked onstage in a line, Glenda whispered, "These guys are a bit much, but not gonna lie, they're cute."

"Sure, I suppose," Stephanie said quietly. "But look at the definition. The legs on number five — they're extra cut. I wonder what he did to get that kind of definition. And the biceps and triceps on number three, what vascularity!"

After the first line of men were introduced and posed in front of the judges, who were sitting just offstage, and the audience, they were dismissed from the stage. The next set of competitors were then brought onstage.

As that group of bodybuilders was introduced, a particular name stood out to Stephanie. "Number four, from right here in Detroit, Michigan, Marshall Corbin!"

As an oiled Marshall showed off his physique, she was almost speechless. "Oh my God."

"Nice, huh?" Glenda said.

"No, not like that. I'm pretty sure I know that man."

"You do?"

"Uh-huh. I knew a kid named Marshall Corbin who lived on my block when I was maybe six or seven years old. We went to the same school and we always played together outside. He was one of my only friends back then, but he moved away, and I haven't seen him in years. I wonder if that could be him."

"Okay, well, after they get offstage, go talk to him."

Stephanie grew nervous. "No...Glenda...I can't."

"Why not?"

"Because...I can't. What if it's not the same Marshall? Or what if it is and he doesn't recognize me? I'ma look stupid."

"Nah, you got this."

After this group of men left the stage, they each put on black tee-shirts with block letters that read "Mr. Chiseled Detroit Contest 1978," and joined the previous competitors, mulling about in a section in the room reserved for the sales of supplements, diets, and other wares purported to give the regular Joe the body he so desired. She took a deep breath, got up from her chair, and motioned to Glenda to come with her.

Upon making it to the merchandise area, she found the man she was looking for and waved at him weakly. When she got his attention, she shakily said, "Uh, hi. Marshall?"

The man squinted his eyes. "Uh, do I know you? You look familiar."

"Um, I think so? I'm Stephanie, uh...Stephanie Fields. Did you ever live over on the near-west side, um, y'know on Gladstone near Woodrow Wilson?"

"Yeah, I did. Oh shit, Stephy?"

She smiled. "Yeah – Red!"

He laughed and gave her a huge hug, lifting her from the ground. "Oh, sorry Stephy, I hope I don't get oil on you."

"It's fine — I can't believe I'm seeing you again!" she exclaimed.

"I know!" he agreed, as he put her down gently. "What are you doing here?"

"Uh, well, I saw this poster about it at work. And since I enjoy working out and lifting a little bit, I wanted to come down here and check this out."

Marshall looked at Stephanie and smiled. "I see, I see, you definitely have been working out. My buddy and I have a gym over on Davison near Dexter. Here's the address." He grabbed a piece of paper and pen at one of the tables and wrote down the address, as well as his phone number, then handed it to her. "Ask for me."

"Thanks, Red. I'm gonna check it out."

Glenda sipped her tea and smiled, recalling the story of how Stephanie and Marshall found each other again as adults. "They loved working out together, and they would talk about all kinds of other things too — politics, religion and spirituality, music — and then they got married."

Ann sat there, bewildered. "Uh...it sounds like an amazing story...that they knew each other when they were kids and then found each other when they were older. But I don't understand why my dad wouldn't have told me that, or that they had things in common besides the fact that they were single and liked each other."

"I don't know, I wish I knew. All I can think of is that maybe he was trying to minimize their bond for some reason. People sometimes do that when they're hurt, when they feel a kind of way about their ex or how things ended between 'em."

"Um, I guess that makes sense. So, they knew each other, they lost touch, they reconnected and got married. I was born. Was that over a few years? How'd all that happen?"

Glenda shrugged. "Not a lot to tell there. They weren't together all that long before they got married, maybe a year if that. But they went down to Toledo — that's where you went back then when you wanted to get married quick — they didn't have a wedding or nothin.' Stephanie hated having all eyes on her, and Marshall wanted to make her happy."

"I kind of get it."

"Then, he bought 'em a house on my block just off Joy Road on the west side, we were living on Sorrento at the time...this was when my first husband was living. It seemed like things were going fine. Maybe another year or two later, you were born. Then, they broke up."

"Do you know why they broke up? What happened?"

"Marriage is a funny thing. The only folks who know what's going on in a marriage are the ones in it."

"Makes sense."

"And here's the other thing. Stephanie's got a lot of pride. She never told me why they broke up, and I doubt she told any of her other friends. But I'm guessing that at least some of it had to do with her baggage."

"Baggage?"

Glenda hesitated. "Well...you know you have an older half-brother, right?"

"Yeah, my dad told me I have an older brother named Lionel, he was like ten or so when I was born."

"Okay, so that's not something you don't already know. That's good. Stephanie had him right after she turned eighteen. She ended up going to summer school to graduate high school, but she was determined to graduate and raise her son."

"That's pretty admirable."

"Yeah, she did what she had to do. Now, Stephanie and Lionel's father, his name was George, they were on and off a lot, but George always made sure his son was taken care of. He was determined to make sure Lionel didn't grow up without a father. But the police had other plans."

"The police?" Ann had not been told previously what happened to her brother's father, but her heart broke with the feeling of what was coming next.

"Have you ever heard of the STRESS unit?"

"Uh, no."

Glenda explained. "You heard of Larry Nevers, the cop that was part of the Malice Green killing back in '92?"

"Yeah."

"Well, he was part of the STRESS unit — STRESS was a special unit of the Detroit Police back in the early seventies. The politicians sold it as their plan to make the streets safer, but what they *really* did was that they set us up and put a target on the backs of Black men, and because of them, a whole lot of our young men were sent behind bars and even killed."

"Oh wow, Miss Glenda, I had no idea."

"Yeah, well, Lionel's father got caught up with them, and got killed in, I wanna say...'73. Lionel was real young, around three or so, barely even had a chance to know his father."

"Aw man, that's so sad." Ann shook her head mournfully.

"Yeah," Glenda sighed. "See, that really messed with Stephanie's head. She was different anyway, she struggled with talking to a lot of people. But after George was killed, damn. She felt so bad, she didn't know how to deal with it. She had nightmares; she'd occasionally do things to try to forget. You know, it *was* the seventies. But the thing is, she didn't wanna go see a shrink."

"Why?"

"She didn't want to end up like her mother. She was sent to Eloise and never came back."

"Eloise?"

"Eloise — the mental hospital, it's long closed now, I think they closed it down in the early eighties."

"Oh, okay. Wow."

"Yeah, Stephanie was so afraid of being sent there just like her mother. And she didn't want to do that to Lionel since he already lost his dad."

"Uh...that's a lot to deal with. I can't imagine."

"Yeah, I can't either, but the thing is, Stephanie was strong, still is. She just kept going. Figured she had to. She eventually found fitness, and it was her outlet. I guess it was a way to get out her anger, a way to gain some control where she didn't have a whole lot of it in other parts of her life."

"I can see that."

"Yeah, but anyway, all of that with her mother and her son's father, that's what I mean by baggage. She had quite a bit of it and some days were better than others. I don't know for sure, but I would imagine that factored into why her marriage to your father fell apart."

"Um, I could see that. I know my dad would say she had mental health issues, so that would make sense."

Glenda nodded. "Yeah, it does. But what really upset me is what happened *after* they divorced. Baby girl, I know you love your father, so I don't want to make you upset with what really went down. I don't know if you're ready for all of that," Glenda warned.

"My dad's not here anymore. And besides, Miss Glenda, we've gone this far." Ann shrugged. "I guess the truth will make me free."

Glenda laughed along with her. "You remind me a lot of Stephanie, she's the kind of woman who insists on staring at the needle going straight in when she gets a shot. She'll tell me, 'Glenda, gimme the full-on truth, straight no chaser!'"

"Yeah, I feel that."

Glenda began recounting the story. "So, after your parents got divorced, Marshall moved back in with his mother for a while to have somebody he trusted to be there to care for you while he was at work, and they shared custody of you while the courts were sorting it all out. And I guess that was real messy."

"I know, I've seen the custody papers."

"So, you have some idea. Well, here's the thing. Court was full of drama, but at the time they had joint custody and both of 'em kept it together and didn't fight in your presence. I respected that a lot. And then, one night, I got a call."

September 1981

On a cool September evening, Glenda was settling into her soft brown couch in the living room to watch "Archie Bunker's Place" on television. She was waiting for her husband to arrive home from work when the telephone rang. She leaned over to the end table to answer it.

"Hello?"

"Uh, hi, Glenda — it's me, Stephanie," a distressed voice uttered on the other end of the line.

"Oh, um, hi, Stephy...sounds like something's wrong. What's going on?"

"Marshall didn't bring Ann back home."

"What?" Glenda sat straight up, alert.

"He didn't bring Ann back. He had her for the weekend like he normally does, and he's supposed to bring her back every Sunday night by five o'clock. And he's always good about that. But this time he didn't show up, and nobody's answering the phone at his mom's."

"Okay. I'ma come over as soon as Reggie gets home."

Once Glenda's husband arrived home fifteen minutes later, she advised him of the situation, donned a blue cardigan for warmth, and left. She quickly walked over to Stephanie's house, which was halfway down the block from hers. The home was a small brick bungalow with mint green awnings shading the front windows.

She headed up the concrete stairs to the front porch and rang the doorbell mounted next to the white-painted metal security door.

Stephanie answered the front door, her face streaked with tears. All she could do was open the security door to let Glenda in. She quietly took her place on the couch while eleven-year-old Lionel was sitting on the floor watching *CHiPs*.

"Hi, Mrs. Townsend. Have you seen my sister?" Lionel asked in a soft voice.

"No baby, I haven't, but we'll find her, I'm sure of it," Glenda responded.

She then spoke to Stephanie. "Have you gone by Marshall's house to see if he's there?"

Stephanie silently shook her head.

Glenda spoke to Lionel. "Lionel, put on your jacket. We're all going for a ride." She then directed Stephanie. "Wash your face and put a sweater on. It's a bit windy outside."

The three took a short walk over to Glenda's tan Dodge Aries and got in. Glenda drove them to the home of Estelle Corbin, where Marshall was now living. The house was located in the Boston-Edison District, an older neighborhood with large, manicured homes just north of Detroit's New Center area.

The K-Car came to a complete stop at a stately Italianate house on Chicago Boulevard. The home was adorned with a beige stucco exterior and dark caramel trim. Glenda turned around and told Lionel, who was sitting in the back seat, "Wait here."

The women got out of the car and walked up the stairs to the front door. Glenda knocked.

Several seconds later, an elderly, light-skinned petite woman answered the door. She trained her eyes on Stephanie, who was at eye level with her, then on Glenda. Her slate grey eyes shot daggers into Stephanie. She spoke curtly, "Marshall is not here."

Glenda responded. "Mrs. Corbin, we're looking for Ann. Marshall didn't bring her back to Stephanie's house earlier when he was supposed to."

Estelle glanced at Glenda, then stared at Stephanie, lips pursed. "Ann is just fine. She is with her father. He'll bring her back when he's ready." She then slammed the door in their faces.

The friends returned to the car. Stephanie broke her silence, whimpering, "How am I gonna get my baby back?"

Glenda suggested, "Let's go to the cops."

"Oh no, I don't wanna deal with no cops. They won't do shit."

"I know, I know, Stephy. But look, we might as well give 'em a try. It's better than doing nothing."

The friends next stopped at a local police precinct located a few blocks from Estelle's home. With Lionel tagging along, they all walked in. A woman in a light blue police uniform and brunette bun sat at the front desk equipped with a typewriter. After several seconds, she looked up at the group. "Hello, how can I help you?"

Stephanie spoke. "Uh, hi. My daughter is missing."

The officer grabbed a piece of paper, fed it into the typewriter, and began typing. "What is your name, ma'am?"

"Stephanie Corbin."

"And you said it is your daughter that's missing?

"Yes."

"What is your daughter's name?"

"Ann Leigh Corbin."

"What is her age?"

"She's seventeen months."

The officer typed in the response. "Black?"

"Yes."

"Female," she said slowly, typing the description. "Hair?"

"Brown."

"Eyes?"

"Grey."

The woman looked up and hesitated. "Grey?"

"Yes, grey, " Stephanie reiterated.

"Alrighty then." The officer hesitantly continued typing. "Any identifying marks?"

"A birthmark on her right arm, uh...upper arm."

"When was she last seen?"

"A couple days ago, Friday morning."

The officer inquired, "Was she last seen with anyone?"

"Marshall Harris Corbin."

"Can you describe him?"

Stephanie stammered, "Y-yes."

"Age?"

"Twenty-eight."

"Height?"

"Six feet."

The policewoman started on her next piece of paper, feeding it into the typewriter. "Weight or body type?"

"He's three-hundred and forty pounds, so um...big."

"Race?"

"Black."

"Complexion?"

"Light, very light."

"Hair color?"

"Red."

The officer looked up at Stephanie, eyebrow arched, then kept going. "Eye color?"

"Hazel."

"Is he related in any way to you or your daughter?"

"Yes, he's my ex-husband and my child's father."

The officer stopped and stared at the distraught mother. "Ma'am, you said she was last seen with her father?"

"Yes."

Glenda interjected. "He was supposed to drop her off today at five o'clock, but he never showed up."

"Well, if it's a matter of your daughter being with her parent in a shared custody arrangement, that's a civil matter," the officer explained to Stephanie.

"But if he didn't drop her off, aren't y'all supposed to look into it, you know, make sure nothing happened to her? Isn't that what police are supposed to do?" Glenda pushed back incredulously.

The woman sighed and turned back to Stephanie. "Okay, ma'am. One of our officers can call up the local morgue and hospitals to see if anyone fitting your daughter's description has turned up there. But if that is not the case, we would consider this a civil matter and we won't be able to help you."

The officer then picked up the receiver of a glossy black telephone and rotary dialed a few numbers.

"Officer Stanczyk, come down to the front desk, please." She then hung up and said to Stephanie. "Ma'am, you'll wanna have a seat over there," pointing to a small waiting area with white plastic chairs. "We're going to make some calls, and we'll be back with you in a moment."

Stephanie, Lionel, and Glenda sat in the waiting area. Lionel was growing tired and leaned his head on his mother. A tall male police officer with a bushy brown mustache came to the front desk and briefly conversed with the desk officer. She then handed him the report she typed, and he walked away with it

After about two hours, the male officer returned.

"Which one of you is Stephanie Corbin?"

Stephanie raised her right hand.

"Hi, Ms. Corbin, I am Officer Will Stanczyk, and I was given the missing persons report for your daughter Ann."

Stephanie nodded.

"We've called all the hospital emergency rooms within a thirty-mile radius of here, as well as put in a call to the morgue. The good news is that no one fitting her description has turned up in any of those locations."

"That's good, but what does that mean? How can I find my baby?"

Officer Stanczyk sighed. "Welp, in the vast majority of these cases, children turn up within a few days. Especially since she was last seen with her father, he probably decided to spend a little extra time with her, maybe went on vacation, took her with him and he just forgot to mention it to you."

"A one-year-old, though?" Glenda pushed back.

"Yes, these things happen, we've been seeing it more and more the last few years. At this point, without any evidence to the contrary, our hands are tied."

"What?" Stephanie was exasperated.

Glenda spoke up. "Really, you're telling us there's nothing else that can be done? Are you for real?"

"Ma'am," he said, "How are you related to the missing person?"

"I'm a family friend, I brought her over here."

Stephanie cut in. "It's fine sir, she's like a sister to me."

Officer Stanczyk nodded his head. "Ma'am," he told Glenda, "I understand your frustration. There is only so much we can do on our end, but it doesn't mean nothing can be done at all." He then turned back to Stephanie. "Ms. Corbin, is there a custody agreement in place?"

Stephanie responded, "There's a temporary one. We got divorced a short time ago, and we're still working on a long-term custody arrangement. Right now, I have Ann during the week, and Marshall gets her on weekends."

"Okay, what you'll want to do is this. First thing tomorrow morning, if your ex-husband still doesn't bring back your daughter, call your attorney and let him know what happened. He can then file papers and go back to the judge. The courts can compel your ex-husband to appear, and to produce your daughter. At that point, we would be able to step in if needed. But not before then."

"Okay, sir."

"We'll get a few more details from you, and then we'll file the report. At the very least, we'll have something on file documenting this matter. I'm sorry we're not able to do more for you right now."

The group left the police precinct and returned to Stephanie's home. They walked inside and Glenda quickly straightened up the living room and kitchen, while Stephanie sat on the felt orange couch, stressed and speechless.

Glenda instructed the boy, "Lionel baby, it's late, and you have school tomorrow. It's time for you to go to the bathroom, and wash your face and hands, and get ready for bed.

"Okay, Mrs. Townsend. Do you think I'll see my sister again?"

"I'm sure you will. We will, baby. Say your prayers and go to sleep." She hugged him. He then hugged his despondent mother before disappearing into the hallway to get ready for bed.

Glenda cleaned up the kitchen table and called out to Stephanie, while she lay on the couch. "Stephy, you'll want to call your lawyer now."

"But I'm sure they're closed, it's Sunday night."

"Well, they should have some kind of after-hours number, or at least an answering service. They're a law firm and situations change quickly."

Stephanie leaned over, grabbed her address book, and found her lawyer's phone number. After several rings, a professional female voice answered.

"Cipriani and Stone Law Firm after-hours answering service, how may I help you?"

"Hi, um, I'm a client of Mr. Stone, he is representing me in my divorce and custody cases. We're in the middle of the custody case, and my ex-husband has taken our baby and hasn't brought her back from visitation. I figured he should know now rather than later, um, so the court can order him to bring her back."

"Yes, what is your name?"

"Stephanie Corbin."

After a few seconds, the after-hours receptionist told her, "I have written down your message and will relay it to Mr. Jeffrey Stone so he may call you back."

"Thank you."

A few minutes later, the phone rang. Stephanie answered it.

"Hello?"

"Thank you. I will connect you to Mr. Jeffrey Stone's home phone. Please hold."

After another few rounds of rings, a deep male voice answered the phone.

"Hello?"

"Hello, may I speak to Mrs. Stephanie Corbin?"

"Uh, yes, this is she."

"Hi, Mrs. Corbin, I'm Jeffrey Stone returning your call. How may I help you?"

"Yes, thanks Mr. Stone for returning my call. Marshall didn't bring Ann back from visitation earlier. I went by his mother's house and she said he wasn't there. We made a police report and everything, but they said it's civil, that I need to let you know."

Mr. Stone cleared his throat as if he were perking up. "Oh, I see Mrs. Corbin, that's not good. I can file a motion with the court to have Marshall appear. But if I do this, this will become a more protracted court case, and the retainer won't cover it."

"What? How much more do you need?" Stephanie asked.

"We're looking at another fifteen hundred dollars."

"Are you serious? There's no way. I work as a financial aid clerk at Wayne State. There's no way I can come up with that kind of money," Stephanie responded, exasperated.

"I understand and sympathize with the position that you're in, Mrs. Corbin. Unfortunately, we don't work for free, and when we start getting into trying to locate a respondent, protracted disputes, kidnapping, things like that, those actions do cost quite a bit of money."

She sighed. "I understand. When do you need this by?"

"Once you're able to send us the money, we can get to work bringing Marshall back into court and forcing him legally to produce your daughter."

"Thank you."

After the call, Stephanie began crying uncontrollably.

"What's wrong?"

"The lawyer wants another fifteen hundred before he does anything else. There's no way I can come up with that. I can barely keep the lights on with how much this case is costing me. There's no way! What if I never see my baby again?"

Glenda rushed to the couch and held her broken best friend.

Ann was blown away. "Oh wow. That's so heartbreaking...I really can't imagine. Did anything else happen after that, Miss Glenda?"

Glenda sighed. "Not really. Your mother had a real hard time dealing with you not being there, she wanted to keep fighting but she didn't have the money and nowhere to get it from. We were all living paycheck to paycheck at that time."

"That's rough."

"Your mother was so broken. Not long after that, she was sent to Eloise for a little while, about a month or two. After they let her out, she felt like she had to keep it together for Lionel, so she left well enough alone after that."

"Oh wow. I don't know what to say."

"I hope you know, Ann, it's not your fault. Your mother didn't just abandon you. She didn't just disappear; she really did try. In a perfect world, could she have done more? Maybe...I don't know.

But the way I see it, your mother did the best she could given her situation. She didn't have as many resources as your father, and she had a lot of ghosts she was battling. I think she deserved a better hand than she was dealt, but sometimes life is like that."

Ann felt stirred up with emotion.

"She moved on as well as she could. For a while, she would drive by your grandmother's house, and she hoped she would see you outside, but she never did."

"Wow..."

"She ended up earning a master's at Wayne State and became a math teacher for several years. Later on, she had two more kids. You have another half-brother and a half-sister as well. They're twins, a little bit younger than you but they're both grown, graduated high school last year. They're in college now."

The young woman was a bit overwhelmed taking in all this new information. "Where is Stephanie now?"

"She's still in Detroit. We still talk quite a bit, mainly over the phone. I still go up there every once in a while and I stop by and see her when I'm in town."

Taking a deep breath, Ann felt a bit of courage. She always had this one question but was afraid of the answer. Now, she finally asked it. "Do you think she would ever want to meet me?"

Glenda smiled. "Of course she would. She's still in the same house she lived in when your father took you away. She's never said, at least to me, but I figured she wanted to stay there so you could find your way home."

Ann was verklempt.

"I know your mother still thinks about you a lot, she still brings you up when we talk. She'll look at the sky, and see the moon, and think about how, no matter where you are, you're under the exact same moon, so you're not that far away from her. Even though you left her arms, you never left her heart."

The tears fell from Ann's face. Glenda leaned over and gave her tissues.

"There's somebody else that you'll want to talk to. I think it would be even better if Stephanie learned from him that we found you." She picked up a notepad and wrote down a telephone number and a name.

Lionel (317)555-0224

Ann read it, noticed the area code, and remarked, "Huh, 317? Where's that?"

"Indianapolis," Glenda advised. "He lives only two hours away."

"Oh wow, that's not that far."

"Nope, not at all."

"Does he know you found me?"

"Yes. Yes, he does."

EVERYTHING DIES HERE

JUNE 2003

A week after the conversation with Glenda, Ann drove to Detroit for the weekend to spend time with her family. The road trip gave her a chance to think.

The story Glenda shared regarding Stephanie's disappearance from Ann's life was much different from what Marshall had told her years before, and admittedly, he had not told her much. But one aspect that bothered her about Glenda's account was that if it were true, her father's behavior sounded out of character for who she had always known him to be – an empathetic person who had a passion for keeping children physically safe and emotionally well, and to Ann's knowledge, had a whole lot more friends than enemies.

Once in the Detroit metropolitan area, Ann made her way to Sherrye's new home in the northeast suburb of Saint Clair Shores. Since Marshall's untimely death, Sherrye struggled with the overflow of memories of her husband everywhere in the family home in the city and could not shake the horrifying flashbacks of his end from a hemorrhagic stroke. Feeling that she needed to escape Marshall's ghost and reclaim some semblance of peace, she sold the house on Grayton Street and moved north of Eight Mile Road, settling down in the bedroom community of Saint Clair Shores. Since the suburb was only a few miles away from the old neighborhood, it allowed Michelle to stay at her high school and maintain cherished friendships.

The new home was a brick mid-century modern ranch with one main floor and a finished basement. It was somewhat smaller than the old house but had three bedrooms, so Ann would still have a bedroom when she came to visit.

Once arriving, she fed Charlie and had a seat on the front porch. Sherrye came out to join her, sitting down on a matching beige plastic lawn chair.

"Annie, remember when you were a kid, and you and Michelle would have to rake the leaves and mow the lawn on the weekends when it was warm?"

"Yeah, Mom...and Dad would come outside and just watch us do work and direct us – he would be 'supervising.'" Ann recalled with a laugh.

"Oh, I *know!*" Sherrye chuckled.

Looking out on the much larger plot of land the small bungalow sat on, Ann quipped, "At least the lawn on Grayton was smaller. I can't imagine us mowing the lawn over here!"

Both laughed, then Sherrye switched the topic. "How was your visit with Stephanie's friend?"

"It was fine."

"I know you're secretive and you don't like me prying in your business. You're just like your father."

Ann shook her head, "You know, I'm not secretive Mom, I just don't always think to tell you everything." Yes that, but really, it's that I want to figure out how to do things my way. Mom means well and she cares, but I don't need her to push me to do things I feel uncomfortable doing, like talking to people or discussing something with others as if I'm incapable of doing it myself.

"Okay, darling."

But I'm probably going to tell her anyway because she's Mom and deep down, I care about what she thinks. Damn, I'm messed up.

Ann opened up. "Well Mom, the meeting was fine. Miss Glenda talked about how Dad and Stephanie knew each other as kids but they lost touch until they became adults. They found they had fitness and bodybuilding in common and reunited at an event downtown in the late '70s."

"Oh wow...I didn't know that."

"Neither did I. So, she talked about how they got married, I was born, they got divorced, that part you already know."

"Uh-huh."

"But according to her, Stephanie didn't give me away. Dad had me for visitation one weekend and didn't return me. And she wanted to fight, but she didn't have the finances to keep going, and that was that."

After Ann finished, Sherrye shrugged. "Yeah, sounds like your father."

"Really?"

"Oh yes. Think about it. Your dad was very stubborn. You don't get to be a lawyer like him without being stubborn. And you know he worried a lot about you. When you were younger, especially when we lived in Florida, the thing he was scared of the most was the thought of you going missing...you ending up on the side of a milk carton."

"I remember him saying that, but I thought it was because he was overprotective and it was the eighties."

"Yes, dear, it was the eighties and a lot of kids went missing back then, but it was more than that. He was so deathly afraid of losing you. And when he and Stephanie got divorced, he was afraid that would happen."

"Ah."

"Did he do the right thing? Probably not, but I don't know. I wasn't there, and knowing him, he probably shared as much with me as he did with you. But I believe that at the time, he thought he was doing the right thing."

Ann nodded. "Yeah."

Sherrye continued. "You know, I've seen pictures of Stephanie with you when you were a baby. You looked very well taken care of."

"Okay, that's good."

"As a mother, I truly believe that she loved you just as much as your father did. I really do. But people oftentimes do the best they can with the hand they've been dealt. Your father did the best he could with the understanding and the knowledge he had at the time. And I think she did the same."

"Mom, if I end up having the opportunity to meet Stephanie, will you be okay with that?"

"Of course. I always felt like it was important for you to meet your biological mother. I know your dad didn't like that idea, but I *always* felt like you should. And really," Sherrye added, smiling, "I'm not worried about being replaced. You're not going to replace me!"

They both laughed and hugged.

❧

During Ann's visit to the Detroit area, she paid her uncle Louie and aunt Eliza a visit. The day after her arrival, she stopped by their home in Palmer Woods. After being let in, she entered the spacious kitchen and sat at the chrome-lined table with her uncle and aunt.

"Would you like anything to drink?" Eliza asked.

"Sure, Auntie Liza. What do you have?"

Eliza scanned the counter, then briefly checked the refrigerator. "We have pop...Pepsi and Faygo RedPop, we have lemonade, and we have water."

Ann paused for a moment to decide. "I'll have some RedPop please."

Eliza stood up and grabbed a glass from the dark-stained wooden cabinet above the countertop. She then filled it with ice from the refrigerator door, poured from a previously unopened two-liter pop bottle on the counter, and handed it to Ann.

"Thank you." Ann took a sip of her pop.

"You're welcome, Annie." Eliza then poured lemonade for herself and her husband and sat at the table.

Louie turned to Ann. "When I drink pop, I like to dilute it with a little water. That way it cuts down on the sugar. It's better for my diabetes."

"Thanks, Uncle Louie. I'll try that sometime. I don't want any part of diabetes."

"I don't blame you. I don't want that for you either. I would try to tell your dad, but he wouldn't listen. Hopefully, you'll learn from what happened to him."

Ann nodded.

"So, I know you wanted to learn more about your mother, Stephanie."

"Yes, I do. Um...last week, I met with her best friend Glenda who now lives in Losanti, and we talked awhile."

"Hmm, small world, isn't it?" Eliza quipped.

Ann chuckled. "For sure. So, Glenda told me her version of what happened between my dad and my birth mother. According to her, he basically took off during a visitation and didn't return me, and that was that."

"Hmm..." Louie slowly nodded.

"It's kind of confusing, you know? My dad would always say she had mental health issues and she *chose* to give me to my dad."

"I don't know if your dad took you during a visitation or how all that went down, but it wasn't like he was that hard to find. He had moved out of the house he shared with your mother after the divorce, and he took you over to your Big Mama's house. You both stayed there the whole time until the custody case finished up."

"Oh, okay."

"Yeah, that custody case...you know, your dad being a lawyer himself, he had a lot of money for good representation and he could afford to wait her out. Stephanie...she was kind of shy and soft-spoken, but she wasn't crazy."

"Yeah, that's what Glenda was pretty much saying."

"Now, could she have come by the house while y'all were still in Detroit? Probably. But Annie – I really don't believe your mother let go of you willingly."

"From what her friend said, she did go by the house, but Big Mama didn't tell her where I was."

Louie shrugged. "I don't know. I would guess though that with them having problems, she wanted to protect her baby boy. Your dad was always your Big Mama's favorite. But see, I remember when your dad decided to move to Florida and take you with him. Mama and I both told him not to do it, but you know your dad, he went and did what he was gonna do."

April 1982

On a rainy Sunday morning, sixty-eight-year-old Estelle Corbin attended morning church service at Zion Hope Missionary Baptist Church. After four hours of the main service and Sunday school, she returned to her home on Chicago Boulevard in the early afternoon. Louie was visiting, chatting with Marshall in the living room, while two-year-old Ann was sitting in a brown metal walker next to the plastic-covered tan and orange-striped Davenport. She was content after being fed a meal of chicken and peas from baby food cans.

After Estelle entered and greeted her boys and granddaughter, she took off her plastic headscarf, lowered her umbrella and closed the door. She then placed her brown leather purse and worn Bible on the polished wooden coffee table. She picked Ann up from the walker, sat down, and held her in her arms.

"Hey, baby Annie," she cooed to the smiling, quiet child. "I hope your dad fed you and changed you while I was gone."

"Of course I did," Marshall mused. "You know I take good care of her."

"How was church?" Louie asked.

"It was good," Estelle responded. "Pastor Jenkins was talking about patience. That sermon stirred me in my spirit. I know you're worried about Annie not talking yet, but we've got to be patient. It'll come."

Marshall inhaled deeply. "I know, Mama."

"The church is praying, too."

"Tell 'em I appreciate it."

"Now, on a Sunday morning, you both should be going with me, instead of lounging around. It's never too early for Jesus, and it shows him you're faithful."

Louie sighed. "You know, work's crazy right now, I gotta get my rest when I can. Tell Pastor Jenkins I'll be back once things calm down at the plant, I promise."

"I will. Now what about you, Marshall? Maybe you should come and bring Annie with you. Maybe being around other kids will help her get to talking."

"Ugh...I dunno," Marshall uttered wearily. "So, Mama, I wanted to talk to you about something."

"Of course. What's going on?"

"I'm looking to move back to Florida."

Estelle shot her youngest son an angry look. "Why would you do that?"

"To be real, it'll give me some distance from things here."

"Distance?"

"Yeah. Everything reminds me of what Stephanie and I had. But then she started falling apart. I tried so hard to keep us together, but love wasn't enough. I couldn't keep living in that misery and I don't want Ann to grow up seeing that."

Louie cocked his head to the side. "Marshall, that don't make no sense. She's still at the house on Sorrento. It's not like you're gonna run into her over here, and you know she don't go nowhere."

"Nah, brother. You know we're not that far from the old neighborhood. You forget...I've known her since we were kids. And I've loved her since then, too. I still do. Y'all think that it was easy for me to leave her, to get a divorce. It really wasn't. You don't get it. I *need* to start over."

"I hear you, Marshall, but—"

"And then, I had to sell my stake in the gym to pay the attorneys for the divorce, and last month, my partner ended up having to shut it down."

"You know I could've helped you with those lawyer fees. You did not need to sell your business," Marshall's mother reminded him.

"Mama, I could never ask you to bail me out like that. I'm supposed to take care of *you*, not the other way around, and I already feel bad enough that I'm living with you right now. Everything dies here." Marshall paused for a moment to gain his composure. "Anyway, I *really* need to start over."

"But what about Annie?"

"I'm bringing her with me," Marshall said.

"Oh no you won't!"

"Your family is *here*. You're a single father and you need to have family around," Louie calmly advised.

Marshall tried to reassure his family. "I mean, it's not like I won't bring her up here to visit."

"You're really taking Annie away from her *mother*. You're wrong for that, Marshall. Dead wrong," Estelle admonished him.

"When's the last time she's come over here to see her?"

"She hasn't, but maybe give her time and she can be there for her baby. But it's hard to do that if y'all are in Florida and she's still up here. Look, now that you're done with court, maybe you can bring Annie over there sometime."

He shook his head. "No...no Mama. I can't do that. It's like I told you, Stephanie needs *help*."

"I know...but if she sees her baby, that'll give her the strength to get that help."

"No...no way. She's not going to get it, even for the sake of the baby. I'm Ann's father, it's my job to protect her. Ann needs stability."

"Annie needs *her mother*."

Marshall silently stared at his incensed mother.

"Whatever happened between you two, Stephanie is still her mother. She might not be perfect, and she might have her problems, but she's still her mother."

With that, Estelle stood up while carrying the baby and left the room.

"So, Annie, your father ended up moving you down to Florida anyway, and y'all were there for four and a half years before you came back," Louie explained.

Ann shook her head. "That's crazy. Why did he decide to finally come back?"

"Well, he met Sherrye while he was down there...she was working down at the courthouse, and they got matched up by a mutual friend. You know, she's from Michigan too, Benton Harbor, and she got sick and tired of Florida and wanted to be closer to her family. So, after a while, he finally gave in and moved back up here."

"Okay...but Benton Harbor's on the other side of the state. If that's why, I'm surprised he didn't just move us there instead of coming back to Detroit."

"Well, Detroit's a bigger city, probably more clients, easier to practice law and make a good living," Eliza noted.

"Uh-huh, and after your Big Mama died, I think he finally realized he needed to have family around, especially as you were getting older," Louie added. "But I wish he hadn't shut your mother out of your life. You deserved to know her. You still do."

UNAVAILABLE
JUNE 2003

The weather was heating up on a humid Friday in late June 2003. The streets of downtown Losanti were filled with hordes of Green Sox baseball fans excited to experience an evening interleague matchup between the hometown team and the Detroit Tigers.

Due to the game, employees at the Nichols Agency were encouraged to wear sports-themed clothing to work. After hours, the agency's analytics department planned a happy hour outing at the Losanti Shanty, where the outdoor seating area was reserved and they would be provided food and drinks.

At one of the tables on the patio sat Ann and a few of her colleagues. All were served beer, wine, and spirits courtesy of the agency.

"So, how is the world of academic analytics?" Rob asked Gwen and Brian.

"It's great," Gwen answered. "We're gaining so much insight into the worldview of college students and how that affects their buying habits and political behavior. Brands do well with them as a demo when they cater their messaging to their concerns."

"Oh yes, of course."

"Yeah, and we're also seeing a lot of good data regarding their political behavior and how candidates can get them engaged, because young people typically don't vote as often. It's an untapped demo," Brian added.

"That's great and all," Jason chimed in, "but it's the weekend. Do we really wanna talk shop?"

Everyone at the table shook their heads.

"Let's talk about the game," Jason said. "The Green Sox have got to win this."

"Anything to get closer to .500," Rob responded. "But I know you feel differently, Ann."

Ann, who was wearing a cap with an old English "D," laughed. "I mean, I root for the Green Sox unless they play Detroit. Can't go against my Tiges."

Jason understood. "I feel you."

Trevor, who had been sitting at another table, came over to the table where Ann was sitting and placed his hand on Gwen's shoulder.

"Gwen...you're so hot. I know I'm just a regular nice guy...but give me a chance, let me take you out to dinner, and after that...we can go to my place...and...I'll rock your world!"

Her face contorted as she brushed his hand off her shoulder. "Trevor, how many have you had?"

"Uh...only like three or four. I'm fine. I...I mean it. Offer's still on the table."

"We've only been here an hour," she pointed out to him. "You're drunk. Call a taxi. Go home. Chad's coming down soon. Do not let him see you like this."

"Ugh, don't be such a bitch...you're missing out," he slurred.

"Bro, you heard her," Jason told him forcefully. "She's doing you a solid. Go down the street, catch a cab, get outta here."

To that, Trevor stood and ambled away. A few minutes later, he could be seen entering a taxi cab that stopped along the same block.

As the night flew by and more drinks flowed, the coworkers continued to enjoy each other's company.

"Gwen," Brian looked over to her. "I heard you recently broke up with your boyfriend. So sorry to hear that."

"It's fine. Things weren't working out for quite some time. We just needed to go our separate ways."

"That's understandable," he commiserated as he took a swig of his ale. "I'm sure you already know I got divorced last year. My wife and I...it was hard. We just weren't compatible, if you know what I mean. A guy's got needs."

"Bro, we don't need to hear about your needs!" Rob yelled.

"Yeah yeah. I know, man. Too much info." He then turned to his right. "You're an enigma, Ann. We never hear about your relationships, any dates, or anything."

"Well, uh..." she began while nursing a Cuervo and Sprite. "There's not much to tell. I've gone out with people, but nothing of note at this point."

"Huh. Not surprised."

What's that supposed to mean?

Then, Gwen turned and asked, "Have you thought about Trevor?"

"No, why?" *They have no idea. Ugh.*

"I mean, he's a little young and he comes off kinda stupid, but y'all work together well. Your brains can make up for his dumb."

"Hell no."

"Oh, why not?" Brian inquired. "I know Black girls aren't into white guys, but it's something to think about. Are you mixed?"

Ann narrowed her eyes at his continued audacity. "What? No, I have two Black parents, I'm just light. We come in all shades. And there are Black women who date white men – I never said I wasn't open to that – just not Trevor."

"What's wrong with Trevor, though?"

Ann shook her head, and having had a couple of drinks, the booze began to hit, loosening her tongue. "Do you even hear yourselves? We literally just saw him hit on Gwen. He was fawning all over her and acted like a dick when she said 'no' to him. Why would I even be interested in that? Do I look that desperate to you? And we're literally on the same team. I don't shit where I eat."

Brian took a long sip of his beer and shrugged. "Fair enough."

At the end of the night, Ann offered to take Gwen and Brian home. She had cut herself off early and had since sobered up, and her colleagues lived fairly close to her apartment.

When they arrived at Gwen's apartment in Mount Eve, she asked, "Hey guys, why don't you stick around a little bit before you head back?"

Ann accepted the invitation. "Yeah, sure. Are you good with that, Brian?"

"Yeah, that'll be fun. Not like I have anywhere to be."

After parking on the street, they followed their colleague up the inside stairs to her second-floor unit. When she unlocked the door, they took in a neat unit furnished in various shades of brown and red. She turned on a black CD player on an end table, which began playing "Boadicea" by Enya. A golden Pomeranian jumped around excitedly on Gwen's loveseat.

Gwen gave excited pets and face scritches to the dog as it wagged its tail in exuberance. "Who's a good Killer? Who's a good Killer?"

She then turned to her visitors. "Figure we can hang out a little while, chat, play Yahtzee. Have a seat on the couch. I'll be back in a second."

Ann was unsure of what she heard. "Your dog's name is *Killer*?"

"Yeah...Killer. She's a sweetie. I appreciate the irony." As she said this, the dog's tongue drooped from her mouth and she sat, relaxed.

Once Gwen disappeared down the hallway, Killer hopped to the sofa and sat on the cushion between the two guests. The dog wagged her tail as Ann gave her gentle back pets. "Beautiful dog."

"It's alright, but something about it reminds me of a cat. When I was married, we had a cat. Kind of looked like ol' Killer here. Orange with long hair. It sucked."

"Eh, I don't know about that. I don't have cats, but I think they're cute and they're pretty independent. If I wasn't living in an apartment and didn't already have a dog, I'd get one."

"Ann, you're a woman, that makes sense. Cats are too feminine, too dainty. My ex-wife took the cat in the divorce, I said, 'See ya!'"

The dog looked up at Brian, her expression morphed in the absence of her master. *Grrr!*

He boasted, "Look at this. I'm totally a dog whisperer. I'll get it chilled out."

Ann shook her head. "Uh...I don't think that's a good idea, Brian."

"No, it's fine. Watch this." He lifted his hand and inched it toward the agitated Pom. "Hi, doggy! You're a friendly one, aren't you? Aren't you?"

The dog leapt and sunk her teeth into the cuff of his dark blue dress shirt shirt.

"Ahhh! The fuck!" He shook his arm violently, but the angry pooch held on with a vice grip.

"I told you, Brian…"

"Oh God! Gwen! Gwen! Get this stupid dog off me!" he screamed.

Gwen ran out upon hearing the commotion, dressed in pink plaid pajama pants and a matching demi bra. "What the hell happened?"

"I was just sitting here and your dog came over and attacked me!"

With a sharp "Killer! Heel!" command, the dog stopped, and she scooped her up in her arms.

Brian looked himself over and found that other than two minor scratches and a bit of wounded pride, he was uninjured.

"That's so weird," Gwen said, petting her agitated Pom. "I don't know what happened. I'm so sorry."

"Killer…not a lot of irony there," Brian quipped. "Anyway, it's alright, Gwen. I'm fine." He then stood and stepped into her space, angry canine be damned. "Hey look, I'm thinking we're compatible, you're my type, we should go out and see where things go."

Her voice wavered. "You're a sweet guy and I love working with you, but I don't know about going out."

"Uh…Gwen, we should probably take off," Ann suggested.

"Yeah, that sounds like a good idea."

She started heading towards the door, gently guiding Brian her way. "Thanks for having us over."

"Yeah, thanks for hanging out."

Brian slurred, "Think about it, Gwen."

"Yeah, sure," Gwen replied halfheartedly as she and Ann guided their coworker out of her home.

It was nearly nine o'clock in the evening when they returned to Norris Park. Brian lived on a residential street nearby, dotted with bungalows. Upon arriving at his home, a small white house with a brick porch, she pulled over to let him out.

He stared into her eyes, and then placed his warm hand on her right thigh.

"Ann, you look so cute and sexy. I'm sure you don't hear that a lot, but more men should tell you that because it's true."

She froze up.

"I've always loved caramel goddesses, especially the ones with a bit of something extra. I know we work together, but there's something here and we shouldn't let that stop us."

He just got done trying to ask Gwen out. I'm not gonna be the last call fat girl, some kind of pity lay.

He then leaned in, attempting to kiss her.

She pulled away. "No, Brian. This isn't happening. I'll see you Monday in the office."

He sighed and backed off. "Alright, Ann. I'll see you at work." With that, he got out of her car and entered his home.

As Ann walked through the doorway of her apartment unit after the work outing, her cell phone rang. She picked it up in haste, neglecting to check the display to see who was calling.

"Hello?"

"Hey, AC. It's Luke."

"Oh, hey Luke."

"Is everything okay? It's been a few weeks and you haven't called me back."

She rolled her eyes. "Is everything okay with us? Like, our friendship? Apparently not. I don't know why you're even calling."

"What?" He sounded surprised.

"Dude, now you're acting as if you forgot. Paul called me a few weeks ago to tell me that you said I was too dependent on you, but you didn't have the heart to tell me to back off."

He sighed. "Oh, that…"

"Yeah, *that*."

"Ugh," he groaned. "About that…I was in a shit mood, and everything was pissing me off. I've been having a rough term and my parents have been pissing me off. So, I was talking to Paulie and it came up that we were spending a lot of time together…and I got it in my head that, y'know, what if you thought we were becoming more than friends?"

"What? That's stupid." *Is this what we're doing?*

"Yeah, I guess so. But I dunno. Y'know, sometimes I feel like you trigger my obsessions."

Ann was at a loss for words.

Luke continued. "AC, I know you still like me and you wanna be with me, and I can't stop thinking about that, and it really bothers me. So, Paulie was saying that if I wanted us to stop hanging out so much, so you don't get the wrong idea, I should tell you, but I think I told him I'd just figure it out or whatever. I guess he must've gone ahead and told you himself."

"I guess he did. Why does that even surprise you? I know you guys are best friends, but he's my friend too, and you know how he is. It was gonna get back to me before too long."

"True, but I had no idea he did that. We hadn't talked about this since that one conversation. I should've known."

She took a deep breath. "You know, Luke, you could've called me yourself instead of blabbing to Paul. That's some passive-aggressive bullshit. I even told him that. I mean, if you don't wanna hang out with me anymore, I get it. If I bother you that much, maybe we shouldn't."

"No, I'm not saying that."

"Okay...but trust – I'm quite aware we're just friends. You made it clear back in college and I was good with that. It's not like anything's changed."

"Yeah, AC, honestly, I don't *want* anything to change. I enjoy us going places together, and I really like spending time with you. We have great intellectual conversations and you're fun to hang out with."

Ann paused for a bit, then responded. "I feel the same way, but, um...the whole thing confused me because you usually call *me*, and the last thing I wanna be is a burden or come off as clingy or whatever. Not gonna lie, that kind of hurt."

"You're not a burden, and I shouldn't have said anything like that, Didn't mean to hurt your feelings. I hope we're fine now."

"Yeah, we're good."

"So, what are you doing tomorrow night? If you're not busy, we can go to the coffee shop down the street. They're gonna have some kind of band playing."

"Thanks for the invite, but I've already got plans," Ann said. "Maybe next week?"

"Alright, I'll talk to you then."

After the phone call ended, she rose from the futon and entered the small galley kitchen. She opened up the freezer and took out a half-gallon of Dairy Union brand chocolate cheesecake ice cream. She retrieved a bowl and spoon, and doled out about a third of the container. She then pulled out a jug from the refrigerator and poured some milk into the bowl, so her ice cream took on a soupy consistency.

After returning the rest of the ice cream and milk to their rightful places, she grabbed her portion and trudged to her desk in the living room. She turned on her computer and played *The Sims* deep into the night while slurping down the diluted ice cream and her frustrations.

Ann sat on the couch in her counselor Belinda's office, shifting about.

"So," Belinda began, "you've mentioned in previous sessions that part of the reason you moved here to Losanti is because of a man."

"Yes...I mean, it's a bit embarrassing, honestly."

"Could you tell me a bit more about that feeling? Why do you feel embarrassed?"

"Um...I took a gamble with my future that didn't pay off, and it's embarrassing to admit that. I also feel like God lied to me."

"Okay. What led you to these conclusions?"

"Um...Luke – that's his name – Luke and I are friends, always have been, nothing more than that. We met in college up in Michigan, but he's from here. We've never been together – never been in a relationship, never slept together, never even kissed. But I feel like I've always gotten mixed signals from him. He would call me to hang out with me, he would call me more than I call him. He's even said things that sounded like he was open to potentially dating in the future."

"What kinds of things?"

"I remember when I told him I like him, you know, in a romantic way. This was our second year of college. And he said something like 'I don't see you the same way, but my feelings could change six months from now, a year from now,' or whatever."

"I see."

"Stuff like that. We've hung out together a lot, we've danced together, we've held hands, he even almost kissed me, but then he pulled back. Though to be fair, that happened during a stressful time."

"A stressful time?"

"Yeah, it was on nine-eleven."

"Oh, okay. That was a difficult time for all of us."

"Yeah...and I mean, I feel like we really are good together, and other people have mistook us for being a couple. At one point, I felt like God wanted us together, and that's hard to let go of. But at the same time, nothing's progressed. Then last month, he had a mutual friend call me up to tell me he wanted me to back off because I was being clingy, and to find my own friends."

"This mutual friend played intermediary?"

Ann nodded slowly.

"How did that make you feel?"

She sighed and twirled her curls nervously. "I dunno...it really hurt. And I don't even know where it all came from. Like I said, he calls me more than I call him. He initiates our outings most of the time, it's pretty much always been that way. It's like he lied about me to save face or something. It's like I'm being rejected all over again." She wept.

Belinda leaned over with a box of tissues. Ann took two out of the box and dabbed her eyes.

"So that was about a month ago. Then, Luke kept calling me but I didn't pick up. I mean, why would he even call me if he doesn't wanna be bothered with me?"

"Ann, what I'm hearing is that you have a male friend, Luke, that you have known since college, that you have unrequited romantic feelings for. Despite the fact that he's expressed he's not interested in a romantic relationship with you, you moved to Losanti in hopes that he would change his mind, because you feel like you and him are meant to be together?"

"I mean, kind of...but it's not like he hasn't shown that there isn't anything there."

"Well..." the therapist opined, "He could just be a friendly person, and whether any feelings ever existed for you on his side or not, I can't say, but the fact that he has declined your request for a romantic relationship should be enough."

"I hear you. And it is...it's not like I keep asking him to be with me romantically. It was just the one time years ago, and I respected that he said 'no.' He offered to remain friends, and I was good with that. Still am. He's the one who calls me. I hardly ever call him for that reason. I don't want him to get the impression I'm clingy or I'm pushing for something more. If it happens, I want it to be of his own volition. That's why this whole thing feels out of the blue to me."

"Okay, I understand. Have you spoken to him since?"

"Yeah," Ann admitted. "I picked up the phone last Friday by mistake, and it was him. He came out and admitted he had said these things to our mutual friend, but he was going through some things, something like that. He said he got caught up with the idea that I still have feelings for him, even though I haven't said anything to him about it since our second year at UGL. I never bring it up, haven't since then. But I guess he didn't expect our friend to actually follow through with calling me, which is stupid because that friend runs his mouth, so of course he would. But yeah, Luke also said something else that really bothered me."

"What was that?"

"He said that I trigger his obsessions. I don't know, it doesn't even make sense. I don't even do anything but hang out with him when he calls inviting me out. And then when he had Paul — our friend — tell me all that stuff, I honored his request even though he straight up lied to him about me. I gave him space. He still kept calling me. Still does. How is that my fault?"

"It is not your fault, and it's not your responsibility. Luke's mental health is not your responsibility."

Ann looked back at her counselor, listening silently.

"You cannot control Luke, including how he feels or what he does. But you can control yourself, in terms of your actions and your own boundaries," Belinda explained. "How has your romantic life been otherwise?"

"Not great. I've tried online dating and got a hit from this guy. Uh, I wanted an actual date, he had me go over his house once and we messed around, but then I insisted on an actual date, he ghosted me. Then recently, he became my coworker, which is really awkward. And then, there's another guy that I met at a BBW party not too long ago."

"What's a BBW party?"

"Big, beautiful women. Um...there's these parties for heavier girls and guys who are into us. I went to one and met a guy, we started talking, we went out on a date and he's been at my place, but he's married with kids."

"Are you still involved with him?"

Ann sighed. "I am, but I don't feel great about it. Uh, excuse my language, but yeah, I feel like a piece of shit. At the same time, I feel like that's the best I can get."

Belinda scribbled down something in her notepad. "So, what I'm hearing is that you have been involved in toxic relationships with a number of unavailable men."

"Huh?"

"Okay...Luke, your friend, makes an effort to spend time with you, and it sounds like perhaps he's stringing you along for a potential future. But at the same time, he's been unwilling to pursue an actual romantic relationship with you, and he has shifted responsibility for his mental wellness onto you. Then, the man you met online – he wanted to see you as long as it wasn't in public, as an actual date would be, and he stopped speaking to you once it was made clear a date was expected. Then the married man. Well...he's married, which is about as unavailable as you can get."

"Wow, Belinda, never thought about that. It's frustrating, because I mean, I just want to love and be loved back. I don't half-ass love, I fall hard. But I feel like I'm just not good enough for mutual attraction, mutual love. I'm too fat, too weird, too awkward, too unlovable. It's never gonna happen and I'm gonna die alone."

"Ann, I want you to really think about this question before you answer it. Do you love yourself?"

In thought, Ann paused for a few moments. "I don't know. I love things about myself. I'm smart, I think I'm interesting, I have a good heart and I care about other people. But do I love myself? Honestly, not really. It's kind of hard to love myself when everything and everybody out here says I'm not good enough."

"Well, that's what we need to work on. Self-esteem and self-love. How you see yourself comes from within, and we'll need to work on building that up. Does that sound good to you?"

She nodded.

"So, before our next session, you have homework. Continue looking for activities with like-minded people. Don't focus on dating or romantic relationships right now. Just focus on finding some activities that interest you, where you can meet others who share your same interests. The idea is not to find a mate, but to begin surrounding yourself with people who bring positive energy into your life. As you surround yourself with like-minded people who have positive energy, it's likely to rub off on you."

"That makes sense."

"The other part of the homework will be a bit more challenging. You'll want to take time to evaluate your current relationships. Be honest with yourself about those relationships and the energy these people bring into your life. And — this will be the really tough part — you'll want to begin considering ending relationships that bring you down, reinforce negative messaging about yourself and your worth as a person, or otherwise lead you to a negative place."

"Okay."

"I'll share with you a bit of wisdom my mother told me when I was young. She said, 'You never let a man tell you 'no' more than once.'"

"Okay."

Belinda then encouraged her. "I don't expect you to build self-esteem and self-love overnight, but the homework I've given you is a good place to begin. You, Ann, you are worthy and you deserve a good life."

∾

The loud screech of Ann's alarm clock went off.

Beep!

It was a bright and early Sunday morning, and it was time to go to church. Most of the time these days, she would hit the big "snooze" bar and take advantage of the day off work. But this time was different. She felt compelled by an external force to go, even though her body enjoyed the coziness of bed.

Over the past week since her encounter with Harry, the idea of being the other woman, or another woman, was becoming increasingly harder to reconcile with her conscience. Her showers were a bit hotter and longer, as the immense guilt was more difficult than expected to scrub from her loins.

Feeling more disconnected than ever, Ann craved spiritual comfort, but felt too ashamed to speak to anyone. She wanted to see God without being seen, and she was convinced she would remain invisible in a crowd. Once dressed, she made the half-hour trek to Lightway Community Fellowship, a popular megachurch on the outskirts of Losanti she had never before attended.

Arriving at the facility, orange-vested flaggers guided her to a parking spot in the expansive lot. She retrieved her navy leather purse and worn Bible and walked into the church, which looked more like a repurposed warehouse than a traditional house of worship. Crowds of congregants milled about in the bright vestibule, many with their families.

Eyeing several commercial-sized coffee dispensers, she headed over and poured herself a cup of complimentary black coffee. She then added sugar and cream, and sat on a blue plush couch to await the opening of the sanctuary.

Once the ushers opened the sanctuary, Ann filed in along with the other attendees. The room was huge, with rows of theater-style seats divided into three sections, all facing a raised stage. Prayer volunteers were stationed on the outer walls of the sanctuary, available during service for any congregant requesting prayer. She decided to sit in the left-hand section in one of the back rows, at the end of the row closest to the outer wall. This was her first time attending Lightway and she recognized no one, as she hoped, but she was still convinced that everyone could see her sin.

The church service began with the worship band in ripped jeans, flared denim, tee-shirts, and flannel performing contemporary Christian songs with a rock tempo. While many in the audience were singing along, some even standing, Ann remained seated, embroiled in her thoughts and emotions. *I never thought I would go this far with a married man. Ugh, I almost lost my virginity to him. I really am a bad person...I deserve this hell.*

After the band played three songs, an associate pastor stood at the podium to share announcements. He then directed a series of tan wicker baskets to be passed through the congregation to collect the tithe, ten percent of one's income directed to be donated to the church, and any additional offerings on top of the tithe. Ann was too distracted to throw money into the basket.

The pastor, a man named Pastor Dan who looked to be about the same age as Harry, stood at the front of the raised stage to give his message to the congregation. In a conversational oratory style, he shared verses from the Bible, but her internal flagellation drowned them out.

Then, in a kindly voice, he told the attendees, "I'm sure there are some of you whose sin is weighing you down like a boulder. You're thinking to yourself, 'There's no way God would ever forgive me. What I've done is horrible, I can't even live with myself, how can I even dare to think that I can be forgiven?"

From her seat, Ann fell apart, her hands in her face. She felt like her chest was burnished with a scarlet letter "A" for "adulteress," and she was being buried alive.

Harry is a married man. We haven't gone all the way yet, but this is still wrong. It's one of the worst things I've ever done. I can't tell anybody this – not even Terah. And my God, Mom would die if she knew. If people knew, everybody would judge me. If Harry's wife found out about us and killed me, it would be my own damn fault. There is no future with him.

She thought back to Harry's rationales for cheating on his wife.

"She cheated on me first."

"Everybody cheats."

"Humans are not made for monogamy."

If he's lying to her, what makes me think he's telling me the truth? He married her, he owes me nothing. I'm sure a lot of people cheat, but not everyone...I dunno, I guess I'm naïve. But, I do know I can't live with myself if I go through with our planned meetup. I can't do that to his wife. I can't do that to his kids. Hell, I can't do this to myself.

In that moment, memories intruded in her mind.

"They said you ugly, and you know what they rated you? A negative two hundred and fifty-six. Fatass."

"My *girlfriend* Ann, I call her Porkie, it's a cute name, isn't it?"

"Men are designed by God to focus on physical appearance."

"You're a *big* girl. Maybe your standards are too high. You should probably rethink them."

She arrived at the core of her soul.

"We figured that having a baby would bring us closer and save our marriage."

"Stephanie truly loved you, Annie. She just didn't want to confuse you by staying in your life."

Then, she remembered Belinda's words.

"You, Ann, you are worthy and you deserve a good life."

I am worthy and I deserve a good life. I deserve to truly live.

As Ann continued to cry, a few prayer volunteers noticed her and proceeded to surround her, praying over her. Indeed, she was grappling with her past, with God, and the Christianity that had dominated her adolescence and early adulthood, including the bounds of a purity culture that was not made for her. Yet, despite her explorations and willingness to push against its barriers to find companionship, she knew that it would not be found in the person of Harry.

After services at Lightway, she walked to her car. Before opening the door, she flipped open her cell phone and dialed her lover's burner phone. When the phone predictably went straight to voicemail, she left a message:

"Uh...hi, Harry, this is Ann. I just want to let you know that this isn't going to work. I don't want to see you anymore. I wish you well. Bye."

She then hung up, deleted the phone number, and clasped the phone closed. She finally stepped into her car and started for home.

Never again.

LIONEL
JUNE-JULY 2003

On a calm Wednesday evening, Ann was at home relaxing on the couch with Charlie. Her recent conversation with Glenda and her visit to her uncle Louie gave her a bit of confidence and piqued her curiosity. So, she opened her purse, grabbed her wallet, and retrieved the contact information for her brother Lionel. She took a deep breath and dialed the number.

After a few rings, a man with a tenor voice picked up. "Hello?"

"Hi, is this Lionel Fields?"

"Uh, yeah. Who's this?"

"This is Ann Corbin."

There was silence at first, then a little bit of sniffling.

"Hello?" She thought she might have been disconnected.

"Uh...sorry," he responded, sounding overcome with emotion. "This is Lionel. I can't believe I'm hearing your voice."

"Hi, I'm your sister. I'd love to meet you."

"Wow, I want to meet you too. I heard from my mom's best friend Glenda that you're in Losanti where she is."

"Yeah."

Lionel laughed. "It's funny – I'm actually not far from you. I'm in Indianapolis."

She smiled. "That's only like, what, an hour and a half, two hours away? I can come up there sometime this weekend if you're free."

"Yes, sounds wonderful. How about Saturday?"

"Sure, I drive up Saturday morning. Is that good?"

"That sounds great. Lemme give you my address. Come by around eleven. My son Lamar will be here too."

"Oh, I have a nephew?"

"You sure do! You have a nephew and two nieces...one of your nieces is named Leigh."

"Oh, like, my middle name?"

"Yes," he confirmed.

Tears streamed down Ann's face.

The sun peeked through the fluffy, bright clouds on a Saturday morning as Ann pulled over to the shoulder of Interstate 465 in Indianapolis, Indiana. She focused intently on her printed MapQuest directions and became incredibly annoyed.

Why is the Indianapolis Loop so damn confusing? I've been around this thing twice. Can't find I-70 West.

While she was struggling to get her bearings, a police car pulled up behind her, lights flashing.

Fuck.

She rolled down her window and placed her hands on the steering wheel.

The police officer, a tall, muscled man, came up to Ann's driver-side window. "Hello, ma'am. License, registration, proof of insurance?"

"Uh, my license is in my purse, and my registration and insurance is in the glove box." Ann dug inside her purse, located her driver's license, and handed it to the officer. She reached into her glove compartment and retrieved her Ohio registration and proof of insurance. She then handed these documents to the Indiana state trooper, who took the items back to his patrol car.

While waiting, Ann was extremely nervous. She knew she had not done anything illegal, but police stops worried her. She thought back to her father telling her what to do and what not to do when pulled over by law enforcement:

"Be alert."

"Follow their directions. Don't argue with them."

"If the cops want to question you, tell them you want to exercise your right to an attorney and say nothing else."

The officer came back a few minutes later and handed her back her items. "Ma'am, I saw you stopped here, and I pulled over to make sure everything was okay."

Ann relaxed a little bit. "Yes, officer. I'm looking for I-70 West and I somehow keep missing it." She handed him her printed map.

The patrolman reviewed the map and handed it back to her. "I understand, ma'am. It happens all the time here on 465. You just passed it, it's very easy to miss. You'll want to take the next exit, turn left across the bridge, go back onto 465 but in the other direction, and bear right for I-70 West."

"Oh okay. Thank you!"

"You're welcome. You're free to go. Have a great morning, ma'am!"

"You, too!"

Ann drove back onto the freeway in the direction of the next exit. Using the police officer's directions, she found the Interstate 70 interchange without any additional challenges. Ten minutes later, she arrived at her brother Lionel's home, a small ranch-style house with yellow siding. She parked in front of the home, exited the car, walked up the concrete pathway to the door, and knocked.

A bald, heavyset man in his mid-thirties with a medium complexion and dark brown eyes opened the door. He was short, only slightly taller than Ann.

"You must be Ann." The man beamed.

"Yeah, I'm Ann. Are you Lionel?"

"Yes, I'm Lionel, I'm your older brother, can't believe I'm seeing you!" He opened his arms and Ann gave him a hearty hug. While this was the first time they met, she already felt in her core that she was with family.

After they hugged, Lionel welcomed Ann into his house, and she followed him to his covered back porch, which overlooked his large bright green lawn with manicured landscaping. Ann had a seat at a table there. Lionel then went back into the house and brought a teenage boy with him when he returned.

"Ann, this is my son Lamar. Lamar, this is your aunt Ann."

Lamar quietly waved, otherwise displaying little facial affect.

Ann spoke, "Uh, hi, Lamar," and waved back.

"My wife Keonna will be home later on; she's looking forward to meeting you too."

"That'll be great. I'm looking forward to that," Ann responded.

Ann and Lionel began talking, while the boy sat on a bench seat in the same room, immersed in his Gameboy.

"I'm glad you came over here," Lionel said. "I'm sorry to hear about your dad passing."

"Thank you."

"So, did y'all end up in Losanti? Is that where you grew up?"

"No. I only moved there less than a year ago. I grew up in Detroit."

Lionel was a bit surprised. "Oh, I thought you and Marshall left the area."

Ann clarified. "We did, at least for a few years. My earliest memories are down in Florida. I went to preschool and kindergarten there. Then, my dad remarried, and then we all moved up to Detroit when I was six."

"Oh, I see. What part of the city?"

"Far east side, near East Warren and Cadieux."

"Wow! Some of my relatives on my father's side live over that way. My uncle lives on Harvard near Mack."

"That's super close, like next street over. I grew up on Grayton between Southampton and Frankfort. Small world."

"Yes, yes it is, that's crazy. Can't believe you were that close. I mean, Mom and I lived on the west side off Joy Road, but uh...I would go over to my uncle's all the time."

"Oh wow — that's something, for sure. So, how did you end up in Indy?"

"Well, I enlisted in the Army and ended up stationed at Fort Bragg down in North Carolina. I didn't see any action, but it was still a life-changing experience. Anyway, that's where I met Keonna. She's from Indy originally. We got married, and after I was honorably discharged, we moved here to live close to her family, settled down here and we had three kids. I went back to school, got a degree, and now I teach high school English. We're close to Mrs. Townsend and her family, and I still check in on her. So, it was crazy to hear that she found you in Ohio."

"It was," Ann agreed. "I wouldn't have thought I would meet anybody who knows our mom down in Losanti."

"So, how did you end up there?"

"Uh...I went to the University of the Great Lakes for college, and once I graduated, I got a job there."

"Oh, okay," Lionel responded. He then went back to the subject of Ann's parents. "So yeah, I liked your dad, but the thing is, I get why they split up."

"Really?"

"Yeah. In some ways, Mom wasn't easy to deal with. And, now that I'm older and I have kids of my own, I kind of get why he took you. But when he took you, he didn't just take you from her. He took you from *me*. He took you from *our family*, and he robbed us of the chance for us to know you for all that time."

"I think I get it," Ann responded solemnly. "I have a younger sister, Michelle, that I grew up with. We're almost nine years apart. I was so excited when she was born, 'cause I really wanted a sister or a brother. I can't imagine if for whatever reason, my mom, Sherrye, the mom who raised me, took her and never brought her back."

Lionel nodded. "Yeah...it was tough for both of us to live with, but we had to keep on going. The thing about our mom is that yes, she has had her challenges, but she's much more than her problems. She's quite accomplished — she taught for a while in Detroit Public Schools; she taught math in the middle schools. And then she got her CPA and has worked as an accountant for the past few years."

"My dad would always say that I'm smart like her. So, she's a numbers person?"

"Yeah."

"That's so funny. My degree is in statistical math and I'm a data analyst. I'm into numbers too. Such a weird coincidence."

Lionel smiled. "Yeah, the math gene skipped me. But Lamar, though, he's incredibly smart, he's got it. He's been in so many regional math challenges and has done very well. As long as he keeps it up, he'll probably be able to earn scholarships for college."

"That's so cool." Ann glanced at her nephew, who was still immersed in his Pokémon game. She called out to him. "Lamar, what's your favorite Pokémon starter?"

Without looking up, he mumbled, "Squirtle."

"Oh, okay. My favorite is Bulbasaur...it's cute, but Squirtle is a great choice."

"Yeah...everybody chooses fire, so water types give me the best advantage early on."

Ann turned back to Lionel. "So, I heard I've got a brother and sister?"

"Yeah, Lynn and Donnie, they're our mom's surprise twins. They graduated last year from Renaissance."

"Oh, wow — Renaissance is a great high school."

"Yeah, they did good. Lynn decided to venture off to DC, she's studying political science at Howard. Donnie's still at home. He's at Wayne State working on a computer science degree."

"That's pretty awesome. I hope to meet them one day."

"Oh, for sure. You know, our mom, she's got a good heart. She cares for all of us kids — you know, her kids and grandkids, our cousins. She's very much part of the 'village' that helped raise everybody in the family. She's a generous person — she might not have much, but she gives what she has. And you know what? She's never stopped thinking about you, she's never stopped missing you."

Ann nodded. "A part of me really wants to meet herut I'm scared."

"What are you scared of?"

"I mean, I've heard she would like to meet me, too. But what if she sees me and she's disappointed?"

"Why would she be disappointed? You're her baby girl."

"I mean...uh...I read the custody papers when I was younger, and I learned that our mom didn't like that my dad wasn't working out anymore and he gained weight. What if she sees me as some kind of failure?"

"For real, Ann, you have nothing to worry about. You see me, right?" He looked at his protruding stomach, looked back at Ann, and smiled. "You'll be fine. You'll fit right in."

Ann exhaled as if a weight was lifted from her shoulders.

Later, Keonna arrived, and Ann got a chance to meet her. Keonna was a warm, talkative ball of energy in a short, small body.

"I'm sorry you missed your nieces, Rina and Leigh," she lamented. "They're at a weekend soccer retreat. But I'm sure you'll be able to meet them before too long." She proceeded to make dinner for all of them by frying pork chops and making green beans and rice as sides. As Ann, Lionel, and Lamar were now sitting at the dining table in the open-concept combined dining room and kitchen, Keonna was chatting with them while cooking.

"Keonna, what would you like me to do to help?" Ann asked.

"Nothing. Just sit there, you're our guest. Just so glad you're here."

She blushed, feeling awkward about the attention, but at the same time, oddly at home with people she just met. "Thank you."

"I'm so glad you had a chance to come visit us, Ann. I know Lionel's been looking forward to this day for the longest!"

Ann nodded.

Once dinner was served, Ann ate the food, which she thoroughly enjoyed. Keonna was a great cook, and the food reminded her of time spent with family. While this was the first time in this home, and with these people, she felt like she belonged. *These are my people.*

"I'll tell you what – when you're ready to make the trip up to Detroit to see Mom, let me know, and I'll be happy to get the time off to go up there with you," Lionel offered.

"You know what? I'd really like that."

In the early evening, after Ann returned from Indianapolis, she took Charlie to the dog park at the end of her street for some playtime. She entered through the double gates along with her dog, and after closing the gates back, she took him off the leather lead, then walked over to the bench and sat down. A few minutes later, she heard someone talking.

"Laura...here you go, have fun girl!"

Ann looked over and noticed that her neighbor Ian had entered the dog park with his Dachshund mix. After letting her off leash, he made his way over to the park bench and joined her.

"Hey, Ann!"

"Oh, hey Ian! Nice night, isn't it?"

"It's perfect. Your dog's temperament is excellent, so well-behaved. He's getting along quite well with my Laura."

She noticed the dogs running around and playing harmoniously. "Charlie is pretty great. And Laura, you said?"

"Yeah, Laura."

She smiled. "Laura, she's quite well-trained. You do great with her."

"Thanks."

"You know, I'm a fan of dogs with people names."

"Same," Ian concurred. "It makes them feel more like part of the family in a way."

"Oh yeah, for sure."

"So how long have you had Charlie?"

"Less than a year," she told him. "I adopted him when I first moved into our building. He was about a year old when I got him."

"You adopted him? That's cool. I'm all about rescues."

"I hear you. There are plenty of great pets in shelters who need homes. So, tell me about Laura."

"Oh, she's like three now. She's also a rescue, I adopted her when I was still in Pittsburgh. When I moved here, it was so important for me to find a place that would take her. It's hard to find an apartment that will accept dogs."

"Thank goodness you didn't just leave her behind or give her up."

Ian shook his head and looked at Ann with his dark brown eyes. "I couldn't, there's absolutely no way."

"That's a good thing. I feel the same about Charlie. We're connected at the hip, you know?"

"Yeah, totally. So, I see you travel a fair amount. What do you do for a living?" he inquired.

"I'm a data analyst, I work downtown. But I don't really travel for work. Most of my traveling is to see family, most of them are in Michigan."

"Oh, that's cool. Is that where you're from?"

"Yeah, I'm from Detroit originally. What about you? You said you had moved here from Pittsburgh. Is that where you're from?"

"No, I went to college there, Pitt. I was born and raised in Abington, Pennsylvania, just outside of Philly."

"Oh okay, that's pretty neat. What made you decide to move to Losanti of all places?"

Ian smirked. "Very good question. I work in IT, and there was a startup here that recruited me right out of college. It paid well enough, and the cost of living is pretty low, so now I'm here. Been here for three years now. What about you? How did you find yourself here?"

"Same thing, pretty much. Got a job out of college down here, so why not?" Then Ann shifted gears. "Since you're an outsider like me..."

"Yes, the dreaded 'outsider' status." Ian laughed.

"Yeah," Ann chuckled along with him. "So you get it too?"

"Of course. How could I not?"

"True. So, I guess what I'm wondering is how do you find a friend group here? I mean, I go to happy hours with people from work, but it would be nice to connect with more people. How do you do it?"

Ian's side bang moved to the side as he shook his head. "It's not easy, honestly. I'm still trying to figure it all out. All I can say is, it takes time and getting involved in stuff around here. I paint in my spare time, and so I started going to art galleries, starving artist meetings, you know the deal. So now I'm tied into the arts scene here. Found out about a lot of these events in *The Almost Countrybeat*."

"That seems to be where to look, huh?"

"Oh yeah. Anything that's trending or remotely fun here, you'll find it in there."

TRIBE
JULY 2003

Ann found herself working on a routine report for a news media client on a Friday afternoon. Most of her coworkers left early to head to the downstairs bar, but she had a deadline, or at least that was the excuse she gave her coworkers. She was over the bar scene, or at least going to the bar after work with colleagues.

She was just about to plow through the next line of code for her regression model when loud yelling caught her attention.

"Holy shit! You gotta see this!" a voice carried from a room on the other side of the office. An analytics lead, Jamie Spencer, called out to the floor to bring the few who stayed behind into his office to watch what was on his computer.

Ann sprinted into the office with Gwen and Jason, who were also there to work that afternoon. On Jamie's monitor was a zoomed-in grainy image of a man holding a long rifle and pointing it at a clerk behind the counter.

The robbery occurred at the Dairy Union gas station just down the street from the office. The surveillance footage released by police and posted to the local news station website depicted a man of average height and hefty build with a slightly limping gait, wearing a pitch-black balaclava, pants, shoes, and a long-sleeved matching shirt with a stately logo and the words in bolded, all-caps Courier New font, "The Nichols Agency." Not only that, the man wore a ring on the pinky finger of his ungloved left hand, which the clerk described to Losanti Police as "a blue heart ring."

"Are you fucking kidding me?" Ann blurted out.

"Ooh, it's nuts," Jamie concurred, shaking his head.

"Bro is such a moron. Chad needs to stop hiring dumbasses for juniors," Jason snarked.

Gwen added, "I knew Trevor was kind of stupid, but my God, this is next-level idiotic."

The lead then clicked back to the online news article and scrolled down to view Trevor's mugshot. "Shit, Chad's not gonna be too thrilled come Monday morning."

"Welp, if we go downstairs to the bar and tell him now," Ann suggested, "he can have a new ad out for a junior analyst by first thing Monday morning."

Jamie and Gwen stared at Ann disapprovingly. Jamie then said, "Too soon, Ann. Not in good taste."

Jason shrugged and interjected, "Eh, sure it's not in good taste, but it would be efficient, that's for sure."

"Good boy! Let's go bud!" Ann encouraged Charlie as he took a potty break on their morning walk. After he was finished, she guided him with his leash down the street towards the apartment. While on their way home, she noticed a blue newsstand holding a stack of newspapers with covers in full color.

She picked up one of the newspapers on the newsstand. *The Almost CountryBeat*. The cover was graced by an alabaster-toned man with ocean eyes, elaborate makeup, and long, spiky rainbow-hued hair. Then, paper in hand, she and her dog continued home.

In the apartment, while sitting on the fluffy futon, Ann leafed through the paper. The pages brimmed with stories about local hotspots, trends in cuisine, and human interest stories. Then, she turned to the "events" section and examined the announcements. Concerts featuring garage bands, grand openings of new bars and restaurants, and meetups for various interests were listed there. As she continued to peruse each page, a particular event caught her eye:

CELEBRATE STARS & STRIPES WITH LOCAL THEATER: Tiny's Bar, Oaktown, *Saturday, July 5, 2003, 3:00pm. Come out & quench your thirst with our beer specials & eat from our tasty menu while watching a lovely night of community theater on our outdoor patio. Weather permitting.*

That afternoon, Ann showered and put on a lavender empire waist sundress and white flip-flops, then started up her Bug and headed to Oaktown, an eclectic, up-and-coming neighborhood northwest of downtown Losanti. She parked in a local pay lot, stuffed a dollar bill in the slot that corresponded to her parking space in the metal parking payment box, and walked over to Tiny's Bar. She walked over to the bar and perused the giant chalk drink menu affixed to the wall.

"What would you like me to get for you?" asked the tall, pink-haired woman bartender with a septum ring.

"Uh," Ann briefly hesitated, "I'll have your house ale."

"Lovely!"

After a couple of minutes, the bartender came back with a glass of medium-colored beer. The bar's "house" beer was a peach ale with real peach pieces. After leaving a credit card to open a tab, Ann took her drink and made her way to the patio.

The patio was an outdoor area with a wooden stage located through double doors at the back of the bar. The seating on the patio consisted of several metal tables with plastic red and white plaid table covers, with shiny coated metal seating. The seating on the patio was about a quarter full once Ann walked out there with her beer. She then sat down at an open table, sipped on her ale, and waited patiently.

A thick-sized woman with a dark blue hoodie, coal wide-leg rave pants, and white Converse sneakers walked over to Ann's table.

"Is anyone sitting here?" asked the woman, placing her hand on the seat next to her.

Ann shook her head. "Oh no, go ahead."

The woman sat down next to her and sipped on her pale-shaded beer. "Have you ever been here before?"

"Uh, I've been at Tiny's before, but not this kind of event."

"That's cool. I've never been here, but I saw this advertised in *The Almost CountryBeat*."

"Same."

"Yeah, so I sorta figured I'd come by, I live pretty close, right around the corner." The woman's milk-shaded right hand was holding onto her glass, which was starting to show condensation.

Ann took a sip of her own beer. "That's cool." Then she took a breath and introduced herself, "Uh, I'm Ann, by the way."

"Great to meet you," the woman smiled. "I'm Christine."

The two women continued to chat while waiting for the show to start. "What high school did you go to?" asked the woman.

Ann glanced at her glass, then looked back at Christine. "I didn't go to high school in this area, I'm not from here originally."

"Oh, cool!" Christine lit up. "I'm not from here either. People always ask that around here, so much that I kinda learned more than I ever wanna know about high schools in the area. So, since people expect the question, I kinda picked it up."

"Uh yeah, I totally get that," Ann chuckled. "So where are you from?"

"I'm from Phoenix."

"Oh okay, that's pretty cool. I'm from Detroit. I've heard Phoenix is nice with the dry heat. What made you wanna move here — like, Losanti, Ohio?"

"It sure wasn't for the weather!" Christine joked.

Ann laughed. "I know, right?"

"My girlfriend at the time got a really good job here, and I moved here with her. But, it sorta fell apart once we got here. Basically, she broke up with me out of the blue and I had to move out."

"Oh damn, that's rough. Um, sorry about that."

"It's all right. Shit happens. So, how did you end up here?"

"Oh, long story, but pretty much after college I moved down here for both a job and a guy. The job worked out but the guy didn't. So uh…I can sort of relate." Both women laughed.

A woman in a retro A-line white dress with red polka dots stepped up to the microphone located at the front of the wooden stage, which was about a foot off the ground. "Hi, everyone! Good afternoon and welcome to a wonderful night of community theater to celebrate the Fourth of July!"

The audience applauded.

The lithe woman continued. "I'm Tina and I'm the emcee for the show. We have three different groups that will perform tonight. Our first opener is an amateur theater troupe that calls itself..." Tina checked her notes, then continued, "The Sketchy Thespians. Then, after that, we'll have something a little different, an improv troupe called Improv Losanti, and then our headliner, The Piglet Playhouse!"

The crowd cheered. Ann and Christine were both captivated.

First, a collection of five people in street clothes walked onstage and quickly arranged the set. They then acted out two short sketches. The first sketch was about a young man who was brought in as the newest member of a boy band, but could not sing and had two left feet — literally. The second was about a man and a woman who were on a road trip, encountering all kinds of obstacles including a serial killer, a bear, and a lost child, but were arguing with each other the entire way.

"This is too funny," Ann chuckled. "Man, that trip was too real!"

"The bear, oh my God, I'm dead!" Christine concurred.

After about twenty minutes, a diminutive, tawny man with short business-style brown hair took the mic. He said in a calm yet commanding voice, "We are the Sketchy Thespians! We are an amateur theater troupe and we write and perform own sketches in addition to acting out established plays. We are always open to new people. You don't need any experience or talent, we just love having fun. We meet every Tuesday evening at six-thirty at the Oaktown Community Center. Thank you and enjoy the rest of the show!"

During the break between sets, Christine turned to Ann and said, "See, this is what I was kinda looking for. I was in community theater back in Arizona."

"Oh, that sounds so fun."

"It was. I'm not good enough to go to Broadway, but I loved it. Here's the thing, I've come to terms with who I am, and I'll be honest, I'm sorta weird."

"I don't think so. You seem really cool,"

"Thanks, but weird isn't a bad thing. Some people are better at conforming than others. I'm not one of those people who's good at it. But see, that's the awesome thing about a lot of that kinda stuff — acting, improv, sketch, stuff like that. It's usually full of interesting folks."

"Hmm, I didn't know that. I'm having a hell of a time trying to find something to do here that doesn't suck."

"I don't know if this group will suck or not, but I think it's worth checking out."

"Eh, I'd say so."

Both women took the time to get their glasses refilled, along with many others in the audience. Then, the next act came up. Improv Losanti consisted of a group of seven improvisers who performed a few improvisation games.

The troupe lined up, and a middle-aged man stepped forward and projected, "One-hundred and eighty-five doctors walked into a bar, and the bartender says, 'We can't serve all of you right now.' So, the doctors say, 'It's fine, we've got a lot of patience!'"

Watching the performance, Christine giggled. "That was so hilarious!"

Ann agreed. "Totally! I haven't laughed so hard in quite a while!"

After Improv Losanti was finished, there was another intermission. Ann spotted the small man from The Sketchy Thespians sitting at a table near the stage, along with several from the group. She felt compelled to take this step, so she stood up. "Hey uh...Christine, I'm gonna go talk to the guy from the opener to find out more about the group. You wanna come with me?"

"Yeah, that sounds great."

The women grabbed their beers and walked over to the table with The Sketchy Thespians.

"Hi," Ann greeted the group.

The group waved, and the man spoke back, "Hi!"

"We really liked your group's performance."

"Thanks! We're glad you enjoyed it."

"So I heard y'all were looking for some new people?"

"Yes!" said the man. "Yes, yes we are!"

"And uh...you said we don't need any experience?"

"Nope, we'll take anybody. We just love enjoying ourselves and learning something new in the process."

"Welp, I don't have any experience, she does though," pointing to Christine.

"Yeah, I used to do community theater some time ago," Christine said, "but I'm out of practice."

"Well, you're both welcome to come join us. My name's Tim, and this is my girlfriend Molly." A woman with cropped purple hair turned around and waved. Then Tim continued introductions, "and this is Mariana, Gary, and Alex." A young, plump woman with dark hair and eyes waved, along with an average-sized man with deep tan skin and a shaped afro, and a tall, gangly man with a pinkish tone and short blond hair.

Ann and Christine both smiled. Ann introduced them, "I'm Ann, and this is Christine. It's so great to meet you all."

Christine chimed in. "It's nice to meet everybody. And you said you meet Tuesdays at 6:30 at the Oaktown Community Center, the one on the corner of Oaktown Road and Franklin Hollow?"

"Yes," said Tim. "Looking forward to seeing you both on Tuesday!"

After the conversation, Ann and Christine walked back to their table, sat down, and exchanged telephone numbers before the main event.

"We gotta hang out!" Ann offered.

"For sure!" Christine responded joyfully.

She was excited to meet someone new and take part in a performing arts group. As The Piglet Playhouse took the stage to act out their rendition of William Shakespeare's Much Ado About Nothing, the fast friends enjoyed their beverages and watched gleefully.

Ann was cautiously optimistic. The Sketchy Thespians seemed like fun people, and it would be exciting to try something new and different. At the same time, she worried that much like was the case with other experiences she had in groups, such as Christian Kingdom or even her current work group, she would be made to feel like the odd person out. Still, she would not know if it was a good fit for her unless she tried, and actually taking initiative would hopefully pay off.

The next Saturday morning, Ann decided to take Charlie for a brisk walk. She put on a pair of dark bootcut jeans and paired it with an orange tank top that showed a hint of cleavage, and then donned a pair of brown sandals. Once she made it back, she was at her front door about to let herself in when Ian came outside with Laura.

"Hi, Ann!"

"Oh, hi, Ian!"

"I'm glad I ran into you," he expressed. "So, uh...I have a favor to ask."

"Sure, what's up?"

"I'm taking an oil painting class down at the Losanti Arts Center, and I've been given an assignment to paint another person. I need to paint someone in their environment. Would you be cool with sitting for a painting?"

"Oh, uh sure! What would be involved, and when do you wanna do this?"

Ian explained, "It could just be you in your apartment, like you sitting or lying on your couch with Charlie. And I can work with your schedule, though if possible, sooner rather than later. I would just need you for maybe a couple of hours or so."

"Uh, I'm free now. I don't have anything planned until later this evening when I head out to the movies with my friend Christine. Does that work for you?"

"That'll be perfect!" Ian responded with a smile.

"Uh, is there any kind of outfit I should be wearing? Like casual, or formal, or whatever? Makeup?"

"What you have on is great. You don't need makeup, you're great as you are."

She smiled. "Okay, cool. Just grab what you need and knock when you're ready."

"I was just about to run Laura out, and as soon as she's finished doing her business, I'll be right back and I'll come over."

"Cool, see you in a little bit."

Ann entered her apartment and used the bathroom so she could be ready for a two-hour sitting. After she finished washing her face and hands, she walked out of the bathroom into the living room. She heard a knock at the door, and she answered it.

"Hey, Ian...looks like you're ready."

"Oh, for sure."

"Come on in."

Ian came into the apartment with an easel, a blank medium-sized white canvas, and a set of paints, brushes, and pencils. He then went back to his apartment to retrieve a towel and a small bucket. While Ian was getting set up, Ann gave her dog a blue and white rope to chew on so he could stay relatively still on the futon beside her. When he came back, she was sitting on the couch with her legs off to the side.

He walked over to her, and slightly adjusted the way she held her head, so her face was sitting in the direction of the window. "Okay, that's great. So, Ann, for a few minutes, I'd like you to be as still as you can while I sketch everything out on the canvas. Then, you'll still wanna stay there, but you'll be able to move more. Does that work?"

"Yeah, sure."

For the next twenty minutes, Ann remained still while Ian proceeded to sketch an image on his canvas. Charlie was happily chewing away at his toy. After Ian was done sketching, he told her, "So now I've moved on to painting. So you still want to stay on the couch, so I can see colors, shading, how the light bounces off, things like that. But you won't need to be still."

"That's fine. Whatever you need."

The paintbrush stroked the plain white surface. He looked intently at the canvas, then Ann and Charlie, then back to the canvas.

"So what have you been up to lately? You seem quite busy these days."

"Well, besides work, I took your advice and checked out *The Almost Countrybeat*. And through that, I started getting involved in an amateur community theater group."

"That's so awesome. How is that?"

"It's really fun. It's called The Sketchy Thespians, and uh...so, we practice on Tuesdays in Oaktown, and we're getting ready for a play we're performing over Labor Day weekend."

"That sounds like a lot of fun. I love watching the performing arts, but there's no way I could get up onstage and do it. Takes a lot of guts."

"I wasn't sure if I could do it either at first. I'm not the most outgoing person ever," she confessed. "But stepping out onstage and performing, it's a different kind of energy, at least for me. It's more impersonal, I can be anything and anybody when I'm out there."

"Hmm, that's a different way of thinking of things," he said as he made small brushstrokes on the canvas. "That's the beauty of creatives. We can embody various energies, interpret them in novel ways. And it can look so different, so unique, depending on the medium."

"Oh yes, definitely."

"Ann, come here and check this out."

She walked over to the canvas and took in an image of a curvaceous woman with gorgeous brown hair and smooth skin, staring longingly out of a window to the left-hand side of the portrait, lounging next to a majestic black Labrador. She had never seen herself in such a lovely, artful way.

"You're so talented, Ian. This came out so well."

He flashed a warm smile. "Thank you, Ann. It just takes the right inspiration."

CONFESSION
AUGUST 2003

It was a hot Saturday afternoon in early August, and Ann was playing a video game, *Sim City*, on her computer. Charlie was lying next to her relaxed and calm. Then the phone rang and she saw who was calling on the outer display. She flipped it open and answered the call.

"So, there's this place that's a little bit of a drive down in Kentucky that I wanna go to. It's called 'Loose Lily's' and it's a country bar," Luke explained.

She was surprised. "I never took you to be into country."

"I'm not, but I went with some of my vet school buds last week and it was great. You wanna go?"

"Uh, I'm not doing anything. Sure."

Later in the afternoon, Luke arrived in his trusty Saab to pick Ann up. They headed across the Ohio River to Marbro, a former factory town now known for ramshackle country bars and lax liquor and vice laws. Once there, he drove along a desolate, winding road skirting the southern banks of the river. Then, turning right down a quiet, dark street, he pulled over to the side of the road and stopped the car.

"Are you sure we're at the right place?"

"Yeah, I'm sure."

He stepped out of the car and closed the door. She then got out as well, shutting the car door behind her. He pointed ahead of the car, but it was pitch black with virtually no visibility. The sounds of country and folk songs hung in the air, but no building was in sight.

Ann felt nervous "Luke...it looks like we're in the middle of nowhere. Is this the closest we can get to the bar?"

"Nothing to worry about, AC. It's just up there. Really close."

He intently trudged on the side of the paved road up the steep green hill. Ann's short, stubby legs struggled to keep up, her asthmatic lungs burning hot. She tried with all her might to keep up with her friend, staying close to the edge of the road while avoiding the drainage ditch mere inches to the right, but her efforts were in vain. His pace was like a man on a mission, and he continued facing straight ahead, never looking back to make sure his companion was still with him. Night was upon them, and the path grew darker and less visible. Intense, palpable fear crept in as she realized she was left all alone.

"Hey, Luke! Wait up!" she gasped.

No response.

Are you fucking serious right now? Ann followed the seemingly endless road, this time by herself. Luke's visage now disappeared in the dark, she stopped in her tracks and dug into her purse frantically, pulling out her inhaler. She pressed it against her lips, pushed down, and breathed in the rescue medication. After a few minutes, she continued her slow ascent uphill. *I have no choice.*

Every cricket chirp, every coyote howl, and every rustle of grass sounded louder than it had any business being. Goosebumps emerged on her arms, and a chill migrated up her spine. Anger at Luke for abandoning her along this unfamiliar road developed into stark terror. In the dark, the wild, harsh environment made itself known.

Howl!

Squeal!

As the ambiance grew louder, Ann's vision narrowed.

I just have to make it up this hill.

After what felt like an eternity, a small yet lively and populated shack slowly emerged in her line of sight, surrounded by a dirt lot full of pick-up trucks and motorcycles. Her eyes now on the destination, she found the strength to pick up the pace. A painted white sign with the red words stenciled "Loose Lily's" and a silhouette of a pin-up girl donning a cowboy hat were held up by wooden two-by-four planks on each side. The signs were posted right next to the road marking the destination. A companion sign with "Loose Lily's" printed in block letters hung just above the front doors of the tavern.

Once she arrived at Loose Lily's, she walked in and searched for her lost friend. She then spied him sitting at the bar while the bartender was sliding him a Budweiser. She sat next to him and placed her order.

"Could I get a Cuervo and Sprite please?"

"I'm sorry, we don't have that, little lady," answered the bartender, a grizzled man that looked to be a hard lived fifty. "All we have is what's right here on tap."

Ann was a bit embarrassed as she did not notice the lack of a full bar behind the bartender. It also did not help that she felt awkward in the unfamiliar environment Luke had brought her most of the way to before leaving her to walk the remainder alone. She read the stickers on the bar taps. "Uh, okay, um, I'll have a Stella."

"Sounds good, comin' right up."

"Thank you." She then turned to her friend and quietly yelled, "What the hell dude? You walked off without me!"

"I thought you were keeping up. The bikers park in front so I figured down the street would be better for us. It was getting a little chilly so I was just trying to hurry up and get inside. My bad." He took a sip of his dark stout. "I mean, it *was* straight ahead. Wasn't hard to find."

After paying cash for her Stella Artois, she tasted it and enjoyed the slight hoppiness. "You know, Luke, that's really not the point. I've never been here before. *You* brought me out here and *you* left me on the road."

"Look, it's not like you would've been kidnapped. What are they gonna do, carry you away?"

She took a sip, and then after a few seconds, she picked up what he was putting down. "Uh, that's a bit of a low blow there. Is this what we're doing now?"

He sighed. "Eh, that was kinda stupid. Didn't mean it like that."

Choosing not to harp on it and opting to avoid ruining the evening by continuing the argument, Ann changed the subject.

"So anyway, how's class treating you?"

Luke took a deep breath. "Not great. I mean, I'm doing well enough, probably enough to pass and continue through the program."

"That's good."

"But y'know, AC, I keep feeling like I don't wanna do this anymore. I'm just...so tired of vet school. I wish I had become a documentarian like I always wanted to do. I love standing back, having other people become the story...the surroundings be the story. There's such beauty in that."

"Sounds like an awesome dream, Luke...it's creative, and I've always thought you'd be amazing at that. Why don't you do it?"

He took a deep breath. "You *know* why."

"Your parents?" She rolled her eyes as she received her drink.

"What was that for?"

"Okay, not trying to be judgy or anything, but at this point, you're twenty-three. I understand wanting to make your parents happy. On some level, just about everybody wants that, even if their parents are the worst people to ever exist. But at a certain point, you've got to live your own life."

He grew furious. "AC – look, you don't get it. You don't have to deal with your parents' expectations the way I do. Your dad's dead and you don't even know your birth mom. Making your parents happy? That's not something you gotta think about. *You* are free to do whatever you want, and nobody's around to judge you. Nobody's around to call you a failure and to say you're gonna amount to nothing. But see, *I do*."

She was taken aback, tears welling up in her eyes. "What the hell, Luke? You really had to go there, didn't you? Just because they aren't here doesn't mean nobody expects anything out of me. You act like I'm Orphan Annie without a fucking family. That's not true and you know it."

"Look, A—"

"And yes, my dad is gone and my birth mother didn't raise me. But I have had to live with the expectations of ghosts. Sure, they aren't here to call me a failure, but they can't tell me they're proud of me either."

"AC, I wasn't trying to go low. That sucks. But here's what I'm trying to say. I have had to live in my brother's shadow the entire time I've been alive. My brother was the star athlete, the honor roll student, National Honor Society, the valedictorian and class president, the world-famous scientist. The motherfucker pretty much invented GPS. And my parents have always looked at me as a failure. No matter how good my grades were, no matter how well I did in sports or clubs or anything, I was always a failure...because I could never be anywhere as good as my brother. Vet school is my way of showing them that I'm not a failure. I can make my own mark in the world in a way they'll actually respect. See, my parents *expect* things of me. Doing what I wanna do is not exactly an option."

She finished her glass. "You know what, Luke? You can do that. But we all only get one life, and we don't get to choose how long it'll be." With that, she hopped off the barstool, walked outside, and opened her cell phone to make a phone call. A few minutes later, he followed her outside.

Once catching up to her, he inquired, "What are you doing?"

"Um...I called a cab. I'm going home."

"Why? Look, I know I shouldn't have said all that shit back there, but I was just so pissed you started in on my situation. My God, I know my parents control my fucking life. I'm well aware of that and I hate it. Paulie tells me that, you tell me that. Everybody tells me that, and it's just annoying as fuck."

"You know, you left me in the woods and I almost had an asthma attack, and when I called you out on it, you acted like it was a joke. And what you said back there was very hurtful."

Luke shook his head but remained silent.

"I'm sorry I made you mad about your parents, but I thought it was fine for me to be honest with you 'cause you asked me about my reaction, and we've talked about it before. I said the wrong thing."

"No, AC, I shouldn't have said those things. I went low...it was mean."

"You know, I'm not even mad right now."

"Okay...so why are you going home?"

"We were talking, and what I said to you, about having one life to live, it was like, all of a sudden, a light turned on in my head."

Ann looked away as her cheeks turned red and she cried in earnest. She then faced him and continued.

"I know it sounds crazy, but from the first time we met, I started having feelings for you. And over time, I truly felt like I was falling in love with you. And there were times when it seemed like you felt the same way. I even thought you were The One."

"Fuck...really?"

"Yes, but at some point, I realized that it wasn't gonna happen between us. Then, when you put Paul up to telling me I'm clingy and I call you too much, even though we both know that's bullshit...that really broke my heart."

"Ugh...I'm sorry."

"You shouldn't apologize. Maybe it was the right thing after all. Maybe I needed to hear that. I've never been great at reading people and I always get it wrong. But anyway, I've always felt like even if it was just as friends, I wanted you in my life."

"AC, we have a lot of fun together. You're a great person, you truly are. I hope you know I truly do value our friendship."

"For sure. And I value it too. But the thing is, there will always be a ceiling because you don't see me as enough for more than that. I'm a *big* girl, after all. But there's might be a great guy out there who will think I *am* enough. Not just enough to be friends, but to actually be *with me*. Somebody who will love me, accept me, and value me as I am, who will be proud to be with me and call me his."

Luke nodded his head and replied softly, "That's fair. You deserve that."

"Yeah, but when we were back there, I realized that as long as my heart is still in your hands, I will never find out for sure. There's no way I'll be able to completely get over you as long as you're still in my life. And just like you, I only have one life to live. Goodbye, Luke."

A yellow cab pulled up to the door of the bar. Ann entered and closed the door, and the taxi sped away, leaving Luke outside the bar stunned.

LETTING GO
AUGUST 2003

Bzzz!

Ann rolled over in bed and smashed the alarm clock. It was seven o'clock in the morning. *Goddammit.*

It was the following Saturday morning, and it was time for Ann's weekly counseling appointment.

She sat on a couch in the therapist's office fidgeting with her hands. "So, uh...Belinda, I cut Luke out of my life."

Belinda smiled. "Hmm. Ann, that's a big step for you. Could you tell me a little more about how that came about?"

"Um, we were hanging out, and I was pretty much over it. I was over all of it."

"What precipitated the decision?"

"So, uh...we had gone across the river to some dive bar in Marbro. He had parked at the bottom of a steep hill, the bar was at the top of the hill so it was a bit of a walk and it was after dark. So anyway, he was walking too fast and he left me behind. I almost had an asthma attack trying to keep up with him. So, that pissed me off."

"That's not a friend. I can understand how that upset you."

Ann nodded. "So, then I caught up with him at the bar. I tried to let it go, but we had gotten into an argument over something else. I said something that upset him, and it was a whole thing. But at one point, I told him that we only have one life to live. I was telling *him* that...but I had this 'aha' moment, and it clicked in my head that I should've been telling *myself* that all this time. So, I told him that for me to move on, he couldn't be in my life anymore, something like that. And then I caught a cab and I left by myself."

"Alright. How do you feel right now about that decision?"

"At first, I was sad and I was angry. I mean, Luke was pretty much a constant in my life for close to five years. I enjoyed his company and we had some amazing times together. We were there for each other during some low points in our lives. I also felt like I wasted those five years on someone who could never truly love me. But at the same time, I know it's strange, but I finally feel *free*. I'm no longer stuck, you know, waiting for God to do something that's never gonna happen."

"Okay Ann, what I hear is a few things. I hear that you can appreciate the good times in your friendship with Luke, yet you feel free of the burden of waiting on him to progress it into a relationship, when the reality is that it's unlikely to occur. I also hear that you feel a sense of regret from being invested in the idea of a romantic future with him for several years, and that it hasn't worked out for you."

"Exactly, Belinda. A part of me feels lost. It's like, now what? I moved down here for Luke. That's fucking embarrassing — sorry, excuse my language."

"It's okay, Ann. Express yourself in any way you feel comfortable."

"Um...thanks. But yeah, it's embarrassing. We were never together, and I believed so hard that God wanted us to be together. It's like I heard it, and I believed it to be as definite as the sky is blue. And I told my friends, I told my family. Now I have to take it all back. And it's like, letting that go is like letting go of certainty. It's like letting go of God."

"So, what I'm hearing is that your romantic interest in Luke, and your belief that you were destined to be with him, was wrapped up in your religious faith. Do you believe that stepping away from the friendship with him, and letting go of the belief that you're destined to be with him, is leading you to reevaluate your faith?"

"Yes, pretty much. I'm starting to realize that my entire life is a lie. Ever since my dad died..." Ann then had a realization. "Belinda – that's exactly what it is! My dad told me all my life that my birth mother just gave me to him and just stopped bothering to see me. I have always felt like my birth mother just left me behind, and then I find out that might not be true. Then, I was taught to trust in God and have faith. My mom, at church, in Christian Kingdom – I was taught that God is all good, all-powerful, and he wants good things for his children. But I saw my dad get sicker and sicker, and I prayed for him to live and get better, and that didn't happen. Then, I moved to Losanti because I trusted that God would bring me and Luke together. That didn't happen either. I am just up here looking like a damned fool. What is even true anymore?"

"Hmm. I'm hearing a couple of things. I'm hearing that you feel that your father deceived you, and so did the people in your life who taught you about God."

"Yeah."

"It's natural to connect our feelings regarding our faith, and our relationship with our parents. You spent a great deal of your life believing your birth mother abandoned you, which already leads to a baseline of trauma at a young age. Yet, you held onto your relationship with your father and believed that if you could trust no one else, you could trust your father. And once he died, you found that his story regarding your birth mother's absence may not have been completely accurate, and that is a huge breach of trust. Is that accurate?"

"I would say so."

"And you feel that, because of how you have understood God, after your father's death and the ending of your friendship with Luke, you don't feel that you can trust God either. Am I understanding you correctly?"

"Yes...that's where I'm at. I feel like now, I'm questioning everything. I feel like I'm invisible to God, and I'm on my own."

"In what ways?"

"God allowed me to live a lot of lies. I believed that Stephanie had just lived her life forgetting I even existed. God allowed me to believe that my whole life up until this point. He never intervened. They say he heals, but he didn't intervene when my dad got sick. And then, I guess when God told me...or I thought he told me...that Luke was The One, it was like at least he recognized my womanhood. But come to find out, even that's bullshit."

Belinda took a deep breath. "There's a lot here to unpack. I believe you're questioning your faith and your relationships because you're processing trauma. Losing a parent is trauma. Having an absent parent is trauma. Broken relationships, regardless of the type, are trauma. As far as your parents are concerned, a helpful thing to remember is that when it comes to conflict, everyone has their own perspective, and human nature is complicated. I get the sense you see things in black and white, is that the case?"

"For the most part, I guess. The way I see it, the truth is the truth."

"Ann, reality often lives in shades of grey. And that's okay. We'll want to get you to where you can live with a greater degree of uncertainty, so you can give the people in your life grace, and give yourself grace. Does that sound like a good plan?"

"Sounds good."

"Also, you can take the opportunity to deconstruct your religious faith and your conception of God as you understand him right now. And as you do that, you'll be able to rebuild your faith, if you so choose, apart from trauma. You can start to redefine your conception of God, a deity, or a spirituality apart from an unhealthy attachment to another person. If you explore and find that religion is not for you, that's a valid conclusion as well."

"Okay, I understand. I think I want to do that."

"The difficult part about desiring an outcome that involves the will of another person is that they have agency. They can make their own choices, and if they don't consent to your desires, then the outcome won't be what you expect or want. Unfortunately, another person's agency is outside of your control."

"I get it."

"But Ann, what you want to begin embracing is that *you* also have agency. In other words, you have choices, and what you need and want matters. I'm not recommending that you necessarily focus on dating. Focusing on having a solid, positive social circle seems like the more immediate course of action."

Ann nodded in agreement.

Belinda continued. "When you *do* begin dating again, you'll want to reframe your thinking. Focus less on whether or not the men you date approve of you or see you as worthy of a relationship, and more on whether or not you see the men you date as compatible and worthy of a relationship with *you*."

"Okay...but how do I do that? It's not like I have this long list of male prospects."

"Honestly, it doesn't matter if you have zero suitors right now or fifty. When you focus on pleasing men or gaining their love and approval, you give away your power and your agency. And what ultimately happens is that you might still meet someone who wants to enter into a relationship with you, but he may not be the kind of person you're truly compatible with. I know it sounds counter-intuitive when you feel that you don't have a lot of prospects, but when you focus on the qualities *you* want in a significant other, that projects more confidence, which increases your odds of finding the right person."

"Okay, I suppose I'll try that."

"On another note, I've noticed you've mentioned your weight quite a bit in our sessions. It seems to be an aspect you feel self-conscious about. Is that accurate?" Belinda asked.

Ann tilted her head. "Uh, I guess so. Look, I know I need to lose weight. I mean, my dad died early because of it. But it's so frustrating that it's, like, the only thing that matters to everybody else, like my family, guys, Luke. I'm more than just my size."

"That's a valid feeling to have. You are more than your size or physical appearance. And, believe it or not, size is not keeping you from having a partner. Women of all sizes get into relationships and marry all the time. That said, developing proper eating habits and consistent physical activity are great steps for anyone to take, regardless of weight. It doesn't *cure* depression or anxiety, but it can help you feel a little better and improve your quality of life overall.

So, it could be a valuable step for you to reach out to a nutritionist or dietitian, or hire a personal trainer that can help you determine the right exercise regimen for your body and lifestyle."

"Sure."

Belinda then reviewed her notepad while Ann sat cross-legged on the couch, fidgeting. "Ann, I do want to briefly discuss one other thing before we end today's session."

"Okay," she whispered, looking out the window.

"Over the past several sessions, there have been several observations I've made. May I ask you a question?"

Ann stopped fidgeting and stared at her counselor. "Uh, okay."

Belinda inquired, "When you've been in counseling or therapy in the past, or even when you were a child in school, has anyone suggested that you be tested for Asperger's Syndrome?"

The client was perplexed. "No. What's that?"

"Asperger's Syndrome is a condition that typically includes difficulty with social cues and interpersonal interactions, social awkwardness, intense focus on specific interests, and repetitive behaviors."

"What? If I have this, um, Asperger's, does that mean I'm mentally delayed or something?"

The therapist shook her head. "No, not at all. Typically, people with Asperger's Syndrome don't show intellectual disability and can live independently. It's just that oftentimes, people with this condition may have some trouble understanding body language, or other people's intentions or emotions, so they may respond in a way others might see as odd or inappropriate. So, because of that, people with Asperger's Syndrome often have a difficult time with socialization, and may be viewed by others as strange or odd."

Ann raised an eyebrow. "Hmm, that's...something."

The therapist shifted in her seat. "Sure. Ann, the reason why I thought to bring it up is that a lot of what you've shared in our sessions, such as your telephone anxiety and other social-related anxieties, your challenges in your friendship with Luke, your struggles connecting with others including your coworkers, or even the issues you have faced in dating and relationships, appear to come down primarily to not being able to understand the signals of others, and not being sure how to form a lot of positive relationships. Is that accurate?"

"Uh, yeah."

"It may also explain your discomfort in standing up for yourself or extracting yourself from situations you might find unpleasant or suboptimal."

"Eh, like the married man, or my four-and-a-half-year mistake?"

Belinda nodded, "Yes. In addition, there may be a genetic component to the disorder. It often runs in families. So, some of the traits you have, you may find other members of your family have similar traits. In any case, this may be a direction worth looking into further."

Ann, still a bit confused, responded, "I don't know, I guess. Nobody in the family I grew up with was like me in that way, but I kinda see it with my brother and my nephew especially, and I heard my birth mother is like that too, so maybe."

Belinda made notes in her steno pad.

"Anyway, I know I have a hard time being social, but thinking back, my parents would always say I'm just shy, and I have to talk to people more and be friendly, and it seems like that works okay, as painful as it is. But sometimes I wish I could read people's minds.

At least I wouldn't feel like, you know, like with Luke. I would always wish he would just be clear – say what he means, mean what he says, not be wishy-washy. I dunno. I wish people would just be straightforward, and I didn't have to guess, I didn't have to interpret or read people. You know, some people, a lot of people, just don't make sense."

"What I hear you saying is that you feel that the people around you tend to provide mixed signals, or are not always straightforward in their communication with you. And that is a source of frustration for you."

"Yes, that, exactly."

"Okay. On one hand, many of my other clients have shared similar frustrations, and some have been diagnosed with Asperger's Syndrome. Not by me – that would require a diagnostic evaluation by specialists in disorders such as Asperger's or autism. But typically, this would be diagnosed in childhood, and from what I've seen, Asperger's syndrome is most often diagnosed in boys, especially Caucasian boys."

"Hmm."

"Yes, there may be a bias there, but even with that, it still could be a possibility worth exploring, and I can refer you for a formal evaluation if you wish."

"Eh, I don't know. I'll have to think about that."

Belinda nodded. "Of course. There's a lot that goes into it, and it can take a lot of time, and may or may not be covered by insurance. You also have a lot on your plate as it is. But if you do decide to explore this and pursue a diagnosis, just let me know and I can provide a referral."

Ann smiled slightly. "Thanks."

∽

Ann was departing the office late Tuesday afternoon when her cell phone rang. She checked the display on the outside of the phone and noticed it was Luke. She let it go to voicemail.

I meant what I said. She sighed, opened her phone, and blocked his phone number. She then deleted his voicemail without listening to it and cleared his name from her address book.

She got into her car and left work. When getting close to her home, she noticed the McDonald's restaurant she always frequented. As she approached it, she was strongly considering a meal.

That sounds really good right now, and it's dinner time. A large fry and a twenty-piece chicken nugget. Might add a Big Mac and another small fry. Do I want a drink? I dunno, maybe a sundae instead. Eh, I can get the food and the pop and then go next door to Dunkin' Donuts and get a half dozen double chocolate donuts for dessert...

She was primed to turn into the parking lot so she could enter the drive-thru line, but something stopped her.

No...I'm not going to do this. Can't keep doing this to myself. I need to take care of me.

She took a deep breath, continued past the fast food restaurant without stopping, and went home.

Once in her apartment, she dusted off a decorative cookbook and followed the directions to cook a sensibly-portioned chicken stir fry with onions, peppers, and mushrooms from the back of her freezer. She then plated it and thoroughly enjoyed her creation. Then, she cleaned up and left for Oaktown.

In the large meeting room at the Oaktown Community Center, members of The Sketchy Thespians were practicing for their Labor Day weekend performance of Oscar Wilde's *The Importance of Being Earnest*. Ann had been attending practice sessions for a few weeks and was tapped to play Gwendolen, a lead female role in the play.

That night, she was sitting on the edge of the raised stage, along with Alex, who was playing Cecily, Gary, who was playing Algernon, and Tim, who directed the scene and also played Jack. Christine and Molly were sitting in beige folding chairs in front of the old stage, as they had parts to play in other scenes.

Tim, a fifteen-year veteran of community theater and sketch comedy, gave an explanation to his compatriots. "So, a skill we want to work on as a group is our physicality. It's not just about memorizing our lines. It's about *how* we say them, it's about our body language, and it's about utilizing the physicality called for by the scene. This scene is a good example. So, let's start with the Second Act, Scene I, and the line from Gwendolen, 'Personally, I cannot understand...'"

The group members involved in the scene stood up and went onstage, then turned their scripts to the correct page.

Tim barked, "Gwendolen, go!"

Ann recited her line with a smidgen of Victorian flair. "Personally I cannot understand how anybody manages to exist in the country, if anybody who is anybody does. The country always bores me to death."

Alex, a slightly plump brunette woman, spoke Cecily's line. "Ah! This is what the newspapers call agricultural depression, is it not? I believe the aristocracy are suffering very much from it just at present.

It is almost an epidemic amongst them, I have been told. May I offer you some tea, Miss Fairfax?"

Ann amped up the high-society air in her voice. "Thank you." She then looked out towards the audience to give her aside. "Detestable girl! But I require tea!"

"Sugar?"

"No, thank you. Sugar is not fashionable any more."

Alex, pretending to hold a mug, motioned as if she were placing several lumps of sugar into the cup, and grimaced at Ann.

The actors continued the scene, and after several minutes, Tim stopped them. "You folks are doing great. Ann, you've come a long way so fast. It's like you're a natural at this."

Molly agreed. "Yeah, Tim's right. You're so freaking good at this. I'm surprised you haven't been doing this longer."

"Thanks, guys!" Ann slightly blushed at the compliments.

After practice, the group socialized and imbibed at their usual spot, La Bonbonita Taqueria, a Mexican restaurant with a Tuesday margarita special.

Over drinks, members of the group enjoyed each other's company.

"With being from Philly, Tim...how did you get used to living in Losanti?" Ann asked.

"Such a good question, Ann. Losanti is a family town, and originally, I moved here with my son and daughter. They're both grown now, but there was so much for us to do, so many activities, attractions, and programs. And being a single dad, it was easy to find entertainment for my kids. But as they got older and started doing more of their own thing, it did become a little harder. There are a lot of bars here, not a lot else. But it gets better. I met Molly, she's so neat and carefree, and it's like a match made in heaven."

"Oh, for sure!" Molly agreed. "To be fair, though, I'm from here, and I can't say I 'fit' in this town either. Honestly, Losanti is the perfect city for people who peaked in high school. For the rest of us, we just come to terms with this place and we make the best of it."

"And really," Alex pointed out as she was slurping on a peach margarita, "you're in the right place. We're all a bunch of nerds and misfit toys."

Ann grinned. "Then you're right, I'm very much in the right place. You guys are awesome!"

"Really, Losanti is what you make of it," Gary chimed in, while finishing his drink. "It can be hell, but if you find your crowd, it's not so terrible."

Christine lifted her glass and gave a toast. "To Losanti's nerds and misfit toys — cheers!"

The others at the table raised their margarita glasses in solidarity. "Cheers!"

EARNEST
AUGUST-OCTOBER 2003

Labor Day was just around the corner, and the first performance of The Sketchy Thespians' four-night run of *The Importance of Being Earnest* was about to begin. The play was held at the Piglet Arthouse across from Ohio Valley Technical University. Due to its proximity to campus, the shows were heavily attended.

Before the Friday evening play, The Sketchy Thespians, costumed and ready, stood in a circle.

Tim spoke up. "This is opening night. All of the hard work we've done over the past couple of months has led us to this moment. You've worked your asses off, every single one of you. Think of this like practice, but we're doing this for real. And let me tell you this. No matter what, remember that I'm so fucking proud of you. Now let's kill it!"

During the first act, Ann was backstage waiting for her entrance as Gwendolen along with Christine, who took the role of Lady Bracknell. Both were in flamboyant Victorian costume and stage makeup.

"Uh, I don't know if I can do this..." Ann sputtered through clenched teeth.

Christine gently touched her shoulder. "You've got this."

"But what if I forget my lines?"

"You won't, but if you do, just wing it. Don't even think about the audience. Just put yourself on the practice stage in Oaktown. It's just like you're at practice."

"I got this...I got this...I got this..."

Just then, the cue was spoken for the actresses to enter their initial scene. Ann took a deep breath. She and Christine walked onstage and began their performance.

After the play and the curtain call, The Sketchy Thespians were backstage changing back into their street clothes.

Tim ran up to Ann. "Let me tell you...you were so amazing out there. When Molly and I say you're a natural, we're not blowing smoke up your ass. We mean it. You have a lot of talent and you can really go far with this. We're so thrilled you're a part of the group."

She blushed and smiled. "Thank you so much, Tim. That means a lot to me. It really does."

In the background, Alex yelled, "Hey y'all! Let's head to the Taqueria!"

"Yeah," Gary said, "sounds good, but give us like fifteen minutes! We don't just jump into our clothes like you bro!"

As the troupe cleaned up and continued to get ready, Molly came up to Ann. "Hey, there's some guy looking for you. Do you know an Ian Evans?"

Ian – my next-door neighbor? Why's he here? I hope it's not about Charlie...or the apartment...

"Ian? Yeah."

"Is it cool if he comes back here?"

"Sure..." she responded in confusion.

A moment later, as she looked up, she viewed Ian, wearing a deep purple button-down dress shirt, khakis, and brown loafers. She smiled and waved to him to come over.

"Howdy neighbor!"

"Hey, Ann! You've been telling me all about this play and I just had to come out to see it."

"I'm glad you did, Ian. I hope you enjoyed it."

"It was great...and *you* were the best part."

Ann laughed. "Thanks! Flattery will get you everywhere."

Ian chuckled. "Touché. So, I'm here because I wanted to check out the play, of course, but I also want to ask you something." He then inhaled. "Ann...you're fun, you're beautiful, you love dogs, which is a huge plus, and you're an artist. You're cool as hell. And I would love to take you out."

She was pleasantly surprised. "Take me out, like..."

"Like on a date. I want to see where things go. No pressure, but truly, I think we'd make a great pair."

With a flirty grin, Ann nodded. "You know what Ian? I'd like that."

One Thursday evening in late October, Ann and Terah relaxed at Norris Cafe, a local coffeehouse a few streets over from Ann's home. They were seated in dark brown cushioned lounge chairs opposite each other behind a large window. Outside, groups of children in costumes walked past the establishment with chaperoning adults, holding pails and pillowcases filled with candy and other treats.

Ann moved in her chair to get comfortable. "Wow, it's Halloween and we're actually out of the house."

"Yeah, I know, Annie. That's one thing we had in common back in the day," Terah noted. "Our parents didn't let us celebrate Halloween."

"Uh-huh. No trick-or-treating, no nothing. 'Halloween's the devil's day,' that's what they'd always say."

"Ooh yeah, I know. And then, my mom would say that we should know Halloween's the devil's day, since the night before was Devil's Night!"

The friends laughed.

"You know what though?"

Terah nodded in acknowledgment.

"Apparently, 'Devil's Night' is only a thing back in Michigan."

"Really?"

"Yeah. Mention Devil's Night here, and folks'll look at you like you have three eyes!"

"Oh damn!"

"Yep." Ann turned up her cup for a swig of Americano black. "It's so good to see you Terah — it's been forever. Glad you came down."

"Oh, for sure. It *has* been forever. Jimmy and I have been talking about going on a trip out of town for a while, and what better place to go than to Ohio to see my bestie?"

"Glad you're here, Terah."

"Just so happens he has relatives here we get to visit, so it works out for the both of us. By the way, girl, you look great."

"Thanks. I feel great. You won't believe the weight lifted off me once I stopped talking to Luke."

"You know what? I'm glad you finally did that. I get why you held on, I know you wanted to be with him so bad, but God's not gonna promise something that's to your detriment. You needed to move on from him. Even being by yourself is better than getting stuck on a man who takes your presence for granted."

"Oh, for sure."

"So...I have some news, and I just *had* to tell you in person. Jimmy and I are getting married!"

Ann smiled and gave Terah a huge hug. "Congratulations, girl! That's awesome! When's the wedding?"

"We're looking at this coming summer. We're checking out venues right now, and we'll probably have a definitive date within the next few weeks once we book a place."

"Oh, that's so cool. I'm so happy for you!"

"And I got one other thing to ask. Annie, I would love for you to be my maid of honor. Will you?"

Ann beamed. "Oh my God, yes, of course, Terah. I'm so honored!"

The two continued to discuss wedding plans.

"So, I'm guessing I should add a plus-one to your invite?" Terah commented.

"Yeah...uh...maybe. It's a bit early to know for sure, but Ian's awesome."

"It sounds like you two are quite compatible."

"Yeah, we are. He's terrific. We have quite a bit in common, and you know, he's such a great guy. He's so fun, Charlie's crazy about him. And he's cute, too."

"I saw the pictures you sent me...real nice-looking dude, not gonna lie. Blows Luke out of the water. Looks a bit different for a white dude. Kind of looks like Keanu Reeves."

"Hmm, never thought about that, but I guess I could see that. Ian's mom is half-Chinese."

"Oh, that's neat. Now, I've gotta ask you, since you asked me when I got with Jimmy..."

"Oh shit, I think I know what's coming."

"Of course, Annie...is Ian a Christian?"

Ann shook her head. "No. He's a bit skeptical of organized religion, but he thinks something's out there. It works though, 'cause I'm trying to figure it all out myself. I've told you about that. I've had to undo a lot of toxic beliefs over the last year or two."

"Yeah, I get it. Hopefully, you'll be able to pick out the truth of Jesus from the cultural mess that is evangelical Christianity."

"I know where you're coming from. My mom said pretty much the same thing, but the way I'm approaching it, it's like my dad used to say, 'Take what you can and throw the rest away.'"

"Fair enough." Terah looked out at the street while taking a swig of her vanilla latte.

"Anyway, Ian's great and we're having so much fun together, but I wanna try to live in the moment and take things for how they are right now. I don't wanna get too far ahead of myself."

"I understand. I will say, y'all do look happy together, at least from the pictures."

"We truly are. Looking forward to tomorrow when the four of us'll go out to dinner, and you'll get to meet Ian."

"That'll be great – looking forward to that. Oh, by the way, you're gonna need to give me some weight loss tips for my wedding. I'm looking at you and you've dropped mad poundage since the last time I saw you."

"Well, I did drop a hundred and seventy pounds," Ann joked.

Terah laughed along with her. "Yeah, Luke had to go, and thank God you moved on."

"For sure, but for real, about the weight, it's not like I'm trying all like that. Living in the 'now' and having more to do has helped a bit. I'm still doing things with community theater, and I've met friends locally through that, and I hang out with them. And then, Ian and I have our quality time and we walk our dogs together quite a bit. I mean, it's only like, thirty-five, forty pounds. I still have a long way to go."

"Welp, you are doing something! I gotta get on that!"

DOOR
MARCH 2004

Ian gazed out of the window of his apartment unit while relaxing underneath the slate grey comforter of his full-size bed. "The leaves on that cherry blossom tree are growing in quite nicely."

Ann, lying next to him, leaned into his chest. "For sure, Fave. It seems like such a short time ago we were ringing in 2004. Can't believe it's already March. When the tree turns color in a couple months or so, you might wanna think about painting it."

"That'll be awesome. But I especially look forward to painting you in front of the Pantheon."

She blushed. "That trip is gonna be amazing. I'm especially looking forward to the Sistine Chapel and Saint Peter's Basilica."

"That'll be cool, though the religiousness of it..."

"It's not so much about religion, but more about the artistry of those sites, and what they meant historically, can't take that away from them."

"I get it, Anna Banana." He kissed her forehead. "Either way, it'll be a trip of a lifetime."

"Can't wait to travel through Europe with you, Fave...June can't come soon enough. Anyway, Charlie's gonna be so excited to be hanging out with you and his best bud Laura while I'm in Detroit."

"He'll be in great hands, as you know."

"Of course. He's always excited when he gets a chance to hang with you."

"It's awesome. I've gotta say, it's so brave that you're doing this."

"Eh, I don't see it as brave. I'm getting a chance to meet my birth mother, not climbing Mount Everest."

"But Anna, I see it differently. She didn't raise you and you grew up without her, and you've told me how you've avoided dealing with that part of your life for a long time. You could've kept ignoring it."

"I suppose so."

"I mean, my family sucks at dealing with conflict and difficult issues. It's really bad...there's so much that's unspoken and it stays that way."

"I know...hopefully that changes for you."

"Hopefully so...it's pretty dysfunctional for sure. So, in a way, I kind of get it, but you got a chance to find out the truth – or at least what you could. You could've buried it and kept going on with your life. But you chose to pursue it, to find out more and see where it leads. I admire the strength it takes to do that."

"I guess I never thought about it that way. I appreciate that, Fave. You always have a new way of seeing things."

"Of course," he said, giving her a kiss on the lips.

Ring!

Ann turned over to check her phone. "Oh, that's my brother texting me. He's getting close, so I need to get ready."

"Everything will be fine here, and I'm sure things will be okay when you meet your bio mom. Don't forget that no matter what, I'm here for you."

The couple embraced. "I'm thankful for that, more than you know."

He kissed her on the lips. "Call me when you get there."

"I sure will."

She climbed out of bed and retrieved a clean towel from his built-in linen closet.

"I'll miss you, beautiful," he called out.

"I'll miss you too, but I'll be back soon enough." She then slipped into the restroom to prepare for her brother's arrival.

As Lionel drove up Interstate 75 North with Ann in tow, the long-lost siblings engaged in conversation and listened to music on the radio.

"I appreciate you being willing to take me to Detroit so I can meet our mom."

"Oh, of course. I'm glad the weather's finally turning. This winter was so brutal. But spring is here, and it even feels like it. We sure lucked out. And it's spring break for Indy schools, so I'm glad to be able to use that time for this."

"How was your drive to Losanti?" she asked.

"Not bad at all. It took a minute to get out of Indy, but once I got onto I-74 headed to Ohio, it was all good."

"Okay, cool. So, have you ever visited here before?"

"Oh, no," he admitted. "Before this, I never had the occasion to go there. From everything I've heard, it's about as plain as Indy."

She laughed. "No place is as plain as Losanti, not even Indy."

As the road trip continued through the vast cornfields of mid-Ohio, Lionel asked, "How about some music?"

"Um, sure, do you want me to find something on the radio?"

While keeping his eyes on the open road, he nodded. "Sure."

"What do you wanna listen to?"

"Uh, it doesn't matter, whatever you want to listen to."

Ann leaned forward and flipped through the FM radio stations. She passed by several country western stations, until landing on a frequency playing easy listening music. "I Can't Tell You Why" by Eagles was playing.

She began singing. "Every time I try to walk away..."

Listening to his sister croon, he guffawed.

"Was I singing aloud? Sorry about that..."

"You were, but it's fine, don't apologize," Lionel reassured her. "I was just laughing because Mom does that too. She loves singing along to her favorite songs."

"What kinds of music does she like?"

"Oh, she likes funk and disco, like Maze, Earth, Wind and Fire, and eighties pop and dance too, like Prince and Madonna. And she loves soft rock like this stuff, Eagles, REO Speedwagon, Genesis, Fleetwood Mac, she loves Stevie Nicks."

"She's got excellent taste."

A few hours later, they crossed the state border into Michigan. Ann stared out the window, entranced by the maple and oak tree leaves in early bloom.

"I only spent a couple of short years with your dad, but when he was with our mom, I liked him. I would tag along with him sometimes when he went to the gym, and it was the first time I saw men putting in work towards a positive goal, and really working together. It made an impression on me that I never forgot. I'm sure you know, but my dad died when I was young, so I barely remember him."

"Yeah, I heard that. I'm sorry about that."

"Thanks. Anyway, for that short time our mom and your dad were married, he taught me things. He showed me how to throw a football and even taught me how to ride a bike. He didn't replace my father, but he was such a role model for me."

Ann nodded.

"So, when y'all left, I lost my baby sister, but I also lost my father figure. That was a tough time in my life. It hurt."

"You know, I'm sorry that happened. Know that he didn't forget you. He said you were like a son to him, and he regretted leaving you behind. I always thought it was neat that I had a brother out there, and I wanted to get to know you."

"I'm glad you told me that, sis. I really am."

"Before we go to our mom's house, do you think we can make a couple of quick stops first? They're not exactly on the way, but I would appreciate it."

"Of course...anything for you, sis."

The burgundy Caravan slowly passed through the front gate of Woodlawn Cemetery. The sky was thick with cloud cover, and a light, crisp breeze drifted through the air. After a couple of minutes meandering down the quiet, desolate road, Ann directed Lionel to their destination.

After he pulled over to one side and stopped the van, the siblings exited and walked up the grassy incline, careful not to step on gravestones. The grounds were neatly mowed, with holly, maple, and pine trees dotting the landscape. Ann clutched a bouquet of pink roses, while Lionel held orange and yellow marigold stems.

They located a flat, grey gravestone, partially shaded by a tall white pine tree. The name "**CORBIN**" was clearly visible on the polished, yet modest stone in bold letters, with Marshall's first name engraved on the left-hand side and the dates "**1952-2001**." The stone also included "Sherrye" on the left, stamped "**1953-**" – the death date left blank. A metal vase, installed above the family name, sat empty.

Ann dusted off the gravestone with her hand, and she and Lionel placed the flowers in the vase. He crouched down and lightly touched the stone, while she sat in front of it, legs crossed in front of her.

He spoke softly while looking up at the overcast sky. "I hope you're doing alright up there. Know that I never forgot you. Say 'hi' to my dad and my grandma for me. Rest easy, Marshall." After that, he stood up and touched her shoulder. Before returning to the minivan, he voiced tenderly, "Ann, take as much time as you need."

This was the first time Ann visited her father's grave since the burial. She felt his presence in her solitude.

"Dad, I don't know what to say. Or I guess, maybe I do. I miss you every day. I miss the times we would ride around the city, and you would tell me stories of growing up, or about Detroit, or your travels around the world. When I was down, you would know just what to say, or the right story to tell, to make me feel better."

She paused and took a deep breath. "But I've gotta be honest. I wish you had been honest about Stephanie. I wish you hadn't made it sound like she was just a fleeting memory in your life, and that it was just easy for her to make the choices she did. When you told me she just gave me up, it made me feel like I was just abandoned, left behind, and unwanted. And you know what? That's probably not true."

She closed her eyes as she continued solemnly. "More than anything else, Dad, I wish you were here for me to ask you 'why?' I don't know if I'll ever completely understand why you took me away from Stephanie...from Lionel. They're my family, too. But what I *do* know is that you loved me, and I believe you did the best you could. I have to believe that."

Hot tears fell onto the cold granite, but determination filled her soul. "At this point in my life, I need to meet her. And I'm not gonna lie, a part of me is freaked out. I don't know how things will turn out, but I want to get to know her in the here and now, and I want her to know me. I'm never gonna know everything that happened, and I've got to live with that. At this point, it makes no sense to relitigate the past. I hope that as I get to know her more, I'll learn more about myself. Hopefully, you understand. I love you, Dad, and I'll miss you always."

With that, Ann stood up, dusted herself off, and departed from the gravesite, finally ready to meet Stephanie for the first time.

Less than twenty minutes later, the siblings were closing in on their destination. It was shortly after three o'clock in the afternoon, and the Dodge minivan was on Meyers Road heading south, approaching Joy Road.

"Oh wow, we're getting pretty close."

"Yeah, we sure are. Just a few more minutes and we'll be there. How are you feeling, Ann?"

"Not gonna lie, Lionel, I'm kind of nervous. I don't know what to say. At this point, I've decided I just wanna get to know Stephanie as a person, build a relationship based on who we are now, not based on what could've been."

"Do you have any questions for her?"

"It's funny you ask that. When I was growing up, I remember how I was just dying to ask her, you know, 'Where have you been?' or 'Why weren't you in my life growing up?' – things like that. But at this point, I don't think that's necessary. The way I look at it, everybody did the best they could with what they knew and the tools they had. I can't fault her for how things turned out. I can't fault anybody. It is what it is."

"I hear you, sis."

"And really, all in all, I've had a decent life. Never needed to struggle, my parents – the ones who raised me – they're not perfect, they've got their issues, but they've showed me they love me and care about me. Honestly, at this point, I want to get to know Stephanie on her own terms."

Lionel nodded.

A few minutes later, the minivan turned off Joy Road onto a residential street, Sorrento Avenue. The block was quiet with brick two-story homes and bungalows. He then parked on the street.

They exited the van, and Ann followed her brother up a small concrete path leading to a brick bungalow with painted white trim. In front of the house was a full porch with a white and blue awning providing shade. A 1996 forest green Ford Taurus was sitting in the driveway.

As they climbed up the small set of stairs, Lionel pointed to a white metal bench on the porch in front of a large window. The bench was painted white, and the seat was cushioned by a yellow, white, and light blue floral cushion.

"Ann, have a seat right there. I'll call you in once Mom's ready."

"Does she even know I'm coming?"

He shook his head. "She knows *I'm* coming. But she doesn't know *you're* coming."

Ann's eyes bulged in terror.

"Don't worry though, it'll be fine. She's been praying for this day for over twenty years."

Ann leaned back on the bench, took a deep breath, and calmed down.

Lionel used a silver Kwikset key to open the white-painted metal security door, and then the cerulean front door. He entered the home, and the security door swung back noisily, though the front door was still open. Ann could hear the conversation through the doorway.

"Hi, Mom!"

Ann could barely hear the muffled older female voice responding to her brother. *That's my birth mother. That's Stephanie. That's her voice.*

As she sat on the bench, she looked out onto the street, viewing the houses on the humble block. *I wonder what this all looked like in the 1980s.*

"Where's Donnie?"

"He's in his room, on the computer as usual," a weathered yet sweet voice responded.

It's weird to think that when I was a baby, I lived here. Almost twenty-four years ago, I was born at Hutzel Hospital, where it seems like everybody from Detroit was born, and my parents brought me home. They carried me right here.

She now heard the strong, upbeat voice of a young man. "Hey Lionel, you wanna play Mortal Kombat later?"

"Yeah, sure we can, Donnie. But before that, I gotta unload."

This feels unfamiliar, but familiar at the same time. It's a homecoming of sorts, I suppose.

"Oh, did Keonna and the kids come with you?" Stephanie asked.

"No, she had to work, and the kids have got school and their activities." Then, after a brief pause, Lionel told his mother, "Mom, I've got a surprise for you. I want you to sit down."

"Okay...what's going on?"

"Look who's finally home!"

Still outside on the bench, Ann's palms grew sweaty and her heart was racing with a combination of extreme nerves and great anticipation.

Lionel walked back to the security door and opened it. With his right hand, he motioned to Ann to enter the house. She took a deep breath, rose to her feet, then walked through the door to meet Stephanie.

This is real, and this is now. I'm home.

ALSO BY JAYE POOL

The Losantiverse Duology

Book Two: *To Die is Gain* (Spring 2025)

Short Stories and Poetry

http://www.jayepool.com/blog

Love *Make Me Free*? Subscribe to the Newsletter!

http://www.jayepool.com/newsletter